-B1 00

CLEOPATRA'S NEEDLE

CLEOPATRA'S NEEDLE

STEVEN SIEBERT

A TOM DOHERTY ASSOCIATES BOOK
NEW YORK

This is a work of fiction. All the characters and events portrayed in this novel are either fictitious or are used fictitiously.

CLEOPATRA'S NEEDLE

Copyright © 1999 by Steven Siebert

All rights reserved, including the right to reproduce this book, or portions thereof, in any form.

Design by Victoria Kuskowski

This book is printed on acid-free paper.

A Forge Book
Published by Tom Doherty Associates, Inc.
175 Fifth Avenue
New York, NY 10010

Forge® is a registered trademark of Tom Doherty Associates, Inc.

Library of Congress Cataloging-in-Publication Data

Siebert, Steven.
    Cleopatra's needle / Steven Siebert. — 1st ed.
        p.   cm.
    "A Tom Doherty Associates book."
    ISBN 0-312-86748-4
    I. Title.
    PS3569.I362C58   1999
    813'.54—dc21   99-21931
                                                    CIP

First Edition: June 1999

Printed in the United States of America

0 9 8 7 6 5 4 3 2

To my mother, Jean Siebert, whose heart
has been weighed against a feather and
now waits across the western desert.

PROLOGUE

Dreamlike, the shape crossed the Gallery of the Eighteenth Dynasty, finally resting behind a case of lion-headed votive statues to the goddess Sekhmet. Malut Feisal noted the movement at the edge of his vision without budging his bulk.

Instead, he tossed a handful of toasted watermelon seeds into his mouth and, with a click-clack of his teeth and tongue, freed the meat from their shells. The small portion of his brain set aside for his guard duties reasoned he had caught shadows of night clouds flitting over the full moon.

It was a standard effect, he thought. One that always frightened the new boys into believing that the ancient gods were stirring to life.

The summer before, one young guard ran screaming from the museum after the shifting clouds caused a long-dead pharaoh to wink at him.

"Alexandrian peasant," grunted Feisal as he spit out a few stray seed hulls which cascaded down the rolls of his belly. These ignorant, superstitious children could be fooled by a weird shadow, but not an old hand like him.

In his nine years patrolling these cold stone corridors, Feisal had learned everything about the Cairo Museum. Nothing scholarly, of course.

He knew the important things: when to doze on his shift, when to be alert for his supervisors' surprise visits, and where to hide his food so he would never starve on his rounds. And, despite his size, he became skilled in disappearing into the walls at the first sign of trouble.

Feisal prayed to Allah twice daily, thankful to sleep during the day's desert-driven heat and wander the cool marble galleries each night.

In his earlier years, Feisal occasionally gaped into the showcases bright with the rainbow treasures of some dried husk of a pharaoh, like those propped in their sarcophagi along the far wall. His eyes might widen then, letting yellow reflections dart and prance from the golden statues and the dazzling jewels. During those long-past moments, unspecified envy and vague feelings of greed pricked at him. But now, even those thoughts were gone.

His atrophied imagination rarely dwelled on the glories he was charged to protect. He walked his circuit oblivious to the fifty centuries of priceless art and history at each turn. Kings and warriors were merely musty, wrapped corpses and their eternal monuments only so much weathered stone.

It was a thing for young men, these dreams of wealth and god-sanctioned power.

One floor below, two young men were crouched in the dark of the stairwell. Ali would have been thought a child in most Western cities, but in Cairo a boy of eleven earned his own bread or starved.

He made a move to stand, but an older boy, Mina, pulled him back and placed a grimy palm over his mouth.

He hissed in Ali's ear, "When I say!"

Ali nodded and Mina let him go. They were an odd pair. Ali, with his huge, sorrowful brown eyes staring out from a face that might have belonged to a bone-china figurine; and Mina, older by seven years, cursed by skin the color and texture of a black walnut.

Ali was small but certain to grow into a tall and tight-muscled man. Mina's teenaged body had settled into the same short, stocky form it would carry until he bloated into his middle age like all the other males in his enormous family.

Zamir Qader, one of Mina's uncles, hatched the plan that had brought them to the museum. He bribed one of the museum's invisibles who swept the tile floors after the day's tourists had tracked in half a desert. Qader wanted one small artifact for himself, but beguiled the boys with talk of the trove of riches shut away in boxes and catalogued in drawers in the museum's storehouse. If half of them were stolen, Qader remarked, they might never be missed.

Never be missed? Yes, if the thieves were quick and quiet enough not to be caught!

Qader chose his nephew and the child Ali for the job because they were audacious street hustlers. They could steal one of those perfumed Europeans blind with such swiftness and skill that he might be back in his own country before he realized how poor he had become.

The sweeper let them inside before he signed out for the night and ushered them into a hiding place he'd prepared in the closet where his mops and brooms were stored. There they slept until well after midnight and then crawled out into the vast stillness of the museum on quivering hands and knees.

Feisal shuffled past overhead, and they heard him turn into another gallery. Mina pointed and Ali scurried to the other side of the stone staircase, his bare feet making no sound on the cool floor. Once there, the boy waved and Mina followed. They hugged the wall to stay out of the shafts of moonlight and found a simple wooden door set into a spot directly below the landing. Mina felt for the lock.

"If my uncle fouled the catch like he said . . ." he muttered under his breath. "Yes!"

The door swung open with a slight creak, and the boys slipped inside. They found themselves in complete darkness, but Ali was quick to open his lighter. Its tiny flame disclosed a planked stairway leading to a lower level of the museum. Mina dug out his flashlight and aimed its beam downward.

"It's just as he said!" whispered Mina. "Go down the steps, and we'll be in the treasure room!"

Ali led the way. At the base, he held the light up high to see the chamber. The ceiling was barely a foot above Ali's light. A tall man would have to walk hunched over through the narrow corridors created by the wooden storage racks. No gold reflected in the orange flame of the lighter. The boys went from bin to bin, but found only broken crockery and old scrolls that thickened the air with a rotten, yeasty smell.

"Trash!" spat Mina. As he continued his rummaging, he told the boy to find what his uncle had ordered. Ali was more interested in booty, but nodded and dutifully tip-toed to the bin where Qader had said they would find a broken fragment of an Egyptian cross, an *ankh*. They'd recognize it, said Qader, because it was carved out of rose quartz.

Out of the corner of his eye, Mina noticed Ali's lighter flame spark. He turned, but Ali's flame must have blown out and his beam could not locate the boy. A shudder passed across his chest just above his heart.

"Be careful with that! You want to burn the place down on our heads!" No answer came.

Where is that dung-brain? What's he getting into now?

Although Mina would deny it to any of the other boys who roamed like packs of wild dogs through the filthy maze of the Cairo alleyways, he felt responsible for the boy. Ali was only seven when Mina caught him begging at his prime corner outside the Victoria Hotel.

At first, he boxed his ears, but the next day the boy was there again. And the day after that. Eventually, Mina gave him the eastern entrance after the eleven o'clock checkout time when the take was lightest. Even so, the sweet-faced orphan child regularly returned with a cup full of coins. No one, either European infidel or devout Arab, could resist those eyes.

"There you are!" Mina saw the boy, his back turned, kneeling behind one of the chests of scrolls. The contents had been dumped onto the floor, and a few of the ancient papyri were unrolled at Ali's feet like so many party ribbons.

"Ali?" Mina stepped closer. "Did you find any of the jewels? Any gold?"

As Ali pivoted on one knee to face him, Mina saw an odd red glint bounce back in the beam of his flashlight. Then, it seemed that the entire room was washed in a pale yellow glare. Ali held tight to what Mina perceived as a shimmering arc of crystal. Mina craned his neck trying to catch what was going on behind the boy. A shape, undefined and ghostlike, appeared at the center of the light. Mina's arm shielded his eyes as it grew too bright for him to see. Then, he heard screams, but not from Ali's throat. These were birth sounds. He tried to open his eyes as a wave of heat struck and transfigured his body to ash.

And when the brilliance subsided, from above, thumping against the low ceiling, came the sound of wings.

Feisal groped for the chunk of goat cheese he'd left on the counter top. Finding it, he shoved it between his puffy lips, barely chewed the remnant, and let the salty piece slide down his throat without ceremony. He wiped the greasy residue on his shirtfront, then drifted on

toward the archway that divided the corridor from the rich Gallery
of the Eighteenth Dynasty. Once inside, he checked the windows—
more out of boredom than conscientiousness.

His handlight searched out the locks. As expected, they were undisturbed. Feisal let the beam skim the hieroglyphed walls and climb
down a basalt figure of Thoueris whose large drooping breasts and
hippopotamus head blocked a ventilation grating.

All secure.

The light passed a length of rope near the statue's granite base.
The rope trembled at its tip. It was alive.

A snake?

Feisal wobbled backward. Snakes had been discovered in the museum before, especially at the rainy season. It always meant more
work, not that he had to dispose of the creature by himself. That was
left to the government snake catcher.

But he would be forced to stand by, unable to nap or eat until the
thing was safely in a sack and any of its relatives were hunted down
and escorted out of the building.

Feisal steadied the torch. He was not fond of snakes. This one
lacked the markings of an adder. It was a silvery tan, colored like the
cobras they sometimes found near the Great Pyramid.

The "snake" turned around, curling between furry hind legs. It
lifted its curious face to the light, blinked twice, and meowed.

Feisal let out his breath with a heavy chuckle, allowing his stomach
muscles to relax. In a friendly gesture, he bent and extended his
cheese-flavored fingers to the cat. The animal pulled back its head in
caution.

"Here, pussycat, come out from there. I won't hurt you."

The cat stretched its slim body and took a step forward. It rubbed
its shoulder against the corner of the pedestal.

"Puss, puss, puss . . ."

The cat turned away and lapped eagerly at one of its paws. Eventually, it stopped preening its short, dusk-colored fur and sauntered
in Feisal's direction. The big guard eased down on his haunches to
meet the haughty feline. Their eyes met.

Feisal smiled, tickling the cat behind its ear. A purr started deep
in the cat's chest as it leaned into Feisal's chubby fingertips.

"Ah, you like that, huh?" Quite unconsciously, Feisal pursed his
lips and made drawn-out kissing noises until he realized how ridiculous he sounded.

"Enough, now, you foul beast." He straightened up, scooping the cat into his palm in the same motion. Feisal lifted the animal's lordly face close to his own. The cat stared at him, calm, unblinking, refusing to squirm.

"Now, how'd you sneak in, little fellow? See? Nothing here you can use. Can't eat those old dead people. Too tough. Outside's where you belong. Where the rats grow big and juicy!"

Feisal laughed and turned to escort his captive to the door. Behind him, old wood creaked. Feisal heard and looked back through the archway into the Eighteenth Dynasty. From his angle the large relics looked disordered—a trick of the moonlight, probably.

The whole gallery felt alive. Contours of the god effigies shifted under the filtered moon. On one wall, the upright sarcophagi of eight noble personages melted in and out of the darkness, alternately exposing then hiding the carved faces of extinct ministers and peers.

One, perhaps more, of the coffins rocked, or seemed to. Ancient, dried wood strained as if some force pushed from within.

Feisal shook his head. He stepped backward, unable to confront his senses. Night sounds, he told himself, the sort that scare the new boys. He had heard them all before.

Could this be another cat?

"So, naughty pussycat, what's this? Is your girlfriend waiting for you back there?"

The cat hissed in answer and lashed out his paw. Feisal heard the whoosh of air, but barely felt the razorlike talons enter his neck and slice through his carotid artery.

He tried holding the ten pounds of now-thrashing and yowling fur, but it was damp and slippery from his own warm blood. The angry feline leapt onto Feisal's head, tangling itself in the fat man's black curly hair.

Feisal spun about, hitting the screaming animal. But the cat dug its claws deeper into his scalp. Trying to run, the large man skidded on a puddle that had quickly formed from the red fountain pouring from his neck. He fell, catching himself awkwardly on one wrist. He heard the bone snap.

Slashing again, the cat opened a neat tear below his brow. Another whip of its paw ripped through one lid and plunged a needlelike claw through Feisal's eye. The man writhed, shrieking on the stone floor, rolling in his own vital juices.

Half-blinded by gore and tears, Feisal thought he saw the ancient gods beginning to move. Their shadows walked by him as his life drained out.

But it couldn't really be happening. It must only be those clouds passing across the moon. You know, a standard effect.

Only a new boy would be scared.

PART ONE

CHAPTER ONE ☥

The light morning rain wasn't keeping the bums indoors. Four of New York's most ragged were huddling under the footbridge as Dan strolled by on his way to work. One of them, a stout fellow about sixty with black axle grease lacquered through his hair, looked up and waved.

"Hi ya, Doc," he shouted. "Got any change?"

Dan waved him off. "Sorry, Georgie. Only packing my credit cards today." His bleeding-heart-liberal guilt stopped him for a second while he considered his obligations to his fellow man.

"How about I leave a hot dog for you at Sammy's stand?"

"I dunno. The cops don't like us out front of the museum, Doc. Freaks out the tourists, y'know."

"I'll clear it," said Rawlins, hurrying off, his conscience assuaged.

Georgie hurried after him onto the footpath. "I won't eat no sauerkraut! I didn't fight the fuckin' Nazis so I could make 'em rich eatin' their stinkin' cabbage!"

"Sammy only sells Hebrew National, for godsakes!"

"He just does it so he can sell that Fascist kraut!"

"Whatever you say, Georgie," yelled Dan as he turned onto the upgrade leading to the knoll. Dan sat down to rest on one of the benches on Greywacke Knoll next to the fence surrounding New

York's obelisk. It was the highest point in Central Park and Cleopatra's Needle capped the slope.

The pillar made a perfect landmark for Dan's occasional morning walks to the Met. At that point, he knew he was less than five minutes away from the building. After a minute, he rose, saluted the obelisk for luck, and cut across the grass for the jogging path down to the street. He followed a couple of Rollerbladers at a safe distance and soon he saw the rear of the museum, looming like a hazy granite giant crouched against an approaching storm.

An enormous raindrop struck Dan square on the nose. He wiped it dry with the cuff of his jacket, but another hit his cheek almost immediately and more were splattering the top of his head. He dashed for the back door, hoping to get there before the downpour made him look like a dog after a flea dip.

One lousy drop falling through the New York atmosphere must have to pass through ten times its weight in grunge, Dan decided. Even his very expensive Nikes with their tire-tread soles were little help against oil and water on a downhill lane of asphalt. He minced through the flower bed and hopped across the low wall, figuring the shortcut would give him more traction and less chance of skidding on his ass where the entire staff would see him.

He raced around to the side steps and steered under the awning, coasting into the glass door with a squish. He was soaked past his underwear. Dripping, he pressed the buzzer urgently. An old security guard peered out, straining to recognize him through a fog of condensation.

"Open up, Lloyd," Dan shouted. "I'm drowning out here!" Dan brushed wet ringlets away from his forehead as the guard unlatched the door and held it for him to enter.

"Sorry, Doc."

The second person in five minutes to call Dan Rawlins "Doc." It happened all the time, of course, everyone assuming that one of the most famous names in Egyptology must have earned his doctorate. But Dan hadn't. He never found the time.

"Professor" went down easier. And it was nearly true. At least during the one semester each year he was committed to deliver his lecture series at Georgetown. Down in Washington they treated him like a celebrity with his own condo at the Watergate and a sackful of cash for his trouble. He was encouraged to spend time with all the fawning young archaeology majors he could bear.

Even so, Dan knew sleeping with a graduate student thirteen years his junior—*no matter how discreet they were*—meant that everyone would soon be talking. That bothered him. He had spent a lifetime building a reputation among his peers as a dogged researcher and an innovative scientist. He shuddered at the prospect of being labeled academia's answer to Joey Buttafuoco.

Especially when the problem with his father had just begun to die down.

The two of them had been feuding for years, but with his father spending most of the year half a world away, they had recently called a truce.

A decade before, Gunther Rawlins was the leading Biblical scholar in the world. Then, one night he had a revelation that the Scriptures were the literal, revealed truth of God. It was a point of view that many Vatican and fundamentalist scholars held, but it was a rare conviction for a secular researcher.

All Dan saw was his aging father's fear of stepping from life into oblivion. Gunther's perspective was that every new theory of God uncovered new mysteries. Mysteries that only faith could resolve. It might have stayed a family debate if the Rawlins weren't world-famous scientists. The media picked up on the secular/religious conflict because it was such a good story and had no shame about dividing the Rawlins clan.

Dan's mother, a leading authority on the prehistory of the Nile Valley, thankfully kept out of the verbal battles, but it was a terrible time. Clashes between Dan and his father aired for three straight nights on *Hard Copy* and, during Dan's last book tour, talk of the father-son discord dominated the interviews. The tumult was only now dying down in favor of political sex scandals and movie-star tragedies.

None of this seemed to bother the Jesuits who hired Gunther, since it helped their bottom line to have their science lectures play to a packed hall.

Dan's real joy came from the small condo group. With them he could hold court like his father. And often, after one of these informal get-togethers, one of the prettier girls would stay on for the night. His friends on the faculty called them Professor Rawlins's "excavations."

That's why!

A delicious moment of revelation struck him. Whenever one of his girls murmured to him, or panted or screamed, she called out "Professor!"

Never "Dan," or "Doc," or any little pet name she might have
devised. No, always "Professor." No wonder he liked the title. Invariably, the next morning in class, his topic would turn to the bizarre
sexual practices of the Egyptian court at Thebes. Most of his class
would sit stone-faced and earnestly take copious notes. Except for
one young lady in a front row. She'd giggle.

"Watch yourself, Doc. The floor's slippery, and you ain't making
it any drier."

Dan nodded. "I'll try, Lloyd."

Dan dripped down the thirteen stairs to the corridor that led to a
maze of offices and workrooms under the museum. He passed an
open door, and a broad man in an immaculate blue suit looked up
from a pyramid of papers on his desk and waved.

"Ha, you got caught, huh?"

"Not all of us can afford taxis to drop us under the canopy, John."

John Erman, the curator of Egyptian and Middle Eastern Studies,
provided a desk and a grad student for Rawlins's office when he was
in town. It was a nice symbiotic relationship. "We're the pilot fish to
your shark," Erman was fond of saying.

In fact, Dan enjoyed his connection with such a prestigious institution. He felt legitimized by it, despite the inevitable talk by his more
academic colleagues that he was merely the product of famous parents, and his standing in the profession was mostly media hype.

"Why does he write only those popular books?" they said.

"All this exposure on television trivializes the science of archaeology," they said.

"Is young Rawlins afraid of publishing in the proper academic
journals?"

"That's poor Danny Rawlins. You know, the one from the TV,
the Jerry Springer of Egyptology!"

Screw 'em, he thought. He knew he came across on the tube in a
way his dull-as-dry-rot colleagues never could. Reviewers were generally on his side. They inevitably remarked on his ability to make
Egypt's past come alive. It was as if he had actually been there, they
said.

However, he did stop appearing on talk shows after a last avalanche of professional criticism jeopardized his work. Museums are
conservative institutions. They rarely dole out consulting jobs or arrange financing for the projects of controversial figures. Still, a famous
man attracts contributions and, in that respect, the Rawlins name on
a museum's letterhead was a valuable commodity.

Of course, snaring D. Gunther Rawlins, Sr., for their stationery was every head curator's first choice, but Dan's father had stayed a fixture at the Israel Museum in Jerusalem for thirty-two years. Although he had privileges at the Met, they could not pry him away from the Middle East. "Not for a trillion bucks and a first-round draft pick," his old man always said.

"Let me go, John," said Dan. "I'm gonna get pneumonia from the chill in here if I don't get dry pretty soon."

"Wait a second. I sent a guy to your office. Sounds Irish, I think. He says he's from Sotheby's in London." Erman grinned, showing all three hundred teeth. In a brotherly gesture, he brushed back the wet strands from Dan's forehead. "We try to cooperate with our suppliers, don't we?"

Dan nodded reluctantly.

"Good," said Erman. "Now, go dry off your head!"

Marcy Lanyard met Dan at the end of the corridor. She stood blocking his office door, her arms folded as she assayed his condition. Dan gazed at her appreciatively. A long, thin colt of a girl, she stood model-tall and wore her glossy blond hair drawn back into an arching ponytail. Marcy had been on loan from NYU for five months. It had taken her three of those months to get into Dan's bed, but at the office, she made an effort to keep everything professional.

Dan felt a breath of cold air from the air-conditioning ducts and shivered. Magically, Marcy produced two towels from under her crossed arms and threw one to him.

"A couple of people are waiting for you, you know," said Marcy, wiping one of his ears with her towel.

"I heard about the man from Sotheby's. Who else?"

"An older woman," Marcy said while helping him dry his hair. "She didn't give her name, but she's got museum privileges and she's wandering around."

"Okay, I'll see Sotheby's first," he said. "Just give me a couple of minutes to change."

"No problem. I stashed him at the reception desk. He'll be happy. Gloria's wearing her pink sweater today, no bra."

Dan leered back at her. "Then, remind me to escort him in personally." Dan pulled off his sweatshirt as he headed into his private office. He felt Marcy's hand patting him on the rear as he swept by her.

Inside, he stripped off his wet shirt and changed to one he found in his office closet. He had just finished combing his damp hair when he heard a knock at the door. "Yeah, I hear you!" he shouted. He peeked through the spyhole in the door and groaned.

Dan opened the door. The woman standing in the dark hall flashed her ice-gray eyes at him.

"Hello, Mother," he said. "I didn't know you were back from Israel."

"You look like shit, Junior," she said, pushing the door wider. Dan moved aside and gestured for her to come inside. She marched to the center of the office and planted herself next to the leather couch against the far wall. Evangeline Beecham Rawlins, at sixty-three, could still dominate any room she entered. She was thin, even scrawny, with her bone-white hair worn long and free, a style she hadn't changed since the sixties.

Dan ambled in behind her, wishing he had organized the clutter of his latest researches before it had spread out into clumps over virtually every flat surface in the room.

"Son, have you considered hosing this office down?"

Dan didn't answer. Instead, he picked up the papers from the couch and piled them on top of a low bookcase. "Sit anywhere you like, Mother. Sorry there's no throne."

Eva Rawlins, although a foot shorter than Dan, managed to look down on him. "Unworthy of you, Junior." She perched on the edge of an old ladder-back chair. It was made of hard oak. Typically, she chose the least comfortable seat in the room.

"Can I get you a cup of coffee?" asked Dan. "I think there might be a Twinkie, too. I had one for lunch last week, and they come in twos. They don't get stale, do they?"

She shook her head. "I don't have much time before my preinterview at PBS. Your father and I are booked on that nice Charlie Rose's television show when he gets back from the Megiddo excavation."

"I didn't know you had a new edition coming out?"

"We don't. We're plugging Resurrection Unlimited. That's the gathering of all the world faiths in Washington next month. We're on the board of directors."

"Well, I'll avoid that little party like the plague."

"Mustn't let your emotions cloud your judgment, son," she replied, folding her hands on her lap. "All we need do is mention that we both accepted Christ as our personal savior, and you get irrational."

Dan knew he was outmatched and gave up his combative stance. "Sure you don't want any coffee, Mom? I only had a few hours' sleep last night. I could use about a kilo of caffeine."

She shook her head. "No wonder you're so testy."

Dan stepped into the outer office to the tiny kitchen area that serviced the Egyptology Department. The Mr. Coffee was plugged in, so all he had to do was pour a couple of glasses of tap water into the top and wait for the coffee to urinate into the Pyrex pot.

As the coffee started to drip, Dan poked around the half-sized refrigerator looking for the fabled Twinkie to have with it. Instead, he found a calcified Fig Newton behind a jar of five-month-old Smuckers grape jelly and put it on his last clean saucer.

"Ma? I've got Perrier, if you're still on your ascetic kick."

Eva suddenly appeared in the portal. "It's fine. Nothing."

The coffee was ready, and Dan poured himself a cup. He dunked the cookie, and when it sogged-up into edibility, he ate it in one bite. When he looked up, his mother was staring at him.

"What?" he asked finally.

"I won't beat around the bush, Danny. I don't want you to be this way when you see your father. Something is worrying him about his new dig. He's been calling Cairo almost every day about an ostracon they found. You may have heard about the robbery at the museum. Only a few minor artifacts and some of the less notable mummies in the collection were taken, but they found an interesting shard that mentioned Megiddo when they were inventorying the loss."

Dan stuck out his chin. "You know him. He keeps everything to himself when he's on the scent of a big find. It's just like it was in the desert. Rawlins-Pasha never sleeps until the mound is flat and all of its secrets revealed."

Eva handed him a manila envelope. "He'll want your opinion on this. Why don't we talk over dinner the night he gets back. Is that a deal?"

"Deal." Dan put down his cup and joined her at the door. "Don't concern yourself about Dad," he said in a comforting way. "He's just tired. And the work hasn't got any easier over the last thirty years. He's probably looking for one last discovery to cap his career and maybe then he can relax at the beach house like you two always planned." He kissed her on the cheek and she smiled. Then, she turned to go.

"I'm opening up the Montauk house. I'll phone you about that dinner." She passed Marcy and a short, red-haired young man on her way out.

"Who was that?" Marcy asked.

"My mother," said Dan flatly.

"Your mother? You mean Evangeline Beecham?" Marcy was very excited and looked back down the corridor, but by then Eva was gone. "Damn. If I'd known that's who it was, I would've asked for her autograph."

"Who's your friend?"

The man at Marcy's elbow spoke for himself. "Gunther Rawlins? Name's Liam McMay, sir," he said with a trace of an Irish lilt. "I'm with Sotheby's."

"Gunther's my middle name," said Dan, standing. "My father uses it, so we don't have to deal with the 'junior-senior' thing."

"Oh, a thousand pardons. I heard Rawlins and naturally I thought—"

"No problem, everybody does it." They shook hands. "Call me Dan. Come on in." Marcy turned to go, but Dan waved for her to stop. "When you get a minute, call Sammy's cell phone and tell him that Georgie's coming for lunch on me."

She leaned on the door frame after the two men entered Dan's office. "He'll probably bring 'the Council' with him."

"Yeah. I'll spring for them, too. Thanks, Marce." As she disappeared, he turned to McMay. "I'm treating my fans to a couple of hot dogs. They live in the park, but they hang around the museum all the time. I call them the 'Citizen's Art Council.'"

Dan glanced back to the closing door. "And Marcy," Dan shouted, "Tell Sammy to hide the sauerkraut."

Marcy shut the door behind her, and Dan eased back into his plump executive chair. He surveyed the Irishman with practiced eyes and smiled. This one looked green (read ambitious). And he worked for Sotheby's, so he had to be good.

Be careful of that open, freckled face, Dan thought. He didn't want to be seen as shilling for the same people who were driving the price of artifacts out of the reach of most museums.

"Sorry you had to wait, Mr. McMay," said Dan, looking at him steadily.

"It'll be worth it, I'm sure," he replied.

Dan again noticed the blarney in his voice. *Trouble.* "What can I help you with?" asked Dan, as if he meant it. "I warn you, our budget's tight this year."

McMay dug a sheet of paper from the welt pocket of his jacket and handed it to Dan. "Have you ever seen this piece?"

It was a color printout of a damaged artifact on black velvet. "It's a broken ankh," Dan answered as he passed the paper back to

McMay. "You can buy a whole one in the gift shop if you like."

"I mean this specific one," said McMay. "There's some talk that certain shadow groups, Palestinians and such, are anxious to get the other half. We at Sotheby's think if we could get all the pieces together, the bidding could be astronomical."

Dan frowned. Sotheby's had more important business than scouring museum vaults for fractured antiques. What was his real purpose? "Why come to me?" Dan wondered aloud.

"I thought you might check your inventory. Next to the British and Cairo Museums, you've got the biggest Egyptian collection on the planet."

"True."

"I think this cross may be very old."

"Doesn't mean the thing's valuable. It's busted in half, for godsakes." Dan saw that the Irishman looked crestfallen, so he relented and held out his hand. "Okay, give it here." He accepted the picture of the ankh and flattened it on his desktop. Except for the side-to-side motion of his eyes, Dan remained still for almost two minutes.

When he could hold himself back no longer, McMay blurted out, "What do you think, mate?"

"There are some interesting things about it. See how big it is? This is only a picture, but it looks carved out of gemstone. Not expensive ones like diamonds. Probably a crystal geode. Notice the internal faceting."

"And its age?"

"Carbon dating a mineral won't tell you when it was fashioned. There are clues, though. The size makes me think it was made for ritual purposes, not decoration. It's also inelegant in its shape, but the quartz is highly polished. That might mean it's old. Almost all the later ankhs were made from some ore: gold or silver for the upper classes, base metals for the commoners. If I were to guess, I'd say it came from the Holy of Holies of some temple. Except . . ."

"Except, what?"

Dan pulled a book off his shelf and flipped through the pages until he found an illustration of an ankh. "This is an ankh from the Twentieth Dynasty. It's representative. Now compare it with your ankh. Usually, the crosspiece under the loop is shorter. On yours, it could almost be a handgrip."

McMay squinted at the image. "Oh, I see. You could hold it like a divining rod. Could you look for water with it, then?"

Dan wasn't listening. "I'd like to see the rest of it. You know, a lot of ritual ankhs were destroyed by early Christians. But this one's cut cleanly in half, not smashed."

"Is that odd?"

Dan smiled. "No, not particularly. In the ancient world, that top loop was symbolic of life's journey. Cleaving it this way might be a clue to its origin. I'd guess it was used in mummification ceremonies. There is a tradition that the early bishops of Egypt wanted all the ankhs smashed because they were signs of eternal life and therefore an affront to the resurrection of Jesus."

"Well, now, nothing like talk of eternal life to perk up the bidding," mused McMay with a sly grin.

Dan held up the printout and put a loupe against a spot near the bottom of the image and shouted, "Marcy!"

No reply.

He went to Marcy's desk in the outer office and sat in front of the computer. Dan placed the picture on the glass of the flatbed scanner and tapped a few keystrokes to transfer the image onto the screen. He zoomed the picture to two hundred percent. Dan saw McMay at his elbow. "I thought I saw something," Dan said to him. "And there it is, a part of a cartouche carved into the base."

"A what?"

"A cartouche. It's a king's name. The Egyptians wrote it inside an oval drawn to look like a rope, like this—see?"

"Yeah. I never noticed it."

"It was hidden in this shadow area, but when I punch up the contrast, you can read it."

"Speak for yourself, my friend. All I see are little birds and squiggles and things."

"Classical hieroglyphs," said Dan with his eye glued to the paper. "Well, this doesn't necessarily tell us when it was made—it could've been an antique when this king got a hold of it—but at least we have a start date on it. The ankh belonged to Tuthmosis III. He's an Eighteenth Dynasty pharaoh."

"Is that good?"

"They call Tuthmosis 'the Napoleon of Egypt,' but it doesn't begin to measure how truly great he was. He invaded most of the known world and took it all as his own personal fiefdom."

"And that adds to the price?"

"I couldn't possibly put a dollar figure on it."

"Oh, try."

"A damaged artifact rarely brings top dollar."

McMay pressed on. "But if I had both pieces—?"

"Under five hundred dollars. And that's only because it's a big ankh, and it's carved out of quartz, which is unique."

"Five hundred? That's hardly worth the trouble, Doc."

"You asked."

"If you don't mind," he said, "as long as you're at the computer, perhaps you might check the inventory to see if you've got the other half."

"Two seconds," said Dan, gliding his mouse to the inventory icon. When the dialog box appeared on screen, Dan entered the parameters of his search and double-clicked. A number and a description winked onto the monitor. A hit.

"This looks like it." Dan leaned back in his chair. "What do you know." Liam McMay flashed his brightest smile, then pushed back his cuff to note the time on his watch. "You've been a marvel, Doctor. I think I've got all the help I require."

"Sure?"

"Absolutely." He paused for a second, then leaned forward slightly. "Now that I know you have the matching piece, I was wondering . . . ?"

"Yes?"

"I could give you a good price for my client's half." Now, Dan was convinced McMay was hiding his agenda. Sotheby's would never make a preauction deal on a piece like the ankh—not if clients with Middle East oil money were so hot for it.

"I'll be happy to take a look when you have it on hand."

"Great, darlin' man," McMay said in his heaviest Lucky Charms accent. "I understand it's en route." He raised a finger. "How do I get out of this bone farm?"

"C'mon, I'll show you the way." Dan stood. He came around the desk smiling benignly and held the door open for McMay. Marcy was just coming back, and they passed in the corridor. Dan stopped her, asked McMay to wait for a moment, and took Marcy aside.

"Marce, when you get back to the office, you'll find a partial artifact on your computer. I found the catalogue number, so if you get a chance, go down to the bins and bring it up to me."

"Right now?" she asked.

"Naw, it's no big deal. Leave it in my desk drawer, and I'll take a look at it tomorrow." He started off.

The tiled corridors were busy with staff on their way to coffee breaks and Xerox machines. One or two faces poked out of their cubicles, checking out the foot traffic. Dan turned into a dim side hall, deserted and bare. He escorted the Irishman to a featureless double door and pushed it open.

They stepped across the doorsill and back thirty centuries into the rich, black land of Qemet, where they stood, facing the stern granite figure of Amun-Re. McMay let out a small gasp as his eyes accustomed to the half-light. It was as if they had been trapped in an ancient tomb.

He followed Dan through a short passage into the main gallery. The room was huge with shafts of smoke-filtered sunlight bathing the ancient exhibits from high clerestory windows.

"Through the double doors. Leads you right into the lobby."

"Perhaps we can talk again," he said.

Dan excused himself, but turned back before leaving the gallery. McMay was hunched over one of the showcases. It held the scrolls of Nekhen, the ones Dan had unearthed from a First Dynasty mastaba which had served as the crypt of a holy man. These papyri were perhaps the oldest copy of the Book of the Dead ever discovered. That one find had sealed his reputation in Egyptology.

The Nekhen scrolls formed the crux of his often-challenged theory that the Osiris legend was, in fact, a much mythologized version of the lives of an actual Egyptian clan that may have ruled the Nile delta in prehistory. Dan wondered, as he walked back to his office, if the Irishman from the auction house was aware of the significance of the exhibit, or was simply looking at the drawings of the brown naked girls that had been propped up behind the scrolls to show the daily life of the period. He voted for the naked girls.

Dan left and McMay walked off a moment later. He blended with a bus tour of people and disappeared through the gallery doors.

CHAPTER TWO ☥

Colonel Avram Halevi and five men crawled around a sewage trench at the perimeter of the Palestinian encampment. They advanced on their bellies, inch by inch, communicating by hand signal. Halevi touched his watch stem, and the time flashed red. He held up two fingers, and the others hurried forward to join him. They bunched under the overhang and waited.

After a few nervous heartbeats, the shelling began. The six-man team of Israeli commandoes heard the sounds of panic and instantly buried their heads against the falling debris. Explosions and screams echoed through the open drain. From the pitch, they knew the shells were raining true.

Halevi counted to twenty in intervals timed to his pulse, then rolled over the top of the ditch. His men vaulted after him, and they ran as a tight unit toward the barbed wire.

Boaz, the dark-skinned sergeant-major, rushed ahead with wire cutters. Two snips, and they were into the compound.

As planned, the force split into three groups of two. Halevi and a corporal cut left, using a storage building as cover. The camp heaved with each deafening artillery blast, fire and smoke camouflaging the Israeli advance as man-made lightning flashed in the night sky.

The attack was working well, drawing the Palestinians to other parts of the camp. A woman cried and stumbled blindly past Halevi, calling for her children and searching for a way out.

"I see it, Av," whispered Halevi's companion. "That low stone bunker."

"Right. Let's be in and out quick." Halevi paused until the instant of the next explosion, then amid the chaos, he raced for the hut. He flattened against the cool rock face of the side wall. Edging to the corner, he saw the floodlight still burning over the entry.

Too bright.

The sergeant-major aimed his Ingram and spit two rounds into the bulb, exploding it. Secure in the darkness, Halevi paused until the next artillery blast decoyed attention from his movements. A shell flew close and blew a small Toyota pickup into the air on a pillar of flame. Before it came down, Halevi was inside the bunker.

He swung his gun barrel in an arc covering the single room, but found no targets. The empty bunker was the size of a formal parlor, but its low ceiling made it appear wider. A single table dominated, reminding Halevi of a corporate board room. A map showing the borders of Lebanon, Syria, and Israel hung from a crossbeam. Another map was draped carelessly over one of the benches.

The colonel stood for a moment examining the chart, before footsteps from behind him made him crouch and whirl around. His corporal was in the doorway.

"The silence worried me," said the young man.

"Not having you at your post worries me more!" Halevi glowered, and the corporal colored under his commando's blackface.

"I'm gone, Colonel." And he was. Halevi ripped down the map and jammed it into his haversack. He folded the smaller chart and took it also. Dashing about the room like a sneak thief, he examined everything. Good went into the bag; trash onto the floor. He noticed a tin file box on the side table and dumped its contents in with the rest.

Only seconds before he must go.

With practiced eyes, Halevi quickly scanned the interior one last time. The bunker was disappointingly spare. Its walls were decorated in terrorist-chic, posters of Qadafi, Khomeini, and Arafat. He picked out a smaller photo of a man he knew well. Mahmoud Salameh. Last of the Munich Olympic butchers. The picture leaned between a large bronze brazier and a statuette of an ugly Egyptian god.

Probably nothing worth bothering with.

"Avram!"

Halevi hurried to the door and peered out. Through the smoke, Boaz waved at him to start back. After a quick nod, Halevi raced into the open and dived behind a pile of tires. He twisted onto his stomach and pointed his machine gun to cover the corporal's retreat.

"Go!"

The younger man darted across as a Palestinian ran out of the mist firing a hand weapon.

"Down!" shouted Halevi.

The corporal hit the ground as Halevi blurted a line of gunshots into the enemy's midsection. Seeing his deliverance, the corporal proceeded like a frightened lizard toward Sergeant-Major Boaz. "Hurry, hurry!" urged Halevi.

A shell landed close by. Halevi glimpsed a silhouette of a man in the momentary flash. Before he could warn his friend, the figure attacked.

Leaping from the thick smoke like an insane wraith, the Palestinian seized the young soldier's neck in a death grip. The corporal arched his back and, using commando tactics, threw the man aside. The figure regained his feet remarkably fast and lunged again for the Israeli. Halevi jumped from behind the tires, firing a spray of bullets that ignited like small flares along the figure's dark chest. The man stopped, but did not go down.

Using the moment, the corporal drew his knife. With a swift, offhand motion, he slit the Palestinian's throat. Halevi saw his dark form turn incredulously and fall into the cloud of smoke and mist that spawned him.

"Come on! We've wasted enough time!" Halevi shouted impatiently.

The corporal smiled and stepped toward the safety of the tires. Then he was gone! A dark powerful arm sprang upward and yanked the corporal to earth.

For seconds, the dust and smoke obscured them. Halevi could detect only the outlines of a struggle, then stillness.

Warily, Halevi stood pointing his Ingram at the fight scene. The smoke floated off. Both bodies were indistinct, seeming like discarded duffels, open and scattered in the dirt. Halevi crept forward, not more than five steps and halted.

His corporal was all broken, his body strewn at odd angles. But the other man—what was happening was impossible unless he had been hit by an incendiary shell. His body's contours were fast fading into the black soil; his flesh crumbling and falling away from the bone.

And his eyes. He had no eyes!

"Lord God," muttered Halevi.

The color drained from his face. He turned, running into the confusion of the night.

CHAPTER THREE

Liam McMay stood by the window of the ninth-floor corridor of the Madison Hotel and stared down at South Street as the city lights winked on. It had grown dark quickly, as if a curtain had been drawn on Manhattan.

One of the pay phones near him rang.

It jarred him from his thoughts, and out of habit he went over to the empty booths and picked up the phone on its second ring.

"McMay," he said, clearing his throat.

"How is my friend with the crimson hair?" The voice on the line was deep and heavily accented.

"Zamir?"

"Of course, Liam. Did it go well today?"

No one was about, but his voice slipped into a hush as he answered, "It worked out."

"Did he recognize the ankh, you think?"

"He didn't seem to when I showed him the picture." McMay went on to give a detailed account of the entire meeting, ending with his suggestion that Zamir provide a crew to help him with the theft of the ankh and the Nekhen scrolls.

Zamir either chuckled or coughed, McMay was not sure. "I've taken steps personally about that. Trust me that if all goes well, you will have no trouble at all. Go to the meeting place for the details. Ask for Natalia."

"Zamir, I'm not really in the mood."

"Be there within the hour, Liam."

A click ended the conversation.

"Zamir?" McMay slammed the receiver home, muttering. "That bloody Arab bastard! Go here; go there! He thinks he's James bleedin' Bond!"

McMay caught a cab quicker than he expected and made it crosstown in twenty minutes.

He got out a block from his destination. Partly from the caution Zamir expected from his operatives, but more out of Irish shame. A life of Catholic education had made him uncomfortable walking toward a red awning with a half-nude harem girl painted on it. He stood for a moment bathed in pink neon from the sign blinking the words "Sultan's Delite" above him.

McMay jerked open the outer door and entered fast, trying to exceed the speed of recognition. Inside, he exhaled. Opening the door to a massage parlor was always the toughest part.

He found himself in a tiny entranceway, cheaply paneled and dominated by a two-way mirror cut into the walnut veneer. A solid inner door was latticed with ornate iron work. He felt trapped in the small space.

He heard muffled voices. A flash of movement passed behind the mirrored glass.

"Please come in when you hear the buzzer." The words came from a speaker in the ceiling. A raucous, rusty chainsaw sound followed, and the heavy lock released. He entered quickly.

The interior was such a dark contrast to the bright entrance, he could actually feel the tug of his irises straining wider. Effectively blind, McMay jumped when he felt a soft, unexpected hand snaking around his arm.

"Hi. I'm Sunshine. Welcome to Sultan's Delite."

McMay's eyes were getting better. He could pick out gray shapes.

The girl attached to him seemed to have colorless, frizzy hair, no apparent face, and a body that seemed thin as shirt cardboard. She led McMay firmly to the only white light in the room. It was a desk lamp, and McMay was almost positive that a man was sitting in a chair beyond it.

"Let me introduce our manager, Eugene," said Sunshine.

McMay could make out her face now. He liked her better invisible.

"Hi, guy. I'm Eugene." Eugene stood and extended his hand. McMay guessed he was in his late twenties, awkwardly tall with blooming acne. His nose descended at a weird angle. All that, combined with his pastel polyester suit, made him resemble a flamingo.

"What may I call you, sir?"

"My name's . . . Newt Gingrich," McMay said.

"Oh, no need to use last names here, Newt," Eugene replied. "Have you ever been here before?"

"Once. A while ago."

"Well, why don't I refresh your memory." Eugene's eyes glazed over as he went into a standard spiel. "Sultan's Delite is a men's relaxation spa and a private membership club. In order to take a treatment, you must be a member. Our treatments are not medically based. They are solely designed to relieve sexual tension . . ."

"I hear there's a lot of that about."

"Uh, yeah," Eugene mumbled and stopped talking. McMay had the sinking feeling that Eugene might have to start again from the beginning. His lips moved for a few seconds, but he was able to go on without much delay.

"So, Newt, if you care to become a temporary member, which will entitle you to all of our privileges and facilities for the day, it'll cost you ten bucks."

Eugene produced a mimeographed document from his desktop. "And I'll have to ask you to sign this confidential release form, Newt. It's required by the management."

McMay signed without reading it.

"Our treatments start at twenty-five dollars and go to one hundred dollars, depending on how long you wish to spend with the young lady—and what form of gratification you'd like to obtain from your encounter. Y'understand?"

McMay nodded.

"Good," said Eugene. "So, why don't you go back with Sunshine, here. Let her show you the place, and she'll tell you about her services in more, uh, intimate detail."

Eugene placed his arm on McMay's shoulder, trying to lead him toward a beaded curtain behind him. McMay turned to face him.

"Look, Eugene, a friend sent me here. He said I should try a girl called Natalia."

Eugene screwed up his face. "Aw, why didn't you tell me that before? I wasn't expecting you for an hour."

"I made all the lights."

"Okay. Your session is paid for. Just go back to the Champagne Room, last curtain on the right. I'll send the lady in."

"Thanks."

"You can hang your clothes on the wall rack in there."

"Okay." McMay walked down the long corridor, dimly lit by red bulbs. The Champagne Room was decorated like Larry Flynt's wet dream. Two walls of the windowless cube were covered with shiny drapes, finished in red scalloped fringe. Dime-store nude paintings were hung randomly on the pale paneling, two of them painted on black velvet. A heart-shaped bathtub was sunk into a raised platform against the obligatory mirrored wall. A double bed dominated the wall opposite.

McMay made himself comfortable. He hung his coat from a hook and took out the tapes and small recorder from the pocket. He set them on the small end table beside two squeeze bottles of scented oil.

The curtains parted suddenly.

"You asked for me?" said a striking dark-skinned woman posing in the door frame. One arm hung loosely from the curtain rod, the other caressed her bare thigh. She wore a T-shirt cut off just below the smooth curve of her breasts and a bikini bottom that rode high on her prominent hip bones.

"You must be Natalia," purred McMay.

She almost smiled. Stepping inside, she let her arm slide seductively along the rod, closing the curtain behind her.

"And your name is . . . ?" Her voice possessed a halting quality, shaded by the hint of her foreign birth.

"Liam."

"A poet's name," she said, dropping her chin a bit to give more impact to her liquid brown eyes.

"All Irishmen are poets, darlin'," said McMay.

"Take off your clothes, Liam."

McMay snickered nervously. "That's not my reason for being here. Zamir told me to . . . you know him, don't you?"

"Yes." She sat on the bed and patted the mattress for McMay to join her.

"He said he made arrangements—."

"And once you're naked, I'll explain to you what he has in mind," she said, removing her top. Her breasts fell into place, set off by a gold, bird-shaped pendant between them. They were beautiful, light brown with dark, jutting tips. The sight of them made McMay swallow hard.

"Naked . . . uh, you want me naked?"

"Zamir requires it. He wants proof that you're not wearing a radio transmitter. He has a thing about secrecy. The phone in your hotel is equipped with a scrambler."

Natalia rose and untied the only wisp of blue cloth that covered her. It fell and she kicked it away with her heel. Nude, she bent over the bathtub and reached for the taps. The view sent a bright flush to McMay's face. He turned away as he struggled out of his pants.

"You like it hot, Liam?"

"Excuse me . . . ?"

"The water," said Natalia. "Hot or lukewarm?"

"Oh, tepid's fine. With my pale skin I end up looking like a lobster when I'm in hot water." McMay was unbuttoning his shirt. "Honestly, luv, is it absolutely necessary to get into that thing? I'd feel like bloody cupid in a box of Valentine candy."

"It's best to talk while the water's running," she said easing into the pink porcelain heart. "The walls might have ears, too."

McMay tested the water with his finger and joined her in the bath.

He sat in one of the top lobes of the heart with Natalia in the other. Their feet met at the point of the heart.

"Well, here we are! Can you talk to me now?"

"Of course."

McMay nodded. "About getting the souvenirs, luv. I haven't been paid as of yet."

"That disappoints me. I thought you Irish were motivated purely by love. Now I hear you talking of money."

"Even the IRA has to eat. Besides, I am only on loan to Zamir. I don't give a red hind of a baboon about you A-rabs."

Natalia's arm went behind McMay's head. She began to stroke the hair on the crown of his head with her damp hand. "Zamir has worried over that."

"Hey!" he yelled as Natalia pulled his hair.

"Zamir says it is time for you to become more involved. I believe the expression he used was 'body and soul.' "

McMay snorted, "Didn't I just bloody tell you that I don't bloody care about you Palestinians!"

Natalia interrupted, "I'm Egyptian."

"Who gives a shit! A bloody Arab's a bloody Arab!"

"Liam," she soothed, "Zamir wants an operative with more . . . flexibility." She leaned over and showed him her gold necklace. "Do you know what this is?"

"That charm? It looks like a bird with a man's head."

"It is the *Ba*. An eternal spirit. He is the great go-between. Through him, the dead can interact with the world of the living," said Natalia.

"Get to the point, hon," said McMay. "My skin is pruning up."

Her hand touched his stomach and moved lower. "Zamir wants me to give you release as a reward for all you've done for us. So, relax."

Natalia pressed her lips hungrily against his. The kiss silenced him, but McMay didn't care. Her mouth soon wandered across his cheek to his earlobe. "Liam, believe me," she whispered, "you will be more powerful than you ever could have conceived."

"Natalia . . . ?"

His eyes closed. He chewed on his lower lip. Natalia was exquisitely expert. It felt as though she could tease and excite each nerve ending individually.

"Let go, Liam . . ."

A low laugh escaped McMay's throat. Natalia shifted so that her body pressed against the length of him. With an easy movement, she unhooked her necklace and draped it around McMay's throat.

"For you, Liam."

He looked down at his chest. The tiny man-headed bird seemed to stare up at him. Then, an odd guttural sound hit his ear.

Was she having an orgasm?

But when McMay looked at Natalia, her eyes were shut and her lips were forming words—strange words—chanted in a cadence McMay had never heard.

Suddenly, her lids opened! Their eyes locked, and McMay heard a deep hiss escape her throat.

"Are you all ri—" McMay stopped speaking as she moved on top of him and smiled. The water splashed over his chin. A drop tickled his nose, and he returned Natalia's smile. Her thighs wrapped around the sides of McMay's legs, drawing them apart. He sank another inch or two into the tub, the water lapping against his nostrils. But he didn't care.

Natalia's thin fingers stroked and squeezed up and down his shaft. It was almost time . . . almost . . . almost . . .

"Promise me," she said urgently. "Promise that all your soul will serve the Horus . . . Promise me . . ."

Natalia's free hand lifted the bird amulet to McMay's mouth and gently ran the gold across his lips. She pressed the charm into his mouth.

He didn't care.

"Promise, Liam . . . and you will be his . . ."

His heart beat so fast, his breath so shallow. "Yes-yes . . . *YES!* I promise."

Without breaking rhythm, Natalia's hand dropped to McMay's testicles, toyed with them for an instant—then crushed them with a single powerful squeeze.

McMay's body convulsed as if hit by a lethal electric current.

His distorted mouth tried to scream, but Natalia's forearm held it underwater. He couldn't think—only pain—inhuman pain!

The amulet slid into his windpipe. He swallowed water and might have drowned—if the shock had not stopped his heart first!

All agony and life left him in ninety seconds, but Natalia stayed on top of him for a full five minutes to be sure. Then, she stepped out of the tub and grabbed a towel. She was dressing when Eugene walked in.

"Any trouble?" he asked. Natalia shook her head.

"Take his body out of the wet. It mustn't be allowed to rot."

"No problem." Eugene pulled the plug and let the water empty from around the pale body. He deposited McMay in a laundry cart and started out. He turned at the door. "Hey, I still got a business to run. I want you to clean up good In here!"

"Yeah, yeah . . . ," said Natalia.

Eugene pointed his finger. "I mean it. I want that tub spotless when I come back here. And don't think I'm not gonna check on you!"

"Don't forget these," she said and tossed McMay's clothes into the basket on top of his body.

As Eugene wheeled McMay down the red-tinted corridor, Natalia reached under the bed and withdrew a can of Bon-Ami. After shaking out a light snowfall of cleanser into the bath, she crouched on her knees and scrubbed the caking soap scum from the sides of the pink porcelain.

She stretched her back after a minute and muttered, "A woman's work is never done."

CHAPTER FOUR

ISRAEL

The bright morning had long since become an oppressively hot afternoon as the Land Rover entered the welcome shadow of the mound. It followed a narrow trail that ended in an old drainage ditch. There, the driver stopped to take his bearings.

Once a paved road curved up here, he remembered. One that led to the gates of the city. But it wasn't a city anymore. This he remembered, too. They called it "a site." And the village at the base bore no relation to the fortress-state that once commanded the Plain of Jezreel. Its only commerce, at present, centered on the dig.

In summer, the townsfolk were tourist guides; in spring, they planted; in fall, they harvested and, whenever the archaeologists left for their own homes, the men lowered themselves into the hill and cut away thin slices of the past.

A dust devil in his side mirror caught the driver's eye. It spiraled from the trail behind him. He twisted in his seat and riveted his eyes on the source of the sand cloud.

An old pickup was speeding toward him, and he could see a man hanging out the passenger window, his arms waving wildly. The Land Rover's driver estimated the pickup to be no more than three minutes away. No time to run, not that flight was ever a serious consideration.

Instead, he grasped the top of the windshield, lifted himself out of the cab, and waited.

Standing, the driver was impressive, tall and thin with the outline of tight, powerful muscles under his thin khaki shirt. His face was plainly Arab, but possessed of elegant features accented by the aviator sunglasses he wore.

He relaxed against the fender until the small truck pulled alongside him. Before it had fully stopped, a large young man in a camouflage shirt jumped from the passenger side. He waved his arms with palms forward, indicating for the Rover to stay where it was. The driver nodded, noticing the gun handle jutting from the young man's belt.

"Civilian militia!" he shouted in Hebrew and Arabic. The driver understood both. "Stay where you are, sir!"

He drew his pistol and leveled it at the driver, who relaxed easily against his Land Rover, saying not a word.

"Don't make any quick moves!" ordered the militiaman.

The driver, slowly, without any show of fear, placed his hands in clear view. The man remaining in the pickup gunned its engine and cut in front of the Land Rover, blocking its path. With escape impossible, the swarthy man got out, flanking the gunman and the driver.

The darker man with his curly brown hair and sun-baked suspicious face was certainly a sabra, a native-born Israeli named for the prickly pear that grew in the Negev Desert.

"What exactly is your business here, mister?" he said as he came closer.

The driver responded in a deep, mellow voice. "Have I made an error?"

"You drove here cross-country over the desert, like a thief, instead of using the road, didn't you?" said the young militiaman, his hand at his gun. "And here you are, trespassing on our land."

"Your land?" asked the driver. "Forgive me, sir, but from your accent you hardly seem Israeli. English . . . no, American I would guess."

The sabra spoke up. "Saul's as Israeli as I am!"

"Yeah, since '94," said Saul. "But you're the one who's got to come up with the answers. Who the hell are you?"

The detainee shrugged. "Excuse my impertinence. I have not been in this land for many years and did not realize that I was under interrogation. How may I help you?"

"How about your name for a start?" said Saul.

"Hammad al-Kahlil."

"Arab," the sabra snorted. Saul's hand tensed on the handle of his automatic.

"Palestinian?" Saul asked.

The man called Kahlil smiled indulgently. "Egyptian," he said, "of the purest blood, I assure you. May I sit and have a drink of water?"

"Okay."

Kahlil leaned on his front bumper, stretching his long legs out in front of him. He picked up a bottle of Evian water from the sand at his feet. He offered the water to the American. "Join me, Mr. Saul?"

"Rosenstiel . . . Saul Rosenstiel. My friend's Yacov. We're part of the security force at Kibbutz Bethshad."

"You know, Mr. Rosenstiel," Kahlil began, after taking a sip, "with peace, you must expect more of us to appear among you. Is that not true?"

"We've been a long time enemies. And when Sadat put out his hand in friendship to us, it was you, the Egyptians, who shot him dead!"

Kahlil eased an identification wallet from a front pocket and handed it to Saul. "You have nothing to fear from me."

The two Israelis conferred. After a minute or so of exchanging whispers, Saul let his gun drop to his side. "Looks official," Saul said.

Kahlil raised his sunglasses to his forehead, revealing penetrating black eyes. He regarded Yacov, but the sabra kept back, still suspicious. Finally, Yacov spoke. "Those papers don't say why you were tearing up our sorghum field instead of coming by the road."

"My friend," Kahlil answered, as he gathered his papers and climbed back into his Land Rover, "Egyptians have always approached Megiddo with the sun at their back." He glanced back at Saul. "May I continue to the tel? I wish to arrive at the excavation before the light fails."

Saul motioned to Yacov, who returned to the pickup, started the engine, and let it roll out of Kahlil's way. Saul didn't turn to leave, instead remained by the door of the Land Rover.

Kahlil started his vehicle and drove off. In half a mile, the trail became a road. As it snaked upward, a group of low buildings became more distinct through the dust-laden desert air. The kibbutz.

Another settlement appeared above, near the flattened top of the mound. Arab diggers stayed in them. Its structures were cruder than those built in the Israeli commune below.

The pickup ahead of Kahlil was kicking up a thick dust cloud, so he dropped back a bit. As he did, a range of jagged foothills to the south attracted his attention.

His heart leapt.

A gray-white turnpike cut straight and wide through a natural parting in the high rocks. He recognized it immediately—The Conqueror's Road, Via Maris—The Way of the Sea!

Blood had, at one time or another in its ten-thousand-year history, covered every inch of that ancient highway. Joshua traveled it, as did Alexander the Great.

And thirty-five hundred years before, a young pharaoh, barely out of his teens, killed a fatted calf on that road to celebrate his first victory.

———————————

"What brings you to Megiddo, Mr. Kahlil?"

A weather-browned, sixty-six-year-old gentleman was bent over his cluttered work space drawing a metric grid onto a photo of what seemed to be a featureless pile of rock and dirt. Dr. Gunther Rawlins had not looked up when Saul Rosensteil and Yacov escorted Kahlil into the trailer, and only took his eyes from the picture when the Egyptian had been introduced.

"My reasons for coming are sensitive, Dr. Rawlins. That call from Cairo was only partially true. If we could speak alone?" Kahlil presented his papers, including one with the seal of the prime minister at the bottom.

Gunther did not examine the documents until after he traced an intersecting line on his graph. He saw Saul waiting expectantly. "Wait outside, son," said Gunther, dismissing him. "Our conversation would only bore you."

Saul motioned to Yacov and they left, taking up positions in the shade as they closed the door behind them. Yacov circled to the window and watched Kahlil lean forward and speak words he could not hear.

"It was partially excavated before this obelisk talk, but we had to stop at the end of the season," Gunther said. "Funds for Biblical field research are erratic these days."

"Yes, I had heard you had begun a trench on that level."

Gunther sighed heavily. "I made a mistake and set the dig between an inner and outer wall. It was not a promising spot, and I ordered it abandoned."

"Then you are doubly in error, Dr. Rawlins. I believe the obelisk has fallen and lies on its side in that very location."

Gunther combed ten fingers through his gunmetal hair and ended the gesture with one palm clasped firmly at the back of his neck. "Go on."

Kahlil stood easily and stepped toward a wall-sized aerial photograph of the tel mounted beside the window. He pressed a thin finger on a section of trench hidden in shadow. "Why don't I show it to you?"

"Why this help, Mr. Kahlil? What do you gain?"

"You caught me, Doctor," said Kahlil. "The Israelis have recently allowed our archaeologists to examine records of Egyptian artifacts found at sites in this country. We at the Cairo Museum think that a damaged ankh you discovered here, at Megiddo, during your 1972 season may match a piece we have in our collection. Our own studies disclosed a possibility that you've overlooked a very interesting find, and I propose a trade. Our information for your half of the ankh."

"The trade seems lopsided in my favor."

"Oh, we expect to negotiate the proper credits and, after you spend your money digging it up, perhaps we might both profit from a joint traveling exhibit."

"Tell me about this secret artifact. It sounds impressive. What is it?"

"Let's see if it's where we think it is, first," answered Kahlil and went out the door. Gunther followed.

The terraced pit dropped over one hundred fifty feet from the crest of the tel. Kahlil glanced over the edge, seeing rope ladders and scaffolding that led to a series of irregular stone steps. They went further down, fading into a powdery darkness.

"The tel is quiet this time of year," said Gunther. "You see, most of our best workers come from Bethshad. Very smart and thorough. But it's harvest time for them now. Besides, all the academics are starting their fall classes."

"Your son would be one of them, I assume."

Gunther's expression clouded over. "I have no idea what he's doing," the old man replied stiffly. He stood near the rim and pointed to a sheer masonry wall exposed beneath them. "That side wall was part of the city's defenses. Our base level has hit about 1500 B.C. There is a siege wall across the way . . ." Gunther indicated what appeared to be a random stone heap. "Shall we go down?"

Kahlil nodded. Gunther jumped a foot to the scaffold with the agility of a man thirty years younger and opened a locked wooden box. He removed two hand lanterns and handed one to Kahlil.

"We'll be needing these," said Gunther. "It's black as pitch at the bottom, even at midday."

Gunther guided Kahlil down three ladders that brought them to a stairway cut into one of the side shafts. They were steep, but Gunther took them confidently.

"Careful," called Gunther. "One or two of the steps are flaky."

Kahlil nodded, grasping the sides of the trench for support until he reached a landing on the third stratum. Gunther continued downward without a rest stop. He boarded another ladder that was braced against the ledge. Kahlil noticed its uprights had worn grooves into the rock, it had stood there so long.

Kahlil gripped the top rung as he backed over the side, following after him. One step, then another. Each rung equaling how many years? Centuries per yard . . .

The Crusades . . .

The birth of Christ . . .

Alexander . . .

Shadows closed in on the two men. The pale dirt walls reflected some sunlight into the pit, but not enough. Gunther turned on his lantern and pointed the beam into the gritty darkness. The light hit bedrock about twenty feet below them.

"We are nearly there," said Kahlil as he reached the bottom. Gunther followed the Egyptian's torch around a forty-five degree angle in the trench and found him kneeling at a long, high step in the wall.

Only it wasn't a step.

"If you brush off half a meter of soil, you'd see it yourself. Intact, laid on its side."

"Yes." The word escaping as a hiss from Gunther's lips. He scraped off a clot of dirt from the end of the pillar and paid Kahlil little notice. "Look here, where it's been chipped all about the base. It didn't fall in an earthquake. It was moved deliberately from its original spot."

"It was in the central courtyard in front of the temple of Astarte."

Silence.

When Gunther spoke again, his voice wavered with uncertainty. "How could you know such a thing?"

"I am Egyptian. I know where to put an obelisk."

Kahlil rose to his feet. As he stood, Gunther tilted up his lantern, keeping it full on Kahlil's face until it appeared as a disembodied head floating over him. Shadows blocked his eyes.

"How did you know there was an obelisk hidden here?" Gunther asked.

"Obelisks have power. It drew me."

Gunther was not convinced. "And what credit did you expect for its discovery? Full or shared?"

Kahlil shook his head in a single, economical motion that hinted at much more. "Neither. All I ask is that you uncover it. Then photograph the inscriptions and have them translated. I wish the story carved on this monument to be told to the world by an eminent scientist and theologian such as yourself. And more, I want this miraculous tale believed."

A sound coming from around the angle of the trench interrupted them. Gunther rose and held his lantern toward the noise.

"Yes?"

No answer.

Gunther went to investigate, Kahlil following. At the ladder, he raised his light. A man stood on a rung ten feet from the floor. The dust at the bottom of the pit scattered the beam, making the figure indistinct.

"Mr. Kahlil? Are you there?" asked the man.

"I am."

"Will you please step closer, Mr. Kahlil."

Kahlil strode away from Dr. Rawlins, responding sharply, "Who is up there? I tell you, I resent this intrus—"

Five flashes of light! Bap-bap-bap-bap-bap. More explosions followed instantly, echoing against the packed dirt walls!

A machine gun burst!

Percussive blasts of point-blank hollow-point bullets drove the body of Hammad al-Kahlil sprawling backwards, smashing into the earth at Gunther's feet! Kahlil's flashlight hit the floor and cracked. Gunther dropped his hand so that his lantern now shone low on the Egyptian's gaping chest wounds. Gunther froze until a sound brought him back to his senses. Above his head, shoes scraped on the metal rungs.

The killer was climbing down the ladder! Coming for him!

Gunther threw the flashlight and ran blindly into the darkness. His fingertips trailed along the walls, leading him into the labyrinth of trenches. He entered an auxiliary tunnel that jutted roughly at a right angle to the main axis. Each narrow shaft had its own escape route in case of cave-ins, but in his panic Gunther could not remember where. The piercing beam from a lantern rounded the corner behind him.

Whoever it was—the assassin or terrorist—had picked up the castoff light and was after him! Gunther slid into a ten-foot crevice, the remnant of a false start. His hand hit a thick length of rope. A rope ladder! It hung from the masonry wall.

Gunther reached up and grabbed for it. His hands were wet, slippery from fright. The killer passed a few feet away and down the main passage. Gunther breathed easier. He pulled himself off the floor, but his grip slipped on the horizontal rope, and he fell into the dirt.

Shaken, Gunther tried to crawl, but suddenly, the light was there! The doctor gulped air in spasms as the man found the niche and blocked it with a wide stance. The round, glaring light came nearer until it was directly above him. An arm reached down.

"Dr. Rawlins," he began, "it's Yacov, sir. You are safe now. There is no need to be frightened."

"Y-Yacov?"

The Israeli lifted Gunther to his feet. "We had to take action. The man was a murderer."

"Kahlil?"

"His name is not Kahlil, sir. I thought I recognized his face when Saul and I met him, but I couldn't place it."

Yacov paused to help Gunther to his feet. He continued as they started back to the ladder. "While you were entertaining that devil down here, I drove down to Bethshad to look at the files we have. And there he was! Practically on top!"

"There *who* was?"

"My mother's cousin Danny was killed at the Munich Games. That's where I knew *that* Kahlil from. He was one of the Black September group that was caught after all the athletes were slaughtered at the airport."

Yacov paused as the Egyptian's body came into view, then went on, spitting the words out with contempt. "Later, our friends, the Germans, caved in to a hijacking and set the murderer free. I suppose they thought he had only killed a bunch of Jews, so what did it matter. But we had good photographs of him by that time."

"Then he's—"

"The planner, the worst of them. Salameh."

Gunther and Yacov stopped beside the body, looking from the oozing chest wounds to his hideously open eyes. Gunther, now composed, returned to his Cambridge accent and manner with full force. "I hope it is not your intention to bury him down here!"

"No, sir. But I'd rather not move the body before notifying the army."

"Oh, I see. You can machine-gun down an unarmed man—not two feet away from me, I might add—without consulting a single person, but it takes a bloody proclamation from the Knesset before you can clean up your mess!"

A voice came from the scaffolding above. "That is hardly fair, Doctor." It was Saul Rosensteil at the top of the ladder.

"Yacov worried that terrorist might kill you. He's ruthless and he's gotten away before. Maybe when he got the bastard in his sight . . ."

"If he was actually the man!" interrupted Gunther. "What makes you so certain he was this Salameh character? Merely that he resembles a fifteen-year-old snapshot? His papers were quite impressive and perfectly in order!"

"Doctor—"

"You idiots! We may not simply have a corpse here; we may have an international incident of cosmic proportions!"

Yacov tried to take his arm, but Gunther shrugged him away. Yacov stepped back, anxious.

"Please, sir. I don't know why he wanted to speak to you, but Salameh is, was, a madman. An anarchist. You couldn't believe anything he said. Let's go up to the field office. We can talk this all out when the soldiers get here."

Suddenly, Gunther remembered the obelisk. He could see the entire Israeli army swarming into the trench and all over his discovery. He turned to Yacov.

"As long as I am down here, there's some work I'd like to finish. Now leave me alone, both of you!"

"But, Doctor, you can't stay in this hole with . . . *that!*"

Gunther pushed Yacov toward the ladder. "Out! I've been around cadavers before. This one's just a bit fresher than most."

Dr. Gunther Rawlins sat on the side of the obelisk and clicked off the lantern light. He leaned back against the cool earthen wall and closed his eyes.

It was much too black to see and, frankly, Gunther preferred it that way. This year marked Gunther's thirty-eighth in archaeology, and after all that time he found it very comfortable being underground. The sun could bake Jezreel with one hundred and twenty degree heat, but it always remained cool in a deep dig.

Five thousand years of insulation.

He pulled the air of the pit into his nostrils and smelled the foul sweetness of blood. The body of Hammad al-Kahlil still lay around the corner. Gunther opened his eyes, seeing nothing but the dark. He sat alone with his thoughts, as dark as the trench itself.

"Rawlins? Oh, yes. . . . Involved in that Megiddo affair, wasn't he?"

"Terribly sorry, old man. But renewing our funding would be clearly impossible. That Megiddo scandal, y'know."

"Rawlins allowed some kibbutz hotheads to murder an innocent Egyptian official under his protection. On some sort of a peace mission, too, I hear."

Gunther groped for his lantern. He trained the light on the obelisk. The stone could be protected by a bit of dirt and a few of the sandbags lying about. An hour's work or so. By the time Saul and Yacov drove down to Bethshad and radioed the incident to Jerusalem, Gunther could finish. He assumed the army would send a team by helicopter at once, but they would be more interested in the body around the angle of the trench. With any luck, they wouldn't come near the obelisk.

With luck . . .

As he dragged a couple of sandbags onto the granite step, Gunther thought again of Kahlil.

If he were some innocuous bureaucrat, could anyone truly blame me for the Egyptian's death? Surely it would be considered a tragic mistake.

Unless, of course, Kahlil *was* the terrorist Salameh. Gunther smiled. He'd be a damned hero, then. But, certainly, Kahlil could not be Salameh. Salameh had been at Munich. If the fugitive had been a teenager at the time, he would be nearing sixty now. Kahlil was no more than forty, or perhaps younger.

After seventy minutes, most of the obelisk was disguised by sandbags and soil. Gunther took a short break to catch his breath. A minute or so later, he decided to walk back to the ladder and check for any activity overhead.

As soon as his lantern's beam turned the corner, Gunther saw the body had vanished. He ran over and checked the ground. The imprint of Kahlil's body was still plainly visible in the dust.

Instinctively, he looked up the scaffolding. He saw two figures silhouetted against the sky. He shouted up at them.

"Saul? Yacov? I thought you boys were so keen about keeping that body down here until the army came!"

It seemed to Gunther that they were leaning on the metal guard rails, baiting him. They made no attempt to answer, an attitude that offended him greatly. Angry, Gunther climbed up the ladder to give the arrogant kibbutzniks a piece of his mind, but when he reached the planking and pointed his lamp at the two shapes, he staggered back and almost fell.

Was he hallucinating? Had his mind been unbalanced by the horrid stress? Surely, the two corpses were Saul and Yacov. But it was hard to tell, because both men had been charred to the color of coal. Their bodies, twisted, tangled, and fused to the uprights and crosspieces of the scaffold, must have been subjected to a sudden and incredibly intense heat.

Gunther pulled himself up and stood beside the dead young men. *What in the name of Heaven could have happened?*

His hands shook as he searched the platform with his lantern. Perhaps, he reasoned, a power line came loose, hit the metal pole, and electrocuted them.

Except, there weren't any frayed wires that he could find. It was then that Gunther realized he was not alone. He swung the beam to see Hammad al-Kahlil grinning at him—a line of bullet holes still oozing red from his chest.

"Follow me, Gunther," he said in an almost intimate whisper.

Dumbstruck, Gunther took half a minute to respond. "I-I saw you die . . ."

Salameh fixed an unblinking stare at him. Gunther let his light fall from his grasp, but he still saw those eyes—those strange, magnetic eyes.

Salameh tilted his head at a strange angle. "Isaiah said, 'The dead shall live; the bodies shall arise.' Did he not, Biblical scholar?"

Underneath his false calm, Gunther was frantic. Why was this crazy man quoting Scripture? The wounds in his chest looked fatal, but what did he know of such things? He had heard stories of men living with horrible trauma.

Adrenaline or something.

Gunther saw a red shimmer underneath Salameh's jacket. He watched the man withdraw an oddly-shaped crystal from an inside pocket. Its glow sliced through the darkened trench as Salameh held it out to Gunther.

"Follow me."

Gunther nodded, his will nearly gone. But one last question escaped through his dry lips. "Who . . . what . . . are you?"

CHAPTER FIVE

Jacinda el-Bahri lay still, concentrating on the ceiling of her cramped hotel room. The moisture clung to her bare skin, a tiny rivulet trailing between her breasts. She wiped it away as she eased out of bed and moved to the window.

With some effort, she opened it wider and let the night breeze fan her nakedness. Then, she reached to the night table for her hashish and rolled a cigarette. Her hand fidgeted with a box of matches. She struck one. The flame flared, for an instant exposing her exquisite body to the Egyptian night.

The aromatic smoke relaxed her, but not enough. She craved sleep and rented this cheap hotel room as a burrow where she could hibernate until her control picked her up.

Once she was in his hands, she might not be able to close her eyes for days, depending on the escape route Malamat had planned. It could be a feint to the south on a tourist steamer or a dash east across the Gulf.

After a time, she returned to bed and sat rubbing her hands along her thighs to loosen her muscles. It didn't work. For all her training, she was a knot of nerves. Jacinda took her automatic from the drawer and hit the catch on the magazine. The clip fell into her palm. Quickly, she checked the bullets and the spring as she had done an hour before. Slapping the clip back, she ran the cool metal barrel along her damp throat.

She suddenly shivered—not from the temperature. Cairo's air was a hot, foul mix of city fumes and desert wind. Her shiver came from inside—some pestering instinct that came on her when things weren't right.

She shoved the gun into her bag with a loud sigh and rose from the mattress. She made it to the sink in the corner and splashed a handful of dark, tepid water over her face and let it roll down her neck into the reservoir above her collarbones.

"I've got to get out of here," she announced to herself. With the four walls closing in on her and no chance for a nap, there wasn't any reason to stay barricaded inside. Among Cairo's millions, she thought, she would be anonymous and as safe from Salameh as she would be buried in that room.

She reached under the curve of the basin where she had taped her black vinyl pouch. It was filled with her forged travel papers, money, and one ancient artifact, a fractured half of an Egyptian cross. She wasn't certain if the Arabs were searching for her, yet. She suspected they were.

If the stories were true, Salameh had spent most of his fugitive life searching for that mysterious ankh. And if the most notorious terrorist on Earth wanted it, his enemies were pledged to keep it from him. Jacinda's handlers hadn't confided whatever secret the ruined quartz held, only that it was a priority she steal it. And Jacinda always did what she was told.

She slipped the pouch, like a garter, onto her upper thigh. In five minutes, she finished dressing, dabbed on a bit of makeup, and ran a brush through her hair. She slid the automatic into her bag and hung it casually from her left shoulder. Looking back from the door, she scanned the room. Mossad agents never leave anything behind in foreign hotel rooms.

Jacinda locked the door and walked the seven flights to street level. She let herself out the side exit, bypassing the lobby and the vigilant eyes of the concierge. A sleek, short-haired cat blocked her way. It mewed and rubbed against her leg. She was about to pet it, when she recalled fifteen or so diseases carried by Egyptian street cats and rushed off.

She broke out to the street with an urge to move. An old bread truck was parked in a direct line under the room she had just left. It seemed to her too late at night for a delivery, but her heightened sense of caution could have led her to suspect anything.

However, an inner urgency told her to run, and as she quickened her stride—the entire west wall of her hotel blew out in a confusion of light, fire, rubble, and finally, clouds of gray-brown dust!

Though halfway down the block, the blast threw Jacinda to the pavement. For an instant, she was suspended, her mind refusing to react to the sudden danger.

But her body did.

She tucked and pressed herself against the only available cover, an old Fiat parked at the curb. Glass slivers and debris rained into the street as Jacinda braced on the car door. Beside her, one of the tires burst as a daggerlike shard of glass sliced into the rubber.

Jacinda screamed as the sound of the explosion pierced right through her. Her eyes clenched shut for seconds that lasted forever. At last, cries and moans began to replace the echoes of the bomb. She noticed herself start breathing again and when she stood, dust and glass fragments fell from her shoulders.

She walked a few steps toward the hotel, but nearly lost her footing on the brick-strewn sidewalk. Only then did she look up to the seventh floor to gasp at the blackened inferno that had been her room. She backed away for a few feet, then turned and ran into the night.

As sirens blared in the streets, Jacinda managed to find an empty phone booth in the lobby of the nearby Hilton. Her nerves had settled to a silent shriek as she dialed Malamat's number. No answer. She tried the emergency line. It picked up after one ring.

"I'm alive," she said.

"That's interesting." The voice was male with a neutral accent.

"I have information about the—"

"Are you speaking from a secure line?" the voice interrupted.

"I'm at the goddam Hilton!"

"You shouldn't be calling at all!" the voice chided. "In any event, please refrain from using specifics."

"All right, all right!" she hissed. "Get me the colonel."

"He's unavailable."

"What do you mean? There aren't any cell phones? Satellites don't exist?"

"The colonel has placed himself out of reach for reasons of security. Do you wish to be brought in?"

"It's my right," she whispered into the receiver. She tried to sound controlled and assertive, but she felt like a frightened little girl. "Don't you understand? They tried to blow me into bits—"

"Can we assume they think they have succeeded? If so, you will certainly be safe for a time. Do you have a contact in Cairo?"

"Not in Cairo exactly. But not too far out of town. At Malamat's."

"Not there. Malamat's dead."

Jacinda blanched. "H-how?"

"No details, remember."

"How?" More emphatic this time.

The voice paused, then spoke quickly. "Ritual murder with an Egyptian theme. They took out his organs and put them in old olive jars. I'd suggest you go to one of the tourist towns on the Red Sea. Don't tell me where. Go there. Stay hidden for a week or ten days until the colonel returns."

"A week? Don't you get it? I have the ankh on me. I lost my cover! They know I've betrayed them, and terrorists don't have forgiving natures. If they see me, they kill me."

"I understand, but your refuge contact is dead. You have no options."

"What if I tried for the coast? If I get back to Israel . . ."

"Call in a week." He severed the connection immediately.

For a good twenty seconds, Jacinda held the buzzing handset to her ear. They had abandoned her. In a fury, she smashed the phone down on the hook.

Her refuge contact!

It was Mossad's method to limit the damage a captured agent could do. In every territory, the field agent was given one person to go to for refuge and a telephone number as backup. Given the choice, Jacinda would have chosen the phone option first, because her refuge contact was Joe Malamat, a man she loathed.

The prospect of ten ceaseless days under his roof almost made her happy that he was dead. She'd never have to suffer his stinking breath or his roaming hands ever again.

"Lady?"

The voice startled her, and she looked up. A young Saudi man wearing a dress jellaba with a white flowing kaffiyeh on his head was blocking her exit from the booth. Jacinda slipped her free hand into her bag and found her revolver.

"Have you finished with the telephone?" said the Arab politely. "I am late for an appointment, and I need to call my friends to explain and beg their forgiveness."

"Oh," was all she could manage to say.

"I noticed you were no longer speaking," he added, "and all the other booths seem to be occupied."

Jacinda realized that she still grasped the receiver tightly in her hand. She flushed when she saw that the man posed no threat to her.

Nervously, she placed the phone back on its cradle and rose with a slight bow of apology. She hurried by the young man and left quickly by the employee's exit. The door opened to a narrow, dark alley where a number of Cairo's derelicts huddled around the garbage rummaging for food from the hotel kitchen.

One of the beggars noticed her and nudged the even shabbier man at his elbow. Both flashed gap-toothed grins at her, but made no move in her direction. She deliberately marched away from the main thoroughfare to a crowded side street and headed south from the hotel district toward a residential neighborhood. Less people would be on the streets at that hour. The fewer the better for what she had in mind.

As the people thinned out, she began searching the curb sides. She found a fast-looking car parked in the shadow of an apartment building.

Its driver's window was open far enough for her to snake her arm inside and unlock the door. In the driver's seat, Jacinda fished a screwdriver from her bag and cracked the ignition lock in thirty seconds. One turn of the handle started the engine, and she drove off.

The traffic along the narrow lanes was light at that late hour, but she maneuvered the stolen auto at a leisurely pace. For the first time since the shock of the bombing, her training began to govern her actions.

Colonel Halevi's rule one: When you're in trouble, go slow!

She eased the car onto the northern road, following the Nile toward Said. She went faster, but kept her speed under ninety km. The well-paved highway, wider and straighter than most Egyptian roads, allowed for it—a legacy from Nasser.

She glanced at her watch. Four hours to daylight. Just enough time to reach the port and hide the car before anyone would notice. Fifteen minutes into the trip, a cramping pain crept up from her shoulders. She massaged it with one hand, and it felt better. But the ache tired her, making her drowsy. She opened the windows to let in the cool air coming off the great river.

Her long black hair sailed back, whipping wildly in the rush of wind.

She drank in the oxygen. It cleared her head. She adjusted herself in her seat, wiped perspiring hands on her thighs, and tried to make sense of the last two hours.

Egypt has more factions than a jigsaw puzzle has pieces. How could she be certain that the hotel bomb was meant for her? Maybe it wasn't a bomb at all! Gas heaters explode in old hotels all the time!

She laughed out loud. Not when it is ninety degrees outside, they don't! No, there had to be a bomb in that truck!

Her mood changed once more, probably due to the hashish. Her features tightened into a stony mask. Resolute. What had really happened?

Was she truly a target? Couldn't it be a—*no*. For agents, there was no such creature as a coincidence.

Each instant of the past year, the terrorist underground had shaped her life, but recently she had been noticing a strange tension around her "brothers." It seemed that conversations would drop into whispers or stop entirely when she entered the room.

Five days before, rumors started that their leader, Mahmoud Salameh, had left Libya and gone to Israel on a private mission. If only she could pinpoint where the Mossad could find him, Jacinda might help trap the most devious and dangerous terrorist in the world.

The previous night, she had staked out Shafiq's antique shop (which served as headquarters for the faction) from a one-room apartment across the alley. About ten, she caught sight of Shafiq arriving at the back door with a heavyset man she recognized as Zamir Qader, a spokesman for the political wing of the organization. He was also the only contact with their master, who had been a shadow man for thirty years.

Jacinda's window presented an excellent view of the two men in Shafiq's office. A pair of high-power binoculars allowed her to focus on the details, and a bug hidden in the light fixture enabled her to record the conversation.

"He was wounded," she heard Qader say, "but he is recovering quickly. Miraculously, I would say. As befits him."

"May Allah protect him."

Qader handed Shafiq what appeared to be a square of dark velvet. Shafiq wore an awed expression as he removed an object from the soft pocket. Jacinda knew of it, but had always thought it never left Salameh's hand. It was the symbol of Salameh's movement, the broken ankh.

The emblem was half a loop and a crosspiece that, if whole, would form a ubiquitous shape in Egypt, sold at every corner souvenir stand.

But the ankh was the most ancient of symbols, associated with the Aten, the face of the sun. As an image of the daily renewal of sunrise conquering the black of night, it stood for healing and resurrection. Broken, it represented the lost grandeur of Egypt, and by extension, the entire Arab world.

Most ankhs were cast in gold or bronze, but this relic, larger than most she had seen in the store, was fashioned from a piece of quartz with currents of light that oscillated in color from pale pink to a deep blood red.

Although, Shafiq smuggled stolen artifacts to help finance the cell, holding the ankh, he appeared nervous. Presently, he took it into his workroom. Jacinda watched him disappear through the beaded curtain, but figured that Shafiq was taking the ankh into his small photography studio to shoot an 8x10 Polaroid using the fifty-year-old Deardorff camera set up in there.

"It must be the exact size it is in life, Shafiq," Qader ordered from the office.

"Yes, yes. One to one."

Jacinda heard a phone ring. Qader took a tiny handset from his top pocket, listened for a moment, and yelled at Shafiq, "How long is this going to take?"

"Give me half an hour."

Qader mumbled something into the receiver and replaced the phone back into his coat. "I've been given an errand, Shafiq. I'll be back in twenty minutes, and I expect the photograph to be sent!"

"Yes, yes. Rush, rush, rush."

Qader left and, for a few minutes, nothing was seen or heard. Then, Jacinda saw Shafiq reenter his office with the ankh in one hand and an instant print of it in the other. He set the ankh on the desk beside the computer and hit the speed-dial on his phone. Jacinda was amazed when the cell phone in her purse started to ring. She answered, and Shafiq was on the line.

"Jacinda, are you close to the store?"

She pretended that the call had awakened her. "I was dozing with the television on, Shafiq. I thought I had the day off?"

"Things have changed," he said. "I have your new courier assignment, but that's not why I phoned you. I need to send a picture over the e-mail, and I have no idea how to work this tool of Satan."

"Is it business, or something else?"

"It is Allah's work," he said. "I will be forever in your debt, dear girl."

"I'll be right over," Jacinda said, but waited five minutes before she left her listening post. She walked around the block before appearing at the back door. Shafiq let her in and led her to the computer.

"I had two minutes' notice on this, or I would have called you sooner," he said.

"What can I do?"

Shafiq handed her a still tacky photo of the ankh. "Scan this image into the computer and e-mail it to a man in New York with an Irish name. I have it on a Post-It stuck to the monitor."

Jacinda found the name, which she assumed was bogus, and performed the task. Shafiq removed the Polaroid from the flatbed scanner and hurried into the back room.

"Don't worry if you smell smoke," he shouted. "I'm getting rid of the picture."

Jacinda had seconds to work. She grabbed the velvet pouch, slipped out the fragment of ankh, and dropped it into her purse. Then, she grabbed a fake medallion from the shelf and slid it into the pocket where the ankh had been. It was of the approximate shape and weight as the ankh and, with luck, no one would check on it until she was gone. And this time, it would be for good.

Jacinda casually wandered back to Shafiq's desk and looked over the stack of invoices. Three pages down, she found a waybill for a number of crates scheduled to leave from Port Said in four days on a freighter named the *Xenophon*. She noted the details so that the Mossad could check on it. The size and number of crates suggested arms to her, not artifacts as they were labeled.

Jacinda inventoried the rest of Shafiq's desktop. A Christian Bible lay open next to his old portable typewriter. Odd reading for a Shiite, she thought. Leaning closer, Jacinda saw it was open to the last chapter, The Revelation of St. John the Divine.

She heard a footfall and moved. When Shafiq entered, she was standing by the dirty rear window gazing at the spires of the al-Hakim Mosque. Out of the corner of her eye, she saw him purposefully close the Bible and cover it with some papers. Then, he bent down to his floor safe and opened it. With the dexterity of a magician, he swept the velvet pouch from his desk, placed it into the steel compartment, and slammed it shut.

"That will be all, dear," said Shafiq as he got to his feet.

Jacinda nodded and started for the door. Shafiq stopped her and touched her cheek with the flat of his fingers. "Jacinda, my lovely bird," he whispered, "I would rather you not tell anyone you helped me with the computer tonight. I have spent a long time convincing others that I know what I am doing, even if we both realize I have no idea how to work that machine."

"If anyone asks," said Jacinda, "I'll deny I was ever here." She smiled at Shafiq and slipped away with her prize. Shafiq raised his hand and called after her. "May Allah accompany you!"

Jacinda pulled over to the shoulder for a moment and sat rocking back and forth on the front seat. If she had lingered five minutes longer in that hotel, her one life would be over. After all her training, it had come down to that—dumb luck, the oppressive heat, and her bad habits saved her. Otherwise, she would have been vaporized in the explosion. Instead, she found herself alive and thankfully nameless in teeming Cairo.

Safe.

For now.

Her muddled mind managed to grasp a few inescapable facts about the night's events. The bomb had sent a message. They could find her, and they wanted her dead.

Jacinda stepped out of the car and took a few tentative steps onto the gravel. The lights of the Great Pyramid shone in the distance. Subtly, her stance widened and her chin rose to face the stars. She had to make the best of it and get a message to the colonel in Jerusalem that the symbol of Salameh was now in Israeli hands.

Quite a propaganda blow, she thought.

A year before, Jacinda woke in her Amman apartment with a persistent tone in her ears. It was the telephone. Western phones had raucous bells, but the Middle East seemed to prefer the even more annoying drone of the buzzer.

Colonel Avram Halevi was calling. Although he made an attempt to hide it, his voice belied an edge of excitement. "Can you travel to Cairo, Jacinda?"

"I suppose—"

"Good!" said Halevi. "Joe Malamat needs a courier. One with good Palestinian credentials."

Jacinda smiled. She had been living as a expatriate in Jordan for eight years, infiltrating fanatic factions of the PLO with surprising ease. Her papers were flawless, of course, but her success was certainly due to her chameleonlike ability to adapt as the power bases shifted. At the start, she worked as an Arafat loyalist. Her cover: the radicalized daughter of a West Bank family killed in a bus bombing.

The *real* Jacinda el-Bahri had been burned by the explosion and sent to Haifa for treatment.

She lost one arm, but would have survived if not for a patriotic young intern who described to her in sickening detail how her parents and two older brothers had been ripped apart in the blast.

The young doctor, a member of one of Israel's more rabid orthodox sects, tried to show her God's retribution working through her tragedy. It was a symbolic defeat of the vile doctrine of Islam, he proclaimed.

With her remaining arm, she broke a Coke bottle and ground the sharp edges into his righteous face. As he fell across her, she sliced open her own throat with the jagged glass. The nurses found them slumped together, her dead eyes staring into his; their blood mingling on the bed sheets.

Halevi confiscated her body and her past, giving the latter to a bright female army officer recruited as a student from Technion University. The new Jacinda resembled the old, both having the olive skin and sultry features of a Hashemite princess.

After a few months studying the life of the dead girl, the new Jacinda was sent across the Allenby Bridge to Jordan, her face wrapped in bandages. Her cover story artfully mixed the facts with the colonel's fantasies.

Appropriate "humanitarian" messages to King Hussein's government explained that she was a poor, orphaned Palestinian girl injured by a bomb planted by her own people. But Israeli plastic surgeons had restored her face with their great skill.

As a gesture, Israel was allowing the girl to emigrate and live with her only relatives in Jordan.

Of course, these relatives had never been able to enter Israel and had never seen Jacinda el-Bahri in the flesh. Any photos would be of her as a child, and the "plastic surgery" would answer any questions of resemblance to the dead girl. Jacinda "recuperated" with an elderly second cousin for a few months before returning to school at the college in Amman. There, she joined in demonstrations and became active in many pro-Palestinian organizations headquartered in Jordan.

In a year, she joined Fatah, eventually working herself to a position in Arafat's office. There, she was recruited as a courier, for much the same reasons the Mossad chose her. Often, she traveled the Amman-Beirut-Cairo triangle with valuable information.

When Arafat's star began to wane as the PLO split over the Lebanese civil war, she infiltrated the Syrian factions and reported to Israel on terrorist activities based in the Bakka Valley.

But ten years living a lie began to tell. The colonel caught her in a few minor mistakes. Minor, yes, he told her—but had they been noticed, she would be in for a messy death. She took some time off and found herself staring at the setting sun each evening, dealing with the wave of sadness the sight brought with it.

Why is that emotion, she wondered, *so beautiful?* But she knew. The sun set in the west. The sun set over Israel.

Jacinda had nearly resolved her longing for home when the colonel called again. The reason was Salameh. He had been busy. A lot of his activity was centered in Cairo, Malamat's territory.

Four or five years had gone by since she had set eyes on Malamat. He was the one who recruited her at school. He went back to her origins, and that posed a problem. When she saw him again, would she kiss him or use his testicles for target practice?

She did see him, of course, and he was all business. Their past, it seemed, had never existed. He briefed her and set her up with Shafiq's cell. That was all. No more gourmet kosher meals eaten on the cold brick floor. And no more love made as tenderly as she had ever known the act could be.

Jacinda shivered and looked away from the road for a second. Despite how coarse he had become over the years, she had held that man, felt him inside her. Death had never seemed so real—or so close. And now Malamat was dead. She veered off the main road, and her headlights led her up a rocky side trail that qualified as little more than a cart path. She had taken the shortcut before, but never at night and rarely in the dry season.

Since the Aswan Dam project, the Nile rarely flooded as it had through the millennia. The constant river might help the farmers, but it also allowed the desert to encroach onto the highlands.

Driving on, Jacinda was all but engulfed by the parched earth kicked up by her tires. She glanced at the green glow from the odometer. Needing a moment to think, Jacinda stopped the car under an outcropping of rock and searched behind the boulders where the lights of the town colored the horizon to pale blue.

The moon hung high, about the size of a pearl onion held at arm's length, casting an eerie toplight over the rockscape. And the sounds were all wrong. A soft wind made a low whistle through the tangled branches of a terebinth tree, but Jacinda saw none of the tiny birds who usually slept there and weighed down its thin limbs.

Has something frightened them away? she wondered.

She visualized Malamat splayed open with his organs in jars around him. That kind of death took time. He must have died before they bombed her hotel. And both were linked. Of that she was certain.

She knew something else. It was Salameh's work.

Though she had never met him, she knew of his mystical bent. He had forced Malamat to tell him where she could be found. If control checked the phone records, she bet there would be a call from his house to Cairo an hour or two before the explosion.

So, she knew that there must be many men looking for her.

What could she do? She had to take Malamat's advice. Get out quick and clean. The car started, and she turned the wheel hard before looping back on the trail in the direction of the highway. Her only hope now was to put space between her and the faceless killers. Space and time were all she had on her side. Time before they (whoever they were) found out she was alive.

She left Cairo behind, heading for the busy harbor at Port Said. Jacinda never noticed the sleepy, short-haired cat curled up under the backseat, waiting.

CHAPTER SIX

A drop of perspiration fell from Marcy Lanyard's forehead onto the letter *J* on her computer keyboard. She wiped it away with her finger causing a line of little *J*'s to scurry across her screen.

Marcy heard the old building groan. She knew it was an inadequate air-conditioning system straining to force air through ducts that hadn't been cleaned in fifteen years, but to the romantic part of her it was the sound of the Met exhaling to life. She only wished the old museum didn't have such hot breath.

To save money, they turned up the thermostat at night when only the late crew was inside. It was supposed to be cooler after sundown, but in the offices at least, it never worked out that way.

The night was so muggy that the guards could lead the "geeks-on-parade" (Marcy's term for tourists) through the computer room, tell them they were in a rain forest exhibit, and the idiots would believe it!

Three hours before, she had packed Dan Rawlins up and shoved him out the door, so she could get her real work done. She just had to finish that one tiny chore Dan wanted. She called up the catalogue number of that fragment of a crystal ankh, circa 3500 B.C.E., on the computer. All she had to do was fetch it from the storeroom and take it back to the office. She'd get to it in a minute. Dan probably wasn't in much of a rush. The ankh would likely stay locked in his desk for a month before he got around to examining it.

Marcy ran a long, darkly polished fingernail along her damp eyebrow. She cleared the screen with two taps of her middle finger, and her reflection replaced the columns of inventory on the screen.

Not half bad, she thought as she saw herself, especially after baby-sitting Danny Rawlins all day and working on her correlations most of the night.

She wore large glasses with round frames and blue-tinted lenses to accent her icy pale eyes. Her prescription magnified her eyes slightly, giving her an innocent look that tended to disappear when she took them off. The effect never failed to surprise her lovers.

"Hey!"

The voice came from a man standing in the dim light of the doorway. "Still at it, Marce?" he said.

Marcy swiveled in her chair. She saw the paunch and the guard uniform, but not the face. "Wally? Is that you?"

"Yeah," he said as he squeezed through the door. "Am I bothering you?"

Marcy laughed. "Shit, no! You're saving my life! I've been loading plot coordinates and strata levels for two hours now. And—I'm sweating like a stuck pig in here!"

"Tell me about it," agreed Wally. He was wiping the moisture from his second chin with an old stained handkerchief. "It's an oven in here, and it must be twenty degrees on the street."

"What's their excuse this time?"

Wally shrugged. "They said the rain this morning mucked up the roof fans. At least that's the story the maintenance staff is handing out."

He grabbed a stool and perched next to Marcy's computer console.

"Anyhow, I was on my break," he said, "and I figured I'd look in on my favorite girl."

Marcy scowled at him over her glasses. "I thought Hilda was your favorite girl."

"She's my favorite wife!" said Wally with mock seriousness.

"And how's Laurel?"

A grin brightened Wally's face. "Oh, my baby'll be coming in from Boulder for the holidays. I paid for the tickets this morning."

"Great. How'd she like it out there? Some change from Queens, I bet."

"She said it was okay, but I hear that first semester is hardest on the new kids, being away from home and all."

"Sure."

"Hell, but you'd know more about that than I do. You're a college girl yourself."

"Grad student, Wally. I can't even remember back to when I was a freshman."

"So sue me," said Wally. "I had to go to work after the tenth grade. What do I know from this higher education crap."

Marcy smiled. "Has Laurel decided on a major yet?"

"I dunno," answered Wally with a shrug.

A squawk came from Wally's walkie-talkie. He unhooked it from his belt and brought it close to his ear. After seventeen years on the job, he easily picked out the crackling voice hidden amid the static— "G Section. . . . Status. You're late, Wally. Over."

"Control? Wally here. I'm downstairs checking on the computer room. Didn't Carlos buzz you guys? He was supposed to cover me. Over."

"Not a peep out of him. Where'd you split up? Over."

"I left him on the main level by the Arms Gallery. What's the matter, Jeff?"

"He's not where he oughta be. The camera scan shows the Medieval Arms section empty. Tell you what, Wally, I'll call you when we track him down. He's got to show up on the monitors somewhere! Station One—out!"

Wally released the button and set the radio onto the console. His eyes went to the ceiling, as if he could look through to the floors above.

"Damn that Carlos! I bet he's jerking off someplace with his radio turned down."

Marcy's eyes followed Wally's, but only saw the acoustical tile. She turned back to her screen and noticed that the machine had called up a few possibilities. She typed in a hard-copy request and waited for the drone of the printer to begin. "It must be spooky up there at night with the lights out," she said to Wally.

"Oh, it ain't bad," he told her after a moment's thought. "Nice and quiet, mostly. And it's fun when they set up a new exhibit. We got the first crack at King Tut when it was here, and you know what a tough ticket that was! I even touched that gold head they brought. I mean, I wasn't supposed to—but, what the hell . . ."

A harsh squeal came from the radio.

"Excuse me," Wally said as he flicked the switch to *talk*. "G Section. Wally here. Did you find the little prick? Over."

Jeff's voice answered a second later. "I don't know. I saw a movement when the camera was panning the main level. Probably just a shadow. But it's right up the stairs from you, so how's about checking it out? Over."

"Hey, Jeff," said Wally grinning, "I'm still on my break here! What if the union hears about this? Over."

"Fuck off! Get your smart ass up there! Out!"

Wally eased off the stool and returned the radio to his belt loop "That guy's got no sense of humor." He gave Marcy's shoulder an affectionate pat and ambled toward the door.

"Oh, Marce," he called from the corridor. "Buzz me when you want to leave, and I'll walk you to the cab."

Marcy glanced up from the keyboard and smiled. "Thanks, Wally. I'm just waiting for this printout, then I have to pick up something down in the storeroom. Shouldn't take long."

Wally stared back blankly. "Whatever ya say, kid. It's Greek to me."

"Coptic, actually," said Marcy.

"Brat," said Wally and he left, walking briskly toward the stairs.

He was puffing by the time he climbed all the way to the main level, one floor above. Whatever he was feeling, fear was not part of the mix. What in the hell could hurt you in the middle of the Metropolitan Museum? After all, the place was more secure than Fort Knox. Sure, it was dark this time of night. (After the museum closes for the day, the light drops automatically to one-fourth in the corridors and, except for some low-wattage work lights, shuts off entirely in the galleries.) But Wally had his flashlight, and even if he didn't, with seventeen years in, only a bat could maneuver around the place at night better than he could.

When he first started "night work" as he called it, he had heard stories about the dangers of the job. Every few weeks, it seemed, some smash-and-grab artist would hide in the bathroom or behind one of the French tapestries waiting for the place to clear out. Mostly they were dumb junkies who'd seen *Madonna and Child with Saints* by Piero della Francesca and thought they could pawn it for fix money.

Since they put in the surveillance cameras, heat sensors, laser-beam trip wires, and the rest of their high-tech security into the Met's fifty-two picture galleries and thirteen exhibition halls, not one piece on display had been lost or significantly damaged by vandalism or theft.

Oh, Wally still caught bag ladies shoplifting from the souvenir counters and, every once in a while, one of the construction workers fell off something and broke a bone. But accidents could happen anywhere. Wally, as he reached the landing on the main level, shared one conviction with his buddies upstairs at the monitors:

The Met was safe.

He took a jog to the left that brought him next to an ornate pair of entrance doors. They were huge. When open, an elephant could walk between them, trunk high.

Each door was coffered and had brass plates etched with classic hieroglyphs set into its teak frame. The stone lintel above them was incised with Roman letters proclaiming, "The Egyptian Pavilion."

Behind him and above, Wally saw the surveillance camera. This was the angle that Jeff had when he saw that shadow on his screen. Wally stepped back to the doors, wondering how Jeff could have missed anyone going in or out.

They were open a crack.

Carlos weighed about one hundred and forty-five pounds. He could have slipped between the double doors easily. Wally's belly would need another six or seven inches to fit, but he didn't try. He yanked the doors wide and strode in.

"Hey, Carlos," he called. "You in there?"

No answer.

Wally squinted into an expanse of dark hall. A bit of indirect light bounced in from the corridor, but it didn't do much to illuminate the statues of gray granite and obsidian guarding the general gloom.

Something moved to his right—Wally threw the strong beam of his flashlight onto it. "Carlos?"

It wasn't him. Only a shadow—*Are we all seeing shadows tonight?*—playing on one of those stiff Egyptian figures, the sort that looked like the guy posed for it with a rod up his ass!

At its base, the sculpture supported an inscription in red plastic with white letters cut into it. It read:

STATUE OF PHARAOH TUTHMOSIS III
DYNASTY XVIII

Red Granite, Height 86 inches

Actually, that's what the sign would have read, if part of it hadn't been blocked by something lying against it, something long and tapered. Curious, Wally went over and picked it off. A feather.

A feather? He twisted the thing around with his wrist, examining it. *Must be from the tail or maybe the end of the wing,* he thought. *Damn feather must be a foot and a half long!*

"And the damn thing's all sticky, too!"

Wally shined his light on it. The edge was red. As if it had been dipped in—

Blood!

He dropped it, and it fluttered to the floor. Wally was at the far side of the statue now.

There was more. A pattern of fine red droplets had splattered across the pharaoh's carved feet and ended where a small pool of blood had collected at the pedestal.

Wally decided to check in with Jeff. "Control? Wally here. I'm in Quadrant E, Section 5. I found blood down here. Over."

"Blood?"

"No, wait a second, Jeff. There's feathers right by it. I figure a pigeon or somethin' flew in today and got trapped. Y'know how they sometimes get crazy. Go banging into walls . . . you know. Over."

It took Jeff a few seconds to get back to him. "I was checking the monitors. But I hear you. It gave me a thought. You think maybe Carlos found the dead bird and went out back to toss what's left of it in the Dumpster? That possible? Over."

"If I know that taco-bender," said Wally, "he's prob'ly out back cooking it! Over."

Jeff laughed. "That's a good one, pal. But try to track him down for me anyway. Out."

Wally snapped the radio back into its holster, then pointed his light into the farthest corner and made a smooth arc around the perimeter of the glass-enclosed pavilion. The streetlights filtering through the wall of windows only made the shadows deeper on the dark side of the exhibits.

Little bright points, like catchlights from a dozen eyes, bounced back from a spot near the center of the room, from where there shouldn't be anything reflective. All that was in that direction was an old temple.

Just dull rock.

Actually, it was a reconstruction of the temple at Dendur in Upper Egypt. It was a two-tiered limestone box with a pylon angled in front, forming two separate structures. It had been a river-front temple dedicated to Hāpi, the Nile god, and dated from the Roman occupation.

The modern Egyptian government sent it as a gift to the Metropolitan Museum for helping raise money to rescue the temple of Abu Simbel from flooding when the Aswan High Dam created the five hundred kilometers of Lake Nasser behind it.

Wally didn't care. As he approached the pylon his only question was, what made it sparkle?

He stopped near the temple's entrance, close enough now to see a cluster of dots on the light stone—shiny red dots. Wally realized what they were. His head shook a bit as if to deny it to himself, but no getting around it. He knew fresh, wet blood when he saw it.

It's the bird, he thought. *Smashed its stupid head on the stone . . . and crawled inside to die.*

Out of instinct, he eased his revolver from his hip.

Put it out of its misery. Only, that feather, it's a foot long. Much too big for any damn pigeon I ever—an owl! Yeah, must've been one of them. A damn big one!

Wally circled the pylon, for some reason unwilling to take the direct path through the cleft at the center where the twin trapezoidal shapes joined. Instead, he approached the side wall, sucked in some air, and mounted the two steps to the sanctuary.

Wally lifted his flashlight and played the light over the entranceway. Its dark opening was flanked by a pair of lotus-tipped columns, still elegant after twenty centuries. Between the columns, the bright circle vanished, absorbed into the murky heart of the temple.

Wally leaned closer, peering in, but it was as if someone had painted the inside walls flat black. While he could not see anything, a smell greeted him, musky and sweet. It wasn't the first time he had smelled it. He holstered his gun. Whatever was in there could never hurt anyone.

"Shit," he muttered and screwed up his face. "That owl's gotta be dead in there."

He took one tentative step in. On his second, the sole of his shoe squished when it touched the floor, sinking into what felt like three inches of strawberry preserves. Not Smuckers. More like the store brands that are runny in spots.

His foot skidded out from under him. He pitched forward, trying to balance, and grabbed onto one of the lotus columns for support. But the stone was slick with whatever covered the floor, making Wally's fingers glance off and catch air.

He fell, fell hard in a half-split parody of an acrobatic dancer, his hands cushioning most of his bulk as he landed. As he did, his side struck a large, greasy lump, and he rolled off to the right.

His ankle absorbed this second impact and cramped when Wally tried to raise himself up on it. He dropped back for a moment, panting. He waited, hoping his racing heartbeat would return to a steady thump, and that the pain in his legs and arm and hip would go away.

For one horrid instant, Wally had no idea where he was. The pain sliced into his knee and he reeled back. His shoulders hit the wall, and he pressed his weight against it for support.

It was sticky, too.

After the shock dulled—less than three minutes later—Wally realized how dark it was in that small square room, how tomblike. A cold shudder twitched along his shoulder blades.

Where'd that flashlight go to?

It had sailed out of his hand when he tripped, and he vaguely remembered a sharp crack and the light blinking off. His hands groped around, searching for it. He needed it now, needed to see!

What if his ankle—as he suspected—was broken? What could he—?

Stupid! Stupid!—The RADIO!

Wally reached to his belt and found the radio's leather case, but it was empty! The radio probably popped out of its holder when he hit his side—popped and pirouetted and tumbled to God knows where! It could have skittered across the temple. Groping about, his fingers landed on a familiar object.

The flashlight!

The rubber handle seemed slimy, but not hard to get a grip on. He jiggled it a little and heard the batteries clack into place.

The light snapped on.

At first, Wally couldn't do a thing except stare. Then, his belly began to move. It bounced and jumped and heaved like a jolly fat man, like a bowl full of jelly.

Until he threw up.

Over and over, in long, nearly continuous spasms.

The small sanctuary bore a thick, rich, black-red coating from a height of four feet down to the viscous floor. Every inch had been covered—like those granola bars dipped in chocolate that he liked.

Finally, Wally pushed his fist into his mouth to stop the vomiting. "Oh, my sweet Jesus!"

What had once been a twenty-two-year-old Puerto Rican lay floating in congealed blood. His chest had cracked open at the sternum and the two halves wrenched apart, so that most of the skin of his upper body fell away. His rib cage stood straight, like a rack of lamb.

CHAPTER SEVEN

A level below, Marcy Lanyard searched the computer inventory. Finding a specific ankh in the collection was needle-in-a-haystack stuff. If it had been made of bronze or lapis lazuli, the hunt might take a week. This one was larger than most and made of an odd material, so correlating the elements would make the quest a lot easier.

There it was. A fragmentary rose quartz ankh, 1.6 kilograms in weight, dated to the reign of Tuthmosis III, Eighteenth Dynasty.

"Christ," she cried. "The printer!"

She forgot to turn it off and, if she didn't stop it, the machine would try to spew out a hundred pages of data for her thesis when she only needed the first ten. She must have been so tired that she added an extra zero when she set up the print function. Marcy scooped up the sheets in the tray, bent at the knees, and angled her elbow so it would hit the toggle switch. That done, she warm booted the computer back to "Main Menu" with a free finger. Three key strikes later and the computer was shut down, also.

She shoved the pages into a gap between two ledgers that sat on a shelf behind the filing cabinets. That was the cubbyhole she staked out for herself. All her thesis notes were there and most of her own research into the "King Lists of Ancient Egypt."

Dan Rawlins had been encouraging her plan to create a computer database to correlate all the random snippets of information about the pharaohs with other sources. Egyptian history is too often clouded by myth and the vanity of one pharaoh trying to obliterate the name of another. By feeding in Babylonian battle accounts, court records from the old Syrian capital at Ebla, Bible stories, and thousands of odd facts, she might create a more accurate chronology of the Egyptian kings than those available from the Egyptians themselves.

And the work was about finished. Maybe one more hard night in front of the computer. But not tonight. Tonight it was a long hot bath and sleep, sweet sleep.

Marcy pulled on her raincoat, a nice London Fog her father and stepmother sent her for her last birthday, and flipped her hair off her collar. A master at doing more than one thing at a time, she gathered up her notes and dialed 8 on the phone for security. She waited six rings with the headset jammed into the crook between her neck and shoulder before giving up.

"Assholes," she shouted into the phone, and slammed it back onto its cradle. "Probably having a circle jerk up there!"

There wasn't an iron-clad rule for the female employees who work late to get an escort to the parking lot, although they usually did.

Marcy stopped at the water fountain to wet her throat and take a breather before dropping the printouts on Dan's desk. As she strolled to his office, Marcy stopped short.

Damn! I forgot to get the ankh!

Marcy dropped the printouts on the credenza behind Dan's desk. *No big deal,* she thought. The ankh was only one floor down. She knew that because each artifact in the building was given a three-number designation. The first number told her what wing or gallery in the museum, the second was the room, and the third directed her to the right shelf or drawer.

She hurried down the back stairs and into the lower storage area for the Egyptian Gallery. Turning into the corridor, she blinked as a shape whizzed past her peripheral vision.

She whipped her head around in time to see a door click shut at the end of the hall.

Whatever it was, it was in the Artifact Depository, a restricted area. Only the staff Egyptologists and a few of the curators knew the keypad code on the lock. In a place as vast as the Met, the professionals needed a central storage area close to their workrooms for the hundreds of priceless artifacts that they might be working with at any one time.

The maintenance and clerical people were barred from there and not even the guards could enter unaccompanied. *So who could be in the depository?* she wondered.

Marcy crept closer. With her ear to the doorjamb, she heard a scraping sound from the other side. She tried the knob and the door opened effortlessly. She took a tentative step inside. Her hand instinctively went to the light switch, but she pulled it back and kept the depository dark.

Catalogued clutter was stacked on floor-to-ceiling shelves. Marcy had been in there earlier with Dan and could not detect any disturbance.

But she smelled something—smoke!

Scared of fire in the depository, she hurried to the back of the room where a ray of moonlight caught a smoky ribbon rising from behind a metal storage cabinet. She stopped when she saw it.

One of the pre-Coptic stoneware lamps had been removed from its bin and sat on the floor. For the first time in centuries, it held a burning wad of foul-smelling incense. Marcy kicked it over and ground out the smoldering ashes. The tip of her foot hit something solid, and she separated it out with her shoe. She stooped to pick up and examine her find.

She brushed the soot away and rolled the charm between her thumb and forefinger. It was nothing, a green basalt scarab, the most common amulet in Egyptian ritual. The museum had drawers full of them, ten thousand at least of these tiny carvings of the dung beetle, in granite, marble, glass, and porcelain from every dynastic period. To the ancients, they were symbols of creation and regeneration. Marcy turned the scarab and read the "words of power" cut into its base. *Definitely Eighteenth Dynasty,* she thought.

SCREEEEEE . . .

A sharp, high-pitched shriek made her look up suddenly. She couldn't see a thing. Slowly, quietly, she backed out of the depository and ran to the nearest phone. Again, she dialed *8.*

This time Jeff answered quickly. "Security."

"Jeff, it's Marcy," she whispered into the receiver. "Do you have one of your guys in the depository?"

"What do you mean?" he said, with an edge to his voice.

"I know you were looking for Carlos and I saw . . . I think I saw somebody go in there. And I heard him in the dry room. . . ."

"Get out!"

"What?" she said.

Jeff spoke firmly. "Marcy, Carlos is dead! I just got back to the board here. I was in the gallery calling for the cops. The thing is, Carlos was hacked up. And Marcy, I got nobody to cover the offices."

"You sure?"

"I'm damn sure. But you've gotta get out of the building as quick as you can. You see, my panel says nobody came in or out since right after closing. You know what that means? That butcher must still be in the museum!"

Marcy felt all her muscles tense. "Holy crap!"

"Listen, Marcy," Jeff continued, "stay cool. Go to the lower exit and . . . You have your keys, right?"

"Right."

"Good. Then let yourself out. Stay in the parking lot; it'll be crawling with cops any minute."

"Okay," she said.

"One more thing. Lock the outside door behind you! Now, scram!"

She didn't need more encouragement. Marcy let the phone drop and bolted from the room. Her heels made a fast click-click on the tile floor all the way to the landing, their noise echoing off the hard granite facing of the walls, louder to her ears than it had ever been.

The hallway was longer, too. Miles long, it went on and on, until she was certain it would never—then, there they were! She jumped the three stairs down to the double glass doors.

Her left side hit the doors. They strained to open, but the chain between them held strong, the links snaking between the door handles and secured with an imposing padlock.

My keys!

She opened her purse and dug for them. They were easy to find, being attached to a six-inch slab of Plexiglas with her name etched into it in hieroglyphics. The key was the smallest she had, except for the one to her letter box. They gave it to her in case she had to get out of this rarely used exit in an emergency. And with another Jack the Ripper on the loose, this qualified as an emergency to her!

Though she had never once tried that key, it rotated in the lock as if it had been greased. The shackle arm fell from the case, the padlock opened, and the chain fell away.

The metal bar across the door said "Press Down" and she did, with all her weight as her shoulder pushed out on the glass.

And it was over—

She was outside!

She hurried to the center of the parking lot where it was easy to convince herself she was safe. With all that space around her, nobody could even get close without her seeing him.

Marcy decided to collect herself for a second and sought the warm pool of light from the street lamp in the center island. Her shoulder blades rubbed against the pole as she took a calming breath.

Whooping sirens announced the arrival of the police on the Fifth Avenue side of the building. There'd be an ambulance, too, if Jeff wasn't wrong about Carlos being—*He couldn't really be?*—butchered.

She decided to make the long walk around to the front to get the truth behind all that scary talk. Murder? She doubted it. With her heartbeat returned to normal, Marcy reminded herself of the practical jokes Wally and Jeff loved to pull.

She looked at the museum, rising like a carved escarpment above her.

All those black windows . . . with the only light coming from the locked glass doors facing her. She had a clear view down the corridor.

And something, a shadow, a black, batlike shape, raced down the center hall toward her. Above the floor, twisting between both walls—*Lord God, the thing is flying!*

Marcy whirled, the terror welling up in her throat again, and ran across the parking lot to a line of low shrubs. She burst through them and into the trees that separated the museum grounds from Central Park.

There, she turned for a quick look—at the instant the shape struck the glass doors. They shattered! Jagged pieces of glass fanned out into the night air like a comet with a tail of ice. The black thing rose into the sky, flying near enough to the street lamp to block the light for a moment, casting a giant-winged shadow across the museum's granite facade.

Marcy stared horrified as the shape seemed to curl and shrink as it banked and soared above her and into the trees.

The sound of splintered glass cascading onto the pavement shocked her into flight of her own. She had to get away! She tore into the undergrowth, trying to clear a path with her hands. The bushes scraped her arms and legs as her lungs cried for air. She raced on blindly. Panting, she threw her arms around a tree trunk and clung to it for support.

A shriek came from above!

The sound cut through her like a spear, and she held the tree tighter.

Then, silence. Marcy felt so alone, so vulnerable. Looking around the dim forest, it could have been a dream. A light fog caressed the ground and reflected the moon as tiny pinpoints of light on the leaves. Under her feet, the damp rug of grass pulsated with a life of its own.

She felt a small bite near her ankle. *A bug*, she thought. She swatted it, but her hand came back covered by a mass of shiny beetles. They swarmed onto her shoes and began to crawl up her calves as she ran screaming toward a clearing. She broke onto a section of rolling grassland and stopped.

Looming seventy feet above her stood an obelisk, now a featureless black spire against the lights of the city.

Cleopatra's Needle!

Suddenly, she felt very cold. The insects continued to bite, though she had no sensation of them anymore. Her eyes were fixed on the pyramid that crowned the obelisk. Behind it, a dark wing stretched out and tested the air.

Talon-tipped feet gripped the point and scraped the stone, making a noise as unsettling as fingernails against a chalkboard. Two huge wings unfolded, and the shape leapt into space. For a moment, the form merged with the night sky and disappeared.

Then, she saw it, blocking a bright constellation as it fell—directly toward her!

Closer . . . and closer . . .

And still, she stood rooted. Watching.

The bird-creature dipped and hunched in its shoulders to accelerate its dive. It came fast, and up to that last instant Marcy searched it for details. The bird had a white head with russet plumes capping the crown. Except, she noticed that it seemed to have no beak. As it crossed into a shaft of moonlight, she saw it clearly for the first time.

Marcy gaped at it, unable to move. And a split second before the bird reached her, she recognized it for what it was.

"You don't exist! There's no such thing as a—" Her words were drowned out by an unearthly screech.

Razorlike talons tangled in her long blonde hair as the monster's great black wings flapped in powerful, agitated strokes above her head and neck. For a fraction of a second their eyes met, Marcy and the dark thing.

The creature opened its mouth, as if to speak, but didn't. Instead, it lowered its huge wings and folded them over Marcy's upper body like a shroud.

The head jutted forward from its thick feathered neck, and it bit down. Marcy went limp with only a single muted cry as it cut into her bloody throat like a carrion vulture.

CHAPTER EIGHT

PORT SAID, EGYPT

Jacinda made the one hundred and forty-five miles to Port Said in under three hours. Arriving midmorning, she drove directly to the Suez Canal. Once there, her instincts told her that it was time to abandon her stolen car. She double-parked on a cramped side street near the docks.

Remembering to wipe the steering wheel and mirror for fingerprints, she opened the door with her handkerchief wrapped around the handle and stepped out.

On the street, she turned her back quickly and waited for a clutch of Italian sailors to pass before joining the crowds in the squalid waterfront fish market. She noticed the twin funnels of a large ship rising above the corrugated tin roof of a warehouse a few blocks off and walked toward it.

In the car, the sleek, steel-gray cat jumped to the front seat to watch her. He pulled back his muzzle, exposed his teeth, and hissed like a cobra as he leapt atop the headrest. He stepped, with intricate balance, to the side window. Then he sprang, vaulting to the street with such grace that his long body seemed to stretch beyond fur and muscle as if in slow motion. He landed softly as cats do, stirring up a powdery veil of dust. The wind scattered the puff instantly, and when it was gone, the beast had vanished with it.

The day had turned stifling hot. The steamy breeze across the canal did not help at all. The air stank. Jacinda's dress was damp and clung to her, dotting her back with wet splotches.

She turned sharply, passed through a low archway to the next avenue, and found an open market teeming with people, both Arab and European. In the safety of the crowd, she paused to think.

Can I risk another call to Control?

She reasoned that even if Control had made an honest mistake, Malamat's killers had been ahead of them. Now, she was not about to trust anything they told her. After mulling it over, her best bet appeared to be to pick a boat at random and get lost for a week or so as it crossed the Mediterranean. Then, when the heat was off, she could fly back into Israel and simply walk to Mossad's doorstep in Haifa unannounced.

She knew that if she spent too much time calculating her escape, her pursuers might trace her thought process and use her own cleverness to find her.

She shivered. No more than a slight clenching between her shoulder blades, but enough to alert her to the pair of immense green eyes following her from a dark alleyway. She passed, then quickly glanced back.

A cat, the color of the shadows!

The animal paced his prey, silently matching Jacinda step for step. Suddenly, he darted ahead, through the legs of a fat Frenchman in walking shorts and turned on her.

The cat snarled, whipping the air with its claws. Jacinda jumped, flattening her side against the nearest wall. The cat locked his stare onto her eyes. He began walking toward her, slowly, relentlessly.

Thoughts of rabies and other diseases crossed Jacinda's mind again. She was having déjà vu. The cat looked like the one from Cairo, but they all looked alike to her.

She inched backward, away from the surly feline. Then as her back touched an ornate portico in front of a row of shops, she watched as the cat suddenly hissed and leapt at her! She spun around as he sailed by her ear, and then lost her balance. She hit a door, lurched through to the other side, and slammed it shut.

The cat noted where she had gone, then lost interest. It melted into another doorway close by, stretched, eased itself into a furry semicircle, closed its eyes, and slept.

Jacinda made tracks to the headquarters of Kostos Ship Lines and rushed into the comparative safety of its large terminal. She looked around. The Greek line's Egyptian offices lay in a converted, century-old villa, originally built as a seaside resort for one of the local pashas. Steady use had made the place considerably less regal.

She noticed that cardboard partitions did little to hide the decaying walls. The old tile flooring had come up in patches, and she could tell that it was rarely swept. About thirty persons, mostly peasant families, sat waiting for their departures. Some had spread out blankets along the walls under the peeling travel posters and the faded Victorian mural depicting great British seafarers. Children played in the corner near three old Arab men who ate dried fruit from one rattan basket.

Other passengers stared blankly, read, or rested on the three rows of wooden pews.

A ceiling-high chalkboard hung behind the ticket counter. Jacinda left the doorway and checked the sailing schedule. The boat she was looking for would land her in Cyprus in two days.

Jacinda strolled to the counter and approached a swarthy bear of a man who was struggling to jam a stack of index cards into a green metal box. He cursed in a low-island dialect Jacinda suspected was Cretan. She coughed to get his attention.

He looked up at her with a smile, his eyes settling about nipple height. Every tooth in his head was yellow, two made of gold and the others stained by Turkish tobacco.

He leaned familiarly across the counter, wiping off a glob of spittle from the corner of his mouth before he spoke. "I may be of service, sweet lady?" he said drawing out each *s* sound in a leering, snakelike lisp.

Jacinda answered with authority. "I need a single stateroom. Minimum accommodations will be fine. Now, when's your next ship sailing to Cyprus?"

The big man consulted his cards. "Of course, you mean the cruise ships . . ."

"I mean your next ship! I don't care if it's a garbage scow!"

"Well, our absolutely first departure is the *Xenophon*. But that is a merchant vessel with very limited cabin space. It is quite inadequate for a woman of your . . ."

"I'll take it!"

The man yanked a yellowing card from the file box. "Yes, we have one cabin. A very tiny compartment, though. A sink, but no bath or toilet facilities."

"When does it leave?"

"This afternoon. They are loading their cargo now."

"That'll do." Jacinda remembered the *Xenophon* from the bill of lading on Shafiq's desk. Those mysterious boxes had intrigued her. The colonel would want her to check on them if she had the chance. It was risky, but she doubted if anyone she knew from Cairo was baby-sitting the shipment. Besides, escaping Shafiq on one of his own boats was simply too delicious to pass up.

She pulled a wad of bills from her purse, paid for her ticket, and counted the remainder before returning the cash to her bag. She would need enough to get passage on another boat from the port of Kyrenia to Israel. If she made it back with that trinket she stole, Halevi would owe her a long holiday in Europe or America.

The Cretan stamped her transit forms and put the papers and her ticket into an envelope. With a wet, yellow smile, he passed the documents over the counter to her.

"May you have a very, very pleasant journey, my dear."

"You're very kind. Thank you."

For an instant, both held the envelope, with the clerk's fingertips just touching Jacinda's hand.

"You have two hours before you sail," he said. "And if you are tired, I have comfortable cot in the back room."

She snatched away the ticket and jammed it into her purse. "I'm wary of strange beds, sir. You never know when you fall asleep, what manner of vermin might be beside you when you wake up."

His grin disappeared, replaced by a sneer. He hated fancy modern women always ready to make a fool of a man. "You can board anytime you wish. Pier Seven."

Jacinda pivoted on her heels and left quickly. The street outside flowed like a human sea with midday shoppers and peddlers. She searched the road for the cat, but it was gone. For some reason, she breathed easier.

Screeching seabirds were flying overhead. Mediterranean waters met the Suez Canal a mere four blocks away. She strode into the open marketplace, ignoring the shouts that came from all sides.

Figs . . . almonds . . . pomegranates . . . bolts of bright cloth . . .

One black-skinned Arab cooed at her like a pigeon. When she turned, she saw that his teeth jutted at odd angles from his purple gums. Before she could move off, the vendor waved frantically, exhorting her with passages from the Koran. His wares, all touristy items of Moroccan leather, held no interest for Jacinda until she realized what he was sitting on.

Luggage!

Customs might remember a single woman traveling without luggage. A tan overnight bag caught her eye, and she bought it without haggling. For the next half hour, she ranged the bazaar purchasing clothing and souvenirs to fill it. An old peddler sold her an ornate box, a mediocre copy of Nefertiti's toiletry chest with ancient Egyptian symbols cemented to the lid.

Following the dictum that the best hiding place was in plain sight, Jacinda placed the ankh fragment in the box with all the junk jewelry she bought. With a set of huge ankh earrings on top of it, the authentic piece blended right in with the souvenir schlock. She stuffed the box in her overnight bag along with more intimate female items. Customs agents, almost exclusively a job for men in Egypt, tended to avoid those items.

A horn blasted nearby, startling her.

When she lifted her eyes, she saw a building glide across the road not a hundred yards from her! It took a second for her to grasp that it was actually the bridge of a supertanker. She had stumbled on the Suez Canal.

Jacinda sat on her new leather bag and watched for a while as the tanker steered into the harbor. The water splashed against the gates of the lock as it closed.

Sadly, she reflected that the canal had become the port's open sewer. She stood and walked along the waterfront. Tiny boats darted among the larger ships, selling food and souvenirs to both sailors and tourists.

Except for the outboards on their small open boats, the same scene must have been played out since ancient times: the poor pleading for alms from the rich who were floating by them in splendor.

Almost an hour had passed since Jacinda purchased her tickets.

She counted out seven wharves, five behind her and two ahead. She started for the last. Closer, she saw a big 7 decorating its side. The Kostos warehouse dominated the dock, but Jacinda had to pass through the central Customs Office before being allowed onto it.

Inside, the Egyptian officers treated Jacinda solicitously as she passed their stations. The area, designed to examine hundreds of passengers an hour, held less than thirty. Even so, the baggage search proved cursory, except for one nervous moment as the examiner mentioned the lovely jewelry in Nefertiti's box.

Jacinda smiled and said they were national treasures. Then, she pointed to the "Made in Taiwan" sticker stamped on the back of a charm in the shape of the falcon, Horus. The inspector laughed heartily and let her through.

On her way to the ship, she checked the giant wall clock. She would be out of Egypt soon, according to the posted schedule. But, of course, she understood that punctuality did not rank high on the list of Middle Eastern priorities.

Walking onto the open pier, she caught her first sight of the *Xenophon*. It was an old freighter, a working vessel designed for cargo with little concern given to the comforts of either passengers or crew.

Few deck hands or stevedores were visible as she climbed aboard. A few long boxes hung in a net over an open hatch, but the rest were surely below decks where the crew would be securing them for the trip. As she stepped off the gangplank, a young man wearing a white uniform rushed to her side.

"Hello. Good afternoon. How are you?" He spoke with a heavy Greek accent.

Jacinda smiled cordially. "I am very well, thank you," she replied. "Am I the first passenger?"

"Oh, yes," he answered quickly, then lowered his voice assuming a more intimate tone. "Our only passenger, in actual fact."

He reached for her leather bag, but she clutched it tight. "Please. I take you to your cabin now." He led the way up a metal stairway to the middle deck. She stayed behind him as he stepped inside a portal and ushered her through a dark corridor to a polished wooden door.

"Here," he said placing a key in the latch. A quick half turn and a gentle push opened the door. He held it wide for her to enter.

The room would fit into a closet of her apartment in Amman. A single bunk was tucked under the porthole with a rod above it. Two wire hangers dangled from the pole.

That is the clothes rack? Pure luxury! she thought.

"Yes, this is our finest cabin," the young man said proudly. "It is only two doors down from the water closet."

Jacinda exhaled wanly. She went over to a small cabinet hugging the interior wall. She lifted the top and found the basin.

"Uh, miss . . ."

Jacinda turned to the young Greek. He waited, one foot in the room and the other in the companionway. "Anything you should want, ask for Alexandros. That is me. Second Officer."

"I will. Thank you . . . Alexandros."

"You may come to the bridge, the captain say. It is very beautiful, the sailing from the harbor. You would enjoy it."

"Perhaps I will."

The second officer bowed and started to step out of the cabin. Jacinda raised a hand to stop him. "Oh, there is one thing . . ."

"Yes, miss?"

"Where is the dining room?"

Alexandros looked stricken. "How stupid it is of me! You must have not eaten!"

"Uh, yes," she answered, "it's been a busy morning for me."

"I see." He furrowed his brow, straining for the correct words. "The problem is that we will not dine until the evening meal. B-but, I will go find the cook right now and have him open the galley for you."

"Please, don't bother."

"Please, please. If you wish, I will bring food back here for you. Do you like Greek food?"

"A sandwich will be fine."

"Souvlaki? It is very good. Lamb, onion, tomato."

"Okay. If it isn't any trouble."

"It is my duty and also my pleasure, miss. And tonight for dinner, you must sit with the ship's officers at the captain's table. He insists."

"I'd appreciate that. Now, I'd like to freshen up."

Alexandros blushed, backed into the hall and shut the door. Jacinda locked it after him and kicked her bag into the corner. She adjusted the taps on the sink to a steady flow and cupped the warm water in her hands. She splashed it onto her face and neck. It felt heavenly.

Maybe a shower later! The very thought relaxed her. A coarse towel hung from a hook beside the mirror. As she reached for it, she caught her reflection for the first time since Cairo. The only makeup left on her face was smudged eyeliner.

She shook her head and moaned. Something had to be done about that poor weather-beaten creature looking back at her from behind the glass. She grabbed her purse and spread her makeup out on the basin.

Espionage would have to wait while she fixed her face.

First, she took her blouse off and tossed it on the bed. Then, she scrubbed from neck to hairline with the small bar of yellow soap generously provided by the Kostos Shipping Company. She rinsed, patted herself dry, and smoothed on a light film of foundation. Her olive skin rarely needed blush, but she brushed some on anyway. This was therapy, after all, and she wanted to make it last.

A touch of lipstick and then her eyes, darkening her black lashes and stroking on a long dash of color over her lids. She had enjoyed that part ever since she was a little girl. Her mother, a woman of pure Egyptian blood, would take her to see statues of her ancestors and, at home later, trace thick lines around their eyes, pretending they were ancient queens of the Nile.

Jacinda decided to try it again. She ran the liner in a broad stroke around her eye and ended it in a long, thin triangle. When she stood away from the glass and looked at her image, she felt a strangeness that had come upon her before, though not for many years. There had been childhood nightmares and days at school when she drifted to another place.

At those times she knew the eye, all deep with its sinuous black outlines snaking toward her, was beckoning to her. When the visions vanished, they left a longing—a longing for things that never were.

A knock at the door brought her mind back to the cabin.

"Yes?"

It was Alexandros with her sandwich. She told him she was dressing and to leave it by the door. She heard him comply and walk off. When he had gone, she got the tray and brought it inside. He had kindly left a warm Coke next to the sandwich. She drank and ate quickly, then placed the tray in the hall.

As she shut the door, Jacinda closed her eyes and rested her forehead against the warm wood. She felt drained—not unreasonably, since she had barely slept for two days. Nervous tension and adrenalin can only work for so long. Turning around, but still supported by the door, she faced the bed. It drew her, but somehow it unsettled her, also.

It dawned on her that sleep was frightening. If she had surrendered to its temptations in her Cairo hotel, she would have been blown into scattered strips of meat.

Smart girl, she thought. Sleep. Now, she equated it with death. Her heart pounded as she stepped haltingly across the short space to the bed and touched the mattress. It felt so soft, so inviting.

And she was safe, now.

Halevi said to follow your body, and now hers was tired and pleading for rest. She stretched out and kicked off her shoes. Her lids sank heavily over her eyes, but she still fought sleep. *Perhaps only a few minutes of quiet,* she thought.

Quiet.

Quiet.

CHAPTER NINE

She had no memory. How had she come to this frightening place?

Red-tinged fog billowed above and below her, so that looking down she could not see her own body. And yet, she knew her arms were groping inside the angry cloud—and feeling nothing!

The tendrils of cloud arched over her until they formed above her head into a mimicking contour of–an *eye!* An *Egyptian* eye, exactly as in the tombs!

"Jacinda," came a gruff whisper of a voice.

As she stared, the red fog thinned a bit. But the eye remained, growing ever larger. She turned away, but wherever she looked, it was there. Now, at the center, where the pupil in a true eye would be, she glimpsed a human face. The clouds made it hard for her to see. Yet, there was something horrifyingly familiar about it.

"Jacinda!"

"That's not my name!" she cried.

Suddenly, viselike fingers grabbed her calf muscle, tearing at it, trying to pull her down as a second unseen arm circled her waist and squeezed with inhuman force! The first hand crawled up under her skirt and ripped at her panties until it touched bare flesh. It cupped over her pubis as the other, at her breast, was forcing her backward and whispering foul words into her ear.

She fell, landing hard on rocky ground. As the powerful arms caressed her, the red smoke blew away, revealing her attacker.

Malamat!

Grinning, dead Malamat. His smile pulled his gray-white skin across his rotting features, showing his black gums and yellow teeth. He stared out, though his eyes had already decayed and fallen back into his skull. He relaxed his mouth to speak.

It was not easy. His lips had ulcerated and cracked as the blood in his face clotted into blue and rust-colored patches around his chin and left cheekbone.

Malamat said, "They're coming for you, Jacinda, my favorite. Come embrace your old lover. One kiss. Is that too much to ask? One kiss . . . and I'll tell you how I know!"

Malamat's arm began to draw her closer and closer to his cancerous mouth. She struggled to free one hand and began to pound on his laughing parody of a face.

"How could they find me? They think I'm dead from the bomb!"

Malamat licked her face with his large St. Bernard tongue. "Don't they know you stole the ankh, sweetness?"

Jacinda nodded.

"So, follow me, now," said the rotting apparition. "If they want their ankh back, why use a bomb that might blow it to powder?"

"Oh, my God!"

"They didn't detonate the bomb until they were sure you were out of the building."

"Why, Malamat, why?"

Malamat shrugged a battered shoulder. "How could Shafiq know his ankh was taped to your thigh. If you'd hidden it and they blew you to pieces, the ankh might never be found. So they followed you all the way here."

"They're coming for me, then? On the ship?"

"They don't have to kill you now," howled Malamat. "The ankh, by giving life, will cause your death."

She ran at Malamat and struck the laughing corpse. One blow—then another and another—in an insistent rhythm!

Pounding . . . beating . . .

Beat . . . beat . . . beat . . .

Her eyelids burst wide open.

The pounding continued, and for a few incoherent seconds, she had no idea if it came from without, or if the sound was echoing inside her head. Only half-awake, she struggled to calm her heaving chest and focus her eyes. Once she had, she realized where she was: in her small cabin aboard the *Xenophon,* jolted awake by—

Someone was pounding at the door. Jacinda got to her feet, grabbed her blouse and threw it on. Whoever was in the hall must have heard her. He stopped knocking and shouted, "Miss! Please, are you in there?"

"Yes. Alexandros?"

"It is I, miss," he said, sounding relieved. "Bless the cross, you are here!"

It was dim. Had the sun gone down? It seemed mere seconds since her head hit the pillow. She glanced through the porthole.

Endless black water. Not even shore lights reflected in the sky to hint at where the horizon might be. Likely as not, the ship had made straight for the open sea as soon as it cleared Suez.

How long have I been asleep?

She hurried to the cabin door.

"One moment." Her hand had already closed on the latch, when her training took over.

"Alexandros, are you alone?" she whispered. She thought she heard an ironic laugh before the boy answered.

"Most certainly, miss. Please to open the door."

Jacinda gripped tight on the handle and pressed her other hand flat on the wood, in case she had to shove it back fast. She cracked the door open enough to tell that Alexandros was indeed alone in the dark, silent corridor.

"I must come in!" he said anxiously.

"You aren't drunk, are you? I don't want any trouble, Alex."

The visible part of his mouth dropped open in surprise. "Oh, that is not what I meant, miss. I swear by Saint Stephen!"

"What time is it, anyway?" Jacinda asked.

"Late. Very late, I'm afraid." He pushed inside and went immediately to the far wall. "Lock it, please."

She saw the buttons on the boy's white uniform dance with every short breath. Alexandros was shaking as if he were locked in a meat freezer. He stood, his back to the wall, head bowed.

"Forgive me, miss. I would not compromise a young woman in such a way . . . but . . . but . . ." His voice trailed off.

"You look terrible. What's the matter?"

"The silence. You hear it?" said Alexandros, his tone suggesting he doubted his own senses. But it was true, there was no sound.

"I don't hear the engines," Jacinda replied. "Have we broken down?"

"No. Th-that is not the reason I've come."

"Then what?" she urged. "Come on, Alex, make sense. Is the ship in trouble? Are we in any danger?"

"I don't know. We are dead in the water, but," he added, "it is calm on the sea tonight. If there is peril, it will not involve the sturdiness of our vessel, miss. And that is fortunate because, I fear we are the only two people on board!"

"What?"

"I have searched for an hour or more, and not one soul have I seen."

"No one?" she asked, at a loss.

"I swear. You see, miss, earlier I was in one of the storage rooms reading my nautical history. I wish to enter the naval academy after another year, and I can sneak away there to study when my duties are light . . ."

"Yes?"

"I heard some noises and the engines, they stopped. I did not think to go on deck just then. I am not involved with things mechanical. Mostly, I keep ledgers and see that we have enough provisions in the stores. So, it was only later that I left to go to the bridge."

"Why the bridge?"

"To find the captain. Actually, he requested I remind him to come down for dinner. It seems he wanted to meet you. But no one could be seen. Not the captain, the helmsman—nobody!"

Jacinda fought the tumble of strange, disquieting thoughts sweeping through her mind. Could the boy be right? If so, did it have anything to do with her? She thought she was being so clever booking passage on one of Shafiq's carriers, tracking his illegal cargo as a final insult to the men who wanted her dead, but what if she were seen by someone from the cell?

One phone call and she was snared in a tin coffin floating in the middle of a dark nowhere. She might choose her way to die, but even if she gave them back the ankh, there was no way to get out alive

What power was in that ancient ankh to compel Shafiq's—or Salameh's—people to pursue her, even here? Would they detain a ship in international waters and snatch the entire crew without firing a shot simply to ensure the safety of a piece of broken quartz?

A gunboat could have done it. One well-armed launch sending

threats over its radio could have panicked the captain and demanded he abandon ship. Or the captain might be part of the faction himself and might have set this all up on his own. She might never know.

"Alexandros," said Jacinda, her voice cool, but firm, "did you see any other boats nearby?"

He tried his best to answer. "I-I did not see . . . but perhaps if one ran without lights, it might anchor just beyond us. In the darkness, who could tell?"

"Stay here, Alexandros. I want to go on deck and see for myself."

"Oh, but I am come here to protect you, miss."

Swiftly, Jacinda snatched her purse, found her gun, and held it under the young Greek's chin.

"I can protect myself. Now, please, would you hand me my jewelry box over there."

Biting his lip, Alexandros did as he was told, then retreated to a corner. He watched as she sat on the bed and took a pair of comfortable shoes from her survival kit and slipped them on. Then, with her back to the young man, she took the ankh from its chest and stuffed it into her fanny pack.

"I suspect the ship had a mechanical problem, and the crew is off fixing it. But if we're dealing with a hijacking or terrorists, I have to know that fast!" She spoke with a quiet firmness as she strapped the bag around her waist and tucked the gun into her pocket.

His voice wavering, Alexandros said, "It is you? They are after you? But you are only a woman."

Jacinda grinned indulgently as she passed him on the way to the door. "I'll be back soon. Lock it after me."

She gave the boy a quick peck on the cheek and threw open the bolt. Putting her shoulder to the cabin door, she yanked the latch handle and pushed at the same instant.

"Bye!" she blurted.

And she sprang out. Twirling in a tight circle, she landed low and coiled. One hand braced her against the opposite bulkhead; her other swung her gun in a wide arc.

Her bravura performance seemed wasted. The corridor stood empty. She saw nothing from one murky end to the other, got to her feet, and inched onto the cabin-level deck.

A single row of running lights above her made little bright patches that scurried from place to place across the polished planking with each slight pitch and roll of the sea. She looked over the side, straining until her eyes adjusted. Above, the moon hung with its top half neatly sliced off. It shone on the water without much effect.

Jacinda could hear the sound of tiny wavelets lapping the hull, but aside from that, the ship was silent. For all she could see or hear, she could be aboard the only vessel in the world.

She decided to explore. She dashed up the steep metal stairway to the bridge, without regard for danger. The wheelhouse, ringed as it was by windows, would be a good vantage point—and safer than most spots aboard.

Nothing was visible on bridge level, either, as Jacinda stood on the outer platform. She scanned the ship below her for any movement. Everything was quiet.

SCREEE—WHAK!

Jacinda jumped a foot! Her hand jerked back as she whirled half a turn. The hammer on her gun clicked, but she caught it before she fired at—a sliding door! A heavy metal one at the rear of the wheelhouse. It had been left unlatched and rolled open down its track as the freighter pitched in a small swell.

"Calm yourself, girl," she said to herself. "Don't go shooting at ghosts!"

She ventured into the wheelhouse. It was a compact space, designed to hold four or, at the maximum, five men. The work area had a messy, lived-in look, as if the helmsman had just gone out the door for a smoke.

Smoke!

She spied a thin ribbon of white smoke rise from behind a rumpled chart. It was a pipe, sitting in a cheap glass ashtray. She picked it up, sniffing the strong scent of Latakia coming from the bowl. It might belong to the *Xenophon's* captain.

She had met a few Greek men in her time. Most of them smoked and when they did, they liked a lot of Latakia in their blend.

How long, she thought, *can a pipe burn on its own? Not too long. Men were always puffing away on those things to keep them lit, weren't they?*

But Alexandros said he had been searching for an hour. Where was the captain all that time? Could he have returned to the wheelhouse for some reason? Had he stayed longer up here until his crew had left?

Perhaps, he had to stay on the radio and report on the transfer . . .

SCREEEEE—WHAK!

The sliding door at her back slapped shut with a shrill whine and latched with heart-stopping finality. The sudden sound caused Jacinda to drop the pipe. It bounced off the metal lip of the chart stand, cracking apart at the shank as it struck the hard wooden floor.

Stupid! Jacinda bristled with annoyance. *I should've jammed something in that door!*

The radio crackled from an alcove behind the radar console. A red light tinged the walls, but did not cast enough light to work the controls. Jacinda took a chance and turned on the hanging light. It shed a sudden antiseptic brightness over the wheelhouse.

Rapidly, she flicked the radio to "Transmit" mode and sent her code number on a channel the Mossad monitored. Then, following procedure, she twisted the dial to a predetermined frequency that changed every twenty-two days.

She grabbed the headset. It was greasy. Jacinda grinned: *Greeks love their hair oil*. The metal was still warm. The captain might have used the radio notifying Shafiq's men that the ship had reached a prearranged rendezvous point.

She had to speak fast and clear, because anyone listening had their orders not to reply. In her head, she tried to anticipate their questions. But one question she would be unable to answer. She couldn't give them the ship's position. Without knowing how long she slept, or how fast the *Xenophon* had been going, or on what course—Jacinda had no idea where in the world she was.

The charts!

She rushed over to the navigator's station and found them taped to the countertop. There was a line beginning at Port Said and tracing northward to the island of Cyprus.

But there was something peculiar. At a position one hundred km from the Egyptian coast, a second line intersected it. A red line traveling east northeast, ending at a spot off the border shared by Israel and southern Lebanon. There it met a row of dots from some kilometers below Beirut.

So that was it!

The *Xenophon* had changed course to rendezvous with a ship from one of the coastal towns to pick up the arms that were undoubtedly in the hold. Jacinda ran back to the radio and called in a warning. When she finished, she left the switches open, hoping the signal might act as a beacon for the Mossad.

If they gave a damn.

She stood warily facing the dark windows. A part of her hoped to see another person there, but she saw only her own pale reflection and the blackness beyond the glass.

Her skin tightened, its rising goose bumps betraying a growing fear to herself. It was one of those interminable moments when a woman's body has time to be aware of itself and sense the forces pulling at it.

Eyes were on her—her own eyes!

She caught herself glancing behind uncomfortably at each of the six windows angled around her. Jacinda's image stared back from each of them like an accusing jury.

I'd better get out of here, Jacinda realized, *I'm spooking myself.* She stared, wondering what to do next. *Did Alexandros check the hold or the engine room? Maybe I'd better take a look for myself.*

Jacinda tucked the gun in her pocket, tugged at the latch of the sliding door, and yanked it open. She rushed down two levels to the main deck easily, but had to grope down the final few steps when she entered a black shadow caused by a worn canvas awning overhanging the side deck that blocked the running lights.

"Ye—ow!" Her shin hit something hard. Smothering another groan, she stumbled back—

—into a man's powerful, encircling arms!

Jacinda snatched at her pocket, fighting for her gun, but the man's hands held her wrists tight. She lifted one leg for a back-kick to his kneecap—

"Miss? Miss!"

The man released his grasp and withdrew to the railing so Jacinda could see his face. "It is Alexandros, miss. You made me so scared when you fell into me."

Feeling a flush of embarrassment rise on her cheeks, Jacinda decided to stay in the shadows. "You—you shouldn't sneak about like that. I could've hurt you."

"Oh, please forgive me. I would not have left the cabin, only that I thought of something."

"What?"

"Only that, if we are quite truly alone—that would make me captain of the *Xenophon!*"

In spite of herself, Jacinda chuckled. Alexandros heard and drew her out into the dim light. He paced for a moment, then approached, his expression earnest and struggling.

"Perhaps I am not so good at expressing myself in your language, miss. But what I am meaning is that—well, as the captain of this vessel, I am empowered to—sail it away."

"You're not serious," she said guardedly.

"I most certainly am serious. I am a seaman all my life. My father was a pilot for the port of Corinth. I can plot a course that will take us safely to one of the islands."

"Is that possible? This is a big ship."

"Yes. Possible. With your help, miss."

Jacinda glanced downship. From her vantage, the *Xenophon* looked huge and uncontrollable. But if they could get it moving, leave the nightmare behind, it would be worth the risk.

After a quiet pause, she lifted her chin and met the young Greek's eyes. "All right, Captain. What do we do first?"

Alexandros allowed a shy smile to form as he answered. "Start the engines, I suppose."

"Okay, how do we do that? Do you need a key?"

"A key?" Alexandros, perplexed for a moment, suddenly understood. He shook his head, suppressing a laugh. "Oh, no, miss. You do not start a merchant vessel like a Toyota. I must go into the engine room—"

Jacinda, embarrassed, cut in, "We'll both go!"

"If you wish, yes. There is much to do." They started aft. "We can take this hatchway. It is closest. Through the hold and then we find the engine room."

On the way, Jacinda felt her confidence returning. But she took a sharp breath when Alexandros pulled back the heavy steel hatch, revealing a single metal ladder dropping straight into what appeared to be a black, bottomless pit.

"I go down and find the light," said Alexandros. "Then, you climb after me. Okay?"

"You can go first, with my blessing."

Alexandros hooked his instep to the edges of the ladder and slid directly into the heart of the ship. She lost sight of him immediately, but heard the slight ting as he jumped onto a catwalk grating somewhere below. Short metallic footsteps led off until they faded away.

Topside, Jacinda sat with her feet dangling into the hole. Two minutes went by before she began worrying. No sound at all came from the hold.

She made the mistake of glancing up. The high decks, topped by the lighted bridge, rose like a sheer escarpment or some atavistic temple. The wheelhouse windows stared back, an idol watching from its mountain shrine.

Suddenly, one of the idol's eyes blinked at her!

Jacinda gasped. She had only caught a glimpse of the form that crossed in front of the window and momentarily blocked the light.

But a second later, the shape returned, walking by one window to the left. It stretched upright, revealing itself as a cat.

It was only a cat.

Not another damn cat.

At that instant, a light shone through the hatch. Alexandros called that he had found a battery lamp, but told her that the overhead bulbs would not work until the hold's generator could be started.

"—But you can come down now, miss."

The way down was a long tube that dropped one story, but seemed to fall into eternity. Alexandros pointed his spotlight under her. It helped her footing, but because of the glare, she had no idea how far she had to go. At some point, she wasn't exactly sure where, she passed through to the lower decks, and the metal tube no longer encased her.

It made her shudder.

She froze, clinging onto that ladder like a baby chimpanzee attached to its mother. The hold plunged another three floors and if she fell from that ladder—

Jacinda gritted and started again. One rung at a time. Alexandros helped her down the last few feet. She landed on a sturdy catwalk made of widely spaced cross-strips of steel.

No place for high heels, she noted.

"The air's different here," she remarked as her sight became accustomed to the lamp. The walls sweated from the heavy, humid atmosphere. Smells of axle grease and leaking oil mingled, invading her nostrils. She gagged, but kept the spasm in the back of her throat.

Pipes, electrical conduit, chains, and winch ropes snaked everywhere like viscera inside a great beast. Jacinda felt a mild panic as the significance of the place came into focus for her.

She felt swallowed!

CHAPTER TEN

Alexandros took Jacinda's arm and guided her down a set of flying steps leading to the engineer's station. It occupied a large corner area, cluttered with switches, gauges, and rows of dials.

Alexandros propped the light on a desk and began studying the readings beneath their little windows. While Alexandros worked in silence, Jacinda looked down. Through the grating, she focused on a tangle of pipes and steel tendons. Her eyes followed two massive pistons rising from the lower deck like the legs of a huge mechanical locust. The connecting rods met below her feet amid the grimy watchwork complexity of the ship's engine where they joined the main drive shaft.

Suddenly, a sharp vibration jolted the walkway!

A shot of white steam almost knocked her off her feet. She screamed as she stumbled back against the engineering console.

"She's starting!" shouted Alexandros as more puffs of vapor escaped from an overhead line. In a second or two, a chorus of hissing and groaning began as the flywheels sighed to life.

"Good. Good," whispered Alexandros as he increased the pressure, smiling broadly as the drone of the engine pitched higher and higher. The sound settled to a deep murmur, and Alexandros locked the controls. "We can climb back to the bridge now, miss," he said.

"You don't have to tell me twice," said Jacinda with an anxious smile as she hurried to the stairs. She gripped the railings tightly, preparing to pull herself up, when the catwalk lurched and tossed her into the steel balustrade.

A bass gnashing sound rumbled up from the engine in fits and starts, its rhythm madly out of phase. Jacinda held on to the handrail so hard, her knuckles popped out like moonstones.

"What's wrong?" she yelled. "Alex!"

Another tremor spun her flat against the stairs, and she glimpsed Alexandros pinned to the console, watching the gauges as if hypnotized. The dials fluttered wildly like wings on a flock of panicked birds, but the Greek did not move.

"Alex! What's happening?"

Jacinda's scream broke his stare and when he turned his face toward her, there was death in his eyes. "Kristos! They have cracked the shaft! It is over!"

"Quick! We can still get out!"

The lights flickered, and a loud whoosh of steam billowed from below the engineer's station. Alexandros gasped and switched off everything he could on the console.

"Yes. Yes, miss, I come."

Alexandros grabbed the lantern and ran toward Jacinda as the ship heaved. A pipe wrenched free and struck the catwalk, buckling the floor not three feet ahead of him, ripping the steel and making a wide jagged fissure in his path. He leaped over it but caught his trouser cuff on a sharp strip of grate. He stumbled and fell, sprawling.

"Are you hurt?" Jacinda's voice was shuddering now.

"Tip-top, miss." He raised up on his knee, wincing as he drew the other leg up. Jacinda left the stairs and ran to support him.

"We must hurry," said Alexandros, his tone amazingly deliberate. "When the screw shaft breaks apart, it will surely tear through the hull like a razor. And this engine room will flood in seconds. We have very little time to get on deck."

"Don't worry. I'll help you up the ladder."

"That is not such a fine idea, miss. Should we be caught between decks when the sea water hits the hot motors, the boiler will no longer vent. . . ."

"And?"

"It will explode. The steam will shoot up the ladderway and we will be . . ."

"Boiled like lobsters."

Alexandros nodded solemnly. "Exactly, miss. We will have to make it through the hold if we can."

That instant, a roar engulfed them. The catwalk pitched, wrenching some support bolts from the plate walls. Jacinda gave Alexandros her shoulder and somehow managed to reach the watertight bulkhead door before a rod split off and tore a huge gash in the *Xenophon* eighteen feet below the waterline.

The sea poured in, the churning water sizzling into vapor clouds the instant it struck the engine. A geyser of hot metal and boiling air rocketed up the ladder chute. It whined like an immense pipe organ and sent a towering flume through the open hatch to a hundred feet above the wheelhouse.

Below, Alexandros and Jacinda caught their breath in a tiny compartment sealed off from the engine room bathed in red emergency lights. They had escaped a searing death by under seven seconds.

On the other side of the heavy door, water and steam battered and crashed, trying to get at them. The rusty hinges creaked but held, even as small explosions strained it. Inches away, inside, Jacinda managed to show her relief with a tired smile, but Alexandros wore a grave, hidden look. He drew her to her feet and handed the lantern to her.

"Hold this. The generator will fail any moment, and we will lose even this poor illumination."

Jacinda turned on the light, and the beam fell on Alexandros's uniform. His white trouser leg was drenched red from his calf down, and the blood had begun pooling around his shoe.

"Oh, Alex . . ." she said, concerned, but he waved her off.

"It is nothing. Greeks have a lot of blood to spare," he said, but he was worried and did not deliver the joke well. He lifted his hand to the portal, feeling the constant vibration.

"We cannot remain here any longer, miss," he said. "Once the pressure has built enough, none of these bulkheads will be able to endure it."

He dropped his chin, as if in prayer. "The *Xenophon* is doomed. I am so sorry for this. Perhaps the ship line will pay for another vacation for you."

Jacinda laughed. She shouldn't have, but he was so very earnest and she needed a laugh badly.

"Did I say something?" he asked.

"I'm sorry, really I am. It just struck me funny. Here we are. And you're worrying over a refund." She took his hand. "That's very sweet, actually."

"Oh, I see." He smiled with embarrassment, his face getting redder in the red light. Then, he returned to business. "We must find a lifeboat. There is one forward, I know."

"How much time have we?"

"Little, miss. And we waste it here." He walked a few painful steps. "Come, this passage leads to the forward cargo hold. From there, we need only take a stairway to the main deck."

Jacinda followed and slipped under his arm, offering her shoulder to lean on. "I'm ready, if you are," she said, and the young Greek beamed.

They hurried along a narrow companionway. Alexandros's knee made every step agony for him, but he pressed on. Jacinda nearly dragged him the last few paces into the cargo hold. After passing through the thick hatch, Alexandros stopped and asked Jacinda to help him seal it shut. The latch secure, they rested.

"That should give us some breathing space," he said. "I doubt the ship will sink until this hold floods."

"That's not enormously comforting, Alex."

"It is why we have all these compartments."

"Like the *Titanic*," mused Jacinda.

"A bad example," he replied and pointed off into the expansiveness of the main cargo area. "Our way out is this way—there, between the crates."

Jacinda turned her light on it. "You mean that narrow crack?"

The way, about a shoulder's breadth, was surrounded by perhaps thirty long wooden boxes piled erratically near the outer wall. Alexandros took her hand and shifted her lantern beam up. It glinted off a flight of metal stairs that led in easy stages to the safety of the upper deck.

"I am afraid it will be a bit of a squeeze, miss. We must walk single file and be very careful. With the aft section filling with water, the *Xenophon* is quite unstable. If those crates shift and fall . . ."

"But can you walk on that knee? Without help, I mean."

"I will be right behind you."

"No, you go first, Alex. . . ."

"And block your way? No. Please, miss, you have the torch. You show me the path. Quickly, now—Captain's orders."

Jacinda started off but, after a few steps, noticed that Alexandros was not coming as promised. He still leaned against the bulkhead where she left him, bent in pain, his face obscured by red shadows.

"Alex, please! I need you!"

He glanced up and tried to limp toward her. He might have been smiling, but she would never know, because at that instant the hold went black!

Immediately, the entire vessel seemed to twist in violent spasms. Jacinda fell backward, striking her temple hard on the corner of a crate.

She was stunned, but fought to clear her head.

From high on the pile, a box slipped its rope and crashed beside her. The wood splintered and the lid dislodged, spilling its foul-smelling contents onto the floor. She couldn't orient herself as shadows and moldy odors assailed her. Her head ached so, she wished for unconsciousness.

The crates whirled around her.

No, it was the lantern! It had dropped from her hand and now pivoted madly like a top where it fell, its beam splashing over the narrow passage, revealing and hiding with every circuit.

She went to her knees and reached out to stop the turning light—but another hand beat her to it!

"Alex?" she cried, but he had been behind her and the hand was ahead of her. She inched back, her palm pressed over her lips as if it could confine her terror. The hand lifted the lantern by the end, spilling its light from wrist to fingertip. Its skin was black and leathery with dark indigo nails dull and cracked with age. A gold scarab ring was trapped by the bulbous second joint of its thin middle finger.

It turned the lantern and played it over Jacinda, who cowered on the ground by the broken crate. The beam filled her eyes and blinded her. That was the moment the creaking started.

And another sound—a short plaintive cry. It happened again, and once more before she realized what it was. Long ten-penny nails whined as they slowly withdrew from their holes. The crates were opening from the inside.

But they weren't exactly crates . . .

They were coffins.

What had her dream prophesied for her? *"The ankh, by giving life, will cause your death."*

Moving stealthily in the darkness, the bodies crawled out of their cases and staggered to the floor of the hold. Jacinda heard the wood cracking, then, the chafing of dry skin as the shapes closed in, in front of her.

Beside her, Alexandros stirred. He pulled himself to his feet and began shouting in Greek. The only reply was the sound of shuffling feet getting nearer.

"Alex! You okay?"

"Yes, perfect." There was pain in his voice. "I was asking if they were from the crew, but I don't think they are my men."

From what she had seen, Jacinda doubted they were men at all, but she hesitated to mention that to the poor boy. He was trying so hard to protect her. She felt a sensation of heat at her hip. Her hand went down instinctively and touched her pack. Inside, the ankh was glowing red.

"Take my hand," she shouted. "We've got to run for the deck before they block the way out. Can you make it?"

"No, you go. I will slow you—"

"Forget that!" Jacinda reached under his arm and grabbed his belt. She supported him against her hip bone as she launched herself through the narrow passage between the stacks of crates.

Thin arms clutched at them as they half skipped, half ran to the last bulkhead. Fifteen feet from their goal, a body dropped from above and landed directly in front of them. First, it slumped, then drew itself up to its full height. Jacinda had only seen such an ema- ciated silhouette once before.

At the Holocaust Memorial in Israel.

The man, if that's what it was, poked his finger at a spot above Jacinda's right breast. She slapped it away. It felt slick and oily to her touch. And one more thing, its arm had no power behind it. All it had stopped was their momentum. She knew she could take him out.

Jacinda used her forearm as a bat and struck a blow at its neck. Its throat snapped like a rotted branch. The skull fell sideways onto its shoulder, but nothing else even quivered. She pushed against its chest, but it stayed there in the way, sturdy and immobile as a block of marble.

"Behind us! They're coming!" shouted Alexandros. Not a second later, the ship pitched violently. Jacinda and Alex bounced into the wall of crates. Above them, they shifted and began to tip. A crate on top tumbled into the confined space, hitting the body ahead of them squarely and collapsing it as if it was a foot stepping on an empty beer can!

The deck shook under their feet. The crate splintered when it hit, forming a V-shape. Jacinda hauled Alexandros through as the other bodies tore at them, fracturing the wood a second after they passed.

Again the ship quaked and rolled.

Alexandros's leg buckled under him, sending both of them to the damp floor. Jacinda helped him crawl the last yard to the bulkhead door.

Alexandros pulled the grip as they hurried through the opening. It clanged shut solidly. Jacinda rotated the lock and jammed the rod with a short length of pipe.

We'll never get out of here that way, she thought.

Beyond them, they saw a catwalk rising up into the dark at a difficult incline. Jacinda hoisted Alex again, but this time, he was strong enough to pull himself along. In less than two minutes, they made it on deck, appearing at a rarely used access port near the stern.

The young man let go of her and crawled to the edge of the aft gangway. Alex could go no further and eased himself down.

Jacinda knelt beside him. "We need a lifeboat," she whispered.

"They were near the deckhouse. I had not wanted to alarm you before, but when I was searching for the captain, I saw they were gone."

His knee was wet with blood that soaked up and down the shredded pant leg, barely covering the wound. "Much pain?" she asked.

"Numb. I hardly feel it now."

Jacinda did not believe him, but smiled reassuringly and brushed his cheek with her fingers. "Good. Good. Look, I didn't tell you, but I found a chart up on the bridge. This ship changed course after dark. Right now, we're probably a few miles off the coast of Israel. Maybe we could find life vests or something else that floats, and we can swim to shore."

"To Israel? Why would the captain sail so far away from where he should be?"

"Money, Alex. These people are funded by oil money. My guess is the captain was bribed to meet a terrorist force coming from Lebanon. The crew left, or were taken off then."

"No, no," he protested. "That is foolish. Why leave the ship empty? The captain would have left a skeleton crew. Or these others would have taken over running the ship. Is that not logic?"

A deep animal groan rose from the hold beneath their feet. Only with huge effort, Jacinda quelled the unsettling terror that fought to take her over.

"Alex! The life jackets! The boiler's going! It's breaking apart below the water line!"

"There!" Alex pointed to a row of small hatches a few yards away. Getting off her knees, Jacinda hurried to them and flipped the cover on the first one. It contained a length of rope and some sort of harness that was useless to them in their current predicament. The next one yielded gold, four Mae Wests and a two-person inflatable raft.

"Hurry, Alex!"

By the time he limped over, Jacinda had released the compressed-air valve and, with a whoosh, the small yellow rubber boat filled and unfolded. They lowered it over the side just as the superstructure was hit by a series of rumbling shocks. The two of them rolled against the gunwale, but managed to hold onto the line.

"Put on the jacket," shouted Jacinda. Instead, Alex lifted one of the vests up and motioned for her to slip her arms through. She surrendered and put it on. That done, he grinned and grabbed his own vest and swung it around his shoulders.

Awkwardly, he shifted the rope from his right hand to his left to maneuver his hand into the arm hole. Alex didn't see the arm raised behind him until it struck him between the shoulder blades. He lurched forward, his smile changing instantly to stunned amazement. His chin dropped, and he looked down to his chest as a thin hand emerged from his rib cage.

It was red with blood. Ribbons seemed threaded among the fingers, until Jacinda realized they were Alex's veins and arteries. The young man slumped, and behind him rose a smirking death's head.

Jacinda let the rope go, and the raft hurtled to the black sea and disappeared from her sight. Her eyes never moved from Alex's fresh corpse until it dropped into a heap. The figure behind Alex drew itself up. Its torso was impossibly thin. At first glance, it seemed clothed in rags, but as it came closer, Jacinda saw that it was wrapped in strips of filthy linen.

The grisly sight enthralled rather than panicked her. Somehow, the skeletal creature was too unreal. Its face was barely human. A black ooze bubbled from thick cracks in the leathery skin. It looked at her through puckered eye sockets, damp and vacant. Cocking its head, first one way then the next, it presented its hands to her like a benediction.

The ankh at her hip was burning into her flesh. It was the pain that shook her from her immobility. Awakened to the danger, she backed away. The thin figure mimicked her movement, and she realized that it was transfixed by the glow from the top of the pouch.

Again, the sound of twisting metal erupted from the hold. She searched the darkness for any sign of aid, but instead, she saw at least fifteen of the desiccated creatures rise from hatches on all sides of her.

In a flash of insight, she knew why there was no crew on the *Xenophon*. The ship did carry weapons, but not rifles or missiles. It had brought this army of the dead to sail into and attack some Israeli port.

Invincible soldiers.

A supernatural army.

The thought of them, the look of them, the very fact that they existed would accomplish the purpose. Whether or not any individual walking corpse could be blown to dust by Israeli gunfire, the goal of stark terror would be fulfilled if they were allowed to land.

Ten or more of the walking dead came at her, drawn perhaps, like the corpse that murdered Alexandros, to the ankh at her waist.

For a second, she considered ripping it off and heaving it at them. Instead, she ran for the gunwale and climbed on top of the narrow rail. As twenty bony, dead hands grabbed for her, Jacinda closed her eyes and jumped off the ship.

She fell into the black, thinking that if she died in the attempt, the blackness might never end.

Five seconds were an eternity, but she struck the water cleanly and sank far below the surface. The wind was knocked out of her. Her lungs felt like clenched fists. The vest bore her up slowly, but finally, she broke into the air.

It was so dark she was unsure if her eyes were open or closed.

Then, the world lit up like a flare. Jacinda first heard then saw a huge cloud of flame shoot up from the exploding deck hatches on the ship. None of the debris landed near her because the *Xenophon* had floated to a safe distance, but she pointed herself away from the inferno and swam madly into the cold and dark.

A few minutes later, in the orange glow, she caught sight of the rubber raft bobbing only a few yards from her. She swam to it and rolled on. A pair of green eyes faced her. It was the cat, all wet and shivering. He cowered in a tight ball under the lip of the raft.

"Hello, little fellow," she whispered trying to calm the animal. "I guess it isn't only the rats who desert sinking ships."

The cat sniffed, then let out a plaintive wail.

"Don't like being soaked, huh? Here—" She folded the scrawny beast in her arms and wiped his fur with the tail of her blouse. "You didn't follow me from the market this morning, did you?"

She dismissed the thought. "No, you must be the ship's mouser. You just didn't want to be left all by yourself."

Jacinda heard the *Xenophon* vibrate and split apart behind her. She turned and sat watching as the ship ignited into a backdrop of flame and fireworks.

Ten minutes later, the only evidence of the *Xenophon* was a slick of oil, still burning in patches, and a few clumps of floating wood. Jacinda sighed and curled into the soggy bottom of the raft, intending to rest. She closed her eyes. A swell rocked the tiny craft, and a wavelet splashed into her face.

Brushing the salt water from her hair and nose, she felt another, harder strike against the rubber side.

Sharks? The thought crossed her mind. *Are there sharks in these waters?*

She knew that the creatures sometimes bumped their prey before circling in for the kill and, from below, a black raft might seem like a seal or some other shark delicacy.

Jacinda sat up and braced both sides of the raft. It would be morning soon. She had to hold out until then.

Nothing. No more bumps or swells. All was so very calm.

Still, she tensed, clinging tighter to the raft with every slight movement. She squinted into the night and saw a line separating the water from the sky. It was dim, but it was a sure sign that the sun was on its way.

The *Xenophon* had been a roman candle before it sank. Some agency in this most surveilled part of the world was certain to have detected it. One of the spy satellites trained on the Middle East would surely have noted such a bright point of light in the shadows so close to Israel.

Certainly. Surely.

She sat there shivering as the sun's edge surfaced above the horizon, and she stroked the cat. "What am I going to name you?" she asked aloud. "I know. In honor of another brave sailor, I'll call you Alexandros."

As the light grayed the black water, Jacinda saw that her raft was sitting amid an island of flotsam from the sunken *Xenophon*. The wreckage must have been what was bumping the raft during the night. In that same instant, she felt a welcome twinge of warmth. She sighed in relief, twisting around to watch the crest of the sun appear. Soon, its hot rays would dry her and take away the chill as it was doing even now—

NO!

Her hand went to her side with a start! The ankh was hot, much hotter than before. In the gray light, it glowed red as a burner on an electric range.

She screamed.

Rod-thin fingers shot up from the water in front of the raft. A dead face burst from the surface and grinned at her in triumph. Its brown, cracked fingernails dug into the rubber and ripped four long gashes from the top to a point just below the waterline. There, one of the long nails broke through but with unexpected results. As the air escaped the hole, the sudden force acted like a jet engine, propelling the raft ten feet out of the corpse's reach.

"Stay away!" Jacinda cried out. The two black eyesockets stared at her for a long moment, and then the head sank silently until it had disappeared below the water's surface.

Jacinda held no illusions that it was gone. Madly, she tried paddling with her hands. Once, she leaned too far the wrong way and almost toppled out of the boat. She had progressed only a few hundred yards when she realized that the raft was taking on water.

She inched over to the lobe of the raft that remained inflated. She pinched the rubber skin trying to stem the leakage, but she knew it was futile. And worse, the ankh at her waist began to radiate heat once more.

A scraping noise came from below her. She looked down and saw the shape of fingers poking up into the thin membrane of the raft's bottom. Nowhere to run. Jacinda's fear trembled at the edge of insanity, and what happened next nearly sent her over.

From above, a gale whipped the sea in a perfect circle with the raft at the epicenter. *Lord God, let it be true*, she prayed. Jacinda raised her eyes into the downdraft and saw a harness descending from a helicopter.

She grabbed at the heavy line, slipped it under her arms, and snatched up the cat by the scruff of its neck. The cable straightened, and Jacinda flew into the air. As her legs cleared the boat, she stared as the dead thing shredded the raft's underside and sprung at her.

It had her ankle. The winch shuddered at the added weight, and the line slipped a bit. Jacinda flailed about, kicking at the corpse in a panic, trying to throw the monster off. She began to twist and sway in the harness, but the rotted creature held on. As she looked up toward the face of her rescuer, she saw him paralyzed by his own disgust and disbelief.

"Use your flare gun, you bloody idiot!" squealed Jacinda as the thing dug its sharp nails into her calf. It reached up with its other arm, but by then they were only a body length under the helicopter's sliding door.

The crewman produced a flare gun but hesitated. He couldn't get a clear shot.

"Give me that!" Jacinda hollered. She pulled herself up on the cable and, stretching herself farther than she would have thought possible, tossed the cat to him as she grabbed the gun out of his hands.

Instantly, she bent over, pointed the barrel between her feet, and fired.

The flare hit the undead thing square in its forehead. Its skull exploded in a blinding white flash. The body caught fire as if it were a dry twig and plummeted in blazing pieces into the sea.

The crewman pulled Jacinda inside the helicopter. Flecks of phosphorus burned on her leg, but she was beyond feeling more than annoyance. The man threw a blanket over her to put out the fire. He took her face in his hands and lifted her eyelid, looking for signs of shock.

"I'm okay," she said. Out of habit, she spoke in Arabic. A sudden thought crossed her mind that she had no idea where the helicopter was based. What if they were Libyan?

Or Lebanese?

Salameh owned the Lebanese.

Without saying a word, the crewman carried her to a cot and covered her with a second stiff khaki blanket. It felt warm and wonderful. He smiled as he stuck her arm to start an IV drip.

She looked him in the eye. All she could think to say was a universal, Americanized greeting, "Hi."

"Shalom," he said as he swiftly returned the cat to her care. "Here," he snapped in Hebrew. "Your mangy monster bit me!"

Jacinda lay back with Alexandros curled on her chest and laughed. As the helicopter flew toward the port of Haifa, she drifted into sleep, comforted and safe.

CHAPTER ELEVEN

NEW YORK CITY

It had been a long couple of days and two hellish nights for Dan Rawlins. Thankfully, he had more than enough research to keep himself busy during working hours. But at night, he was up and down, sleeping for only an hour or so at a stretch. When he did fall asleep, he dreamt of the obelisk.

Marcy.

Trapped. She was holding onto the shaft. . . . Her life, her blood, draining onto the tall, cold granite. Like some giant's headstone, it rose above her . . . above her perfect naked body. . . .

In the shadow of the obelisk. . . .

Picked apart by birds, John had said. . . .

And if there was anything he could do, just call. . . .

The police had not released the body yet and, when they eventually finished all the dissecting and sectioning and probing of what had been Marcy, her corpse would be sent to Michigan for burial.

Fred Lanyard, Marcy's father, a clinical psychologist in Muskegon, phoned Dan a day after the cops notified him.

"There's a lot of work to be done," he said measuredly, his voice fading into sobs at intervals. "The man who carried out this horror must have been in incredible pain. Marcy's mother and I've thought about how this could have been prevented. We feel every child must receive a nurturing and loving upbringing. It's abuse that creates monsters, you realize. Love . . . that's our only weapon to stop tragedies like this."

Dan agreed, though he felt less touchy-feely toward Marcy's butcher.

"Marcy had talent, sir," Dan said to her father. "She would have been a great Egyptologist. Everybody at the museum will miss her more than you'll ever know."

John Erman arranged a special memorial service at a small church two blocks from the Met. It was held the next day for both Marcy and Carlos Antonio Ramiro Meireles-Todaro, the young guard who died in the Egyptian gallery. Dan said a few words, then John Erman spoke, followed by a representative of the archdiocese who offered a prayer.

Dan returned to a back pew and sat there in a dark mood. He was not aware the service was over when John patted him on the shoulder and asked, "You going back to the office?"

"I guess."

"I'll walk with you."

Georgie stopped Dan outside the museum when he and John Erman were crossing the lot to the employee's entrance. Georgie was shaking as he pulled Dan aside for a private conference. Dan wasn't in the mood, but reached into his pocket for some change. The homeless man drew back and waved away the money.

"They don't want to hear me, Doc. I tell 'em and tell 'em, and they blow me off like I was garbage."

"If I can help, Georgie—" Dan said dismissively.

"Listen, Doc! I was here that night! I sleep on a bench over by the Needle. So I saw it!"

"Saw what?"

"The little girl, that's what! Blondie! The one that gets me the hot dogs—."

Marcy!

"She was runnin' and runnin' until that Nazi got her. The bird with the—"

Dan clapped Georgie on the shoulders in a fatherly manner, even though Georgie had thirty years on him. "I know, buddy. Birds got to her. It must've been terrible to see."

Erman was holding the museum door open for him, coughing impatiently. Dan said, "I gotta go, Georgie."

As Dan passed through the door, Georgie shouted at him from the other side of the glass. It sounded like, "Damn thing weren't no bird, Doc! Birds ain't got teeth!"

Alone in the corridors, Dan passed the outer office which seemed gaily gift-wrapped by the yellow police tape. He ducked under the barrier and went inside. The room smelled odd. When he ran his hand over the desktop, it came up with a layer of gray grime.

The police must have dusted Marcy's office for fingerprints after I left. Now, he realized that cleaning up after themselves was obviously not part of the Manhattan crime lab's job description. He made a mental note to have the museum custodians scrub the place down when they decided to get back to their jobs.

And it occurred to him, he should have Mar—

Yeah, have Marcy check what chemicals the print experts used up in the Egyptian gallery, in case they used something that might harm the exhibits. . . .

Except, Marcy couldn't fit that into her schedule.

She had this funeral to go to in Muskegon, you see. . . .

Without thinking, Dan grabbed an empty carton and started to throw Marcy's things into it. He went at it in a fury, scooping off shelves full of the knick-knacks she always called her "little treasures" and heaping them together in the old box until they were spilling over and falling to the floor around his feet.

Dan could not stop. When he had wiped all trace of Marcy from the desk and bookcases, he sat in her chair and, finally . . .

He wept.

Taking out his handkerchief, Dan wiped his eyes and stepped into his office where he was stunned to see an imposing man waiting for him.

"Professor Rawlins, I assume," said the man with an obvious Israeli accent.

"Who are you?"

"Halevi is my name." Colonel Halevi sat at the edge of the desk and directed Dan to a side chair. He looked military even in his European-cut blue suit. An old scar at the corner of his mouth gave his hard features a perpetual frown.

He spoke softly. "I heard about your assistant. I sympathize for your loss."

"If she were here, I doubt if you'd be taking over my office." Dan asked the Israeli, "Are you an archaeologist?"

"We Israelis are archaeologists in our souls, but that's not how I make my living."

"Are you Mossad?" said Dan bluntly. He had dealt with their agents before in Israel and recognized the type.

Halevi shrugged. "James Bond is the only spy who tells you he's a spy."

"You may or may not be Mossad, but for damn sure you're an Israeli. I've worked with you guys since I was in diapers and don't take this wrong, 'cause I know you've fashioned a great country out of desert and you live in a pressure cooker surrounded by people who want to bomb you to hell, but you are a bunch of arrogant bastards."

Halevi nodded. "True," he said, the scar at his mouth crinkling as his face formed a patronizing semblance of a smile. "You have identified the national trait of Israel. We're insufferable. World's best fighters; world's worst diplomats." Halevi shifted to a more comfortable position on the desktop. He fished into his jacket pocket, found a slip of paper, and passed it to Dan. "Here. This is why I came."

Curious, Dan quickly opened the folded note. It was a stat of the minutes of a meeting, random notes, really. It was handwritten in Arabic.

"I picked up the original in a Palestinian camp in Lebanon," Halevi said. "Can you read the language?"

Dan grinned. "I spoke Arabic before I learned English." His eyes darted across the page. It appeared to detail the progress of some operation, but the purpose was clouded by the flowery phrasing. The page ended with two museum names and was signed Z. Qader. Dan looked up. "Who's Z. Qader?"

The colonel showed him a picture of an overweight man with a shaved head. "Qader is Chief of Operations for a man known as Mahmoud Salameh."

"Salameh?" Dan stiffened.

"Heard of *him?*"

"Sure," Dan countered. "Anyone who's spent any time in your part of the world knows Salameh's name. He's head of some Arab faction, but I haven't heard about him in a while. I thought he was dead."

"No such luck. But you're correct, he's been quiet. Too quiet. We think—"

"We?" Dan interrupted. "You mean you and your friends in the Mossad?"

That drew a sneer from Halevi as he went on. "For some reason, this Salameh has been collecting a strange group of friends. You wouldn't know anything about that, would you?"

"No."

"Why would a known terrorist meet secretly with a renegade Catholic bishop and a radical Orthodox rabbi? Any ideas?"

"Why are you dragging me into this?"

"I thought you might know the answer."

"Maybe he's planning to convert," said Dan indignantly. "I don't know a thing about him."

Halevi answered slowly. "He seems to be aware of you."

"Keee-rist!" Dan exploded. "I've been on the damn cover of goddam *Newsweek!* Of course he's aware of me! I bet Salameh's heard of Madonna, too! Once you get a little notoriety, you kind of lose control of who uses your name. Hell, there are T-shirts that say "Dan Rawlins Digs Me." You should read some of the crazy fan mail I get!"

Halevi flashed a wry smile. "I have."

"You are a bastard!"

"Don't get bothered, Rawlins. We've investigated you quite thoroughly, and we haven't found much sympathy for terrorism in your profile."

"Thanks a bunch. So why are you bothering me?"

In answer, the Israeli produced a small photograph, a glossy headshot of a man sporting a red beard. But clearly beneath the hair, it was Liam McMay.

"You met with this man the day of the mutilations when the Lanyard girl was killed," Halevi announced. The blood drained from Dan's face as the Israeli continued. "He's IRA. We think he's on loan to Salameh."

Dan bristled. "Well, that's news to me. He said he was with Sotheby's. I saw his credentials, so I believed him. But before that morning, I never saw him in my life."

"He didn't reach out to you? Ask you to join him in any endeavor?"

"No! No! I'm not political."

"I don't believe you," Halevi said. "About being nonpolitical, I mean. I wouldn't ask for your help if I felt you were indifferent to the way these vermin do their work."

"I've seen terror on both sides, friend."

Halevi nodded in agreement. "What *did* he ask you?"

"He showed me a picture of an ankh. Half an ankh, actually.

Come to think of it, he said Palestinians were looking for it. It turns out some museum has the matching half. The last thing I asked Marcy to do for me was to get it out of the inventory."

"Check it again. I doubt if it's there."

"What's that supposed to mean?"

"As far as we can make out, the broken ankh is the symbol of Salameh's movement. Like the swastika was to Hitler. It's supposed to represent how far Egypt's fallen since the time of the pharaohs. Modern folklore says that when the two pieces merge, the Arab people will also reunite—under Salameh, I suppose."

"He had two people killed because of a fairy tale?"

Halevi shook his head. "More than that. As ambitious as he is, for some reason, Salameh won't make a try for power without that cross."

Dan turned away. "Even so, I don't know why you're dragging me into all this."

"You don't? Don't you know who found your half of the ankh in the first place?"

"I've no idea. I could find out from the records, though."

"No need. I looked it up. The name of the archaeologist is Rawlins."

"Uh-uh!" Dan got to his feet to confront the Israeli. "I never saw an ankh made of that reddish quartz. I would've remembered."

"Oh, I believe you. It seems," Halevi said evenly, "that you're not the only archaeologist named Rawlins."

"My father?" Dan dropped back into his chair.

"Twenty years ago, Gunther Rawlins was digging at Megiddo. That's where Dr. Rawlins just found a new obelisk, I believe."

"Yeah, he told me."

Halevi folded his arms and spoke amiably. "Do you happen to know where your father is at the moment?"

"Is that a test question?"

"Not at all. I simply wanted confirmation that he is presently at your family's summer house on Montauk Point."

"As if you don't know I'm supposed to go there for dinner tomorrow. How long have you been tapping my phone?"

"I understand the truly sophisticated intelligence services don't tap phones anymore," Halevi mused. "They use digital audio grids. They cover a wide area and are virtually undetectable, or so I've heard. Which may be how they knew your father had an interesting luncheon guest over the weekend."

"Look, Mr.—"

"Colonel, actually."

"Okay, Colonel," Dan continued. "My father and I haven't talked much since we had a fight on *Nightline* a few years ago. My mother usually acts as our go-between so that we can keep up the facade of a family. But, I've got no idea what they do with themselves and, basically, I don't give a damn."

"Their weekend guest was described as an overweight gentleman with a slick bald head and a Syrian diplomatic passport. Zamir Qader!"

Fuming, Dan got to his feet to confront the colonel, but didn't. Instead, he stood with his back to Halevi for a few moments. He ran his fingers over his lips, disbelieving, but sensing that the Israeli's facts were right. He barely noticed as the colonel moved closer and was startled when the man whispered to him.

"I accuse him of nothing, Rawlins, but he and your mother may be in danger. Tell me," he asked, "would you place yourself in harm's way if it would spare your father's life?"

"Any day of the week!" said Dan without hesitation. "I still love the old sonofabitch!"

The colonel was stoic. "There may not be much time now. If Salameh was dealing with your father only to get his half of the ankh, well, he's got it. He has no need for Gunther Rawlins anymore. Salameh might even see him as a threat to his ultimate plans—whatever they might be. So, are you in?"

Dan turned to face the big Israeli and nodded slowly. A heartbeat later, Halevi clapped him hard on the shoulder like an old comrade. Then, the colonel unlocked the door and held out his hand to his newest informant.

CHAPTER TWELVE

Dan unlocked the top drawer of his desk and took out the manila envelope his mother had left with him. He removed a sheaf of photographs and spread them across the flat surface in rows because much of the text they recorded read up and down. One picture showed his father standing at the excavation site of an obelisk. It was at the bottom of a deep trench, toppled over, with three sides exposed. The glyphs on each surface, somewhat weathered but perfectly readable, were documented in a series of tighter shots.

Dan felt like he had at school, cramming for the big test. His father would surely grill him about it over dinner, and he knew he was ill-prepared for a man as intimidating as Gunther Rawlins. He would've loved to beg off dinner, but with everything the colonel told him, he had to find out if his folks were truly in jeopardy.

Dan wanted to get a headstart on the translation before he left. He jotted down a few alternative phrases, trying to fit the proper ones into the context of the opening declaration of the immortality of the pharaoh. As far as he could tell, the inscription followed most of the standard rules, invoking the divinity of the pharaoh, although the artisan who originally chiseled the glyphs onto the stone may have made the Egyptian version of a typo. Not a major error, but some epithets usually associated with Osiris, Lord of the Resurrection, were applied to Horus the hawk—symbol of the pharaoh.

Dan continued translating undisturbed. Ten minutes after opening the envelope, the first signs of boredom were setting in. All these inscriptions had interminable passages praising the pharaoh, the gods, or both. But the instant he read the name Sennemut, he was jarred awake.

Sennemut had held many posts, including Chief Scribe and Architect during the reign of Queen Hatshepsut, and his longevity in her service fueled the speculation that he had been her lover as well. His unique position sparked strange legends that spoke of unnatural powers.

Certainly, as a priest of the highest rank, he was privy to the secrets of the cult of Amun-Re, so many of the stories that came down in the oral tradition may have stemmed from his prowess as a magician in the Great Temple.

Dan knew that Hatshepsut, the infant Tuthmose's aunt, had assumed the throne in his place. Some time after Tuthmose had grown to manhood, the queen allowed her nephew to join her as coregent, but Dan reasoned it had been a stormy relationship based more on political necessity than either duty or filial love.

He was certain of one fact: After her death, Tuthmose ordered Hatshepsut's cartouche chipped off all her monuments and replaced them with his own. Somehow this obelisk was an exception, preserved against the wishes of pharaoh, who was *God-on-Earth*.

Gunther's message was vague on the details. He wrote only that the three revealed sides of the monument would confirm or expand on the story told on the wall paintings from the tomb of Amenemhab, a general under the mighty Tuthmose III. Before he came to the end of the first row of text, Dan saw that the desk was not wide enough for the task. He decided to use the floor and laid the copies lengthwise on the carpet to approximate the look of a splayed obelisk.

He got out a yellow legal pad and a Pilot razor-point pen to jot down any corrections he might want to make. He scanned the symbols to get familiar with the author's construction.

It read vertically in formal hieroglyphics. The body of the obelisk seemed to weave tales that Dan found familiar, but with a very strange spin. Even after a quick perusal, he could tell that the writing contained enough specifics to give graduate students a hundred years worth of dissertations.

The Egyptians had no objective chroniclers. All stories of battles and great deeds were written for the greater glory of the god-king.

An Egyptologist had to sift through a ton of such verbosity to find a syllable of truth. As Dan read the story of Amenemhab and Sennemut, he kept that in mind.

Dan took out a handkerchief to wiped his soaking brow. Sweat was getting into his eyes and running to the tip of his chin, but Dan wasn't sure it was all from the heat. The police had asked that nothing be disturbed in the building, and the maintenance crew took that as an excuse for a paid holiday.

With the thermostat stuck at eighty degrees, Dan removed his coat and dragged it to the closet to hang it up. He whipped his tie from around his neck as he went. No one was around, so he decided to change into comfortable jeans, his Bronx Zoo T-shirt, and an old pair of Reeboks. When he turned back to the floor, he half hoped that the mosaic of Gunther's discovery would have disappeared from the carpet. But the paper squares lay exactly where he left them.

He expelled a long breath, pursed his lips together, and blew out the remaining stale air from his lungs until his chest hurt.

It helped clear his mind. His father had taught him that trick once when they were camped one chilly evening atop some forgotten tel so many years before. Now, Dan felt the almost forgotten rush it gave him as fresh oxygen entered his blood.

But the sensation had always meant more to him—as though his soul were speeding to another place, perhaps backward to an earlier time.

He now viewed the ancient picture-writing in a new way, reading it as easily as a scribe in the black land of Qemet. Reading their words, no one could doubt that these were real men and women. Three thousand years had not brought so many changes.

Dan poured himself a cup of coffee from the pot by Marcy's desk and went back to work. After the first ten minutes, he almost forgot about the murders and, by the half-hour point, the talk with Colonel Halevi about terrorism and the missing piece of ankh also faded. Dan functioned that way, focusing totally on whatever was in front of him. That trait, he always said, made him a terrific scholar and a horrid friend.

By 2:30 P.M. on Sunday, Dan was satisfied his task was done. Considering that his father would be his critic, Dan decided to go over it once more before printing out a hard copy. It seemed tight.

When he had done all he could, Dan stroked the keys to alert the printer and went to bed on the couch. He could hear the clacking begin as his head hit the cushion, but he was asleep before the machine finished typing the monograph. Dan woke an hour and a half later, gathered up his work, and took a taxi home.

Dan hit his apartment running. There would be just enough time to shower, scrape his face with his razor, and change.

By five-thirty, Dan stood in front of his bedroom mirror, checking himself out. He had chosen a conservative gray suit, but decided against wearing a tie, especially not his trademarked knit maroon. He hoped to give his father the impression of a successful, but self-assured professional.

Fat chance.

He caught the Long Island Railroad commuter train from Penn Station with fifteen minutes to spare and arrived at Montauk on schedule. The Rawlins house was only a short distance from the station, and since he was all nervous energy, Dan decided to walk it.

The sun had just dipped below the Sound, ending the day with a quite spectacular show. The darkening sky was still tinted red-orange when Dan arrived at the seaside house. His mother opened the front door before he knocked and led him into the dining room to talk as she finished setting the table.

"Where's the great man?"

His mother lifted an eyebrow. "Tied up," she answered. "He had a late meeting on the Washington convention, but he'll be here eventually. You know how he is."

Dan nodded. "Did you catch the sunset tonight?" he asked to make conversation.

Eva shook her head. "No time. Busy creating culinary magic. Speaking of which . . ." She started off toward the kitchen. As she backed into the swinging door, Eva excused herself politely, explaining that a poaching salmon, unlike a grown son, needed constant attention.

Dan half grinned, then rose and stepped into the library. Moonlight sparkled in through the picture window as it hit the surface of Long Island Sound. The sight calmed him some, but there was still a fluttering in his stomach as he waited for his father to come home. All day the tension had been building in anticipation of the moment when the front door opened and he would be confronted with Gunther Rawlins's stern, weathered face.

Damn it, let's get this over with!

He dropped noisily into a soft upholstered chair and took a deep breath.

Succulent smells filtered in from his mother's kitchen. Dan laid his head back and remembered how it used to be. They had a cook, of course, when the family went on a dig. But Dan recalled that his mother seemed to haunt the mess tent, sprinkling strange packets of spice into the camp's food to the horror of the Arab servants. She loved to experiment, which made her a great scientist but a royal pain in someone else's kitchen.

He would never forget those meals. Even when they threatened to burn the roof of his mouth off, they were so good.

The best.

Dan heard his mother call out something from the other room. "What did you say?"

"I heard a car," she said loudly.

As she spoke, the side door banged open, and a large man strode into view. He stood in the doorframe and filled it.

"Dinner ready?"

"And it's real nice seeing you, too, Dad," said Dan.

Eva's voice called from the kitchen. "Ten minutes, Gun! Why don't you talk to the boy a while?"

The elder Rawlins crossed directly to the bar, poured himself three fingers of Cutty, and turned to Dan. "Want one?"

"I only drink on social occasions," Dan answered with a smirk.

For the first time since he arrived, Gunther Rawlins's face showed a sign of life. The two deep furrows etching his mouth moved up an eighth of an inch and then down again a moment later. It was not an involuntary twitch, but as broad a grin as ever appeared across his cracked, sun-weathered features.

"A good one, *but,*" he chided, "your mother expects a quiet, sociable family gathering."

Dan leaned back in his chair and clasped his hands behind his neck. "Other people have gatherings; you and me—we have summit conferences!"

"Terrible. Terrible thing," Gunther muttered. "That business at the Met a few nights ago." Gunther lowered his voice. "Eva says you knew the girl."

"I knew her. And the guard who was killed," Dan answered. "The police think it was a gang of crackheads."

"But you don't sound convinced." Gunther finished his drink. "Correct me if I'm wrong," he began again, his voice grim. "There's an unimportant scrap of an ankh missing from storage."

"How did you know about that?"

"It was mine. I kept it at the Met because, well, did you read Poe's "The Purloined Letter"? If you want to hide one ankh, hide it among a thousand of them."

"Ankhs are a dime a dozen."

"Ever heard of the Horite Cross?" Gunther asked as he went to the bookcase and pulled a leather folio from a shelf just below his eye level.

"Sure," Dan answered.

Gunther set the tome, unopened, on the coffee table and beckoned Dan over. Dan recognized the stamped gold-leaf title from his childhood, *Hieroglyphic Texts Reproduced from Stelae of the Third Intermediate Period in Dynastic Egypt,* a volume the elder Rawlins compiled three decades before at the British Museum.

" 'Sure' is not an answer, boy," he growled as Dan dropped onto the springy leather of the couch.

Without realizing it, Dan reverted back to when Gunther tutored him as a kid. He knew his father wouldn't be satisfied unless he rattled off all he knew. "The Horite Cross. Nomadic tribal legend from the Sinai. Sent from above; forged in fire. Same as a million other resurrection myths. In some texts it's tied to the story of Isis and Osiris, except all power is contained in the artifact and not the gods."

"My theory," said Gunther, "is that the Cross of the Horites was the first ankh, the prototype for all ankhs. And the one I found might just be it."

"Well, Dad, you finally went off the deep end and hit your head on the bottom of the pool."

"The proof is on the obelisk."

"I read the inscriptions," said Dan with a surprised expression. "The obelisk celebrates the victory of Tuthmose III over the Prince of Kadesh. The same war stories are in General Amenemhab's tomb."

"You only read three sides," Gunther replied.

"It's lying on the fourth side!"

"And I thought you were so modern. Haven't you heard of fiber optics? If they can shove a camera into your colon, they can read the underside of an obelisk buried in sand."

Dan accepted that. "You have a copy with you, or did your proctologist keep it?"

Gunther snorted, untied the folio, and spread it open. He flipped through the vellum sheets covered with the ancient picture-writing until he reached a section where the quality of the paper changed. He lifted the top page and handed it to Dan.

Dan ran his finger down the page, then looked up hesitantly. "Dad, don't take this the wrong way, but how did you find this slab of marble? I thought the seventh level at Megiddo was all played out."

"Evidently not." He seemed annoyed.

"Still, it shouldn't be at that stratum," Dan continued. "You said that yourself. And there's no proof that obelisk's authentic. Megiddo's a tired, old mound ripe for a good old-fashioned artifact fraud. First the Cardiff Giant, now the Megiddo pillar."

Gunther ground the words between his teeth. "It's too expensive to fake an obelisk. It would take a million dollars just to move it, let alone bury it in a well-guarded excavation site. And as for Megiddo, it is more than worthy of study. People have lived on that site for six thousand years. And, yes," he admitted, "I know it happens to be a sacred site for Christendom. This *is* the traditional Armageddon, after all. And every man of faith knows this is where the last great battle between good and evil will be fought, and the Second Coming will be announced!"

"Well, Dad, I'll believe in the end of the world when I watch the tape on CNN!"

The kitchen door flew open with a bang. Both men pivoted their necks in unison and saw Eva Rawlins standing in the doorway patting her palm with the bowl of her heavy metal ladle.

"Gentlemen. Your soup's getting cold."

CHAPTER THIRTEEN

Things had calmed down considerably by the time Eva served her poached salmon entrée. Actually, she didn't serve dinner, as much as stage-manage it. With a word here, or a little cough to indicate her disapproval there, she maneuvered the conversation so that soon Gunther was pouring Sebastiani Eagle and telling funny stories.

However, by dessert, talk had returned to the obelisk.

"The shape gives an obelisk its power, perhaps as a conduit for psychic energy. But there is more to this hunk of granite," Gunther pontificated. "Its significance is not so much what's written on it, but rather that it was found at the seventh level."

"From what period do you date that stratum, Gun?" Eva asked.

Gunther linked fingers and sat back. "Roughly, it corresponds to the time of the two kingdoms of Israel and Judah."

Dan perked up suddenly. "You keep saying that it's not where it should be, but wait a minute. You're telling me that you dug up an Eighteenth Dynasty obelisk at a level five hundred years later than the time it could have been buried?"

"Only if you're a slave to the king lists."

"You can expect the lists to be off a little, if only because they didn't use our calendar. But five or six centuries? That would confirm

Velikovsky's theory, and he's the biggest crackpot in the history of Egyptology."

"Maybe now *I* can claim the title," Gunther cut in, "now that the obelisk proves the old chronology wrong."

"What proof?" Dan threw up his arms, letting his linen napkin fall from his lap to the Persian carpet. "All we have is the obelisk. If Amenemhab's inscriptions date it from Tuthmose's sack of Megiddo, exactly what does that verify?"

"That Egyptian history is misdated by five or six hundred years!" said Gunther triumphantly. "That the man we knew only as the Prince of Kadesh was the son of Solomon!"

"Only if the obelisk was never moved! At Megiddo, new cities were built on top of the old, and possibly a few times over generations, the city fathers dug it up and used it to decorate a new temple or as a way to attract Egyptian tourists! How the hell would I know their reasons, but if they did raise an old buried monument, that could account for the difference between the strata and Manetho's king lists."

"You're constructing implausible theories when the obvious explanation is that Manetho's chronology is simply in error." Gunther appeared shocked that anyone, even his son, would be disagreeing with him on this point. "Really, boy," he went on, "that old priest was a toady for the Ptolemies and a dubious scholar. Any rational person would expect him to add names to his lists of pharaohs! The man has the credibility of O. J. Simpson!"

Dan tried to keep from grinning. "C'mon, Dad, lighten up. This really is ancient history! Besides theories are all well and good, but like I said, some actual proof would be nice."

Gunther raised himself up on one elbow and sent the fist of his other hand crashing onto the tabletop, upsetting his empty wine glass. "*I'm* your proof, goddammit!" he shouted. "You have a question about Relativity, you ask Einstein."

"That's modest," Dan snickered. A little white wine was left in the bottle. Dan picked up his father's glass and filled it. What was left, he poured into his own.

Lifting his glass, he caught Gunther's hard eyes and said, "Sorry, Dad. A long time ago, we agreed to disagree."

Silence for a second.

Gunther downed his wine and wiped his lips with the back of his hand. "Apology accepted. Let's go to the other room."

As his mother cleared the dishes, Dan followed his father's steps back to the library where they took the exact places as before at either side of the portfolio. A slight breeze from the paddle fan overhead threatened to scatter a few loose pages, until Gunther grabbed the errant copies, handing them to Dan, who allowed them to fall limply into his lap.

"Thanks. What do you want me to do with them?"

"Read them for me. I'd value your opinion."

Dan glanced down at the rows of glyphs traced from a photograph of the Megiddo obelisk. Reading the hieroglyphs was not the hard part. Understanding their meaning was. Ancient Egyptians used no punctuation or written vowels. Of course, his mother could read glyphs, too. And hieratic script. *And* the odd five-thousand-year-old scribbling that formed the basis of both alphabets.

It did occur to him, however, that the characters on the obelisk might be too small for his mother's aging eyes. She had undergone cataract surgery only the year before, and Dan wondered if the real reason his father asked for him had been to save his mother the embarrassment of having to turn the job down.

"Am I watching out for anything in particular?" Dan asked.

"The Horite Cross, of course," Gunther said, then added for effect, "and Sennemut."

"Oh, believe me, I found that name all right on the three sides I translated first. Did you know the inscriptions confirm the theory that he was sent into exile? I assumed, like everyone else, Sennemut was killed, if only for the fact he was Hapshepsut's boyfriend."

"Boyfriend?" Gunther looked like he had just smelled bad cheese. "Give the man some credit, son. In all of Egypt's history, it only produced two men of true genius. Im-ho-tep was one—and they made him a god.

"The other was Sennemut. He was an architect, scientist, politician, high priest, magician, and, only perhaps, depending on what gossip you read, the Queen's lover. In his time, Sennemut was so powerful they thought he controlled the spirits of life and death. He was so feared, the priests dared not make him a god lest he take over Heaven itself!"

"Mom taught me that much when I was nine."

"Did you know that hidden behind the door in the dark of Hatshepsut's temple is a relief of Sennemut? In the carving, he holds a red ankh."

Dan edged forward. "You think it was the Horite Cross?"

Gunther wasted no time in answering with a quick nod. "All I know from tradition is that when Tuthmose came to the throne, Sennemut disappears and the ankh was lost to history." Gunther shifted his focus beyond where Dan was seated, off to a netherworld of his own thoughts. "Perhaps," he said softly, "the hidden side of the obelisk will tell us more."

Dan had thoughts of his own. "If the new chronology is true, it brings the Eighteenth Dynasty into the time of Solomon. If that's so, Velikovsky thinks Hatshepsut was the Queen of Sheba."

Gunther raised an eyebrow. "Exactly. And what if their son wasn't Menelik of Ethiopia, as some think, but rather Rehoboam, the Prince of Jerusalem."

Encouraged, Dan finished his thought. "Tuthmose fought the Prince of Kadesh at Megiddo. And *Kadesh* translates as 'a holy place.' And Jerusalem was where the Holy of Holies of the Jews was located."

There followed a lively discussion about how the united kingdom built by Kings Saul, David, and Solomon had collapsed into a civil war.

About 922 B.C.E., King Solomon's son Rehoboam inherited the throne of Judah in a lavish ceremony at the temple in Jerusalem. The rite made him king only in the south. To be crowned king of all the Hebrews, Rehoboam immediately went thirty miles north of his capital to the holy Ephraimite city of Shechem.

There, he met with the elders of the northern ten tribes, who had suffered under the heavy hand of Solomon for the forty years of his reign and sought some relief. Obviously, Rehoboam had not studied diplomacy at the feet of Solomon.

Gunther knew the Old Testament passage by heart. " 'My father made your yoke heavy, but I will add to your yoke; my father chastised you with whips, but I will chastise you with—*scorpions!*' "

The north was more than a little annoyed at being considered second-class compared to the Judeans. So they seceded, proclaiming they were the Land of Israel, the name the Lord gave to their ancestor Jacob after he fought with Yahweh's angel. The ten tribes named Jeroboam as their king. He was an Ephraimite war chief who had once led a revolt against Solomon. He had recently returned from exile in Egypt.

For protection, Rehoboam made alliances with pagan city-states, but that placed the northern tribes in jeopardy and forced Jeroboam to ask for help from his Egyptian allies. That was how Tuthmose and Amenemhab got to Megiddo, they theorized.

Gunther rose. "I'll leave you to your work." With surprising tenderness, Gunther placed his large, rough hand on his son's shoulder. "Son, I wanted you here for another reason. In a few weeks, I'm giving a speech at the opening ceremonies of a religious convention. It will be held at the base of the Washington Monument and I'd like you to escort your mother. I have a truth to reveal."

For the first time in Dan's memory, he saw confusion on his father's face.

"Once I figure out what the truth is."

Dan had a million questions he wanted to ask, but Gunther did not give him the chance. "It was a miracle," he said, "that I found the obelisk. A murderer showed me where it was. At first, I saw it as a sign, like the conversion of Saint Paul. Even a terrorist can be saved. But I'm not the religious fool you think, son. It's about the Cross of the Horites, you see. Now, I think discovering the obelisk may have been the work of the Devil."

Dan suddenly realized the Israeli was right. His father was linked with Salameh.

"Dad, we have to go to the authorities."

"To get my thirty pieces of silver?" said Gunther. He was anguished. With that, he walked out of the room toward the back of the house.

Dan heard the screen door open and held his breath until it slapped shut a second later. He didn't know what to do, so he studied the inscriptions for another five minutes, but he had barely finished the tributes to pharaoh's glory when his mother came in.

"I made coffee," she said.

"Elvis has left the building."

"I know," said Eva. "He's walking along the path down to the beach. The quiet helps him think. But you can join me."

Dan followed her, as he had since he could crawl. In the kitchen, she poured him a cup of the promised brew and sat across from him at the center island.

He ran his index finger around the rim of his cup, waiting for the steaming black liquid to cool. Eva preferred herbal tea for herself. Dan mentioned that there was a time she would slip a shot of rum into it. As she sipped, she confessed that a difficult menopause coupled with a lifetime of Arabic cooking had finally taken their toll on her stomach lining.

Dan always figured his mother's ascetic ways started when she became born again.

"Have a cookie," Eva said as she pushed a plate of his favorite Orange Milanos down between them.

Dan took one and let the chocolate and orange flavors mingle in his mouth a bit before chasing it down with the coffee. He saw his mother watching him over her teacup.

"It seemed to be going well over dinner," she said.

"I probably blew it, as usual!" Dan gave her a short rundown. "I was invited down to Washington."

"He told me he was going to ask you."

"Is he all right? He seems disoriented . . . something about his speech at the convention?"

"It's a big event," said Eva. "He wants it to be memorable. I think the people who are running the convention plan to spring a big surprise. Religious leaders from all over the world are coming, and they expect a media event."

Dan wanted information, especially about his father and Salameh, but he phrased his next question carefully. "He mentioned the circumstances around his discovery of the obelisk."

Her face creased suddenly into a disarming grin. "He sees it as symbolic. Obelisks are associated with sun cults. They're all about renewal and light. It's in keeping with the theme of the convention, to affirm Man's belief in God as the new millennium begins."

"He hasn't been talking to a Mr. Qader, has he?"

"Why, yes. He came over the other afternoon. He's involved with Syria in some capacity, but we know him through the interfaith committee. He's helping to coordinate the Islamic portion of Resurrection Unlimited The Moslems see your father as a Christian who loves the Arab world, respects it. They think he is the perfect man to calm suspicions between the two faiths."

"Ma, Zamir Qader works for Mahmoud Salameh."

"The terrorist?" She sat back, astounded.

"What does he want Dad to do? When we talked after dinner, Dad said he hid this piece of an ankh at the museum. It was stolen when Marcy was murdered, and the man who could've done it, he's working with Qader. You see, there's Dad and Qader and this guy McMay—*and me*. It's all in a circle, connected some way. What's Dad really caught up in?"

"He's been very secretive ever since he found that obelisk. All I'm certain of is, Qader asked him to give the keynote at the sunrise service. A hundred thousand people or more are supposed to be there. But, he's been troubled lately, hinting that he might have to change his speech."

"I want to speak with him straight out," said Dan as he got up from his chair. "First, to warn him about Qader and then to find out the truth once and for all. There've been two killings, and somehow we're tied into them. But, if we're lucky and if the family keeps a united front, maybe we can stay out of trouble."

Dan left quickly through the back porch and went outside to find his father. He hoped he could clear up the situation before he had to catch the late train into town.

The sun was long gone, leaving only the distant lights of New York to gray a low band around the horizon. The humid air carried an unpleasant odor of decaying fish and brine. It was darker out toward the Atlantic, with the moon too low to add much light.

Dan headed in that direction, following the flagstone path that led down to a cleft between the bluffs. The man who built the house sometime during the last days of the nineteenth century had chiseled a staircase out of the white rocks to give him easy access to the beach.

The steps were eroded now, and Dan had to hold onto the boulders to keep his footing. He was amazed that Gunther Rawlins, who had constructed the most elaborate excavations, had never thought to install lights or a handrail at his own house.

"Dad!" he called on his way down. There was no response. He was wondering where his father had gone off to, when he felt the sole of his shoe slip over a bad spot. He skidded a good three feet before landing in a cushion of sand at the bottom.

"Shit!" he said, picking himself up. He brushed off as much sand as he could and walked only a few feet when he heard the scream.

Christ, thought Dan, *What had that colonel said?—Your parents, your father could be in danger—danger—DANGER!*

The sound of the scream distorted as it cut through the air. That made it hard to pinpoint, but Dan wasted no time. He ran down the beach. Further down, there were a few pools of light fanning onto the sand from the other summer homes on the cliff.

He thought he saw a black cloth whip from the wind in and out of the spotlight about two hundred yards away, but it was gone so fast, Dan thought it might be the blinking of his own eye.

Another scream exploded out of the placid night.

Louder now, nearer.

Dan tried to pick up speed, but his feet only dug deeper into the sand, making each stride an effort. He entered the light but instead of letting him see, the effect was to blind him to all that was outside the bright oval on the beach. He slipped his open belt out of its loops and slowly wrapped the leather around his fist with the buckle facing out.

The muscles along his spine shuddered as he stood there, alone and unprotected. The shadows encircling him were suddenly very threatening. He turned as the wind blew passed him. Then, he realized he had not felt the air rush by, he only heard it.

"Dad?" he called. "Answer me! Are you out here?"

From out of the empty black, came an amused cackle.

Dan quickly stepped back out of the glare. In the moment it took for his eyes to readjust to the dark, he glimpsed an oddly formed shape traveling laterally across the shoreline. When he could finally see clearly, the shape had disappeared.

Searching the sand, Dan moved to the high ground near the rocks. The slope was gradual. It led him to a tangle of driftwood and beach debris. He kicked at the largest piece blocking his way. The decaying trunk shifted only slightly.

Something was catching its underside. Dan bent over to clear it.

It wouldn't give—

C'mon, c'mon!

He kicked it. The tangle rolled over once. A bundle of damp cloth spilled out, unfolding. A human head lolled into the sand inches from him.

Omigod—omigod—Christ alive, why him? Dad—Daddy—

Gunther Rawlins's pale face was staring back at him with dry, dead eyes.

Dan jerked away. His movement jostled the body, and it rolled free from the branches. The wood cracked and grasped like witch's fingers. Gunther heaved as if he were alive and flopped in rag-doll fashion to the bottom of the dune.

Dan clung to the rock face, swallowing air in great gulps. His mind refused to function. The image of his father facedown in the sand entered his pupils, but was rejected somewhere beyond the optic nerve.

He might have stood shaking like that all night, if he had not heard the laughter. The sound came from above his head. He pivoted and looked up.

A head peeked over the edge of the bluff. The man was smiling down at him, his features only partially revealed by a yard light from one of the neighbors' houses.

"Who's there?" Dan shouted.

A deep chuckle came from the man's throat. Somehow, it seemed familiar.

"Get help!" screamed Dan. "My father's hurt! Send for an ambulance!"

Whoever it was on the high ground stayed there and said nothing.

"*You* killed him!"

The head, which was all of him that could be seen, moved to an outcrop where a tree jutted over the boulders. Dan squirmed as the head bobbed strangely from side to side with each hidden step. The man's red hair hit a beam of light as he reached the half-fallen trunk.

Like a thunder crack, Dan knew who it was. "You're McMay!"

There was no answer, only a sad grunt from the cliff. Then, with one huge hop, the killer landed on the horizontal branch. From Dan's angle on the beach, McMay's silhouette seemed malformed. The head rested on a torso that was broad at the shoulder but squat, as if he had been cut off at the waist.

What is it? A misshapen dwarf? Or maybe he's like a circus freak born with half a body, so he has to walk on his hands!

Then, Liam McMay spread his wings.

Dan panicked. The sight of the obscene creature would have frightened anyone, but Dan's fear carried an added element. In an insane rush, he knew what McMay had become!

A sharp, savage terror pierced him. He ran, leaving his father's bleeding corpse in the sand. Heart hammering his ribs, Dan fled, feeling nothing but rushing darkness. Above, the man-bird threw back its human head and laughed. Then, it rotated its wings to their full nine-foot span and dropped off its perch into the air.

Its wings flapped twice before it caught the updraft. It soared high over the beach in a slow arc, cutting off Dan's escape.

The monstrous hybrid hung motionless on the invisible current. After a few exhilarating seconds, it folded its wings and pitched downward.

Plummeting fast, it caught Dan on the run. A talon grabbed at his neck, but Dan twisted clear, and the point cut only a shallow slice from his shoulder. McMay flew upwards and swooped around for a second attack.

Dan fell in the shallow waves, clutching his collarbone. The salt in the water stung his wound and shocked him back to himself. He rolled over as a breaker struck him on his side. His face up, he saw the winged shadow coming toward him at incredible speed.

Dan screamed, but didn't move.

The bird-thing became visible at the last moment as it passed through the beam of one of the spotlights. Talons high, it swiped at Dan's chest, burying a razor-sharp claw into his ribs. Dan closed his fingers around the thin bird leg and yanked it out.

A spurt of blood came after it.

Suddenly, Dan's head was buried in a flurry of flapping wings. He fought fiercely. His leather belt was still wrapped across the knuckles of his right hand. Blow after blow found only feathers and air. With one desperate lunge, he connected to the head, and McMay tumbled to the sand.

The monster flailed and beat the ground like a headless chicken for a time, then leapt into the air, cursing. Dan heard it rise higher than the bluffs and then it was gone. He struggled to his feet on rubbery legs.

He'll be coming back, Dan thought, *back to kill me—like father, like son!*

He craned his neck trying to catch a glimpse the thing, but only saw the star-flecked sky overhead. Oddly, Dan grinned. It was crazy, but he knew he was going to die—death by mythology!

Dan laughed out loud, a maniacal laugh as if his senses had all been strained to breaking.

"A myth is as good as a mile!" he hooted.

The night seemed to be getting darker. Some of the stars began to form grayish halos, and the line of houses lining the cliffs was breaking up like the grainy cinematography in a cheap movie.

His shirt was damp.

It oozed when he pressed the material against his skin. Even without a clear head, Dan knew it must be blood. During the fight, a claw could have sunk into an artery. Strange . . . there was no sensation of pain.

No . . .

He felt it now, the rivulets of blood streaking down his leg with each heartbeat. He looked down. A black pool was collecting at his feet, but the tide promptly washed it away.

He was being drained.

A whoosh from behind and it was on him, tearing into his spine and biting the nape of his neck. Dan was far too weak to fight it off and dropped to his knees. A clutch of pain hit him between the shoulder blades.

Huge wings beat at his head and shoulders. One of Dan's eyes shut when blood and salt water got into it, but he could make out a dim shadow with the other one. An errant thought flashed across his mind—it looked like Hawkman's shadow, the comic book character with the beaked mask and the bird's wings.

His other eye closed then. He was still swinging his arms at the creature, but it had become an instinctive effort without much force. Even the sounds were dimming. Wavelets lapped, cool and bell-like, over his ears. The harsh flapping seemed farther away, now.

The bird—*the impossible bird*—was cackling again. At least that was how his brain perceived the jumble of nearly senseless sounds—before Dan Rawlins shut down.

Although he could no longer see through his eyes, Dan's vision enjoyed a clarity his consciousness had never experienced. He had left the beach for an endless desert.

Death or dreams are always depicted with mist and billowy clouds, and yet, there was a sharpness of focus that far outstripped the range of visible light.

The coherence extended to thought, and Dan suddenly understood the tale that the long-dead general had chiseled onto the eternal monument and placed in the city that would see the final battle to end the world.

PART TWO

THE CONFIDENTIAL REPORT
ON THE ANKH OF THE HORITES

CHAPTER FOURTEEN

*Let the four geese fly, carrying the news
to Heaven's four regions I, Amenemhab,
his general, his friend and protector, must
tell the tale of Lord Tuthmose.*

—THE CHRONICLES OF GENERAL AMENEMHAB,
   DYNASTY XVIII

Seventy-five days' march from Djahi had brought the legions of
Qemet to the base of the Mountains of Karmel. There, we camped. I
found my men a spot with shade and water while my servants were
erecting my tent. As was my custom, I ordered a shirker to drink first
from the pool in case the Sons of Amasis had poisoned it. It is a
practice that fosters discipline within the ranks—what foot soldier
would not learn a lesson from seeing a lazy friend die with his black
tongue swelling out of his mouth?—and saves the horses from injury.

This time the water was fresh, but it had fallen from the rocks
above and was sulfuric in flavor. Nevertheless, I sent a manservant
to fill my skins. Water is Life, and a man at war in foreign lands can
never expect to quench his thirst with a drink as sweet as the Mother
Nile.

While still among the god's troops, I spoke to my captains, ad-
monishing them to curb the fighting I had seen in the scramble for
flat ground to set up their lean-tos. Have them save it for the heathens, I told them, and force them to rest for tomorrow's march to
Megiddo.

When I left, most of my men had settled into their nightly routines
of eating, gambling, and complaining. It is the same with every army.
Often, I have wished I could join in a simple game of jackals and

hounds. But how could I get them to die for me, if they saw me as a man like themselves? No, my place was to serve the God-on-Earth as it is their lot to serve me.

After a day's ride in the cruel heat of the sun, I had become impatient to have the trail scraped from my skin and get some rest. The women set out my divan and sleeping mat. My old ivory headrest had never looked so inviting. It had been my father's, a gift to commemorate my first campaign. He had been a general during the time of the Bitch Queen and had accompanied her on her famous journey to this land when the father of our present enemy ruled.

I closed my eyes and let the weariness drain from me.

Our kindhearted gods have granted me the grace to enter their world of dreams easily.

A short while later, I floated back to wakefulness.

Night had descended on the camp. Still muddleheaded, I sat up and called for a slave to light an oil lamp. In fact, he lit two. With the tent bright, I was pleased to discover that while I slept the women had laid out a plate of barley bread and honey cakes for me to have with my beer.

I downed the cup of beer, its acid warmth restoring me. I ventured outside and took a honey cake along. Overhead, the sky was clear, congested with stars. The moon was just appearing over a range of high hills. As it did, its light fell first upon the golden pavilion stationed on a high commanding ridge. Standing as it was against the slope of the mountain, above the multitudes in the encampment, pharaoh's gleaming tent reminded me of the holy of holies inside the Temple of Amun in the capital.

Perhaps the young god had planned it that way. He had the cunning of his aunt-sister, that one. And on the eve of his first battle, it would be well for his army to be reminded that they had the Horus leading them and not some untried youth.

A short time later, the trumpeters signaled all the generals to a war council with pharaoh. I walked there alone. As I was cutting through the grazing cattle that separated the royals from the rest of the officers, I met Menthu of the Chariots and we continued on together.

Menthu was a veteran of nine campaigns and trembled at neither man nor god. From his breath, I surmised his courage that night had come from a jug of good Charu wine.

"How are your horses faring?" I asked without much concern.

"It is always the same," he started. "If you begin a war too early in the season, I tell them, the rivers are too high, and you're bound to lose horses in the fording."

"Will there be enough horses for the battle, then?"

Menthu screwed up his face. "I'm not our whelp-god, friend Amenemhab. Old warriors know their business. I picked up a string of Edomite mares when we passed that caravan from Joppa. At a good price, too!"

I smiled, but since we were fast approaching the king's precinct, I whispered, "I shouldn't let pharaoh hear you calling him a whelp."

Menthu's laughter roared from his throat. "No disrespect, of course. But to me, you're all little puppies. By the fat, ugly face of Bes, here you are a general and I bet you're still sucking your wet nurse's tit!"

"Pharaoh still keeps you around, doesn't he?"

"If he wants his chariots, he does! Ah, the other children have beaten us to the nursery."

He was speaking of the rest of pharaoh's generals, who were milling about waiting for the leave to enter the god's presence. We greeted the others, and with Old Menthu in the lead we moved as one to the council chamber which was set up beside the golden pavilion.

A single guard stood outside, leaning on his spear. He stiffened when he saw all of us approaching, and he saluted. Menthu grumbled a question to the soldier, eliciting a quick nod in response. I assumed the god was expecting us since Menthu marched right inside. My four companions and I went after him like a line of goslings pursuing their mother's tailfeather.

Inside, we found the council chamber empty, save for a pet cheetah tied to the tent post. Menthu patted the animal on the head as he proceeded out the back way. The rest of us followed, but we managed to skirt the cat, who in any event was more interested in gnawing at his rag doll than he was in us.

I opened the tent flap and saw the old man bounding up a rock-strewn foot trail that ended as a natural watchtower on the mountainside above our heads. We trudged the fifty steps up to the promontory where we saw Menthu in supplication to the Living Horus of Qemet. We dared go no further and dropped to our knees.

The god stood where his guards should have been, gazing off toward Esdraelon, the great plain of Canaan. He tugged at his spotted leopard hide, closing it tightly around his shoulders against the night chill. The god did not acknowledge our presence for a time. But when he spoke, the sound was sharp-edged and seductive in its power.

"I have talked with my fellow god Anhur, Who-is-the-Amun-at-War. His voice was quite distinct." He turned to where we knelt and bade us rise.

"It is fitting, Exalted One, to consult that aspect of Amun on the eve of battle," said Menthu in his most formal tone. "Especially when it will be your first taste of the fight."

The god whirled suddenly. His woman's hands gripped the old man by the jaw and held tight. "You must not mock me, Menthu! I am Menkheperre, *Who-Is-the-Third-Tuthmose*. I have the blood of Kamose coursing through me! We are the same Horus, and did we not destroy the invading Kings of Sheep and free Qemet?"

"Yes, Lord."

"Do you doubt I understand the science of war? Am I not the match of any charioteer in your company?"

"Yes, Virtuous God."

The Tuthmose released his grip and smiled as a boy would after winning a game of serpent. "Of course, I am. You were the one who taught me all the secrets!"

"I never had a finer student."

The god clasped the old man's shoulder's heartily, then looked at us. "Gather around. I wish to hold council here."

We stepped out onto the flat ledge and, taking the god's lead, we sat cross-legged as he addressed us. "The Amu who vexed my fathers are gone along with their cursed flocks, but again our sacred borders are threatened by Bearded Ones. I do not worry over these landless raiders who pick their plunder from our outposts. They are like gnats around the eyes of the Hapi Bull, no more than annoyances. Our enemy lies far to the north. We are threatened by conquest, not by these puppets of Israel, but by their puppeteer—Mitanni!"

"Mitanni?" Khnemu of the Javelins was startled. "But that is at the end of the world."

"Too close to the underworld of Duat, they say," Menthu muttered.

"Dead men walk in the streets of Mitanni, they say."

The god drew a wavy line in the dirt. "They live here—in a land of boulders and hot winds, where the locusts eat better than the people. But they have heard of our cool Nile and our rich, black earth. Drool falls from their gaping mouths at the thought of having what Amun-Re has given us. Yet, they believe they are safe there, beyond that open sewer they call the River of Euphrates."

"A mighty spirit rules those waters, Majesty," General Pentaweret called out. "Once, when I was no older than yourself, I rode as escort for your father's ambassador to Babylon. Ten died trying to cross the Euphrates's rapids. It is an angry river."

"We have all been nursed by the Mother of Waters," countered the king. "When I reach out to crush Mitanni, no mere river will dare hold me back!"

"May I speak, Lord?" I ventured.

"Yes, Amenemhab?"

"Surely, we all would fight the daemons of Heaven's twelve nomes for you, but each of us is concerned that we don't have a battle plan for tomorrow. We don't even know how we're going to enter the Jezreel Valley."

The god sat silently for a terrifying moment, then he nodded at me. "Always the practical one. You are right. That is the reason I came up here to speak with the god Anhur. Look over the plain. Can you see the glow?"

"I can, yes."

"Campfires. Rehoboam is there. The princes of Palestine and Syria are there; armies massed on the Plain of Jezreel; conscripts taken from every city from Megiddo to the northern mountains. These are Mitanni's men. Bought and paid for! If we are swift—if we are bold— if we devastate them here, nothing will lie between us and Mitanni. Then, it is simply one great sword thrust into her naked, white underbelly and . . ."

At once, he was on his feet. He ripped off his leopard robe and threw it to Menthu.

"Hurry! You have to see my plan!"

The god scrambled over the edge of the outcropping before anyone could stop him, hung there for a second, then, let go. He landed on the mountain trail and rolled a couple of times before jumping to his feet.

All of us, guards and generals alike, ran after him. He did not wait for us, instead he raced happily down the hillside like a boy at play. Minutes later, we found him at the war table inside the council tent.

"I want to show you something." A servant pulled back a soft, white linen drape to reveal a detailed replica of the Palestinian terrain built with clay on cedar planking.

The Tuthmose spread his hands over it, pointing out the important areas. "These mountains lie between us and the walls of Megiddo.

We have three choices, three passages that lead to the city. Our army might continue west toward the sea, until the hills diminish, then swing about and attack their fortress from the north."

"A sound tactic, O-Ladder-to-the-Gods," intoned Khnemu in a transparent attempt at currying favor.

It failed.

"That would be our deaths!" Menkheperre exclaimed. "In our mad attempt to get near Megiddo, we would be trapped in the open on the barren plain. No cover, our troops tired from the long march, and outnumbered by an army that has only had to wait for us to come to them. They would cut us down like slaughterhouse cattle and leave our bones to whiten in the sun."

Menthu turned to Khnemu, who was red-faced by then. "That damned turncoat Rehoboam's had weeks to prepare for us. And I can't imagine him not setting up an army to guard the northern approach."

Pharaoh went on. "Our second option is the simplest and most direct route. The Way of the Sea—the highway through the Megiddo Pass. Its advantages are obvious, I'm certain, to all of you. The Way is wide and straight, and we come out on the plain to the south of the city."

"Yes, it would be best for the chariots," said Menthu.

The god leaned toward the old man. "Tell me, my dear friend and teacher, what would your charioteers think about the road if I were to tell them they'd be driving through the pass as Syrian bowmen shower their arrows from the cliffs on either side?"

"Many will get by. Losses are inevitable in war."

"Are they?" Menkheperre smiled. "I told you there were three choices. We needn't go around the mountains where an army waits to the north, or take the pass to the south where the Syrians wait. My plan is to go over the mountains."

"You're joking!" Menthu blurted out.

"There is a narrow trail used by traders and goatherds that ends up outside the walls of the city."

All the generals seemed to speak at once:

"I know it; the Aruna Road. It's impassable!"

"Much too arduous. Our mounts could never stand it!"

"And what about the chariots? They're not built for mountain climbing, you know!"

I said nothing. The god noticed and pointed his finger in my direction. "And what objections do you have, Amenemhab?"

"How narrow is it?" I asked.

"The width of two chariots. With a steep drop to one side."

"Then, I see one problem. We can only send a thin, continuous line of men along the road. I'd be afraid our advance troop would be forced to fight before the rear could reinforce them. But your plan could work if the Palestinians and the Syrians weren't alerted to where we are—and if our men aren't bottlenecked at the end of the road and butchered one by one as they pass."

"Ah, that look again. Watch out! Amencmhab has an idea."

"I was just thinking . . . if you sent a small force around the mountains to divert the northern army, Rehoboam would likely order the Syrians to abandon the south and help him. . . ."

"And by the time he learned the truth, we'd have the gates of Megiddo under siege!"

I shrugged. "Thank the gods that the curse of knowing the future is left to Shai. Only that sad goddess is burdened with knowing our fate."

The war council glanced wearily from one to another. Finally, it was Menthu who dared offer their opinion.

"Lord," he said, "each of us has studied this terrain. Our spies have brought back many encouraging reports on these other routes. Won't you reconsider? We would be marching single file along steep shepherd's trails. I agree with Amenemhab's point. Our enemies could simply wait until our force was spread thin and unprotected and pick us off."

"Oh, Menthu, can't you see? Rehoboam's black-bearded generals must've argued just as you have. The Aruna Road would not even be considered an option. They will be aligned to the north and to the south knowing we must come from one of those two places."

"Instead," I added, "we pour out of the mountains and hit them from behind! Megiddo will be ours before they can turn their chariots!"

"Yes!" Tuthmose whooped and pounded on the terrain map. "And then we will control Jezreel!"

I agreed. Without Megiddo to supply them, Rehoboam would be forced back to Kadesh, the holy city known to his people as Jerusalem. But the others were still muttering their disapproval.

"Menthu," said the god calmly, "bind the wheels of your chariots with rope that they may better grip the trail."

"This is folly," he answered.

Suddenly, the Tuthmose flared. "Then I suggest you take your men and your horses and go whichever way you wish. But bind the wheels of my chariot because tomorrow I shall ride that high pathway at first light! And by the gods, you know I mean it!"

With unexpected strength, he heaved the map and sent it sprawling across the tent. The generals jumped back, stunned into silence. He stood in the corner, pale and stiff as the granite statues of his father in the Great House of No-Amun. "Join me," he said.

Menthu and the others fixed their gaze on the god, then lowered their heads and bowed. They all waited, still unnerved at the outburst. Finally, old Menthu cleared his throat. "Command us. And pray for us, Lord, your servants, who have presumed to question their master."

"Lead us," said Pentaweret.

"To victory," I added.

"To victory!" echoed the council.

In the morning they climbed the Aruna Road. I volunteered my legion of Braves to travel west with the mountains between us and the Judaean army. For two nights, I had my men set small fires in a wide pattern that made my meager company appear to be the main army. By day, I tied bushes to the backs of our wagons and our dust trail was truly impressive. At the same time, I sent patrols up the mountainside to intercept any of Rehoboam's spies. I wanted them to return bloody. I thought that if the Judaeans were convinced there were so many of us that we covered the hillsides as well as the valley, it might scare them into sending for Syrian help quickly. We kept this strategy up for the three days the god asked for, while he led the true army of Qemet across the mountains, undetected.

The main force regrouped on a small plateau. Megiddo stood below, commanding a rise that guarded the great valley. It was a knife-sharp morning. Clear as the day, according to the scrolls of Amun, when the Nine Gods created the world. Menkheperre, the Living God, was the first one to the edge. He scurried down the moist rock face with his scouts for a better look. The city was known for its high, solid walls. Lofty towers were placed every hundred cubits or so with archery ports a man's breadth between them. Cultivated fields radiated from the city like a vast mosaic.

Even from that many leagues, the god could pick out farmers at work tending their crops—war season is also the best time for growing—but, strangely, few soldiers. From his vantage point, all the god could detect was a small garrison that occupied a cluster of tents beside the main gate.

Could that be their only protection?

Menkheperre nudged the scout next to him with his flail. "Hardly enough men to get a good beer brawl going, eh?"

The soldier was silent. He had never quite been this close to royalty and was fearful of offending the Master of the Great House with an opinion. The god had been through it many times and knew the cure.

Once back on the plateau, he called the scouts together for a talk. He asked them questions he knew they could answer and made certain to treat them as fellow soldiers, even to the extreme of complaining about the food and the heat. At one point, the Tuthmose placed his hand on the shoulder of a young man, no older than the god himself, who had been standing at his side. The scout, thinking he had caused some affront, reeled back and fell, landing square on his buttocks.

Menkheperre laughed and offered his hand to help him up, but by that point he was trembling too hard to stand up. "I hope that I frighten the Syrians this much!"

After that, they relaxed together, the new god and his men. Needless to say, all that familiarity shocked the other generals and most of the royal household. Even the priests spent a great deal of their time muttering over the propriety of it.

Later, as the Tuthmose walked back to his war tent—he had not set up the golden pavilion for fear that its glint might be seen in Megiddo and alert the enemy to their position—he casually asked one of his men if he and his comrades were tired from the mountain crossing.

"It was a tough road, Your Majesty," answered the soldier, "but we are tougher!"

Pharaoh stopped and hugged the surprised veteran. "That's what I like to hear! Tell your captain there'll be extra rations tonight and a fresh jug of beer to each squad."

"You are too generous, Horus."

"Pray to Anhur tonight, my warrior. And light no fires. Tomorrow, at Aten's rise, is when we attack Megiddo."

Such actions produced the effect the Tuthmose had wanted. Word spread man to man throughout the ranks about the young god. And by dawn, there was not one soldier in any of Qemet's legions who would not have gladly died for him.

On the third day, I scouted the Palestinian positions and confirmed what the spies had reported. Rehoboam had placed his men along both sides of the valley, hoping to catch us in a twin attack if we had ridden between them through the central plain. But our plan to bring the Syrians out of the south had failed. I learned from a captive that Rehoboam was in the south with the Syrians!

He had obstinately refused sending more than a few token chariots to buttress his own Judaeans. His One God had spoken to him it seems, and Rehoboam was thus convinced that reports of my movements had been a trick, the true attack coming through the southern pass. As befitted the grandson of wily King Dawidh, his instincts were right, but as Menkheperre had foreseen, no one believed that any commander would be insane enough to attempt the Aruna Road.

I knew I had to get to Megiddo swiftly to warn the god that he might still be caught between the Palestinians and the Syrians. The most direct route to Megiddo would be right down the middle of Jezreel, but I would be flanked to my left and right by the entire Judaean army.

Suicidal. Like falling down a well of swords!

Then, I happened to look back along the trail we had taken. The scrub bushes tied behind the supply wagons were making a high, billowing cloud.

I thought, *What if the entire company—infantry, chariots, the works—dragged the branches in a wide front, but very slowly, while I and a few chariots rode at top speed for Megiddo? Would the Judaeans risk attacking so few, and lose the element of surprise? No, they'd wait for the main column to pass and try to catch our army unawares.*

At least I hoped that was how they'd think.

I called my captains together and they implemented my plan.

They knew that the Palestinians would attack them in midvalley, so our scheme was to place the wagons and chariots in the center of our wide advancing line with the infantry spreading out as far as they could without making gaps in our great, obscuring dust cloud.

I prayed to Qebui that his north wind stay constant. We had to leave in the dark if we were to get to Megiddo by dawn. As soon as my chariots had raced through Jezreel safely, I explained to my captains that their orders were to turn all the vehicles around and have the infantry make a mad rush for them. The idea was for the Braves to draw the Palestinians to the head of the valley—well away from Megiddo—while I alerted Menkheperre to the danger from the south.

Fingers of light inched over the eastern mountains just before the new day, but the army of Qemet had been prepared for hours. On the plateau, the third Tuthmose adjusted his war crown and braced himself behind the driver of his golden chariot.

As the Aten's disk filled his eyes, the god's arm rose in readiness. His legions were massed below him. Overnight, the infantry had filtered down the gradual slope. The Bows of Pentaweret and Khnemu's spear carriers fanned out in straight lines, looked as immobile as the sphinxes along the Royal Avenue at Karnak. Nobody moved. The men all stared at their generals while the generals' eyes fixed on the slight figure in the golden chariot.

Then, the god dropped his arm like a headsman's blade. A sound rose like a million screeching birds. The war cry! The battle had begun.

Qemet's legions ran forward in bronze waves, spilling onto the plain, widening their front as they ran. Each warrior concentrated on keeping his place in ranks. Of course, they knew the god was watching them, but they had a more personal reason. Running in close formation, a soldier who falls, dies. His brothers will not—cannot—stop to help. The fallen man is trampled and must remain, broken and suffocating, in the dust of the battlefield.

Pentaweret's bowmen reached a ravine that dipped into the plain about two miles from the city walls. There, they took positions. Behind them, the Qemet infantry came on fast. They split in two divisions to avoid the ravine and kept running with swords high toward the walls. The Javelins stopped two hundred cubits beyond the archers and knelt, planting their thick oxhide shields into the ground to protect their chests.

Suddenly, on Tuthmose's command, the war whoops abruptly quit. He drove up to General Khnemu's chariot and asked the general if his men were out of arrow range from the walls.

"As ordered, Immortal One."

"Good. Now, I want the foot soldiers to surround the city at a safe distance, but have them thin the force on the southern gate, will you?"

"But there might still be Syrians to the south," said the general. "If they see a hole, they could pour in to defend it!"

"And then what might happen?"

"Why, they'll be able to fight through our lines and enter Megiddo!"

The Tuthmose grinned. "Exactly, spear-master. I'd rather have them behind thick walls than at my back while I'm laying siege. I'm going to the war tent now. I suspect we'll have a few hours' grace after we take the rise and seal the gates."

He sprang down from the chariot and started up the incline to his headquarters. He turned and called down to Khnemu, "Keep me informed!"

As pharaoh closed the tent flap, a skirmish began near the city. A group of no more than fifteen foot soldiers from the Judaean garrison outside Megiddo decided to attack the grand army of Qemet by themselves. Running at top speed from the rise, the defenders waved their bronze swords frantically while screaming like men possessed.

"Yee-way ehcoot! Yee-way ehcoot!" they were shouting all the way down to what they must have known to be their certain deaths. I heard much later that these fanatics' words were exhorting us to believe in their one god.

Absurd, but true.

A flag from one of our front-line commanders sent our spearmen flat onto their bellies. Another color signaled the bowmen to let fly a fierce rainstorm of arrows. Fully half the defenders fell with that initial barrage. The others dashed to the refuge of some low rocks as a third flag ordered a squad of our best swordsmen to advance on them. On the hillside, unseen by our troops behind the garrison tents that fenced the main Megiddan gate, a lone Judaean horseman spurred his mount to the south.

Below on the rocks, the Bearded Ones fought like daemons. It was only when they heard his hoof beats and were certain that their courier was safely away that the Bearded Ones allowed themselves to die. Later, as our men stripped the weapons, shields, helmets, and breastplates from the circumcised ones, they were amazed at the smug expressions remaining on their pale, dead faces. Unnerved, the men quickly returned to ranks.

When I finally rode into camp, the army had ringed the city and was commanding the heights. I went directly to the war tent and found pharaoh resting on a couch playing his seven-stringed harp. I knew he had acquired the skill as a youth. It was something we were all forced to learn at our military academy, The Stable, but music must have become a private delight instead of a mere hymn to Amun.

So it must be with gods; I never got the hang of it, myself.

Tuthmose was surprised to see me. I explained my reasons for returning and my stratagem for accomplishing it. He enjoyed the telling and was not bothered by Rehoboam being with the Syrians. I was about to go when a Habiru scout was brought in.

"Stay," said the god, motioning me to sit on a cushion by his feet. He nodded to the crouching man. "Speak!"

"Holy One, a lone rider has broken through to the Megiddo pass. The Syrians know we control Megiddo and the access to Jezreel."

"Have all the Judaean defenders retreated inside the gates now?" Tuthmose asked.

"Yes, Horus. In retreat or dead."

"Good!" Pharaoh dismissed the scout and motioned me nearer.

"I'm pleased you're here, Amenemhab. Get some rest and find fresh horse for your chariot. In three or four hours, we'll be having Syrian visitors. I want you on the southern flank to show them how displeased we are that their tribute is so late this year."

"Your will be done, Lord."

"Fine. Take three hundred warriors afoot and a squad of Khnemu's Javelins."

"But, that's only a token ground force. Most of my Braves are in the north with the Judaeans. I can't take a few unschooled infantrymen and expect them to stop a Syrian advance. If they hit us with chariots . . ."

"I'm preparing a siege, here, you know. I can't spare any more men." I was troubled, and must have seemed so, because the god placed his hand on my cheek and said that he trusted me. Then, he said something that I thought strange. "Come back whole, my friend. Don't sacrifice yourself for a clump of dirt."

"I will it you order it, Lord Tuthmose," I said.

"Good, but it's still Menkheperre when we're alone, 'Nemhab," the god said kindly. His smooth cheeks dimpled with innocent fun as I stood, saluted, bowed, and backed out of the tent.

If I dare to speak of sharing anything with one so exalted, it is that we so enjoy the sport and camaraderie of battle. I have seen, since we were children together, that behind the lambish face the sculptors carve was a hungry warrior waiting to be tested. I have been—and I sense that the god both loves and resents me for it.

"Why must I be so frustratingly safe?" I have heard Tuthmose often ask. It is very true that the vizier back in the capital and every one of the nomarchs who have accompanied us on our campaign have conspired to keep the god from the thick of the fight. If they do not, it will count against them when their hearts are weighed by Anubis at their deaths.

So, there is nothing to be done and no one for the Tuthmose to blame, save the crowd of gods in Duat who chose him to be the

Horus-on-Earth. With the bloodletting left to such as myself, Tuth-mose contents himself—if the god is ever truly contented—with his battle strategies and his obsession that Qemet never again be enslaved.

A short time after I left him, as I was choosing new stallions for my foray against the Syrians, I noticed Menthu near the newly erected golden pavilion. He was speaking to a captain of his guard when Tuthmose appeared. He motioned the chariot master to him. When Menthu reached him, he embraced the old warrior warmly and whis-pered some private message in his ear. I noticed a momentary uncer-tainty on Menthu's face, but in the selfsame time it took the expression to register, all doubt had vanished.

Menthu stepped one pace back and crossed his arms over his chest in salute. Then, he left at a pace I would have deemed impossible for a man approaching his fiftieth year.

Coming toward last light, I heard the Syrian chariots rumble in from the southern pass. I watched them from my lookout. Massed men and animals covered the prairie with the bright multicolors of their regional princedoms. It was a savage rainbow that reformed into a wedge. They hit my first line of Javelins without any loss of speed.

It was then I saw the man who mounted the charge riding behind the first wave in his black chariot. He was Rehoboam, son of Solo-mon, ruler of the Judaean state, and Prince of Jerusalem, called "Ka-desh," *Which-Means-the-Holy-City*.

He was easy to spot. His was the largest and heaviest chariot in the field. Constructed of dense ebony and trimmed in polished gold, it held, beside the Prince, a charioteer and two lancers.

Four large Abyssinian mares pulled the war wagon as it smashed through below my position and through the ranks of my foot soldiers. I was close enough to see the prince, wet with sweat that dripped from under his helmet and curly black beard, urging his driver and the other charioteers on.

He steered them toward the weakest spots, where the maimed and dying had fallen and trampled them without a thought under his mighty hooves and bladed wheels.

As I feared, my men—who fought valiantly—were too few in num-ber. The Syrian lancers simply sliced them to bits as they rode past. When I saw their blood spewing like fountains from their neck wounds, I leapt from my chariot and ran for the Judaean.

I thought of nothing but killing that black-hearted prince and add-ing his blood to the highway of gore he had created. But his snorting beasts scattered what was left of my men, and by the time I had clawed through their bodies, Rehoboam had cleared a path to Megiddo's south gate.

I found my chariot and rode for the high ground where the army of Qemet was encamped. Filthy with a mud mixed of earth and blood, I stripped off my armor and crawled half-naked up the steep rock face where the god stood watching the fight.

One of his entourage, not recognizing my rank, tried to detain me, but I clubbed my fist into his womanish face and confronted Tuthmose. "They're gone! All the men you said would be enough!"

"Sit, 'Nemhab. I'm glad you've come. Your report. I need it."

Tuthmose turned from me to watch the plain. He was studying the new patterns made by the running and dying infantry below. *It is all a game of hounds and jackals to him,* I remember thinking.

"Come on, come on! Speak your truth!"

"Yes, Horus," I said without glancing up at him. "The enemy fielded more men at the southern pass than we expected. Many of the Palestinian tribes as well as some northern cities are represented. My captain counted over two hundred colors, armies from Haran and Ugarit and farther."

"Each wanting to get a chance at the boy-pharaoh."

"I warned you there would be chariots. The Prince of Kadesh is known for his skill with them, and when he saw our weakness, he sent them first. We tried blocking them with Javelin and foot, but they rolled over us as if we were stands of wheat and they were the threshers."

Tuthmose nodded. "It's the animals they use. Giant horses, mountain stallions bred in Mitanni. Nothing can stop them."

I rose, stunned at what he had said. "And knowing that, you threw an unprepared rabble at them? I saw a man throw his spear into the neck of one of these horses, but it kept charging until it was upon the man and it crushed him. Brave men are down there dying for your glory, Menkheperre. You owe it to them to send more troops to hold the line!"

"I'll have my women clean you up, 'Nemhab. Your foul smell is clouding your thoughts."

"It's the stench of useless death, O Glorious One."

He waved me away, and a group of servants tended to my wounds, which amounted to little more than a few scrapes, one bruised thigh, and a single gash on my upper arm. I was close enough to hear the god call his adjutant, saying, "They'll lose the light, if they don't bring up their infantry soon." It was obvious to me, he was sorting out his next moves as he talked.

"Send for a torchman for the signal fire. Have him stand by me. I want to give the order to light it personally."

"Yes, Immortal." I followed him with my eyes as he strode to his observation post to survey the progress of his siege and thought, *What else does he have in that mind of his?*

As expected, the Syrians were intruding in a dark triangle upon the city's southern wall. The sun disk cast long, low shadows to the east across the battlefield where the fighting had raised a cloud of tan dust to obscure much of the detail. Tuthmose took a broad stance by the wide pit for the signal fire and scanned our southern flank.

I sloughed off the women who were sponging my arms and went to join the god on his perch. Tuthmose narrowed his eyes and pointed at the trees near the edge of the conflict. I followed his line of sight and saw a broad, sweeping phalanx of Syrian infantry spill onto the plain.

Once they were in the open, the black-bearded warriors regrouped into fighting units. I hurried to Menkheperre, shouting, "See! They're trapped! Our men won't have a sheath fish's chance in the desert if they're caught between Megiddo and Syrian foot soldiers!"

He ignored me; instead, he adjusted his miter so that it sat easier on his head. Menkheperre glanced at the young guard with the torch. "Ready with that, son," he said.

On the plain, Khnemu saw the Syrians speeding toward him and ordered his men to raise the flag of retreat. His Javelins split into two groups and scurried away from the attack, letting the Syrians overrun their lines.

The enemy chariots circled the southern wall of the city as the Syrian spearmen flooded the trampled ground left by Khnemu's men. Yelling their triumphant war cry, they soon reached the walls of Megiddo to rejoin their countrymen.

Tuthmose grinned as if he had won a bet. It had been a game to him. "Yes," I thought out loud, "a game of jackals and hounds."

"What were you saying?" pharaoh asked.

"Nothing, Majesty. Just that it looks like a game of jackals and hounds down there."

He gave me a curt nod. "Yes, doesn't it. Well, now that the jackals are in place, it's time to release the hounds. Light the signal fire—NOW!"

The guard tossed a burning brand into the bowl and jumped aside. With a great animal rumble, the pit exploded into a flame over thirty feet high. The beacon glowed brighter as the sky was darkening. It easily could be seen two days distant.

At that instant, hidden by the low hills, General Menthu lifted his sword arm and his flagmen signaled Qemet's counterattack.

"Can you see there, 'Nemhab?" Tuthmose was standing close to the fire, too close, I thought, when he pointed my gaze south. "In the haze there."

On the plain, Khnemu's infantry was already closing on the Syrians in a enveloping maneuver later called "the Horns of the Sacred Bull," a movement coming from the east and west—as Menthu's chariots struck them from the rear.

"Now, it's the Syrians turn," the god shouted.

"Menkheperre, why didn't you let me in on this? I thought I was your general and your friend."

"Would you and your men have fought with such desperation if I told you? Rehoboam needed to see that look on their faces, or he would never have allowed himself to be trapped!"

"Did Anhur give you that idea, too?"

"No," said Menkheperre, breaking into his most innocent smile. "I thought it up all by myself."

Menthu's cavalry was nearing the city now. His chariots scraped up the injured stragglers and reached the edge of the Syrian infantry, boxing them in. In truth, this enemy was not Syrian-born, but mercenary soldiers from the bondage lands across the Jordan.

Nomads and farmers that they were, many panicked. They dropped their girdles and weapons to lighten themselves, but found no place to run. A number stumbled, dust-blind, under the crushing wheels of Qemet's chariots.

Further back, pinned against Megiddo's walls, Syrian chariots could barely maneuver as a mob of their own foot soldiers crowded them. The Prince of Kadesh was forced under his shield as barrages of arrows struck the black chariot.

The press of fighting bodies came right up to the wheels of the chariot, lifted one and threatened to overturn the carriage itself. The horde surged backward like a storm hitting the sea. The chariot rocked, and Rehoboam's shield bearer tumbled off and disappeared below the mass of churning arms and torsos.

More arrows flew, striking bodies locked so close together the dead had no room to fall. The stallions turned skittish. They began rearing and kicking to keep their balance amid the crush of humans.

The front line of Qemet's soldiers cut deeply through the Syrian defense until some were within reach of Rehoboam himself. In one story that came from the fight, it is told that a burly swordsman of General Pentaweret's guard named Kanakht rushed to within a hair's distance of the prince's ebony chariot. He struck out at Rehoboam with his blade, but, missing his prize, grabbed the charioteer instead.

Despite his armor, the prince's driver was slashed from pubis to collarbone with one hard upward thrust. He fell, screaming, over the rail into the arms of his attacker. Kanakht, in his rage, cleaved the Judaean's head from his neck with two strong chops and threw the twitching body back into the chariot where it continued to jerk and flop about, splashing hot blood all over Rehoboam's tunic.

Kanakht tied the head to his girdle by its long hair and kept it at his side until the end of the Palestinian campaign. The Black Prince was in mortal terror from the experience.

Rehoboam began to shriek, "Make for the gates! Make for the gates!"

He tried retreating as a new horde of Qemeti Javelins hacked their way closer. A knot of loyal Judaeans hurried to the side of their king to shield him, but as Rehoboam ran, one of our lancers managed to graze the royal buttock with his spear tip.

"They are murdering me!" howled the prince as he parried a series of blows with one hand while grasping tightly onto his scratched rump with the other.

The noise . . . the struggle . . . the blood-sweet smells . . . the death . . .

The Syrians were paying scant attention to their host prince. They had massed at the southern gate and were clubbing the high wooden doors, demanding entrance. We learned later, the Megiddans inside were scared of the clamoring soldiers. They saw that the fighting was now hand-to-hand and worried if the gates were opened, a flood of Qemeti could enter the city with them.

The Megiddans were canny.

From their location on the caravan route to the sea, the city's tradesmen had built thriving businesses. None wanted to see them torched. They had hidden wells and large granaries; they had resisted sieges before. But, they reasoned, their chances of coming away unscathed, should a pitched battle be fought within their walls, were nil.

And so, the merchants of Megiddo let their warriors die.

More than two hundred of Syrians and Judaeans were slain in Rehoboam's sight. Finally, in desperation, he ripped his battle flag from its standard. Waving it madly from the rear of his ebony wagon for all his troops to see, he shouted to the Megiddans who were watching from the ramparts above to open the gates. They pretended not to hear him.

"What are you waiting for up there? Are you all women? At least have your bowmen rain death down on the bird-worshipers that are hacking us to carrion."

"And hit our own men?" cried a voice from the wall.

"Yes!"

Stepping back, Rehoboam trod on the gaping neck of his dead driver, making blood spurt from the opening onto his sandals. The prince recoiled as the warm, sticky gore oozed between his toes. He moved too fast and slipped. He clutched at the chariot's yoke as he went down, missed, and yanked the reins.

Feeling the sharp tug on their mouths, his terrified stallions broke into a run. Dozens dived away from the galloping horses as they passed the south gate and up the incline toward the unprotected eastern wall. Only Rehoboam's personal guard gave chase.

The Megiddan elders heard the commotion and looked to see their king speeding off. Below, the Syrians were busy. A cluster of well-muscled warriors brought up a cedar watering trough to use as a ram.

They rushed the gate and splintered one of the upright jambs on their first attempt. Before they could try again, a Megiddan noble yelled from the wall that if they beat the enemy back beyond the slope, the doors would open for them.

"I have a better idea," answered a Syrian captain. "If you let us in now, I won't rip off your testicles and feed them to the dogs!"

The Megiddan agreed to the compromise and ordered the gates flung wide. The Syrians streamed inside and Menthu, following pharaoh's stratagem, let them.

The portals were wide, but still acted like pebbles falling through a hole. Soon, with the fleeing soldiers all pushing, squashing, and climbing over each other, the gate became a death trap for many of them.

But not Rehoboam. He and his small, loyal remnant had been boxed into an angled indentation far from the gate that formed part of the south tower fortifications. They were holding out against our rear guard, who had been placed there originally with the sole purpose of keeping the Megiddans from straying outside their wall.

It was hit-and-run skirmishing on our part. Few casualties could be counted on either side, but there was just enough action to keep the Judaeans where they were till Menthu and his chariots could close in.

Rehoboam's fighters made a tight semicircle around the ebony chariot, blocking our darts with their tall shields. But this could not go on much longer—and they knew it. The Aten was falling below the western range. Menthu jockeyed his horses around the mob of Syrians and led his force toward the prince at a deliberate pace.

He took into account that some might slip away once it was night, but with Qemet owning Jezreel, he believed there was no direction for them to run. Actually, there was one direction.

Up.

Grasping Rehoboam's predicament, a crowd of Megiddan guards and townspeople produced ropes and dropped them over the wall. At the bottom, dozens of hands jumped and grabbed for their deliverance. One Judaean boy had the idea to climb onto the side of the prince's chariot to reach the dangling rope.

It was a bad idea.

Truly, he did find the end of the rope and did begin hoisting himself to safety. But, sadly for the young recruit, that had been the rope Rehoboam wished to use for his own escape. The Black Prince unsheathed his sickle-shaped sword and dug it deep into the boy's belly.

He twisted it, causing the boy's entrails to slop out and hang like red-spackled eels before he dropped. "Hear the Anointed One of Yahweh!" Rehoboam shouted as he tied the line around his waist. "I go up first! And a curse on he who touches any of these ropes before they see me on top of this wall!"

Menthu and his men arrived just as Rehoboam was being hauled out of danger. The old general laughed. "Is that the king of Judah, or a side of beef being pulled up there?"

"I can get a clean arrow shot," offered the archer at the general's shoulder.

Menthu shook his head. "No. Once he's in the city, we'll have someone of importance to bargain with. And if he's scared enough, there's no telling what we might get in return for that pale hide."

"Look to the wall!" came a shout from the ranks.

Rehoboam was swinging the last few feet, trying to catch his heel on the battlement and pull himself up. To help, the townsmen snatched at his cloak. They got a hem and lifted the prince and his tunic at the same time—exposing the royal genitals and the lancemark on the royal buttock to the army of Qemet below.

Menthu did not begin the laughter, but joined in with his rich basso guffaw that echoed off the Megiddan walls until it was deafening. Later, Menthu remarked that rarely had so many men laughed over so small a thing.

CHAPTER FIFTEEN

While the last Syrians either scaled the walls or died, an equine-faced young captain of chariots maneuvered alongside Menthu. He was of the general's acquaintance, being the third son of the powerful nomarch who governed Thinis. The father had despaired of a profession for the boy, whose talents were limited to be sure, and requested that Menthu give him a commission in his service. It must have been the gods' work, because on the expedition to Judah, young Neper flourished.

"May I report, sir?"

Menthu nodded indulgently. "Am I a hero again, Captain?"

"Glories are heaped upon glories, my general," he said. "The bearded dogs are crying for their mothers—or for that single god of theirs . . . I'm not too good at their language. But it's a complete rout, sir!"

Menthu was amused by the young man's enthusiasm. He'd heard the rumors that he and this child were lovers, and that was why he rose so quickly to captain of his own force of chariots.

It wasn't that. The reason did not even include the boy's influential father.

Simply, Menthu liked him. And, perhaps, he had come to an age when he felt the need to pass along what he knew of his trade. Significantly, at the beginning, Menthu had given Neper the job he had first been assigned when he joined the Chariots in the time of the first Tuthmose. The boy was put in charge of the herd of pack donkeys.

The accepted rule was to beat the donkeys to make them keep up with the rest of the animal train. Neper hated the sound of the lash, and he soon realized that using it caused as many delays as it stopped.

The herders thought him insane, but for weeks he stayed with the animals—some nights going as far as sleeping in their enclosure—and watched how they reacted. He found that when he rode atop the strongest male, the others tended to follow.

This behavior was helped when he rewarded the donkeys with water whenever their moods began to darken. The whip was no longer used to spur them on, but only to keep them in line and going in the right direction.

Obstinate as they were by nature, the donkeys responded to this treatment—and to Neper. They accepted being tied to double panniers laden with heavy grain sacks or water jugs with a minimum of fuss.

On the trail, the animals shocked even old campaign hands by fording rivers without complaint, if Neper bade them to follow his lead.

For a time, until the army set out for Judah, Neper's donkeys were the talk of the camp. During the hot trek across the Sinai, Menthu noticed that Neper was spending more time among the chariot horses. He would often leave the donkeys to the herdsmen and ride ahead to help feed or water them.

The horses walked unharnessed behind the marching infantry. At dusk, he would watch the charioteers strap them to their war carts, so they wouldn't lose the feel of being driven in battle.

Looking at Neper often stirred memories from the general's own boyhood when he would spend all his days and nights with the great beasts. Galloping astride their broad backs, like a barbarian holding onto their long manes for dear life, must have been what Re felt when charging from the eastern shore to the underworld.

When Neper came to him, finally, with hopeful eyes, to explain how much he had come to love and respect the warhorses, Menthu understood. His work with the pack animals demanded recognition, and so, he was given a squad of ten chariots.

He repeated much of his methods with the donkeys, and the horses invariably responded. He had a harder time gaining the fealty of his men, however. Most of them were battle-scarred veterans who resented a rich donkey driver leading them.

Of course, they were disciplined and did their work—this was Menthu's command, after all—but that didn't stop the slurs against the boy's manhood or the jests about his long, horsy features.

They told jokes about him as he rode by behind his new team of matching grays—*No wonder those stallions'll do whatever the kid wants them to. To them, Captain Neper looks like a mare in heat!* But only loud enough so that he could just hear his name and the laughter a second later.

"General, do you see what they're doing?" said Neper, excitedly.

"I thought the Syrians were running like sand lizards."

"Not them," replied Neper, on tiptoe, leaning over the side of his chariot. "I meant our own men. They're stripping the dead!"

Menthu agreed and smiled at his protégée. "Come, boy, these are the gifts of war you've heard the men talk about."

"But this is most unseemly. It's common looting! Shouldn't our troops be storming the gates or something?"

Menthu shook his head. "I'm certainly relieved you spoke to me about it first. Understand, Neper, our soldiers are mostly poor men with families to provide for. They're fighting for plunder, not glory. And I wouldn't want to be the green officer telling them to drop their haul to go pound on a stone wall!"

"Then, how will we take the city?"

"Oh, that's the simplest part. Draw your men up in close ranks, out of range of any arrows from the parapets, and circle all their fortifications so nobody can get out."

"A siege?" Neper sounded disappointed. "I thought if we made it inside Megiddo, they'd surrender to us. A siege could take forever!"

Menthu hopped down off his chariot and walked a few steps into the starless night. The temperature had fallen fifteen degrees since the warmth of Re had departed. Neper threw his cloak around his shoulders.

Except for the moans of the dying and the terrible death stench from the battlefield, it might have been pleasant to be there.

"Captain? Are you coming?" Menthu called out from some unseen location. Neper tethered his grays and ran to find him. It was impossible to see. Rehoboam himself could've been standing as close as two spans from him without Neper noticing.

That would not long be the case, for as Neper reached Menthu's

side, the first row of torch-bearing sentries rounded the western wall
to cover the infamous southern gate. Suddenly, he bumped into something solid. He had discovered his mentor.

"Oh, forgive me, sir. I couldn't see you."

"Might as well relax, boy," Menthu counseled. "We could be sitting here all season."

"Have you gone through a lot of these, General?"

Menthu snorted. "Pick a town." He walked on, peering into the
solid black with those cat's eyes of his. A few paces further on there
were bodies sprawled in random clumps. They stepped over them.

Neper was amazed at the smoke rising into the cool air from their
chest wounds. He had never seen such a thing before and assumed it
was their ka escaping to the other world.

He turned back to Menthu. "General. About this siege. How
long . . . ?"

The general cut him off with a wave. "Don't worry. We have to
get back to Qemet before the weather gets bad, and the rivers get too
high. If that happens, we'll just be back next year and fight 'em
again."

"But without the element of surprise, sir."

A torchman went by them as the old general raised his head to
answer.

He looked weary. "The outcome will be the same. Except, more
men will die."

Next morning's light revealed a tight formation of tents ringing the
Palestinian stronghold. Pharaoh's golden pavilion had been brought
up from the foothills during the night and now sat opposite Megiddo's main gate. Our quarters, that of the generals and nomarchs,
were laid in concentric circles outward from the royal complex.

The army had been posted at standard intervals outside the walls,
with added concentrations near the gates and outside wells. Off-duty
soldiers busied themselves with picking over the corpses.

Before noon, most of the swords, helmets, and breastplates were
gone. They had been loaded onto the abandoned Syrian chariots—
and there were many—and carted back to camp. Officers had first
call on arms, at least in theory. In reality, they took whatever had
not been hidden by the slaves or their men.

Latecomers to the battlefield had to content themselves with trinkets. One lucky fellow, a Javelin, I think, kicked up a clot of earth
and uncovered a severed hand. It must have belonged to a Syrian
noble because three of its fingers bore gold rings, one with an emerald.

He brought them back to Qemet where they fetched enough for him to purchase an allotment of land near Dendura where he and his family prospered. I understand that his eldest son is today the Superintendent of Sacrificial and Provision Houses under the Royal Governor of his nome. Such stories have kept Qemet well supplied with willing soldiers since before the pyramids rose at Mennufer.

Menthu personally took charge of the captured mountain horses. He planned to try them out at the head of his lighter chariots. Perhaps, he reasoned, the strength and stamina of the breed would increase when they had less of a burden behind them.

The result—a swifter chariot that could sustain a charge for a longer distance—would have capped his career if he had not . . .

No matter, that story can wait for its proper telling.

During that first tedious day of waiting, the god sent but one message into Megiddo. He made no mention of surrender; rather, he arranged for two hours daily when women of the town might collect bodies from the battle scene and return with them to the city for prayers and burial.

Those with kin in Rehoboam's service were the first out. It was difficult to identify Judaean dead among so many Syrians, especially now that they had lost their armor and lay naked to the drying sun and the carrion vultures.

But the women examined limp, dead cocks for evidence of foreskin and only gathered up the bald heads behind the walls that day.

That night their pyres reddened the moon, and the sparks of the dead could be seen from our watchtowers. Our priests, of course, were appalled at this. Burning a man's shell condemned his ka.

Everyone knew a man's vital, continuing force could not survive without its vessel. How sad that the souls of these foreigners are, through ignorance, denied eternal life in the Realm of the Blessed.

Qemet's casualties were few in comparison to the Syrians, but those who began their second lives included many who fought with me at the southern pass. They were volunteers; not my troops.

My Braves had been busy in the north where they had outwitted the Judaean army and had returned almost unscathed. Tuthmose, who sent us to the Megiddo pass as decoys, ordered full honors for the dead. He sent his high priest to supervise their journey to the western land of Duat.

To this end, a small necropolis grew at the encampment's edge. Each common soldier was carefully cleaned by a crew of strange, hairless ascetics who rarely spoke to anyone but their own kind.

Those of rank had their abdomens cut and their bodies emptied of viscera. Palm oil and ground spices filled the cavity and their organs placed in magic jars.

After the purification ritual, the priests took them to the foothills where the ordinary recruits were buried under three feet of dry soil with two urns of food and a wine jar. Their betters would spend eternity higher up, in comfortable clefts in the rocks above Jezreel.

Later, the cadre of priests invoked the magic for the dead. Seven were assigned to repeat the glorifications over and over until nightfall. The repetition ensured the deceased that Isis and Nephthys would weep for him and ease his living essence into the nation of Osiris.

After a week, the siege of Megiddo had settled into routine. A place had been found for the wounded near one of the wells. Most of the sword gashes, even the deep ones, were healing nicely under the ministering of the priests and physicians.

It seems they used a mold from the still water of the well as a poultice. The cuts I have seen were pink with new skin and had not blackened with poison, so I suppose these magicians know their craft.

Menkheperre had sent his personal doctor into the area, and I accompanied him. Irynufer was short and expansive about his middle, but his strange solemnity, and the fact that he wore the lion's pelt of a Sekhmet High Priest, demanded respect.

Wherever he went, his bearers toted ornate chests with images of his lion-headed goddess. Inside, laid out in neat compartments, were his copper-tipped surgical tools; wax to sculpt fetish dolls of the sick; reed pens for writing incantations; jars with a variety of helpful medicines such as sulphur, acacia, alum, and castor oil; vials containing beetles and moths crushed into powder and, in the largest cedar box, the complete collected papyri of Im-ho-tep, *the-Physician-Who-Was-a-God*.

Irynufer has told me that his scrolls were written before Pharaoh Djoser, *Called-Horus-Netcherykhet*, built Qemet's first pyramid.

I smiled indulgently, knowing it could not be so. "A copy, surely," I said.

"Oh, yes, these are my scribe's work. The originals are back home, safe in No-Amun. Too brittle to risk on a campaign in this climate, even if I were inclined to bring them. You understand."

"Of course."

"They're very rare, Amenemhab. Lasted through a thousand or more inundations, I've been told." Then, squeezing my arm in perhaps more than a brotherly way—for Irynufer was known to dally with his boy slaves at the expense of his bloated wife—he added, "I'll be happy to show them to you when we return. The first feast day, all right?"

"You're very kind. They must contain potent magic."

"Truly, I think they do. But," he confided, "they are writ in the old tongue, and I'm not fluent in it."

"And still you bother to bring them with you?"

He grinned that old politician's grin I had seen so often at court. "The former owner was kind enough to leave translations of the more difficult rites for me."

I asked the question he wished me to ask. "Such a valuable collection, how could a man ever give them up?"

"He could only take so much with him into exile."

"Was he a criminal?"

Irynufer drew me closer until I could smell the anise on his breath. "His only sin was to sleep with the wrong slut. The scrolls belonged to Sennemut, the lover of Hatshepsut—the Bitch Queen!"

"Sennemut? By the gods, it's been a time since I've heard that name!"

"It may be indiscreet to speak of him." The physician shrugged, a tone of regret creeping into his voice as he carried on. "The Tuthmose fears the man, you know. He told me once, he believes Sennemut's body holds the Ka of Im-ho-tep."

"I've heard that."

"I never met Sennemut, personally," Irynufer said. "Did you?"

"No, I was in Nubia when it all happened. My father spoke to him often, though."

"Oh, yes. Your father was at court, wasn't he?"

"He was Superintendent of the House of Silver for the second Tuthmose and continued under Hatshepsut. Sennemut held title as Lord Treasurer, so they were always conferring. My father was seldom impressed by anyone, but he told me he would gaze on Aten's sun disk at midday for that man."

"A sorrow what happened."

"It was never proven he poisoned her," I said.

Irynufer's voice grew firmer—and more conspiratorial. "He most certainly did not. The truth is . . . well, her death was ordained by the gods for her affront to them. A woman should never have presumed to wear the divine beard."

"Surely, you don't give credence to the rumors that Menkheperre had her killed."

"Of course not," he said, choosing his words carefully. "He . . . had great affection for his aunt. Did she not make him coregent when he reached manhood? I sometimes think he was jealous of poor Sennemut for the nights he spent with the woman. Sennemut probably realized it. He was scrupulously kind to the boy and spent years tutoring him in all the kingly ways."

"And yet, after her death, he struck Hatshepsut's name from all her monuments and sent Sennemut into the desert."

"The boy had no choice. They had done a terrible thing. But, no point in retching up old follies. Besides, I'm sure you've heard enough about the whole sad affair from your father."

I turned to the physician, my eyes clear and unwavering. I had heard the hushed whispers recounting the events of three years past, but no one—not even my father—dared speak plain. "Still, the events are unclear in my mind," I lied. "And if I am to serve the god, as you do, without hesitation . . ."

"Yes, dear boy, I understand how you must feel. What Sennemut did was out of love, pure and simple. He could not bear to see Hatshepsut enter the second life and usurped the rights of the gods. What was Tuthmose to do? He was Horus, the god on Earth. A mortal, even a genius prophet such as Sennemut, mustn't take these matters into his own hands."

"But, exactly what did he do?"

Irynufer did not answer directly. Instead, he shut his eyes and tried to recall the scene. "Well, I shouldn't tell tales, but since you're your father's son, I suppose I could fill in the spots that are troubling you. You see, Sennemut had dedicated himself to gathering the old scrolls. He sent scribes to every temple in the realm. From what I could tell, he was most interested in the prayers and rituals to the dead. It was his notion that Qemet's magic had been slowly ebbing away since the first days. He felt, and don't ask me why, that our priests had once possessed a power given by the gods: the power to control the everliving spirit. Rituals to ensure immortality, reanimate the dead, that sort of thing, were all supposedly in those scrolls. Very instructional, but according to Sennemut, phrases were added or dropped, procedures modified or forgotten, and whole passages embellished to the point that the pure elemental magic in them was lost."

"That's quite a radical idea."

"But Sennemut was one fellow I'd never dare dispute. Whether he was the new vessel for Im-ho-tep or not, a mind like his is as rare as water on the Great Desert of Kôm!"

"Did he find these, uh, magic scrolls?"

"I'm not certain. Except, he did try to raise the dead, didn't he?"

The full realization struck me unawares. "Hatshepsut?"

"He dragged her body from the necropolis, crossed the sacred river with her, went to the Estate of Amun at Karnak, and laid her body on the ground at the base of her own obelisk. I don't know what he was doing, but that's where Tuthmose found them."

"Menkheperre? He found them? Alone?"

"With his guard," Irynufer said. His words were grave like the expression on his face. "None of whom are still alive."

"To tell the tale?" I whispered.

He motioned me to silence as a soldier passed, then took my hand. "Do not lose faith in the god, young general. Remember, it was his first days as pharaoh and the scandal might have excited the deltan nomarchs to civil war. What he did was politic. And he accomplished it swiftly, with the confidence and dignity of a true king."

"Life and prosperity to him!"

"Life and prosperity," echoed the royal physician. He held open the flap of the tent that served as the House of Healing and ushered me inside, our talk over. The men stretched out on mats inside were suffering from battle fevers. Only seven days after the fighting and many had died of the terrible sickness.

The screams of the soon-to-die could be heard throughout the camp as their bodies were possessed by tormenting wind daemons who turn their insides first to fire, then to ice.

Irynufer explained the malady thus: Any wound, no matter how insignificant, may weaken a man's ka and serve as a point of entry for a corrupt spirit. Once it invades the body, it quickly travels through the forty vessels to the *Beginning-of-All-the-Members*, the heart. Even a child is aware that the heart is the seat of thought.

Therefore, once it is attacked and begins to race, all rationality is destroyed. At the same time, the daemons may rush to the head to strike the gray, pulpy organ within the skull.

While this densely packed, tumorous mass is of little use (embalmers scoop it out of the head cavity and throw it away), it is known to control the movement of certain muscles by pulling and slackening the cords tied to its base that, in turn, run down the backbone.

If the daemons should squeeze the organ, the muscles will begin to twitch wildly. Eventually, the strain will confound the heart and so frighten the Ba that it will rush from the mouth to escape.

And should a man be separated from his Ba it is essential that the prayers of reunification be performed immediately:

O Udjat-Eye of Horus, Bring my Ba to see my body
From wherever it has flown, take him to rest upon my mummy
But if there is difficulty in finding my Ba, O Horus, support me
in the netherworld of Duat until you have united me with my
Ever-Living Soul

If not, the poor man would not be whole and could not long exist in his Second Life.

There were three kinds of healers in camp to tend the sick. My officers and the nobles of the royal compound naturally preferred the *wabu*, classically trained priest-doctors who had studied in the Sekhmet Temple's House of Life at Dendera.

Most women, when a problem arose, sought out the *magicians* who stayed in the bright caravans at the edge of camp. Their practice has never been regulated in any nome of Qemet, for these men work the mysteries.

Too much of their time seems to be spent in grinding the fruit of the hemayet into wrinkle cream for this soldier to take them seriously. But they have a spell for everything, so I would be foolish to say that their amulets and incantations have no merit.

I, however, would rather be attended by the *sunu*. These lay physicians are not blessed by any temple or god, and so they are relegated to caring for common soldiers.

And the occasional stubborn general.

I think Menthu first introduced me to the sunu on our mission to Kerma. Putting down the black chieftains proved costly to my Braves of the King, who led the attack.

Many were injured severely.

I feared for their lives—and I did lose over a hundred courageous warriors—but many whom I thought would pass across the sacred river were saved by the sunu doctors. Their talents impressed me.

I suppose it was because they, like myself, are practical men. If a spell or an incantation works, they use it. But if they see no purpose in a method, they simply choose to ignore it.

I once fought with a follower of Sekhmet on such a point. I had spent a day finding forage for their donkeys and had made the remark that their pack animals might be better used.

A wabu-priest, it seems, cleans wounds with holy Nile water,

which their donkeys carry with them everywhere in gigantic jars. Sunu
doctors, on the other hand, wash their patients in the very same clear
spring water we all drink, saying that sutured cuts have less tendency
to fester or turn black that way.

Naturally, this offended the priests, who still denounce this exercise
as an insult to Hāpi, *Who-Is-the-Nile, From-Whom-All-Gifts-Flow.*

And yet, I have seen two brothers, alike in every respect, even to
the slashes received on their sides at the joining of their breast armor.
The one tended by the sunu recovered, while his twin suffered might-
ily for a week even though a Sekhmet high priest was called in to
circle the tent with a des-wood stick and drew a line of protection in
the dirt that daemons could not cross. The exorcism failed and the
man died horribly of gash poison as I watched helplessly.

Which is not to say that I do not honor Lord Irynufer and his
medicine. His brothers-in-Sekhmet shared Nubia's fetid weather with
me, and many Braves whom I can name are today restored to life
from no other cause than the succor of the wabu.

I found in following Irynufer around that his presence, by itself,
had a salutary effect on my men's medical care. He seemed to inspire
pharaoh's other surgeons to sew a bit neater and pray somewhat
louder over their patients.

On his later rounds, I was amazed to find certain warriors grouped
together in the shade of their lean-tos, occupied with slave work.

"Broken bones," Irynufer explained.

"It's unseemly for fighters to be fixing sandals and sifting grain,"
I groused.

"These are new times," said Irynufer. He reported that the god
had walked among them after the battle and, seeing their idleness,
commanded the men to work at what they could, or they would not
eat. From then on, he had sent loads of hand work to them along
with his blessings.

They complained, as soldiers do about all things, but after a time,
I noticed that the ones who worked the hardest healed the quickest.

As we were leaving an herb-smoked tent, one of my Braves, Memnet of Buto, called out to me. He held up a small clay rectangle encased in a wooden frame.

"General! This was dropped off the wall."

It was a scribe's tablet. I took it and scanned the impressions on
the baked clay. The message was written in two parts, Judaean symbols on top with a translation in Qemet's noble tongue scrawled
crudely across the bottom half.

I sent Memnet back to his guardpost and continued on a ways with Lord Irynufer.

"For the god?" asked the physician as he passed his eye over the tablet.

"From Rehoboam. Evidently, his wound was not mortal."

Irynufer grinned and patted himself on his right buttock. "Not mortal, but perhaps it will teach him that sitting upon a throne can be painful." I nodded, stifling the loud chuckle I felt coming.

Instead, I asked a neutral question. "Have you seen the god this morning?"

"No," Irynufer said, "his servant said he was gone before the Aten rose. That's not to say he hasn't returned to the pavilion. I've been recommending that he take a short nap at midday while we're in this damp heat."

"Oh? And the god obeys such advice?"

His full lips parted. He almost spoke, but instead his face crinkled into an ironic smirk. "Never," he whispered. "Pharaoh left early this morning to bless the harvest."

I excused myself and hopped aboard a grain wagon rolling toward the wheat fields. I would have taken to horse or chariot, but most of the animals were still out to pasture at that hour.

The message from Rehoboam was not unduly urgent and it would have taken longer to cut out a good horse and ready the beast than to take a peaceful ox cart ride. I stretched out on the soft sacks of wheat, closed my eyes and let the warmth of Aten's morning caress my skin.

When the wagon left the road for the narrow trail through the high stalks, I cracked open my eyelids and oriented myself. The walls of Megiddo rose above the remnants of the morning mist some leagues distant. Our city of tents was also well behind me; its canopies looking like gowns laid out to dry on the bank of the Mother River on washday.

Up ahead, three men in uniforms of the Great House, the Tuthmose's personal guard squatted by the path. As the cart passed them, I eased off the back and walked up to them.

"I am Amenemhab, General of the Braves of the King. I seek Pharaoh."

At once, the guards were on their feet, bowing. The oldest, a coarse-hewn campaigner who had earned his post by valor, crossed his chest and said, "The god is there, sir!" He motioned to the flat land behind him. "See, noble general? By the threshing field."

I strained to see Menkheperre, but couldn't at first. Legend has it that the Horus-on-Earth is a spirit who may evaporate from the sight of men when he is not aware that we mortals are watching him. It was my first thought as I searched the wheat for the god. Then, I caught sight of him.

The Tuthmose stood in clear view and yet, he was invisible, perfectly camouflaged as if by design. His bronze skin and golden skirt matched the sun-rich color of the grain as if all were painted with the same brilliant dye.

Only his lack of movement betrayed him.

While the high stalks around him dipped and rolled in the wind, pharaoh remained still as a statue. With a sheaf of wheat in his hand, I wondered if my master had transformed himself into the body of Min, *Overseer of the Harvest*.

Then, when I had traversed much of the land that separated us, he looked up.

"I beg forgiveness, Majesty," I said as I reached him. "I would not interrupt your prayers without reason."

"I'm not praying, 'Nemhab, so don't concern yourself." The god held out the stalk to me and I took it into my hands. "Remarkable, isn't it!"

I had no idea what he was talking about, but tried to look interested.

"I'm convinced it's a new variety of wheat," he continued. "Very hearty. My guess is the seeds come from the land above the two rivers."

"Mitanni?"

"My northern enemies want their allies to fight me with full bellies. And see, it has survived the worst weather of this foul land and yet, it flourishes."

"I know a few men in the legion who are planters in the delta," I said. "I'll send them to gather the seeds, if His Majesty wishes."

Menkheperre nodded his approval. "But, you came for another reason, didn't you?"

"Yes," I said and passed the scribe's block to him. "The Judaean threw this from the wall."

"Megiddo must be getting too crowded for him. What's his pleasure?"

"He begs an audience with you. King to king, the little toad says. I think he'll trade Megiddo for his life."

We sat down on a freshly cut stack of pharaoh's winter grass. His perfect lips formed into a sly smile. "Rehoboam fears a long siege, then. Tell me, my friend, you've been at sieges before. What would you do?"

"You compliment me, Lord," I said, deciding to restate the premise as I thought of something valuable to say.

"It could be," I began, "that Rehoboam's been watching all of this activity down here from Megiddo's arrow ports. He's seen us building the ramps and siege towers and now, he knows we're serious. If I'm not mistaken, he's more panicked than a scarab beetle running over hot wax."

"Should I meet with him, then?"

"Menkheperre, this Prince of Kadesh is a coward. He waited for the Syrians to come before he dared fight us, and only then, because he believed he outnumbered us. That was the coward's way. And cowards cannot be trusted."

Menkheperre brightened. "My thought exactly!" he exclaimed. "I'm certain Rehoboam intends to perform his magnanimous act for me; falling prostrate at my feet, licking my toes and promising to turn over to me what I have already won! And if I grant him his life? Do you expect he will become my loyal vassal once more?"

My head shook slowly. "The hyena will flee to the arms of Mitanni and spend his time gathering another army to avenge his defeat at your noble hands. He is a proud fool, Majesty."

"Yes. It is a dangerous trait in a coward."

"Shall I answer, Lord?"

"Eventually. But for now, the prince can wait."

"For how long?"

Menkheperre shrugged lightly and tilted his chin so that the Aten shone directly on his cheeks. "Oh, I don't care as long as we've got him boxed in there. Delay my answer and make it noncommittal. Make him think I'll let him stew in the pot all season." He gave me his full smile and added, "Or into the next!"

His deep brown eyes narrowed as they met mine. "I know you were disappointed we didn't make a direct assault on the city. Don't think I doubt your skills. We could've won Megiddo. But at what cost?"

He stood abruptly. He was five strides ahead by the time I got to my feet and scrambled after him. A complement of three chariots awaited the god's will in the threshing area near the road, his golden chariot among them. I fell in one pace behind him.

"Anhur, the War Spirit, speaks through me, 'Nemhab. We know, as gods, that the fate of Qemet depends on our strength, but equally on our patience. However, you can tell Menthu and all of my discontented generals that I intend to march on from here and conquer all of Mitanni and beyond!"

"Yes, Majesty."

"And if any of them ever ask why I didn't storm the damn walls of Megiddo, tell them that I was not about to lose half my force in my first campaign!"

"I understand, Majesty."

"Good!" We reached his chariot. He grabbed the gold rail and hoisted himself aboard. Then, staring down at me, he said, "Megiddo will fall, my dear general. That is destined. Its people will know hunger and slow death for their affront to me. And after I tear down their walls and gain their city, their weapons, and their legions—all without any loss to me—then, we will march north."

"North?"

"It is the god Anhur's plan," said Pharaoh savoring that he had preempted any debate on the matter by laying the design of conquest at the feet of the War God. "Rehoboam's men can either choose death or a chance at life in our front lines. I have used the tactic before with good result. You remember my guard Yishaq?"

"He directed me here, Lord."

"Once a Habiru raider, today, he is the most loyal of my home guard. It will be the same with the Syrian mercenaries. The priests will consecrate them to Amun-Re and they will be mine forever. My warriors will increase by a third; my army will be the most powerful to ever ride across the earth! And at its head, the God-on-Earth and Amenemhab, his general, crushing Palestine and Syria—city by city! Each will surrender to me or die in the rubble of their walls and the torching of their homes! But the men of these lands know nothing of the Second Life. They will choose to save themselves by following me—until our numbers rival the stars in Heaven!"

A strange gleam crossed his wide eyes, as if he saw me no longer. He continued to speak, detailing his strategies as a scribe recites from a prayer scroll.

Listening to the god, I too could see those legions—as dense as a tidal bore, rolling unchecked over our foes—until I shouted, "On to Mitanni! And wherever your dreams take us!"

The Tuthmose touched my shoulder as he often did, but this time I felt a spark like a small jolt of lightning rushing through me. "Not dreams, Destiny!" he said. "Qemet has been folding in on itself since the great cackler, Kenkenwer, laid the egg of the world. We are an ancient people, Amenemhab, but far too insular for these modern times. Qemet must rule the world, or be swallowed up by it!"

"Such a mission will take more than one campaign, my Lord."

"Aren't I the most patient of men?" he said, placing his war crown atop his head.

"You are Horus; you have a thousand times a thousand lifetimes."

Pharaoh's driver steadied the matched pair of whites as Menkheperre took the reins. The god pulled them back as the golden chariot rolled a quarter turn forward. "They're anxious to be fed. Ride with me to the compound, 'Nemhab."

"As you wish, Lord."

The charioteer surrendered his place and I held on as pharaoh snapped the leather reins. The horses charged ahead as the two guard chariots attempted to keep pace. The god laughed as the wind struck his face. Osiris, his spirit sire, surely had created him for action.

My fingers gripped the side rail tightly as we raced down the rutted trail.

After a particularly hard bounce, the god grinned at me and chided, "How can you look so worried? A god is driving!"

"I've driven with you before, Menkheperre, and you always forget that your passengers are not quite as immortal as you are!"

"Hah! I love you, 'Nemhab!"

I lowered my head. "I worship you, Divinity."

CHAPTER SIXTEEN ☥

One month into the siege, Menthu of the Chariots came to pharaoh suggesting a series of frontal assaults on Megiddo's main gates. The men, he explained, were bored and hungered for action. Dodging the occasional arrow from the walls was not enough to excite fighting men.

Menkheperre, who had been reclining on his divan after a tiring trip into the foothills, drew up on one arm and said, "General, if you're itching to make a sacrifice, I give you my leave to pick a fat goat from my private stock and have at it! But I won't allow you to sacrifice any of my horses or chariots or men because you can't think of anything better to do with your time than war on a caged enemy!"

Evidently, the tale of that encounter spread among the foot soldiers, who were quite content to stay alive and pursue other interests. In gratitude, they pooled a measure of their war spoils and bribed a royal artisan to fashion the gold and jewels into a staff as their token to the god.

The head and fetish symbols of the Prince of Kadesh were carved on the crook to recall Tuthmose's great victory over the Judaeans and the Syrians. I was with the god when the legion presented it to him. Tears welled up in his eyes as his men placed the staff onto his outstretched palms.

Pharaoh had dressed in full armor, plaited beard, and makeup for the ceremony and could not hide the streaks of coal black that ran down his cheeks. But men of Qemet weep and laugh and nothing is thought of it.

Only the simple peoples to the north, those corrupted by their bastard religions, think tears unmanly. What can be a better answer to these fools than this: The god cries.

I made the second trip into the foothills with Menkheperre. He brought along a well-armed guard in case of Judaean raiders and a party of noblemen skilled in engineering.

When we found a spot high enough to survey Jezreel, the god commanded we all leave our chariots. The guards stayed on the path, but pharaoh ordered the rest of us to stroll with him to where he'd placed a watchtower.

He called the engineers together and pointed out the far city. Megiddo rests on the northerly side of the Karmel ridge, a fertile ground bordered by a forest of tall, straight trees.

Menkheperre had two questions: Was there enough timber to construct a second wall around Megiddo, higher than the first and, when could it be completed?

"It would take forever!" said the builder of the god's shrine to Amun-Re outside the capital.

"Oh, most assuredly, Majesty," agreed a lesser noble.

"Why, just the time it would take to cut down the trees, not to mention transporting them all the way into the valley!"

"The trees are up here; the city is down there," the god shouted through gritted teeth. "Roll them off the damned ledges!"

We shared a chariot on the way back and Menkheperre's mood was ugly. He cursed his engineers until he ran out of breath, threatening to flail them for their stupidity and lack of invention. I could tell that his outburst embarrassed the spearman with us.

"Tell me, 'Nemhab," he implored with a booming voice that echoed so sharply, I am certain that the poor engineers heard every word in their chariots behind us, "why am I burdened so? Where is my Sennemut? Why can't I have a genius to build my dreams in wood and stone? Do I have to spread my legs for them like my Bitch-Aunt did?"

He went on in that vein the entire ride back to camp.

Djoser had Im-ho-tep!

His architect became a god!

Would any of that pack of ox-brained rock carvers we left on the

*hill ever be reborn as a divinity? Hah! Not one of them has the talent
or industry Khepera gives a dung beetle!*

Later, when we talked alone over a dinner of boiled pigeon and
black beer, he had calmed down considerably. He confided that his
morning tirade had not been directed at me, or even "those goose-
headed artisans of mine," but rather, at Rehoboam.

"He has spies everywhere. Half the farmers we have tilling the
grainfields for us are in his employ. And some prisoners have been
caught signaling to persons on the walls. By now my plan to build a
second wall and my maniacal determination to do it will have spread
throughout the camp. Rehoboam's probably heard the details already."

"I don't understand the purpose, Menkheperre. Megiddo is locked
up."

"Ah!" he said, waggling a bird leg at me, "but there are hidden
tunnels in every city. Rehoboam could escape tonight if he were
frightened enough. He stays in Megiddo because he feels secure there.
He knows I won't bargain, so he sits in his comfortable house with
his mercenaries and his loyal Judaeans at his side and waits for one
of two eventualities. First, we might pack up and go home; or second,
Mitanni and the Syrians gather enough strength to rescue him. I can't
allow either to happen."

I searched his smug mask of a face. What was he plotting in that
child's head? Then I knew, and it was so simple I could have flogged
myself—"You *want* Rehoboam to escape!"

The god bowed slightly from the waist as he summoned the huge
Yishaq with a subtle tilt of his finger. Without being told, the Habiru
poured him another beer.

"Of course," I said as if I had just snapped awake. "As long as
Rehoboam's in Megiddo, he still commands the mercenaries. But if
he runs off alone and scared, his soldiers are left for the taking!"

The god smiled and took another swallow of the thick brew. He
wiped his lips dry with a quick, elegant movement and drunkenly
threw the jug against the tent post. His voice did not seem dulled by
drink, although I was in much the same condition as my Lord. He
staggered to his feet and went to a dim corner where he uncovered a
model of his new project.

"You've heard only part of the rumor I'm spreading..." Menkheperre glanced over to the giant in the corner of the tent. "With
Yishaq's help. Look at this! I'm going to place it on a shrine

underneath Megiddo's main tower, so Rehoboam and all his people can see it every day!"

"It's magnificent!"

"Naturally. My wall, I will say to them, will rise a full eighty cubits above Megiddo's wall, proud and solid, of cedar and acantha wood. Its towers will jut like outstretched arms above my wall and at the top, it will be as wide as the causeways of Babylon! I could ride my chariot around it! From my wall, I could rain fire on the city, or divert one of the mountain streams to drown them! And then, all I need do, is watch them quake in terror at the thought!"

Menkheperre's entire body was wracked by a fit of laughter.

"Lord? What is it?" I had seen him this way before he received the Horus, but I feared how his condition might effect his holy spirit.

He fell onto a cushion and spoke between his gasps and giggles, "That's the best part of the rumor! Yishaq's telling the Judaeans that I'm building this daemonic wall to be their tomb for eternity. I want to starve them to death, he says. I want to drive them so insane from hunger and thirst that they'll drink the blood and eat the flesh of their children, he says!"

"But you don't really . . ."

"No, of course not! But they'll believe it when I unveil my model. You see why they'll cringe, 'Nemhab? My wall won't have any gates!"

Rehoboam, King of Judah and Prince of Hierosolyma, the city known as Jerusalem-Kadesh, waited for a moonless night shortly thereafter to desert Megiddo. The prince, escorted by three vassal chieftains, dug out through an abandoned well site and slipped undetected along a shallow wadi to the foothills.

There, they were met by waiting tribesmen who gave them horses and aided their flight to the Sea Peoples at Simyra. Megiddo was silent for nine days; no doubt jittery days for them. I understood. They knew nothing of Menkheperre except the rumors he wanted them to hear.

Their first and last clear view of the god had been, according to what I later learned of their odd sensibilities, quite shocking.

As soon as the battle ended and the spoils were gathered, General Djehuti of the Infantry ordered his men to hack off the hands of the eighty-three enemy dead and lay them before the king when he arrived to inspect the gate.

At the time, I thought the idea of one hundred and sixty-six severed palms upraised in supplication was a fine joke. But as I have gotten older, I realize that even these sad, uncivilized Judaeans might still weep for their dead. As ignorant and deity-poor as they were, it was not their fault they could never enter the Paradise of Duat.

Late afternoon of the ninth day, a time they believe holy, a deputation appeared. They stood within the man-sized entrance at the side of the city's main gateway. A guard of twenty men surrounded them and sent a message to the golden pavilion that Megiddans had come bearing tribute for the god.

Menkheperre invited them into his presence. We strolled under the portico and the servants placed chairs under us so we might wait for them in comfort. The god offered me a new wine that he said was a product of a far eastern province I had never heard of.

I drank it with a smile, although it was too tart for my taste. The god, however, spent a great deal of time extolling its virtues and promising to send cuttings of the plant for my vineyards at home. I thanked him profusely but managed to spill my second cup when his attention was elsewhere.

The elders of Megiddo had wended along the road from the wall and were nearly upon us when I spied Menthu at their head. His cheerful smirk alerted me. When I noticed him glancing down at the Judaeans, something struck me as odd.

It must be said that the men of Qemet are not as a general rule tall in stature. Even pharaoh, who is certainly the greatest of us all, does not rise much above four cubits even when wearing his war crown. The Judaeans and many of the northern tribes are of a more long-boned stock and so, when the group from Megiddo was climbing the incline toward us, I wondered how these men could be a head shorter than their escorts.

Menthu herded them together as they reached us. With the sun at their backs I could see very little detail, except that they were dressed in desert robes with billowing keffiyehs atop their heads that fell like capes down their backs. I caught a fast look at the face of the leader when the cloth of his headdress fell away for an instant.

He was beardless.

Menthu stepped forward, bowing. In a formal setting, it was an affront to gaze upon pharaoh without permission and the general made the request for himself and his entourage to look at the god. Tuthmose granted this with a wave of his crook and a standard response phrase that he muttered unintelligibly.

"O Mighty Horus," Menthu began, "Conqueror of Nations, Lord of the Sun and Moon . . ."

He droned on, repeating the litany the priests enjoy so much and the rest of us use to catch up on our rest, until finally arriving at his purpose.

". . . that I may inform your Magnificence of the pleas of the subjugated. Megiddo has honored you by sending the most royal among them."

With that, he stepped aside and motioned for the Megiddans to approach. Two of the draped figures crawled on their bellies until they were less than a span from the god's sacred sandal.

"Rise," ordered Tuthmose, "and speak your piece."

They got to their feet easily, but when they found themselves face to face with the Lord of Qemet, they froze. They looked at each other, nodding nervously as if they could not decide who was to speak. Their actions seemed to please old Menthu no end. Out of the corner of my eye, I saw him cover his mouth to hold back one of his sputtering guffaws.

I thought, Could he be dotty enough to play a prank on the god himself? I decided to take some action before we all missed dinner. Drawing my short sword, I poked the nearest Megiddan in the ribs lightly. "Speak, heathen! God-on-Earth waits!"

Quite suddenly, the Judaean on the other side reached over and angrily batted the flat of my blade away with his hand. "He is no heathen, Sun-worshiper!" he screamed in a high-pitched tone. "You are addressing Abijam, a royal prince of Judah, not one of the dung shovelers you usually associate with!"

I must say, I was taken aback. Otherwise I might have run the impudent fool through. Menthu, of course, dissolved in laughter. The Meggidan elders giggled and I detected a grin flare for an instant across the god's stern features.

Menkheperre stepped down from his throne and all gaiety ceased. "What is this game?" he demanded. "Cast off your garments that I might see who you are in truth—for you are surely not the council of the town."

The guards helped them disrobe quickly. And pharaoh was right, they were not the elders of Megiddo.

They were children.

And embarrassingly, my brazen challenger was a girl of no more than fourteen!

"Explain, Menthu," said the god as he slapped his hooked scepter against his palm impatiently.

Menthu was no longer smiling as he stretched out his arms and answered. "See, Majesty! Witness firsthand how your enemies in Megiddo tremble like field mice. Behold! These sorry Judaeans are so scared to meet you, they are ready to sacrifice their children."

"Shall I send them back roasted?" joked the god. The defiant girl in front went ashen, but her young companions reacted not at all. Menkheperre eyed her carefully.

Her face was broad in shape with those high, jutting cheekbones characteristic of her ill-bred kind. And yet, the delicacy of her features, a small bud of a nose and wide brown Deltan eyes, softened whatever was left of the nomad seed in her.

Standing naked, her legs looked thin and stretched tall, not unlike those of a desert fawn. They ended in the barest tuft of curling hair that guarded her woman's crease. It was still the palest pink, so pharaoh knew she had never held a man within her.

But we all thought that would be soon remedied.

She tried to cover herself with her right arm, but it only pressed her breasts together provocatively. They stood out quite a bit from her chest wall; far enough that I thought they should have sagged, but didn't. Both breasts were wide and capped by tiny hard nipples that seemed to mock the god with their bravado.

She grew nervous under his scrutiny and shyly averted her head.

Unconsciously, one hand reached for the tall boy at her side and she may have gained courage from his touch. The god turned to the boy and pointed. "Have all your elders slit their throats? Are only you infants left in Megiddo?"

The girl lifted her chin haughtily. "Glorious Tuthmose was crowned pharaoh before he learnt not to piddle on the floor. Did that make him less royal?"

Menkheperre turned his head so that only I could see his grin and whispered, "A budding Hatshepsut, this one." Then, to the girl, "Are you royal? I'd never have guessed."

"All eighty-seven of us!" she declared. "We are the eldest sons and daughters of Rehoboam, the-Gift-of-Yahweh. We are the grandchildren of Shelomoh *He-Who-Housed-the-One-God-in-the-Golden-Tabernacle.* And our great grandsire was the Mighty *Dawidh-of-the-Thousand-Legends.*"

Pharaoh held up his hand. "Enough of that, girl! We shall all assume your lineage goes back to the Creation." He beckoned her and she took one tentative step forward. "What are you called?"

"Raheal, Majesty."

"Ah! A civil answer. Tell me, princess, have all of your brothers been struck dumb? Why must I negotiate a surrender with a female?"

"My mother is of Qemet, O Pharaoh. I am the only one among us who speaks the Nile tongue."

The god crooked his finger in her direction. "Closer," he whispered.

As she approached Menkheperre, Raheal shivered in the wind. Noticing this, the god bade his servant-priest to doff his leopard cloak and place it around her bare shoulders. She fell at his feet, tears pouring from beneath her tightly closed lids.

Menkheperre raised her up and spoke in his most gentle voice, saying, "None of that, my brave sister. No harm will come to you or those in your care. As I am the Horus, I swear it."

"You are more kind than I had been told, Majesty."

The god placed his sacred palm on her cheek. "My heart is saddened that your father should abandon you like this."

"Oh, no, Majesty, he would never forsake us," she tried to explain. "He sails north to plead for us. He promised to rescue us when the weather turns fair."

As a general, I could not stop the admiring grin that appeared on my face. The Tuthmose had elicited with a tender word what hours of torture might not have pulled from the stubborn whelp.

Her unguarded tongue had revealed that the treacherous Rehoboam was taking the sea route up the coast to Mitanni to gather a force for a spring invasion of the southern plain.

"We have brought tribute, Majesty," the girl Raheal said. "A lot of gold. We all gave our jewelry. But the Judges of the town feared to bring it out. They sent us because we are too royal to be a great insult to you and too young to be of any consequence if you murdered us."

Menkheperre pondered this a bit, then raised his chest up as we had seen him do often before making one of his pronouncements.

"Raheal," he began solemnly, "you will return to the city tomorrow with a scroll that you can translate into Judaean for the elders. It will tell them what they must do. Further, it will place in your hands, and in the hands of your royal brother here, the power to carry out my wishes. Will you do that for me?"

"I am but an unworthy maiden, Glorious One."

Menkheperre smiled. "I do not find you thus. In fact, I will you to stay with me tonight. Share my bed. In the morning, you will awaken transformed and ride forth into Megiddo eager to take on any task."

The blockade of Megiddo was raised the following day.

Menkheperre sent me into the city to escort Princess Rahael and her half-brother, the crown prince Abijam. Pharaoh bedecked the girl in jewels and strung her neck with bands of gilt and lapis. The god's own serving women had worked for most of the morning on her makeup, painting her lids with the black udjat eyes of Re and fitting her head with a plaited wig entwined by slender cords of gold.

I noticed a secret smile on her face as I pulled my chariot up to the palanquin that carried her and Rehoboam's young heir. A sweet, knowing smile. Our eyes locked and with the boldness of a queen, she did not release my stare.

I nodded and urged my horses ahead, aware of her newfound interest in tan, hairless men from the Nile.

I entered the city, the first Qemetan to do so, and was met by a phalanx of bowing men. I shouted at them to stand back and Menes, my interpreter, repeated it, yelling in a manner that would have frightened even myself had I not known what a coward the man was in battle.

The assembly, largely priests and merchant lords, sent up a piercing wail like grieving peasant women. I was unsure if they were cheering me or not, but I acknowledged them with a regal nod as they cleared a path for my horses and men.

I deployed my guards to the walls and called a meeting at the town center. As ordered, during the gathering I deferred to the royal children in most things. At first, this angered the Megiddan elders, who sought to establish themselves as friends of Qemet now that the danger had subsided.

Raheal showed us what passed for a royal palace and we plundered it of anything of value or utility. Quite honestly, the house was less impressive than my own farm back in No-Amun, and my people are of far lower station than these princes who are supposedly anointed in that strange, singular spirit of theirs.

I led my troops on a street-by-street survey of Megiddo.

We took all of their horses, 2232 in total, but it being after foaling season, nearly two-hundred were still showing their birth coats. They proved no problem, however. Most of the colts were happy to frolic about after their mothers on their spidery legs and to follow the mares into our corrals.

The cattle and other livestock were more difficult, if only for the enormity of the task. The Megiddan herd, according to the tallymen, numbered in excess of 21,000 animals, not counting the 1,929 bulls. They needed separate handling, of course.

As did the slaves.

Of war goods, we stripped the entire city. Even taking the bronze and black metal from the armorer's workshops. In all, we found 924 chariots, whole or in parts, and sent them laden to overflowing with bows, arrows, lances, armor, and axes to the foot of pharaoh's golden tent.

There, I gathered all the elders and Judges and priests and Syrian princes who still hid in Megiddo and shoved them down to the ground before his throne. One by one they swore to never again revolt against the might of Qemet.

Pharaoh accepted their pledge and sent the Megiddans back to their ruined city. As for the Syrians, in exchange for their loyalty, the Tuthmose allowed them to return to their homeland.

To celebrate his victory, Menkheperre hosted a banquet that brought together his staff, the generals of the war council, and a few of the Judaean nobility. Raheal requested the honor of presenting a gold candle holder to the god. She said it was the sacred Menorah and among the locals was considered magical.

Not to be outdone, the princeling Abijam provided his father's dancers for our entertainment. For some reason, except for an exposed midsection, they performed fully clothed. This merely bored us Qemetans who are spoiled by the small, nude, acrobatic female dancers of home. To a woman, these Meggidans had thick middles devoid of muscle tone. Their idea of sensuous movement was to roll their layers of fat in hideous quivering waves.

While their gyrations were at their most convulsive, Menkheperre took me aside. "You have spent many hours with the princess of Judah," he stated flatly.

"The girl Raheal?" I said, wondering at his purpose.

"She is a pretty thing."

"A child, Menkheperre."

He shrugged. "Of course, a child. Had her father spoken the same insults to me, his head would be gracing my tent pole. But we must tolerate this lovely heathen princess of yours, 'Nemhab."

"Not my princess, Menkheperre. As I recall, that privilege was yours."

He gave a resigned nod, a sad little gesture I thought. "But not soon again," he said conspiratorially. "I can confess it to you, my closest friend, that the virgin was eager to please and I had looked forward to acting the tutor. But I am to marry Ano, daughter of Jeroboam, as a sign of my support for him and his kingship of Israel. And there lies a problem. My councilors think it might be unseemly and less than politic for me to also take the daughter of Jeroboam's rival into the same House-of-the-Secluded."

"Yes," I agreed. "With the Yahweh-worshipers split into two factions, the last thing you need is a war in the harem."

"Good. Then you'll help?"

"How, Majesty?"

"Well, you know this Raheal is half-Qemetan, don't you?"

"Yes. Indeed." As she led me about Megiddo, all of her questions seemed to turn on what she had heard about Qemet. She confessed to not believing her mother's stories about the temples that rose ten times the height of a man on bright lotus-tipped colonnades, until she had seen the magnificence of pharaoh.

She knew that Queen Hatshepsut, who had bedded down with her grandfather, had carved a huge temple out of a mountainside to commemorate the event.

"I heard that one from the prophet," said Raheal. She had explained through full, pouting lips that she and her brother were taught by an old Qemetan her mother had discovered in Sidon. The prophet, as they called the teacher, regaled them with tales of his home.

Menkheperre beckoned me closer. "Did you know that when old Sennemut designed that temple, he put portraits of himself in Hatshepsut's private chapel? I know it's a sacrilege, but he was clever and only put those portraits behind doors, so when the priests enter, they're hidden!"

"You've removed them, of course."

"What?" The god laughed. "And ruin a good anecdote? Go on 'Nemhab, you were telling me about the girl."

I sat back in my place and continued. Raheal, I told him, begged me for more details of the Black Land. For the ten nights we spent together in Megiddo, she curled up at my feet, rapt. I would close my eyes and it was as if I had released my ba to fly down the familiar highways and hover above the god-scaled buildings of paint and marble and stone.

"Her mother was the only daughter of the ambassador Hatshepsut left in Israel after her assignation with that tribal chief Shelomoh, the one some call Solomon. That makes her of prime stock, 'Nemhab. There would be no disgrace should you take her into your house."

"I doubt if that would be politic either, Majesty. If the girl has noble blood, it would certainly insult her kin were I to bring her back as a slave."

Menkheperre placed both thin hands on my shoulders. "Not as your slave, O dense Amenemhab. I want my sweet Raheal to return to Qemet as your wife!"

CHAPTER SEVENTEEN ☥

As the winds off the Western Sea grew cold, we Qemetans prepared to decamp. The god left General Thutiys and a small, but well-armed garrison to govern Megiddo as his caravans packed and moved on toward Jerusalem and the allies of Mitanni.

The first campaign of the third Tuthmose—*May His Glorious Name Rule For Time Eternal*—had ended in triumph.

It had lasted 175 days.

I did not see Menkheperre for three years. While he took his main force north in pursuit of wily Rehoboam, pharaoh sent me at the head of my Braves into the Sinai and finally home to Karnak.

Raheal, my bride, awaited me at my father's house. I had sent her back to Qemet on the first caravan after the ceremony. I am now ashamed to admit it, but once she had left, I put her out of my mind entirely.

I had driven my chariot unescorted down the roadway of uneven stones that led from the capital. I had lost the Aten by the time I reached our estate and took the last league slowly.

When I pulled into the courtyard, the house was brilliant with torchlight. My servants had gone ahead to prepare, but I had not expected the joyous homecoming awaiting me.

Our old porter ran out from the loggia, but was soon outdistanced by two of my greyhounds who leapt upon me the instant I jumped off the step-rail.

"Stay, you two!" shouted the porter. "Leave the young master alone!" The dogs didn't heed him and I fear that was my fault. I was on the ground enjoying hugging them and kissing them and feeling their hot breath and wet tongues all over my face in return.

"Hah, Ptah-em-saf." I laughed. "What a greeting!"

The reedlike old man pouted until I commanded the dogs to race back to the kennels. He helped me to my feet and had the stablemen attend to my chariot. As he brushed me off, he explained that my father had prepared a feast in my honor.

"I have laid out a fine linen robe for you," he said steering me to the side door. "Why don't we scrape some of that road grime from you before we present you to the old governor?"

Ptah-em-saf led me around to the inside stairs and directly to my rooms where two body servants waited for us. The women stripped me and wiped me down with moist, scented cloths.

The porter handed me a cup of barley beer that was wonderfully pungent. I drank it down as my arms, chest, and legs were scraped clean of my morning unguents and replaced by fresh oils.

My fatigue seemed to drain from me and I suspected that Ptah had added one of his stimulating roots to the brew. My feet were cleansed, massaged, and placed into fine calfskin sandals with comfortable soles of braided papyrus.

I dressed in the white robe Ptah had mentioned and chose a thinly wrought lapis necklace and gold wristbands to go with it. One of the women left, but came back in a few seconds with an exquisite ceremonial wig in her hands. The thin strands of hair were twisted and tied in an intricate pattern fit for the god himself.

"A gift from the governor," explained Ptah.

"I'll be sure to bless him for his thoughtfulness," I said. "Go and tell him I'll be ready to meet his guests presently."

Ptah sent the women away, bowed, and was gone. I sat by my window for a few moments, somehow more on edge than before a battle. Five seasons, perhaps more, had sped by since last I had seen my father.

He would be aged now. I remember the signs of it before I had been called to service under the god. He had taken to wearing tunics and robes of a heavier cloth, even under Aten's heat. I think it was to mask the sagging muscles hanging off his arms and chest.

Not that I remembered him as a vain man, but I believe that he

saw his aging body as a symbol of his waning power as the new
pharaoh ascended to the golden chair.

The man had possessed such a commanding presence. I found it
impossible to stand and walk down the stairs into the central hall,
fearful that this giant of a man had begun a dreadful decline.

Searching for anything to delay my appearance at the feast, I ab-
sently picked up the makeup brush and the polished copper mirror
from the table at my side. The paint pot held a thick green paste, a
green as dark as tree leaves at midnight.

I had outlined both eyes in udjat shape when I sensed a person
standing in the doorway. A serving girl, I presumed. "Tell my father,
I'll be there in a minute or so," I said, waving her away impatiently.

Instead of bowing and backing out, she entered. I looked up, about
to scold her for her impudent behavior, when she reached the light
of an oil lamp. It was only then I saw it was Raheal.

My chamber stayed silent for the endless seconds until she spoke,
her voice soft, but not subservient. "Have I changed so greatly, husband?" she asked.

At first, I could say nothing. In truth, she had not merely changed;
she had metamorphosed. Her face and body had rounded beneath her
thin robe. It seemed that her Judaean blood had all collected in her
chest, but the effect was more than pleasing to me.

"My Judaean princess?"

"Your father's women have taught me the ways of Qemet these
three long seasons, my noble, absent husband."

"Which ways are those?"

She moved toward me, opening her linen grown. "They are not
for telling," she purred.

That night, we did not attend the party in my honor, although I
sent Ptah with our regrets. I said the journey home had exhausted
me. And while it was true I spent that night and much of the next
day on my back, my bride saw to it that I hardly slept at all.

CHAPTER EIGHTEEN

I acted the husband throughout that year. My father parceled his land between myself and Menna, a son by his Second Woman. Menna's life had disappointed him. It was a burden my half-brother carried with him as a fact, never complaining about his fate, but never fully accepting it either.

In fact, Menna never said much about anything. He had turned into a dull, but hard-working man. As far back as my memory shines on my life, I cannot recall when we ever quarreled.

Upon the Emergence, when Mother Nile subsided after the annual flood, I would take Raheal into No-Amun where she could shop for toys and trinkets in the stalls near the temple precinct while I conferred at the Great House with Rekhmire, the vizier.

During those times, my friend and Lord, Menkheperre, rarely stayed in the capital. He was never happier than when on a campaign and often ventured too far into one of the vassal states to safely return to Qemet after the fighting season ended.

I remarked on this one night when the vizier summoned me to his residence on the west bank for a private supper. Rekhmire, who had known the court under Hatshepsut, was not surprised. "He does that on purpose," he said between bites of sweet pink melon.

"Just to irk you?" I teased.

He declined to take the bait. "Doesn't bother me in the least. I'm never happier than when you and pharaoh are off on one of your campaigns. By and large, your little ventures pay for themselves and I'm left to handle the day-to-day as I see fit."

Rekhmire clapped. A second later, two serving girls were clearing the melon rinds from our places. Mine, a dusky beauty no more than fourteen, brushed her young firm breasts across my forearm and allowed one to linger in the crook as she scooped some stray seeds into her palm.

The vizier, so it seemed, chose his slave women for more than kitchen drudgery. His server poured beer into both our cups and left. My girl hurried after her, but spun back at the drape to take a last look at me.

She was there one second, and then she was concealed behind the waving curtain. Someone in Rekhmire's household, perhaps the sly old man himself, had taught her well. It confirmed my suspicions about the evening. The vizier wanted something from me.

Rekhmire drained the last of his beer and we retired to the comfort of the north loggia where the breezes brought the scent of reeds off the Nile.

My host stood at the low wall gazing at the enormity of the Temple of Karnak across the calm waters. Then, he motioned to the northeast.

"Out there, in the savage places beyond our borders, the boy is unencumbered by his kingship. He is glad to leave the minutiae of running his empire to me and the nomarchs."

Unlike pharaoh, the vizier was not a man easily amused by such banter. In that, he reminded me of his friend, my noble father. He reclined with his back against the wall, folding his hands over his round belly. He noted my disturbed expression.

"You don't agree, son?"

I answered bluntly. "You make it sound as if Menkheperre refuses to honor his responsibilities. That's not true, Wise One. Pharaoh loves his people. He fights alongside us. He has never shirked."

"It's not that, young general. Every time he enters the city gates or rides down the avenue of the lion-gods, his stomach pulls tight. He begins to sweat under the double crown—and not from the heat."

"I can't believe Menkheperre is frightened of anything!"

"Oh, it's a child's fear, Amenemhab. The whelp never knew a secure day in No-Amun. At least not after his father's death. You wouldn't remember, but the Second Tuthmose was a huge man, the size of the venerated Kamose, it was said.

"But young Menkheperre saw his father sicken in front of him. He lingered well past winter, but when he finally lost the Horus and went west to Duat, the man weighed less than a sack of wheat."

"It must have been a terrible time."

"Chaos. Everyone suspected pharaoh's sister Hatshepsut had poisoned him, but what could we do? She came upon the name Bitch-Queen honestly, and with the help of Sennemut, held a power over the court that was not merely political."

"Were they daemons? I've heard that."

Rekhmire grinned, shifting his position so he could speak in confidence without a servant overhearing through the window. "I was a young priest then," he said softly. "To me, Sennemut was more of a god on earth than any pharaoh I had known. Imagine—the man appeared one day, a lowly provincial cleric from one of Amun's little outposts up in the delta. They say he traveled south from the old capital at Mennufer with a library of ancient papyri he had discovered in an old ruin."

"And he gained admittance to the Great House?"

The wise vizier sat there like a man under a spell, a spell of remembrance. "A strange time. Not as practical as these days have become. Anyone could petition the god then. I was not there, of course. But I have heard that when the Queen first saw Sennemut lift his eyes to her from where he knelt—she was unable to move. And when he spoke, it was as if the sound had crawled inside of her and was echoing within her heart."

"Then he was an enchanter," I ventured.

"In many ways, my pup. They say he had a phallus as long as Min's—*May-He-Make-the-Black-Land-Ever-Fertile*. But, that too, is not from personal knowledge. My opinion is less carnal. I think Sennemut offered a gift of the Old Magic to Hatshepsut."

"Old Magic?"

Rekhmire held out his hand for me to help him to his feet. "Walk with me, son." He took my arm and we strolled onto the colonnade. A torchlit path led around his sacred pool. The wily old man, a survivor of a lifetime of palace plotting, was clearly not about to come to the point of my visit unless he could shield us from interested ears.

He beckoned me to his gate, which opened to a spectacular view of the Luxor temple bathed in the orange glow of a thousand open torches and oil lamps.

His mood turned reflective. "Today, we sit in our cities, behind these bright walls, entrapped by our comforts," he said. "We are dutiful or slack in our rituals as our fancy takes us. We go to the festivals and ask the gods to ease our way through this Life that we may enjoy the Second Life in even more splendor. Except, we're deluded. Oh, the Old Magic used to work. Qemet was born when the first prophets learned the Mysteries. In those days, we had some control over the Spectral World. But now, our chants are as unheard as screams in the desert."

"What do you mean, sir?" I asked.

"Not here." Rekhmire called for his chariot, a heavy model fashioned from rich Nubian wood that shone purple in the moonlight.

As we mounted, he requested that I take the reins. He made a show of telling his groom that he wanted the young general to test the limits of his new matched Arabians and therefore, we might be gone for hours.

Once we reached the road, the vizier directed me to the southern boulevard. We rode on for some time in virtual silence. Every now and then, the old man would tap my shoulder and point to a side trail.

Invariably, this took us further inland into the foothills. We passed the Village of Tomb Builders near the Valley of the Kings. The chariot had traversed a series of high ridges that separated the Black Land from the desert before I summoned the courage to ask Rekhmire about the Magic.

Rekhmire held tight to the rail and stared back toward the city. "The knowledge of the Second Existence is known only to the hereditary prophet/priest, the Ue'b, and is imparted to our poor pharaoh only upon his coronation." His mouth curled into a deep, unconscious smile that chilled me. "I've learned the truth of that Mystery, General," he whispered. "And as dangerous as it may prove for the both of us, I must share it with you."

"Enlightenment is not for ordinary men," I protested. I admit, the thought of learning pharaoh's secrets petrified me.

Rekhmire agreed, but he grasped my hand and added, "Our motive must never be curiosity, son. I would never ask you to gamble your ka on our success, if saving the Lord of the Great House and Qemet itself was not our sacred duty."

The paired Arabians slowed to a cautious walk as we rolled into a rift canyon. I was navigating by moonlight and the high cliff walls now blocked most of it. The shadows were as black as any I had seen so close to the city fires of No-Amun.

Rekhmire bade me stop. I tethered the horses and joined the vizier, who was striking a flint at the torch. It ignited quickly and he handed it to me.

"Hold it high, son," he ordered. The light revealed a deep cleft in the rock face. Rekhmire trudged toward it and I followed closely behind, kicking sand and stones into my sandals.

"Watch yourself. There's a step here."

In fact, there were fifteen steep stairs cut into the stone, leading down to the base of the fissure. He took the burning brand from me and scurried ahead down the incline to a golden portal decorated with the prayers of Osiris. The vizier pushed it wide, letting me enter ahead of him.

At first, it was too dim to see anything. The air smelled of chalk and damp straw. Looking down at the dancing shadows, I saw why. The floor was covered by spongy reed mats of the kind used by workmen to protect their knees.

"Can you see it?" my host asked.

"See what, sir?" I was reluctant to move out of the small circle of light cast through the doorway by Rekhmire's torch.

"The wall paintings, of course!" he said as he came up by my left side. "My Chief Wife discovered an incredible young artist called Nefretkhau. Ever heard of him? I stole him from work on the Royal Tomb. I know that's naughty, but after all, I'll be sealed in this place ages before the Tuthmose needs his done."

Rekhmire stooped down and touched the fire to the top of an earthenware lamp bowl. Its wick, soaked in sesame oil and salted, ignited to produce a pure smokeless flame. Then, in turn, the vizier went to each floor lamp and lit them, until the room was awash in a bright, warm glow.

"There. Have you ever seen anything so lovely?"

I confessed that I had not been inside many tombs, but that his death home was as splendid as any I could imagine. We were standing in the front chapel, which was largely complete. The curved ceiling had been stained with azurite to represent the starry sky. Below, a frieze of sky deities marched in single file across the horizon. On the far wall, twin udjat eyes were following us from just below the vertex of the arch.

Horus spread his all-sheltering wings over the doorway to the burial chamber. Except for a few patches where the plasterers had not finished smoothing the layers of gypsum and whitewash for the painters, the walls were crowded with images of gods and men.

A younger, slimmer version of Rekhmire sat on his chair of office as his wives and naked children attended him. The Third Tuthmose himself, loomed ten feet high on the wall opposite with a discreetly shorter Rekhmire at his side.

Various nomarchs were facing them, sized according to their rank, accepting their year's allotment of grain. All the figures were drawn in great detail, which was not the current style.

Pharaoh's own tomb, which sadly I have viewed since, was decorated in the old-style stick figures that make the walls resemble the quick strokes made by scribes as they fashion the sacred papyri.

Rekhmire would have none of this archaism.

"My stone coffin is being quarried now down south," said the vizier, his voice buoyant, almost childlike in anticipation. "This will be a marvelous place for my body."

Then, he took up the torch and left momentarily to check, I assumed, the progress in one of the antechambers. While he was gone, I read the inscriptions written vertically down each wall.

It was ceremonial writing, in the old picture manner, but I was able to get the sense of it. They were copies of religious texts recounting the journey of Re's nightly trek through the Underworld. Re was obviously the vizier's personal protector.

One cannot help but say His Holy Name twice each time one says *Rekhmire*!

Rekhmire returned presently with two folding benches left by the painters in the sarcophagus chamber. "We can talk now." He spoke in a harsh whisper. His wet, hot breath stung my ear. "I made my supplications in the bare room. In here, not even the gods can listen through the din of the painted prayers."

I was incredulous. "The gods can hear what's written on these walls?"

"Of course," he said, releasing his grip. "Why else do you think the picture-words are sacred?"

"That's why we traveled all this way?"

"Precisely. Look, earthly spies I can handle, but no one, not even a nosy god can know I'm passing the Mystery to you."

I tried to agree, but my tongue had gone thick and dry. It stuck to the roof of my mouth. Subtle tremors shook me. I wondered what sort of bargain I had struck. The gods made the rules and they sent down the word that only the high priest and pharaoh could learn the Mystery.

What if they were the only humans holy enough to cope with the knowledge and not go mad? Rekhmire knew, or so he said. Might he be the maddest one of all?

"Why me?"

Rekhmire whispered with an unlikely sweetness, "I've judged men each day of my life. The fact I have grown old and still perform my small services for the god is proof enough of my talent for choosing the right men to serve under me and the right friends to assist me with the burdens of it all. I knew you as a naked, suckling infant, Amenemhab. I was often at your father's villa—observing you."

He sat on the bench next to me and took my hand as tenderly as a father might.

"Who do you think arranged for you to take studies at the Great House? And who placed you beside the boy Menkheperre so that you might become his oldest and most trusted friend?"

"Arranged?"

"I take little of the credit. I saw loyalty and intelligence and heart in you. A young god needs an honest confidante, don't you think? A boy his own age."

"And this makes me your creature?"

"No, General. You are your own man. As ever. My confession merely shows that our interests coincide when it comes to pharaoh."

"Give me a moment to sort this all out. A soldier likes to feel he has some control of his destiny. How detailed is your plan for the rest of my life, Vizier?"

"Your name has been mentioned as my successor. When Anubis weighs my heart, I want it known I left a Qemet stronger and more secure for my being there. I would trust you in that, Amenemhab."

Wearily, Rekhmire rose, and with his back turned, stroked the wall painting of Menkheperre as if it were a votive object. He was mumbling a few barely audible phrases, prayers perhaps, then fell silent.

Slowly, his great round head rotated toward me. Tears were in his eyes.

"Let's get this over with, General." His voice kept the same tone of calm confidence I expected. The man was more solid than the onyx statue of him standing behind me. I moved the bench over to it, bracing my shoulders against the dark pedestal.

"I'm ready, sir. For the sake of my friend. Where do we begin?"

"In the delta."

CHAPTER NINETEEN

I had heard the tale of Osiris since my mother first took me to hear my father take his turn as priest at Re's temple in No-Amun. The story told in the chants differed a bit from Rekhmire's version.

The Horite god was never mentioned, for instance, but I put that down to jealousy in Duat. Imagine a foreign god taking credit for the greatest miracle in Qemet's history. I doubt Amun-Re would think kindly of that notion.

Isis and Osiris lived in Qemet before the Black Land had a name. Osiris bore the mark of Heaven. His name would not have been worshiped for all time had that not been so. He and Isis, his sister and Chief Wife, ruled at Dedu, now called Busiris, where the Mother of Rivers enters the Great Sea. Dedu, then, was little more than low, clustered buildings of mud and reed. The city wall would not be built for six generations.

Osiris earned his warrior's reputation by trailing the Horite raiders to their stronghold by the mount of Seir. He met them in the shadow of the sacred crag and—with sword, lance, and fire—destroyed them. In triumph, he climbed Mount Seir, but when he reached the summit, where no Horite had ever ventured in their memory, Osiris saw the glowing face of their god.

It was not an effigy or some crude idol as he had expected. Rather, it was a loop of scarlet crystal that sat on a bar and crosspiece, much like the hilt of a sword.

When he took it in his scraped hand, the bleeding stopped and his wounds folded into themselves until all traces of them disappeared. When Osiris returned from the mountaintop, the strange god was safe inside his pack. Osiris and his clan rode back to Dedu with the Horite nation bound and tethered behind them.

In the city, Isis waited with Set, the king's young brother who itched to kill Osiris, if a way could be found. Murdering Osiris, he knew, could not be done with Isis at his side.

His brother's wife was a witch woman, schooled in the weirding ways. Had she not taken the fabled Horite god into her private chapel?

One winter day, Isis asked Nephthys, her sister and also Set's Chief Wife, to her chamber. Each took a half of the nest of a weaver bird and read the pattern of prophecy inside. "The divination says, my own Lord, Set is destined to rule the Black Land," Nephthys said.

Isis looked at her, puzzled. "But my half says that Osiris will give me a son, and he shall be king in Dedu and all the length of the Nile."

Set overheard them and realized that Osiris must die while still childless, or he would never sit on the throne. Always clever, Set thought of a plan. Secretly, Set stole into his brother's bedroom and, using a builder's rod, took an exact measure of him.

Every year the nine clans celebrated the birth of Re-Horakhty, the blending of the sky and sun which causes the Nile to rise. During the final feast, Set asked Osiris his opinion on the quality of a richly adorned chest he had newly built.

Osiris could not believe its beauty. He wanted the chest, that was evident, but instead of voicing his desire, he simply smiled at his kinsman and replied, "It is well made."

"Good! Then I shall give it away as an example of what we deltans can do!"

Osiris lunged after the bait. "A gift?" he asked. "A gift to whom?"

Set looked thoughtful. "Well, I want it to be a fitting present." All eyes were on him as his gaze circled the hall. And when all was quiet, he began to laugh.

"A fitting present! That's it! I'll give the chest to the man who fits it exactly when he lies inside!"

With that, he had his men come forward and, one by one, they climbed into the box. None were the right size. Finally, only Osiris remained.

"I would not insult your dignity to suggest you enter the chest, dear brother. So, I will have to take it back home with me—"

"Wait!" Osiris interrupted. "We are all comrades here, and I think that prize might hold me." The great chief marched smartly to the chest and stepped inside. "A perfect fit!" he announced. "The chest is mine!"

"Enjoy it!" Set spat out his words contemptuously as he slammed the lid down hard. It was the last thing the exalted Osiris saw in his First Life. The assassins dragged the chest to the Nile and heaved it into the water. A tidal bore carried the chest up the delta and spilled it into the Great Sea.

Set and his followers came to reign in Dedu and all the region of the delta. Nephthys replaced her sister, Isis, as queen, but there was no enmity between them. Nephthys loved Osiris and knew nothing of the conspiracy to kill him.

One of many nights when Nephthys was left alone, Isis came to her balcony. Isis asked if she remembered the prophecy of the weaver's nest. Nephthys did, saying that only her half had come to be. Osiris had disappeared before giving Dedu an heir.

"No," Isis said, "the son of Osiris is in my belly. But I fear he will never see life if Set learns of him."

"Hear me, Isis." Nephthys's voice was soothing. "As Anubis is judge of my heart, I swear the son of Osiris will be born and sheltered from harm."

That night, Nephthys placed Isis under the protection of Osiris's own guards, the trusted Scorpions. Named for the deadly sting of their swords, these seven men fought shoulder to shoulder with Osiris in every battle and were loyal to his clan only. In secret, they escorted Isis through the papyrus swamps to the shrine of Uatchet, *Guardian-of-the-Sky-at-the-Sun's-Rising,* on the floating island of Chemmis, a place Nephthys knew well.

It was where old priestesses went after their fertile days, or when the yearly rites had either withered their wombs or filled them with the children of the raping mob.

At first, Buto, the high prioress, barred the door. She was reluctant to hide Isis, fearing a repayment in blood from Set. One of the Scorpions burst inside and touched his blade to the throat of Buto's young son.

He shouted that Isis was to be the Divine Mother and, if the son of Osiris did not live, all the priestess's children would suffer the same fate.

When Isis heard the threat, she ran inside and slapped away the man's knife. Then, humbly, she bowed to the prioress and begged her forgiveness for the horror spoken in her name.

As she prepared to depart, Buto fell at her feet and blocked her way. "Please stay," she entreated. "I was afraid, but your selflessness shamed me. You kept my son from harm. Can I do less for you? We have skilled midwives and your son can hide easily among all our fatherless boys."

"If you'll be in danger because of me . . ."

"Cousin, we are all of the same clan. Your peril is ours. Besides, we're forgotten here, and the shifting reeds hide us from any stray travelers."

Isis remained and in time mothered a boy she named Horus after an aspect of his sacred guardian, hawk-headed Khensu. With her child safe, Isis decided to hunt for her husband's body. Before she left, she lifted the infant up and rested him on her chest.

"I may not hold you again until after your lock of youth is shaved, but I swear I'll be back. And, little Horus, when I do, we'll be riding into Dedu beside your father Osiris—alive again!"

The chronicles tell endless stories of that voyage and the many adventures of the questing queen and her crew. In time, all save Isis were dead and she was left destitute on the shores of Byblos. There, a young princess of the land took pity on the aging woman and made her nurse to the King's heir.

After many years, Isis discovered that Osiris's coffin had landed on those shores and become entangled in a growing terebinth tree. That very tree had been felled and used as a column in the Hall of Pillars within the Great Palace of Byblos.

The princess discovered Isis clawing at the polished wood, ripping out splinters with her nails. As the princess approached her, Isis suddenly glared into her eyes with an animal fury.

"Woman!" she screamed, "Bring me the king, your father! Tell him that Isis, clan sister and Chief Wife to the noble Osiris, awaits him in the council hall!"

The commotion awakened the Lord of Byblos from his midday nap, and he followed his men into the Hall of Pillars. "Who disturbs me in the heat of the day?" yelled the king, his lips puckering into an annoyed grimace.

Isis rose to her feet and extended her arm in greeting. "I am the queen to your murdered ally, Osiris of Dedu."

The king was not easily convinced. "All I see is an old crone whose head has been cooked by the sun."

"Believe this!" Isis pulled the ceremonial axe from its honored place above the throne and took a whack at the pillar. It split along the seam and the chest shifted, one corner tumbling through the crack.

"By the gods!" The king took a sharp breath of utter astonishment. He turned to his guards and ordered them to pull the coffin from the pillar where it had been entombed. Isis wrapped Osiris's body in gauze and returned with him to the delta. Her first stop in the Black Land was, of course, to the temple of Uatchet on Chemmis to see Horus.

Buto found her at the dock. "He's gone, Daughter of Heaven. My women protected him to manhood, as we promised. To look at him, there is no doubt from whose loins he sprung. He's the image of the great chief, my lady. Horus has one dream—to get into battle with Set and avenge the both of you."

"So, he thinks I'm dead," said Isis. A heaviness weighed down her voice. "I'll see him in Dedu."

Dedu lay inside the convergence of two Nile tributaries.

Two ferries, one to the east and another to the south, linked the village to the caravan routes. North of Dedu the terrain was marshy, but provided a direct land passage to the Great Sea. Without a city wall, Set's stronghold relied on shoreline barricades to protect it from riverborn marauders.

Isis sailed north during one dark night with a squad of Scorpions. A coffin shaped like Osiris was strapped to the deck. The boat took the current and remained undetected as it kept a course to the unlit center of the waterway.

To herself, Isis praised friendly Khensu, the Moon Lord, for not showing the glow of his face that night. As Re's gold chariot neared, tinting the eastern shore, the dhow reached Dedu.

Fortunately, the temple sacred to Isis occupied a small island just south of the town. In the years since she left, the priests had abandoned the wood and mud structure. Set wanted no memory of Isis to remain and left the building to the thick weeds and the encroaching river tide.

Silently, they docked out of sight of the far shore in case Set had erected a guardpost there, but when they came to the front of the temple, the side facing Dedu, they found the island deserted.

The Scorpions placed Osiris inside between the statues of Re and Geb and opened the coffin, so that his wrapped body could be seen. Isis told the men to leave and return to the dhow.

The crew departed, leaving Isis alone with her husband's shell. Without an audience, Isis relaxed. The flames licking from the wall lamps warmed the chapel and gave it a soft orange glow that made the stone gods seem flesh.

Isis fell to her face and chanted to each god in turn, ending with Khepera, the beetle-headed Lord. Khepera was the rising sun, who had been born full grown from his own body.

The prayer Isis sent up to Khepera was especially fervent, being he controlled resurrection and that was her business that night. When done, the old queen struggled to her feet. She spent the next few minutes reorienting herself to the place.

It had been a lifetime since she had used it as her sanctuary, and the priests who had been in charge all that time had moved things around. Half the gods were in the wrong niches, and the altar was turned a full ninety degrees from where it was two decades before.

No matter. The Holy of Holies was where she left it, standing in the shadows under the lowest part of the roof.

It was a cedar booth, curtained at the front and just large enough to house a small god and a single priest. An obelisk, ten cubits tall, guarded its entrance.

It had remained untouched as Isis knew it would be. This was her temple and, as its prophetess, she was the only person permitted inside its Holy of Holies—under penalty of dismemberment.

Isis drew aside the filthy, tattered drape and stepped inside the box. It was like walking into a cave. Her shadow cut off the light from the chapel, and she had to feel around for a lamp. She found one, lit it from a reed brand, and watched as the Holy of Holies began to glow.

In the center stood a platform holding a tiny votive statue of Khepera. Isis felt under it for a hidden catch. Her fingertip exactly matched a notch in the wood, and she pressed down hard. Immediately, a drawer slid out from below the shelf.

The Horite Cross lay inside, wrapped in a papyrus mat.

Isis took it to Osiris. She threw open the lid of his box and stared down at him, squeezed tightly by the bleached cloth strips binding him from his neck to his feet. She placed the cross on his chest and unfolded the papyrus envelope.

The cross lay there, picking up the firelight as it had the first day Osiris showed it to her twenty years before. The prize had not aged. It had been carved from a single block of milky red quartz polished so smooth that the surface seemed wet as a crying eye.

A strip of blue-gray mineral was set into the loop with such perfection that it required no bonding to hold it firmly in place.

Isis grasped the handle as if it were a lifeline. The cross felt heavy in her hand, but she managed to raise it above her head and pronounce the blessing of Khepera to bestow life eternal.

Then, Isis took the object to the front of the chapel and set it facing the front entrance. She returned to Osiris and lifted his thin, stiff body into her arms. With some effort, she dragged his body to the obelisk and propped him up against it like a board.

Finished, Isis opened the temple doors, sat down on the front step, and waited.

Across the water at Dedu, the market stalls were filling with peddlers and traders. They were the first to notice the dhow circling Isis's temple isle. As the Aten brightened the morning sky, a hubbub started among the townspeople.

Many were pointing toward the island.

A woman, a priestess, stood in the tall temple doorway.

"Impossible, but she is the image of the vanished queen," they murmured.

"Could she have returned? Could she really be Isis?"

Soon, they were lining the shore, trying to get a closer look. On the island, Isis stepped aside to let the direct light enter the portal.

When the full force of the sun struck the quartz cross, a strange thing happened. Going through the loop, the quality of the light changed, focusing into a crimson beam that shot in a perfect line to where Osiris stood.

The light seemed to splatter when it hit, until his body was washed in the same warm glow.

It radiated onto the obelisk and crept over the entire surface. When it reached the pyramidion on top, the light refocused again and turned into a stark brilliance the color of rubies.

That moment, Isis rushed inside the temple toward her husband.

The light cascaded downward, producing sparks as it fell across Osiris's shoulders. His body jerked as if struck by a volley of arrows, and Isis ran to hold him.

The light grew suddenly in its intensity. It was as if the face of Re had entered the chamber, erasing all that had been. From Dedu, the temple appeared consumed by the light.

The river around the island boiled, and a hot blast of wind rolled toward the crowd at Dedu. The townsfolk dropped to their knees and cried to a hundred gods to save them. The searing air hit their ears like charging chariots. Deafened by the wind's shrill and blinded from the sand, they braced for death.

Then, as quickly as it began, the tumult ended.

One by one, they opened their eyes. The day greeting them was as calm and clear as any they had ever witnessed. The island was green and new. Mother Nile licked at its rim fondly from a surface undisturbed and even as blue linen. The temple doors were still pushed wide, but the glare inside was gone.

A woman walked into the sunlight a moment later, pausing on the threshold just beyond the doors. It was Isis, but she had changed. She was young again, as young as the day Osiris died. Her thick braided wig was interlaced in gold as befit a queen.

She stood tall and straight, an icon of herself. Her sheer gown picked up the morning sun and, to the crowd watching in Dedu, she was the *Mother-Come-to-Earth*.

A somber moan came from the chapel. Isis's eyes darted to the spot, and she held out her hand. Then, Osiris appeared and took his place beside his wife. He still wore the cloth wrappings of death, and yet, he lived.

This was the first resurrection.

"Every temple has its own Osiris story," remarked the vizier. "In one, Set hacks the king to pieces and throws the parts into the Nile. Isis finds everything except his prick—a fish ate it—and brings him back to life. Of course, she has to strap a wooden one to his crotch so he won't feel deprived. Well, at least he'd be hard for eternity, eh, General!"

I chuckled at the blasphemy, but offered no response. Undeterred, Rekhmire drifted on. "I've always wondered how Isis learned to use the cross. Perhaps, she worked her way on some poor captive Horite priest. In any case, General, the tale brings up a practical question. What happened to that ankh? Where did it go?"

"In the story," I recalled, "Horus cuts off his mother's head. So she wasn't telling."

Rekhmire waved the thought off with a tolerant, yet irritated look.

"Who could she entrust with power over life and death? I say Isis gave the ankh to the sisters of the shrine of Uatchet."

Rekhmire paced as he made his point, stepping in and out of the torchlight, ghostlike on shuffling feet. Then he halted and faced me with his hands outstretched as he often did when espousing the god's plans to the Council of Nomarchs.

"It stays at the shrine until . . ." He paused again and his eyes narrowed to two slices in his face. "This next is speculation. But evidence is like mud bricks. You put one here and one there and eventually the bricks all come together in a shape—and you are standing in front of a great pyramid."

"Where is this leading, Lord Vizier?"

"To Sennemut. The cross stayed where it was since beyond the mists of memory, and then, Sennemut stops at Chemmis," he said. "That is known. From that time on, the mystery is no longer handed down as a fact by the Uatchet Sisterhood, but becomes merely one more ritual usurped by the priests of Amun-Re. Add to that a very intriguing bit of knowledge: The mother of Sennemut was a woman called Meh-Urt-Amam. She lived in Chemmis where, by some accounts, she was the High Priestess of the Uatchet cult."

"You think she gave the ankh to her son?"

"Or he stole it more likely. We'll never know the details, but how else can you explain Sennemut's rise to power?" Rekhmire pointed a finger at me. "He was not the son of a nomarch, after all." He smiled and placed the accusatory hand on my shoulder. "Which brings us to today, my boy. Pharaoh met secretly with a certain exiled priest two seasons ago in Sidon." He paused for effect, then went on. "Sennemut."

"He can't still be alive?"

"Some saw him dead, and yet, the Bitch-Queen's lover lives."

I pondered the concept for a few heartbeats, then asked, "Are you thinking Sennemut has the cross with him?"

Rekhmire drew me closer. "It may explain his longevity and, perhaps, his actions. He has been attempting to contact Menkheperre ever since he entered Judah. Sennemut was pharaoh's tutor, remember, so they are well acquainted. He has designs on returning to Qemet and may be offering the ankh as an inducement."

"What difference does it make if the god gains the ankh? He's already immortal."

"His body stays alive. And youthful." The vizier lowered his voice to a whisper. "Menkheperre has no fear of death, but after witnessing the ghastly deaths of his father and Hatshepsut, he is terrified of growing old and weak and infirm. In dreams, he feels himself in agony, lying in his own filth, screaming, but unable to move."

"You're saying that giving our friend peace is a horrid thing?"

"Yes," Rekhmire stated in a grave tone, "if it means Menkheperre does not experience the same earthly cycle as all other pharaohs. Each time a pharaoh dies, Anubis weighs his heart. If he is found wanting, the Horus returns in a more suitable form. A pharaoh that does not die is out of control. The gods can't work their will through him. And without all the gods in Duat on our side, Qemet is doomed!"

"If the pharaoh wills it, what can we do?"

"Keep him apart from Sennemut," said Rekhmire logically. "I'd kill the old sorcerer if I had the ankh first."

"Ah," I said, "am I finally understanding the reason for this conference?"

Rekhmire snorted. "I built my tomb, and I intend to make good use of it." He led me out into the desert night, and we boarded the chariot. On the way home, he recalled a bit of news.

"Soon," he said, "a messenger will come to your villa. He'll bear an order from Menkheperre commanding you to call up your Braves. Pharaoh has a surprise for you. Nothing to do with what we spoke of, but it will return you to his side. Do you wish to know the nature of the surprise?"

"This night has been surprise enough, Vizier," I said as I whipped the team into a gallop. "How do you know these things? You're probably more of a sorcerer than any of those we talked about."

Rekhmire said nothing, but he seemed amused.

CHAPTER TWENTY

As ever, Rekhmire was right. Menkheperre's command arrived a day later. What the vizier did not know was that the god's frivolous decree would set events in motion that would forever change Qemet and all of us.

The god decided a great hunt would be his gift to me and thirty men hand-picked from the Braves. Each man would gain a full portion of ivory for his effort. My reward would be to bask in the glory of the Horus and try to keep our beloved pharaoh from getting us all killed.

We started before dawn, with scouts from Niy guiding our band along a trail worn smooth by a thousand years of caravans. It meandered from the rock-strewn valley up to a grassy plateau overlooking the lush forest lands of Bashan.

The air hung moist and hot once we reached the tablelands. We angled west, taking advantage of flat stretches to camp, rest, and refresh ourselves. I was thankful that the god had chosen wise hunters as our guides. Using these heavily traversed trails saved both us and our animals from the many faster, but more treacherous, paths into the forest below.

We stopped on a promontory where a thin cascade of mountain water had fallen and collected into a clear, inviting pool. I sent the

Braves to fill our skins as I went over to the god's chariot to check if he wanted to set up an early camp. I found him sitting on a folding stool he had kept with him since we had all left No-Amun together, years past. Yishaq, Menkheperre's big Habiru, was wiping the caked dust off the god's face with a moistened rag he kept for that purpose.

"Ah, 'Nemhab," the god said, "when can we escape the heat of this foolish rock and get on with the hunt?"

"Well, Immortal, I doubt if it's any better down there. I thought the water might be cooling if we stayed . . ."

The god raised his hand. A distance from us, one of the scouts was climbing out on an overhanging boulder. The god sat taller in his chair to watch him. The bearded man pointed over the edge, then, almost simultaneously, he began to shout in his coarse Syrian tongue. Tuthmose tilted his head toward Yishaq, searching for a translation.

The Habiru listened, then said in a gruff whisper, "The man yells their term for abu, O Mighty One. He thinks he's found the herd."

Without a word, Menkheperre jumped to his feet, scurried by the milling soldiers, and vaulted onto the rugged crag beside the amazed Syrian. Yishaq and I ran behind, trying to keep up.

The surefooted Tuthmose edged his way to the end of the projecting rock sheet until he stood at the boulder's tip. I held Yishaq back, fearing his weight might crack the shale and send the god crashing with it to the valley floor.

"Majesty . . ."

Menkheperre seemed oblivious to the danger. "Look!" he said with wide-eyed fascination, "The valley's curving like a huge bowl, 'Nemhab! See how the mist covers the horizon?"

"Yes, Menkheperre. Perhaps you could step back . . ."

Ignoring me, the god picked up a stone and lobbed it high over the side. It did not drop straight down, at least not to our perception. Instead, it sailed out sharply at an acute angle. Mountainsides can fool the senses that way.

"Hah!" he exclaimed, "I knew that would happen! I saw it when Yishaq tried to pour water onto the cloth. But it was funny how the stream of water kept missing it, going off in all directions but down!"

Yishaq could not be held back any longer. He began to inch his way out toward the god, shaking more with each step. As a man of the Negeb plains, he knew his solemn Habiru god El had not meant for him to teeter at the rim of high places. The Tuthmose, of course, hummed and tapped his sandal, unconcerned that he stood a hair's breadth from a straight four-hundred-foot drop.

"Listen, 'Nemhab, this could be useful. Flatlanders need a straight horizon to orient themselves. That's why our archers miss more often in this terrain!"

"Very clever, Majesty. But aren't you a bit close to the . . ."

The god glanced back over his shoulder, calling to the scout from Niy, who had stepped behind Yishaq. "Where are they?"

"Near the . . . bend of the . . . river," he replied in halting Qemetan. "Watch that . . . cloud . . . rising above the treetops. . . . The beasts are there!"

The god turned his back on the expanse of the valley and laughed at what he saw coming toward him. Yishaq had given up any attempt to remain erect and was crawling on all fours with an expression of pasty-faced terror. Menkheperre took pity and met him halfway.

He placed his delicate hand on the burly Habiru's quivering shoulder. Yishaq, whose eyes had been tightly closed, looked up into the tender royal face.

"Oh . . . Glory . . . Never fear, Majesty, I will lead you back to safety!"

Tuthmose grinned. "As ever, I remain in your hands, my dear Yishaq." He watched as the bearded one swung his legs about and started toward firmer ground on hands and knees.

"And may I commend your inventiveness, Yishaq," said the god, smiling in my direction. "How much better it is to climb these steep cliffs by assuming the posture of a mountain goat!"

Actually, as they scrambled to the safety of the ridge, the two reminded me of a master leading his faithful dog. The dog bounded ahead and landed beside me. Before Yishaq regained his feet, Menkheperre had passed the order for the Braves to break camp.

Our hunting party rode down into the first fringe of cedar trees just after midday. Further on, we skirted a wild olive grove. Some of the thick trunks leaned precariously, and their branches lay crushed and battered in the dirt. A Niy scout ran up to my chariot to point it out.

Abu sign.

Menkheperre overheard and called from his chariot which was riding slightly ahead of mine, "Are we behind them, then?"

"No . . . Great Majesty," replied the hunter, stumbling over his words. "Surely. . . . not more than . . . five animals. . . . They are likely . . . a . . . small herd . . . on its way to join . . ." He spoke a Syrian word since he could not remember the Qemetan phrase. Yishaq told us the word meant the main gathering of abu.

"Then where is the path that the big herd takes?" the god asked impatiently.

"Oh . . . They head for . . . river. . . . Water scent draws them."

"Yes, man! But what trail do they travel?"

The scout answered boldly, "Abu take no trail, Majesty. One thousand tuskers . . . these many beasts walk . . . wherever they wish. Trails follow them!"

Pharaoh nodded and dismissed the man with a wave. He peered ahead, studying the terrain with a practiced hunter's eye. When we were boys together, we had often gone into the desert for lion or the marshlands for crocodile, so we were used to and enjoyed the stalk.

I guessed what pharaoh was thinking: The foliage, already quite dense, would only grow thicker as we approached the river. A chariot might easily become useless over such ground.

The god motioned to Yishaq, who had taken the reins, to prod on their twin stallions. His chariot widened his lead as the Syrian hunters ran beside on foot. I drove my own, pacing pharaoh as he and Yishaq tracked a slow, winding course around the gnarled trees that lined the rough road. They took it slowly, trying to avoid the dry gullies that often cut the path.

Suddenly, Tuthmose reached in front of Yishaq and pulled up on the leather leads. The royal chariot stopped abruptly, and I had to yank hard on my own reins to keep my horses from hitting it. Instinctively, I raised one arm high.

"Halt!" I barked.

I watched as Tuthmose removed the soft cowskin cap he wore against the sun and ran his fingers through his black, close-cropped hair. He jumped off the back of his chariot, and when he did, his feet sank into the tangle of ground vines.

The god tried to pull out a handful of the plants, but they resisted until he yanked with his full strength. He looked up to where I waited in my chariot and held the twisted mass of green for me to see.

We both realized that the rich loam composing the forest floor was supporting an uncontrolled growth of tentacled weeds, too dense and spongy for the wheels of our vehicles.

"We'll walk," the god said turning to the company. He walked over to me and pulled himself up on my siderail. "All these damn vines! Get a few men to lead the animals through it. Slowly. I don't want any horses breaking their legs. And we'd better face the fact that we're going to have them falling behind."

"And miss the hunt?"

"I can get more men, General. Horses take time to train."

Tuthmose went back to Yishaq to wait for his wishes to be done. Meanwhile, I tethered my horses, abandoned the chariot to my bearer, and marched back to join my officers.

"The good god has decided to continue the hunt on foot," I told them. "What I want is for two squads to flank him—one on each side—but far enough so that he will not realize he's being protected. Our Lord values his independence."

I left the details to Debhen, a barrel-chested, neckless chief. He assigned his best men and sent them forward. Afterward, when Debhen reported to me, his face bore an oddly hesitant expression.

"Sir," he confided, "I come from Mendes in the delta. And I beg forgiveness for my stupidity, but I have never seen one of these ivory-horned animals we seek. It is difficult for me to reveal my ignorance, but how may I recognize this abu should one come upon me?"

I confess, I knitted my brow and tried to look very serious as I answered the poor man. "If you should spy a huge, granite-colored boulder," I began solemnly, "and if you happen to notice a giant, crushing snake crawling from one end and a long, thin poisonous snake slithering from the other—and if this great rock rises up on what seem to be four thick trunks of olive wood—that, my dear Debhen, will be the abu we are hunting."

Debhen drew back, and I saw him shudder. He bowed, then swallowed hard. "Thank you, General."

"Anytime I can help you, chief," I said. But I was not done. As he stepped back, I added, "And don't forget to watch out for the foul beast's horns. They're longer than a tentpole and sharper than your sword!"

"Oh . . . I'd better return to my post, sir. Uh, thank you again."

I nodded politely, but waited until he had gone to laugh out loud. Only then did I realize Tuthmose was standing by a tree nearby. He had been listening to it all.

"Very amusing, 'Nemhab. Except your description of the abu isn't too far off the target, is it?"

"From what I've seen of them when I was in Nubia, most of them are docile. Only the bulls seem to have a bad temper."

"We'll see about that once the spears start flying," the god remarked. "Follow close. Yishaq and I are going ahead."

"Yes, Menkheperre. I'll catch up as soon as I get my weapons."

The god and Yishaq, trailed by a spearbearer and an archer, pressed on. From a distance, I could detect that the god was watching out of the corner of his eye as the Braves rushed to their positions paralleling him. I ran to his side after a short time. As I slowed to match his pace, I could see his half smile.

"Do I detect a bit of your work?" he said, pointing to the soldiers skulking amid the trees.

"Your men are always anxious to be by your side, Lord."

"Liar."

"Well, I did tell them to keep an eye on you. But they do it gladly. Out of love."

Menkheperre nodded and increased his walking speed. "Smell the moisture in the air?"

"If you mean that stench, I do."

"It's the river we saw from the high ground, I'd guess."

"It must be flowing up from the underworld, then. Foul. It makes me miss the sweet smell of Mother Nile even more."

The god was distracted. He stopped at a black-barked tree and scraped some green coating from its base.

"Lichen. It grows where water's close to the surface."

The Tuthmose looked up. "And mosses are in the branches. Would you care to wager that the river will be in sight once we pass those big rocks?"

I shook my head as we started up again. "No, thanks. I think I learned never to bet against you back at the Aruna Road!"

His lips pouted. "Six campaigns and all I ever hear is Megiddo this and Megiddo that! Look at me, Amenemhab. Am I that same round-faced boy? Have I done nothing of note these six seasons past?"

"You've brought Qemet her greatest glory!"

"Bah!" he snorted. "Even the Bitch-Queen was called the Glory of Qemet."

"But, I'm not insincere, Menkheperre."

"I know that, friend. But can't loyalty be a form of blindness? Remember in class when we read the papyri about Usertsen?"

"The conqueror of Nubia? Of course. The Horus was strong in him."

"Am I as great a pharaoh?"

"How can you doubt it? Usertsen never ventured north. He fought bands of naked huntsmen; you've overthrown nations! Why don't you ask that question after we've crushed Kadesh and the Mitanni? Maybe, after that, I'll personally ask your warriors to follow you south. There's always gold in Nubia!"

Menkheperre threw his head back and hooted gleefully. "I know. They dig it out of my mines!"

"That's no excuse not to mount a campaign!"

"Right!" He laughed. "And when it's over, I'll raise a temple to old Usertsen—who was my inspiration!"

"Good. Then will you let me call you the Glory of Qemet?"

Pharaoh inclined his head in a gesture of sufferance and, in a voice as officious as his vizier's, said, "General Amenemhab, you have leave of the crown to shower the Living Horus with whatever praises you wish. I shall deserve them all soon enough!"

A loud yelp pierced through the woods, cut off by a sudden splash. We ran toward it, finally stopping on the rise and staring down—at Yishaq. He stood waist-high in water. The bottom of his kilt floated to the surface, making it look as though he was sitting on a lily pad. His long, wet curls were twisting and dripping over his embarrassed face.

He had found the river.

A stream of water sailed fountainlike through Yishaq's lips while he grabbed his beard, fiercely wringing out his sopping hair.

We all gathered at the edge of the embankment and stared down at him while he splattered water everywhere. Finally, he found his feet. When he stood, the river came no higher than his upper thigh.

"How courageous, Yishaq," shouted the god, "to test the depth of this unknown river for us!"

I sent four of my Braves into the muck to retrieve him. Yishaq lifted his powerful arms to them, and they dragged his bulk up the mud-greased slope. Yishaq sat shivering, his knees tucked under his chin, until Tuthmose came to him and covered his wide, damp shoulders with the god's own leopard cloak.

"Don't look so downtrodden," he whispered. "You'll soon dry. And no doubt regain that Habiru smell of yours in no time."

The rest of the hunters found us and grouped around at the water's edge. The god assigned a slave to cut a branch and measure the bottom.

Summer heat had dropped the river to a manageable level, still deep in many spots but, overall, averaging chest-high. As I gazed across, the opposite shore was a picture of a marshland so still it could have graced a tomb wall.

I backed away from the lapping wavelets. Turning, I watched as Tuthmose called for the bearers to unlash a three-man dhow from two pack asses tied in tandem. After consulting with the Syrians, he chose an exposed sandbar nearby as a suitable point to launch the small boat.

"I assume you don't expect all of us to cross in that thing," I said as I sidled up to the fallen tree trunk where the god reclined.

"Hathor has blessed us." He cast his eyes above to the branches of a giant sycamore. "I'm having them throw a rope bridge from those overhangs."

Indeed, the spreading treetops reached out toward each other from both banks, making a natural ford. By then, the dhow was in the water. I chose Memnet of Buto and a scout to pole the boat to the far shore and, as the light was waning, to find a spot for us to camp.

Memnet left the Syrian to raise a tent and brought the dhow back carrying a rope secured to a thick sycamore. Pharaoh surprised us by crossing the river on the boat's next trip. He wanted to scout a bit for himself, he said to me with a wink, knowing that I and my Braves would be trapped on the other side unable to protect him.

I personally supervised the bridge construction. When it was done—and it was only a simple three-point affair, so the great architects of Qemet need not fear a change of profession on my part—I tested its strength myself by traversing the river hand-over-hand in full armor.

The rope was harsh, and it chafed my ankle bone until it bled. The pain was sudden, and I nearly lost my balance in midstream as the bridge began to sway. My foot—the sandal now covered with slick blood—shot out from under me. The middle rope snapped up and hit my groin.

The shock almost flipped me over, but I caught myself at the last instant. Had I fallen, I would never have risen to the surface; the weight of my armor would certainly have dragged me into the mud bottom.

Devouring me.

My breath was coming too fast. The wetness of the air was making the bridge slippery. In desperation, I hooked my arms around the top ropes to rest and kicked off my sandals. I was able to make a grab at the center rope with my toes. After a torturesome struggle, I pulled myself upright again.

I hung there for a few seconds, then turned to see my Braves shouting encouragement and sending up birdlike wails from the shore like women do. I released one arm and waved. The sounds of rejoicing redoubled and I continued on.

Once safe on the north bank, I sought out Tuthmose in his gold tent and found him eating the flesh of some animal unknown to me that Yishaq had killed.

"Ah, the bridge is finished!"

"Yes. The Braves are eager to be by your side once more, Menkheperre."

"And my life as a free man draws to a close. And I am a slave to my servants again. Is that what all the noise was about?"

"Likely, Majesty," I said. He offered me a skewer with the strange meat laced through the length of it, but I declined.

"Too pungent for you, 'Nemhab?" he asked.

"I've eaten, Majesty," I lied. The meat smelled like goose marinated for a week in urine. "But if I may have the honor of taking a meal with you at any other time . . ."

"At least have beer."

"I'm not thirsty, either," I barked. Immediately, I thought better of it, but Tuthmose did not react with anger.

"Why are you so testy, 'Nemhab? Aren't we having fun?"

I lifted my foot to show the gash. "I'm sorry. You know how I get when I hurt myself. I should put a poultice on this."

"It's blistering. I'll have Yishaq lance it for you."

"No, thank you."

"Oh, don't take my advice, I'm only the Living Horus, the Glory of Qemet," said Tuthmose, grinning. "All I know is that my court physician always cuts those things."

"And if I know Iryuufer, when the blister is down there, he sucks it out himself." I laughed. "Please, It's already bleeding. A poultice will draw out the poison. Believe me, I'll be fine as soon as I bind it up!"

"And no one cuts Amenemhab unless he's a better swordsman, right?"

"Correct, Immortal One."

"And there is no better swordsman. At least that's what we used to say about you in the House of Soldiers." He patted a cushion. "Sit by me. I have spoken to the Syrians. I hope you'll be fixed in a couple of hours."

"How so?"

"The hunt is about to come to us. At sunset, the abu herd comes to drink at the river. When they do, we'll be here, waiting."

"But didn't the scouts say there could be a thousand animals, Lord . . . ?"

He waved me off. "Yes, yes! But as you yourself said, and the hunters of Niy have confirmed to me, it is sufficient to kill the bulls. Without leaders, the others wander about confused."

"I don't know, Menkheperre. I'd hate to be the man who had to get between their hind legs to find out if its a bull or a cow!"

Tuthmose began to laugh so loud that Yishaq ran in, his sword drawn. The god motioned him over and told him the joke, but Yishaq did not understand it. He did, however, offer to bind my foot and I let him. He took a thick leaf from his pouch and squeezed a gob of sap onto the wound. Then, he tied a clean piece of pharaoh's linen tightly across the cut as he chanted a guttural prayer over it.

Strange . . . Yishaq is such a savage, and yet . . .

By the time the Aten fell below the rough-edged slopes from which we had come, my foot was feeling just fine.

Achan of Niy perched like a lounging cat, high in the crook of an old gnarled sycamore. He threw a fruit of the tree down to his son who awaited at the base. The young man caught it and shouted up to Achan for a report.

Achan shrugged and, with his bare feet conforming to the branch, climbed in ape-fashion to a higher limb. There, he stopped and craned his neck to peer into the dusk's purple light.

"Are they there, Father?" the son of Achan called out.

At first, the boy thought his father was too high and thus out of earshot. He cupped his hands around his mouth and shouted his question again, louder this time.

Achan did not respond. The old scout had heard his son, and could have yelled down some acknowledgement. But, he simply could not find the words.

Westerly, facing the underworld where Mighty Re meets his daily death, there rose a green, luminous mist that covered the valley as far to the left as to the right. Below the churning cloud—in fact, its source—was a mass in the general shape of an arrowhead that had invaded the wood country and it was heading, relentlessly, for our small encampment.

Achan, from his vantage, saw this. At the point of this huge triangle, he could make out spots of gray, felling, rolling, and grinding through the pine forest.

A horizontal avalanche.

The abu had come for water.

CHAPTER TWENTY-ONE

O Holy One!" Yishaq whipped back the tent flap and entered, awakening Tuthmose and myself from our beer-induced dozing. "The Syrian dogs have returned with news."

"Close that!" screamed the god, turning as the last over-bright shafts of the sun hit his tired pupils.

"Oh, infinite pardons, Immortal." He stepped forward, allowing the flap to fall shut and the light to return to a comfortable level. "I had no idea you and General Amenemhah were asleep."

"I never sleep!" Menkheperre said, wiping his eyes.

"Yes," I added. "Your pharaoh bears too much responsibility to waste his time napping. We were discussing our hunting strategy, when pharaoh decided to commune with his brother gods."

"Exactly," the Tuthmose intoned.

"I'll just clear away the beer, then, Noble Ones," muttered Yishaq. Then, he suddenly looked stricken. "Oh, Majesty, I forgot! Achan the Syrian says that the abu are coming faster than expected. He thinks perhaps the beasts have gone mad."

"Mad?"

"A thirst madness. The other rivers may have dried farther north. This one at our back is much lower than it should be."

"Yes," I remarked, "that would explain the high slopes leading down to the water."

"Achan surmises many abu herds may have banded together as the smell of this river reached their great noses. Achan has been a hunter for thirty summers, and he says he has never seen so many animals. Imagine a termite mound in full swarm, he says. Except each insect is ten cubits tall!"

"When will they arrive?" asked the Tuthmose.

"Before the sun is gone."

Menkheperre brightened. "Then hurry, 'Nembab! We hunt within the hour!"

There was nothing at first but the cloud. It billowed up from the earth, reminding me of the wide summer sandstorms off the western desert. It blew closer, and soon terrible low moans penetrated up to us from the churning curtain. Our forward scouts could see immense shadows filtering through the dust and hurried back with a report that surprised no one.

The abu had come.

Within the hour, the beasts were passing us in an unbroken line from one side of the valley to the other. The god stood with his bowmen, squinting from the dirt the abu were kicking up. It made everything as obscure as if the forest land were smoke-choked by fire.

"Give me a true shaft, son," the god whispered to the young soldier behind him. "True enough to send it into the eye of a big bull!"

When Menkheperre's quiver bearer handed him his first arrow, the god's eyelids were pressed together tightly against the gritty air. "Lord, how can you tell the bulls from the abu cows if you cannot see them?"

Pharaoh rose to his feet and took his stance, bow at arm's length. He looked at the soldier. "The bulls lead, everyone knows that."

"Be careful, Horus," the boy hollered. He was frightened for his own safety, given their exposed position, but doubted even an abu would dare harm the Living God.

"They'll turn!" said the god confidently. "We'll kill any of those daemons that come near and let the stench of death scare the others into position for the Braves to slaughter!"

Tuthmose raised his bow high as a signal to the others and brought it quickly back into position. "Archers! Let 'em fly!"

Twenty Braves released their spray of arrows, using the dark, indistinct shapes inside the cloud as targets. Some must have hit, for a string of horrid bleats rose from within the dark center until no other sound could reach any of our ears.

Suddenly, it was as if the great stone Sphinx had risen up on his massive legs and was bursting from the haze. It was an outsized monster, a tusked apparition so fierce that Captain-of-the-Braves Debhen could not stifle his scream.

No man not present has ever truly believed the truth of this brute. He has been described as taller than the temple of Karnak with a head wide as the pylon gate at Mennufer. But the creature was more terrifying for its reality.

At his shoulder, the huge animal was fully the height of four men. His massive skull was broad and malignant with curved yellow horns coming from either side of a single snakelike arm.

A bellow exploded from his mouth with quaking resonance, as the brawny trunk heaved back and struck the crown of his head with a heavy whack. His neck stretched upward, defiantly revealing his most vulnerable spot to the puny humans, as he thundered angrily at the sky.

Thus, I first met the beast-god of legend. Towering above us, emerging from the dry mists as Anubis comes in dreams to the priest-magicians, was Heru.

Heru, eldest of the bulls, red-eyed and scarred from a life of battle. Heru, *He-Who-is-Above-All-Abu*. With Heru at their lead, the herd changed direction, heading straight for our main force.

I ordered my men to disperse and to try to throw the cows and calves into confusion. One company sent a cascade of spears into a tuskless mother, who fell against her own baby, crushing it.

An archer-guard at pharaoh's side managed to sail a lucky shot into the soft mouth parts of a young male, driving him mad. He thrashed and trumpeted, bumping his gray bulk into the females he was trying to protect until they ran hysterically into the center of the tide of abu.

I climbed atop a mound to gain a wider view. The swirling grit was still obscurant, with more sound than sight coming through. My ears were under assault from all around, but one hammering noise rose above the general din. I strained to see its source.

Below me, as he broke from the pack, Heru's eyes fixed on Menkheperre.

The god had gone to stand next to Yishaq on a slate boulder, using it as a platform to prod his men. He did not see the huge abu until it was too close to escape the onslaught.

Yishaq saw the danger first. "Behind me, Lord!" he shouted as he lifted his tall spear to fend off the creature, but his glorious gesture hardly stopped Heru's advance. The end of the brute's trunk struck the center of the shaft, but instead of snapping it, Heru grabbed it with his nose-arm and yanked up!

"Drop it, Yishaq!" yelled Menkheperre, but Yishaq either did not hear or was shocked into inactivity. In any case, his wide brown hands locked to the wooden spear like a hunger-crazed hyena locks his jaw onto carrion. I blinked once and Yishaq was in the air.

The powerful Habiru warrior was tossed, without thought, up and over Heru's back. He dropped as lifelessly as a child's cloth doll, skimming the animal's tough hide as he fell. He landed in a sprawl, much of the skin on his cheek and chest abraded raw. But, nevertheless, he took breath.

Heru stepped back, his rear foot missing Yishaq's head by inches. But the monster had lost interest in the fallen soldier. An instinct, alien and primeval, summoned him to battle with his counterpart.

His blood-dark stare focused on Menkheperre as if to challenge the Lord-of-Men to combat with the Lord-of-the-Abu.

Pharaoh jumped from the rock as the great bull charged. As Heru ran, he flapped his ears, making a sound like a cracking whip. Then, he held them out wide in a glorious display. Broad as leather sheets, the ears added another eight cubits to his breadth as he raced to the far side of the outcropping to confront the god.

I watched in horror as Menkheperre disappeared behind the bulk of the crazed abu. A long moment later, Menkheperre rolled into the open, jabbing at the giant with Yishaq's discarded spear! Heru whirled, raising his forelegs high and pounding them hard to the ground not ten cubits from the god.

Menkheperre threw his weapon at the beast and darted into a stand of low trees. The spear struck above the eye, glancing off the bony brow without breaking the skin. It was no more than a prick from a needle to him, but the bull halted and shook his ponderous head from side to side.

Swinging his thick arm, snorting through it as he pushed those immense triangular ears forward like some huge, aggressive bird, Heru slowly approached Menkheperre. The god straightened his spine and stood ready with his feet wide apart. The mountainous animal stopped and allowed a granular grunt to escape his throat.

His old head cocked as if he were weighing his options. Heru watched with a methodical coolness. He took an easy step, sensing that his prey was cornered against the trees. And yet he was wary.

Men, he knew, could be dangerous.

His hesitation gave me the time I needed to act. I ran from the rise, leaping the final distance and placing myself between the dark-spawned daemon and my pharaoh. Heru shrieked furiously at me.

"Stay back, Lord!" I cried. "I'll distract him! You run for the rope bridge!"

"One sacrifice is enough!" Menkheperre yelled back.

"A thousand of us would pass into the Second Life to save you! Please! Hurry!"

Menkheperre nodded, and I rushed the creature laterally. When he turned to face me, I reversed direction. I made sure to distance myself from the tamarisk trees that sheltered the god. Heru turned, determined to rid himself of this human pest—me!

Ineffectually, I admit, I drew my sword and sliced at the air in front of him. If he noticed, the bull made no outward sign. But as he lowered his head to charge, a flash of yellow caught his eye. It was Menkheperre in his golden armor dashing across an open space toward the river.

I arched my back, stood wide, and shouted a prayer to Osiris that he remember his promise of resurrection and eternal life. All I feared was the pain when my bones were crushed underfoot.

But a smile was on my face, I assure you. I, Amenemhab, am no palace general like those who remain in No-Amun second-guessing those who take up the god's fight. I am a soldier. I cannot count the times my Ba has nearly left this shell. I have met the Syrians and their ten thousands with only my Braves at my back. My body is latticed with scars.

Amenemhab does not shy from jeopardy. I faced the monster, Heru, thrusting my short sword out at him as my final act in this Life.

My sword touched nothing.

Heru was fanning the air with his huge nose, grabbing the scent of Menkheperre. He trumpeted and lurched aside, avoiding the sting of my blade. He sighted the god through his tusks and lost all interest in me.

Moving his bulk with a lumbering gait that disguised his speed, the great abu made up most of the distance between him and the god in a few rolling strides.

So huge was this abu that even Menkheperre, born amid the towering columns of Luxor, lost all sense of scale.

"The daemon is upon me!" he shouted as the great wide head

seemed to loom over him. Actually at that point, the creature was forty cubits off or more. But he was gaining fast on Menkheperre, whose legs were starting to cramp.

The god would later tell me, his mind was racing faster than his feet.

Guardian Horus, don't let me trip!

Watch out for stones!

Mustn't look back . . . not even think about it!

Look to the ground or I'll fall . . . and to fall is to die!

Take the safe path and . . . run as fast as I can!

I could see the point where the mighty Heru would overtake the god. Menkheperre would be trampled less than two man-lengths from the river's edge. The bull knew it, too, and aimed one tusk at pharaoh's unprotected back.

Mehkheperre refused to look back, still concentrating on the ground. The rocks were past him, the terrain changing to sand and clay as the refuge of the river neared.

The god heard the pounding of Heru's pillarlike legs close behind, but still, he would not turn his head, even when the beast's heavy breath blew hot and moist onto his golden shoulders in waves.

"Mighty Horus! Protect me!"

I have no idea if the falcon deity heard, but I did. By then, I was running, too. Trying to make up the distance between us, I was hard-pressed to keep apace with the charging giant, so I ducked through an opening in a tangle of shrubs to where I had seen a smooth decline. I scrambled down, flanking the abu and increasing my forward speed at the same time.

I was close now, but desperately afraid I would miss my rendez-vous by a deadly, irretrievable fraction. I saw the royal sandal splash into a thin layer of water left by a high river wave when it lapped over the bank. The river was so near.

Menkheperre could swim across it as he swam the Mother of Rivers at home, leaving the abu to cautiously wade lest his bulk be caught in a soft, shifting mass of sand to rip either muscle or bone and die.

The river! Menkheperre saw it; smelled its pungency. But at his back, Heru's foot, two cubits across the diagonal, obliterated the god's sandal print an instant after he created it in the moist sand.

He had him!

The Lord Abu bellowed in triumph before lowering his tusk to impale the god with his first and final thrust! I hit the god, driving my collarbone into his waist, and we both tumbled into the shallows.

I whipped my head around to face the bank only to see Heru's leg smashing like a falling obelisk into the water a hairbreadth from my head. The impact knocked me against the god again. We were left knees up, sitting in chest-high river water, both utterly dazed.

Ten tons of rampaging bull cannot shift direction easily, but Heru tried. He dug his hind legs into the silt, trying to use his weight to give him traction to counter the slippery mud. Instead, he fell hard into a pocket of deep water. It made a sound like a thunderclap, and a big wave splashed over us as Heru thrashed and screamed, trying to pull his limbs from the clinging muck.

My scouts have told that the thigh and calf bones of the abu are heavy and solid without the marrow that flavors our own. Perhaps that is why three of Heru's four legs sank low under his enormous weight and held fast.

He roared, not in fear, for fear was alien to him, but with pure, consuming anger.

I caught his eye then. A small red eye, staring from the mass of his sleek, wet, black skull. Blackened by the water that bathed the dust away, I suppose. But the black of him somehow made me shudder.

His ears spread out to their full span, and his great arm smashed the water's surface into shards and beads like lapis. Adornments for a king, and king he was, glowering at the pesky two-legs crawling onto the beach.

His eyes screamed to me a warning. "I will shred your flesh and grind you beneath me until not a piece of you remains."

As the Lord-of-All-Abu trumpeted, I cradled the god in my arms and lifted him higher onto a patch of dry sand. Menkheperre's senses seemed to be returning, but as a legacy of the pursuit, his breathing still came in ragged gasps.

"I . . . I . . . saw my death."

Some grit clung to the god's cheek. I brushed it away as I said, in as reassuring a voice as I could muster, "If Great Amun had wanted us to go to our kas, my dear Lord, surely our souls would be sailing over the Western Desert by now."

Gathering his strength, Menkheperre drew up on one arm. "If my salvation was truly the will of the gods, 'Nemhab, you were the instrument. And that, my old friend, I will never in this life forget."

I shrugged off the remark, but inside I felt an exquisite satisfaction.

I rose to a crouch and placed my hand on the small of the god's back to give him support.

"Come, Majesty. We aren't safe yet. See those twin rocks? We can find some shelter there until we . . ."

Menkheperre tried to pull himself up, but fell back onto my chest.

"Lord? Can you stand?" I asked.

"With your help."

So, we push-pulled along, reentering the river as the easiest route to the protective boulders. We tried to skirt the tar bottom that trapped the great abu by finding our path on the flat stones under the surface. That way, we reached the boulders much quicker than either of us expected.

The two conical towers of granite jutted up from the sand at the water's edge. There was a recess formed at the base. It opened into a shallow cave with a cloistered tidal pool for a floor.

Once inside, Menkheperre collapsed. I sat him in a corner of the refuge so that only his feet touched the warm water. I sat next to him, removed his chest plate, and checked him for broken ribs. There were none.

He was badly bruised but otherwise intact, simply much battered and well exhausted. I rested his head on my lap. An instant later, his eyes opened, and he looked up at me, lips trembling. I thought he was about to say something, but he only stared vacantly at a spot near my left ear.

What vision was he seeing?

It frightened me. I hurried to the five-foot crack forming the entrance and shouted through it to my men on the far bank.

"Braves! Guards! The Tuthmose is hurt! Come! Help the god!"

My lungs, taxed by all that had happened, refused to support the sound.

My words spilled out perfectly formed but without power. Each of my cries were swallowed by Heru's constant bleating. I believe he wanted to keep my men from hearing us, rescuing us.

Over the next hour, whenever I ventured from Menkheperre's side, I glimpsed fewer and fewer of the passing herd of abu as the mass of them scattered upriver.

Occasionally, I saw a man or two filtering back from the ridge through the dissipating dust clouds and guessed the Braves were regrouping.

If that were true, the god would soon be missed. Debhen might at that moment be sending out scouting parties.

I prayed so.

My collarbone was paining me terribly. The area from my neck to my shoulder had gone purple. Hurt, I assumed, when I saved the Lord Menkheperre in that desperate leap.

Quite a time passed before the throbbing began. I had the god's concerns to occupy me and gave little notice to any injuries of my own. I kept him out of the water as best I could, being fearful that he might drown or come to other harm if moved too roughly from his resting place.

I stayed in the tidal pool, waist-deep in the cooling water. My bare legs had gone numb, and my head started to ache. I was becoming listless . . . weak . . . slipping in and out of dreams. . . .

Heru continued a wail accompanied by the drumbeat of his fleeing multitude, the music of a thousand thousand abu pounding the earth as they passed . . .

Arum . . . Arum . . . Arum . . .

My breathing captured the rhythm. . . .

My eyelids were so . . . very . . . heavy. . . .

As a sticky darkness hovered outside, permitting the last gray light its lingering death, I sat holding the god in my arms. As Re's sun boat sailed toward the dark underworld of Duat to endure the twelve or-deals in the valley of Osiris one more night, my muscles went slack, and almost without realizing it, I entered another world.

Swirls of gold and blue-violet melted and reformed into fascinating whirlpool pictures behind my eyelids.

Then, they shaped into a bird . . . an odd one with a gold head, blue feathers, and deep, lapis eyes.

The bird spoke to me.

"Amenemhab? Are you listening?"

"My ears are open. What else can I do?"

"Do you know me?"

I smirked. Of course, I did. Everyone can recognize his own Ba! "Wondrous strange to be speaking to you, though," I said. "I was not aware that I had died."

The tiny bird ruffled the gilt on his neck feathers, squawking and tittering as if he'd heard a grand joke. "You think Osiris needs an-other general in His nation of Blessed Dead? For what reason? Is it not the Land of Eternal Peace and Tranquility? Tsk . . . tsk . . . the Second Life can be so boring for a soldier."

"I'll try to keep occupied. In fact, I plan to spend a very exciting Eternity."

My Ba laughed again. "I shouldn't worry, My Other Self," he chirped. "Few generals, or for that matter most of the nomarchs, make it beyond the Sacred Assessors in the Hall of the Two Truths. After all, what man of such rank has not reviled pharaoh, or stolen what was entrusted to him, or taken another's ox or wife . . . in fact, committed any or all of the Forty-two Proscribed Sins. How do you suppose you'd fare?"

"No worse than others I know. Have you seen how they build tombs to rival pharaoh's? They think they'll pass the test, and compared to them, when my heart is weighed, it'll float on the scales!"

"Doubtless true," conceded the bird.

I waited impatiently as my soul preened his wings. Finally, I spoke up. "You still haven't explained how I can be jabbering with my own Immortal Ba and not be dead?"

"I was unaware of any rules in the matter."

"But, here I am alive, and there you are in front of me . . . released!"

The Ba hopped up and landed back on his perch. "A-Ha!" he said with a piercing squawk. "But, I'm not released! I remain within you . . . and quite comfortably, too. At least I was until you decided to footrace that abu-monster. Exhausting!"

"Would it be possible for you to get to the point?"

"My, my . . . You'd think this conversation were taking place in Time! Well, anyhow, I came out to warn you of great danger. Wake up—or I shall truly be free of you!"

The golden bird opened its beak as if to speak once more. How odd, I thought, when a bass note came of his mouth. It shifted lower down the scale until it became a rumble. Louder, until the vibration swelled into nothing less than an earthquake. . . .

My eyes shot open in time to see an ivory spear thrust toward my throat!

I jerked right and it missed me, hitting the stone behind with a sickening crunch. Still groggy, I looked up and the rock cleft closed like a giant gravestone rolling into place to seal the tomb. Then, I saw that the "stone" had a red eye!

Heru had freed himself from the bog.

The giant's other tusk battered the rock inches from my head. Again, I fell on top of the god just as the ivory tip passed over us. It withdrew, shaking the heavy boulders. Rock chips sprayed over our backs.

I waited, pressing against the damp granite while I fingered the hilt of my sword. Outside, Heru heaved his body blindly at the twin rocks, trying to crack them apart.

They didn't budge, but the layers of accumulated dirt did, showering clots of mud and pebbles into our crevice.

A rain of dust fell in the corner where I'd left the god. He began to stir and inhaled a throatful. I heard him cough, and Heru must have picked up the sound, because a few seconds later his snake-arm was inside, coming at him.

Using all the strength remaining in my two hands, I lifted my sword above my head and thrust it downward. The tip barely cut the surface of his armor-skin.

I bore down harder, slicing into the spongy interior of the lashing forelimb. A spurt of red hit my breastplate. I pulled out the sword and hacked again. This time, I felt the metal slide through to the underside.

Suddenly, that small space, our refuge, was filled with Heru's wail of pain. The thick, boneless arm jerked up, tearing my sword handle from my grasp and flinging my shoulder into the stone wall.

The arm whipped from side to side in blinding pain, and it nearly clubbed Menkheperre. Blood was splashing everywhere. The rocks dripped with it, and red rivulets ran like fountains into the tidal pool.

Heru tried to pull his pierced snout through the small entrance hole but couldn't.

Without thinking, I'd cross-pinned the beast's arm with my sword. The grip stuck fast into the top of it with my sword point gaping out beneath.

Heru twisted and tugged, trying to free himself as his screams careened off the sides of our niche. I watched his ears flap in a frenzy as black tears poured from his widening eyes.

I saw agony collide with primal madness in those eyes.

Each thrashing movement cut a longer gash in his wound. The hand of the abu began to fill with blood, not air, and Heru was suffocating in his own juices. His powerful limbs trembled as his muscles weakened.

One knee gave, and he barely balanced his tonnage. Somehow, though, he kept standing.

Looking at him sway, I suddenly realized that he could drop there, blocking our only exit. His rotting bulk might seal out our air, or even if that didn't happen, we would die when the river flooded the tidal pool in the morning.

I knew what I had to do. I jumped onto the arm and used my weight to hold it down. Next, I straddled it and pulled my sword out with a quick yank.

The arm moved wildly and bucked me off. It shot back from the hole with the speed of an attacking cobra. I followed it out to the river and darted for the shore.

The beast saw me and howled in fury. His lumbering footfalls stayed behind me for a few seconds, but the exertion was too much and he tipped sideways into the shallows.

I turned. He was well beyond the crevice, and I breathed easier knowing the god was safe.

Heru was suffering terribly, trying to keep his massive head above the water. I ran toward him with my sword high, but stopped when I saw him staring at me.

He produced a desolate sob, and I noted his arm was nearly severed. It hung from little more than a rope of tendons, but Heru reached it out to me.

I understood and hacked off the offending arm with one blow. Then, I plunged my blade into his eye.

Heru convulsed and, amazingly, rose to his full height. I see now he wanted to die like a king. He ran a few lengths on wobbly legs, finally crashing blindly into the trees on the shoreline. I heard a grating intake of breath followed by the sound of bone against bone.

Then, silence.

The-Lord-of-All-Abu was dead.

CHAPTER TWENTY-TWO ☥

After the doomed hunt, my beloved god Menkheperre was forced to remain at our Qemetan colony at Sidon, too ill to travel. I had carried him from Niy to the harbor of the Sea Peoples in four days. Two teams of horses died on the way.

In all that time, he never spoke.

I sent scouts to alert Irynufer, and he was waiting with a staff of physicians and slaves at the palace of Zimrida, the king, who had given up his residence as part of his annual tribute. There, for the first time since the hunt began, I was separated from the god.

I waited until the morning of the tenth rising of the Aten and, when I still had not been allowed into the god's presence, I strapped on my short sword and crossed to the king's apartments above the central hall.

I caught sight of Irynufer as I stepped onto the stairs from the upper loggia. He was dogging a comely local boy who was trying to carry a heavy grain jar back into the food stores.

The physician stopped him at the far wall, ordered him to set his burden down, and whispered in his ear. With the exception of myself, they were alone on that side of the main house, so I was wondering what the whispering was about until I noticed the tip of Irynufer's tongue flick at the boy's earlobe.

"Physician!" I called out. "Speak with me, here!"

Irynufer glanced around nervously, then, discovering me at the head of the staircase, shot me a frightened look and screamed, "Please! Don't kill me!"

I joined him at the bottom of the stairs as the serving boy scurried away. "Now, what's the matter?" I said.

"He's gone."

"Gone?" I was confused. Irynufer had shut the god away so effectively over the past days that Menkheperre's safety was hardly a consideration. Even after hearing the healer's words, my mind refused to grasp the meaning. "The boy?"

"The Tuthmose! I was just sending the servants for you."

"You mean Menkheperre's out walking somewhere? If that's the case, I'm certain Yishaq will protect him until he returns."

"No, no. He's left the city. Last night according to the gate men."

"Why wasn't there an alarm? You told me the Sidonites were adequate as guards, and now this? How did you allow this to happen?"

"Not I! No, definitely not I! Please, Magnificent Amenemhab, I did not desert my pharaoh. I . . . I was called to minister to a member of King Zimrida's family. And then, when I checked on the god, a priest told me that the god had ordered that I not attend him that night. I assumed he was simply tired."

Shakily, he rubbed one eye with the nail of his middle finger, trying to push back a tear. "But, but the next morning, my assistant woke me, and we ran to the king's chambers . . . and they were empty."

"Yishaq, too?"

"And the slaves. And part of the Sidonite guard. It must have been an intrigue."

"Tell me about this priest who gave you the message. I've never seen a priest anywhere near the royal apartments. Did the god request one?"

"No. He just arrived one day. Tuthmose seemed to recognize him and invited him in. Of course, I left them alone. Devotions are a private thing."

A terrible thought entered my mind. "Was he . . . old?"

"Very. That is why I considered him no threat."

I turned away from the physician and wandered onto the terrace. "An old priest. Of Qemet?"

"Oh, yes," Irynufer assured me. "I am quite certain. He had a fine Qemet face and such soft eyes. And no accent in his speech at all. He was definitely from home."

I whirled back at him. "We do not send old Qemetan priests to outposts of the empire! Conquest and occupation is the business of young men!"

"I don't understand—"

"What would he be doing here? We've only held Sidon for five seasons." I returned to his side and stood over him, glaring. "Unless, of course, this priest had been here all along—in exile."

Irynufer seemed appalled. "I never thought," he murmured.

"Yes. I should've made the connection. Rekhmire said he was in Sidon, said Menkheperre had seen him, but after the hunt—"

"You know who he is?"

I nodded. "The Bitch-Queen's debaucher has returned, and we've delivered the god into his hands!"

"No, Amenemhab! Not that I ever saw him, but how could it be Sennemut after all this time? He's dead! He must be dead!"

"Oh, he's still breathing. Until I cut out his foul heart with the point of my sword."

CHAPTER TWENTY-THREE ☥

I took a company of eight, including three of my best desert hands, and left Sidon as the first rays of Glorious Aten appeared over the far hills to the east.

We took the King's Highway down the coast to Ashdod where we had a decision to make. Sennemut was certainly returning the god to No-Amun by water, sailing along the coast to the delta and from there, down the Nile to the City of the Hundred Gates.

By traveling overland on the coastal road with the Great Green Sea at our right hand, we could never hope to catch even the main force. I had, however, scouted a southern route after the second season at Megiddo.

It led through the Wilderness of Zin to a tiny gulf town. There, the gods of the West Wind smiled, and we took a fast skimmer to Aqaba where I commandeered a merchant vessel.

The boat seemed to pitch in three directions at once without any sensation of forward progress. Spending most of the voyage poised over the side rail, I marveled that the boatmen were able to perform their tasks with such ease, until I learned that they were related by blood to the Bynu sailors who ply the Great Sea.

Here they are called the Phoenicians because the bynu bird is called the phoenix in their home region.

We landed at one of the villages on the Qemetan coast where the eastern desert highlands meet the Red Sea. From there, we dashed straight across the sands to the Nile shore.

Our band made it by the first month of Akhet, when the inundation began. If fortune guided us, we would reach the capital before any barge could arrive from the delta. The god, despite his lead, was traveling against the Holy River's flow while our passage would be more direct.

"And ten times as arduous," answered my Braves.

That dawn, my men and I left with a caravan of linen sellers across the eastern desert through the Wadi Gasûs toward the city of Coptos, where fully a quarter of Qemet's gold is mined.

The flooding Nile spilled so far into the gullies near the town that our trip was shortened considerably. The rivermen of Coptos had already begun to use their inland docks, which were only serviceable for one-third of the year.

From there, I was told, it was less than a day's sail to No-Amun and a bit longer overland. So, I left my men to travel with the horses, and I boarded the barge to the capital.

The high columns of Karnak were visible two hours later, but it did indeed take the better part of the day to arrive. The bargemen let me off at the dock of the Temple granary amid a crowd of bustling workmen and vendors.

I walked home by the onion-field road in less than an hour. Being the first week of flood, that path had just begun to muddy, and the farmers had ceased to use it. I saw no one and prayed to Amun no one saw me.

There was nothing more to be done until my remaining six Braves arrived at my villa the next morning. The wide walls of home were a welcome sight, gleaming orange in the late light of the Aten as I drew near.

They looked smoother and cleaner than I remembered. Raheal must have taken my suggestion about giving the place a new facing of plaster.

It is not my habit to enter by the front door, preferring instead to enter the side gate and stroll through the garden by the bathing pool.

A servant girl peeked at me from around a column on the upper balcony and ran off, obviously thinking I was an intruder, for in a few moments Old Ptah blundered out with his cane raised high against me.

His half-clouded eyes could not recognize me until we were nose

to nose, but when he did, he dropped his stick and embraced me
tighter than the wrappings of the dead.

"Master! It is you!" Tears ran down his face. "Home! Home at
last from the filth of the north!"

"You are a sight to see, old man!"

"Half-blind as I am," said Ptah as he drew back from my arms.
"And look at you! You smell like a goat and have the beard of the
unclean heathens you've been living with!"

"Three days' growth. No more."

The old porter grabbed my wrist and pulled me toward the draped
portico. "I knew I should have gone with you to keep you civilized.
You are a disaster! Come, I'll throw you in the washing room and
have the women scrub you down. Then, I, myself, will shave those
black bristles off you so you'll look human again."

"Where is my wife?"

"Well, thankfully, Lady Raheal is away at the Great House, so she
cannot see you in this condition!"

Old Ptah, who had been porter to my father, limped up the stairs
ahead of me. He leaned on a cane upon which was carved "Support
me, O stick, as my own limbs fail me."

I had given it to him as a gift on my last feast day at home. As
usual, Ptah fussed, and I allowed him to help me unbuckle my skirt
but had him call for a boy to strip off the rest and carry the bundle
to the cleaning vats.

After I had been showered and scraped, Old Ptah approached.
"Lord Amenemhab," he whispered, "if the general wishes, I will send
for your wife to greet you properly."

"Why is she at the palace? Do you know?"

"She is often called to attend the Lady Ano, sir."

"Lady Ano? Oh, yes, the First Wife's eldest sister. Strange. Ano
and Raheal never seemed friendly."

"They are quite close, now. Many nights, the Lady Raheal stays
in the women's chambers at the Great House. I am certain she is with
the god's family as we speak. I can easily send a girl to fetch her."

"No, it can wait," I said. "Why don't you bring me some of that
honey-dipped sparrow of yours."

Ptah bowed. "That dish takes quite long to prepare, Lord."

I placed my hand on Ptah's frail, bony shoulder and said, "Well,
don't you dare rush it, old fellow. I'll use the time for a nap."

Ptah left, but sent in the boy with my headrest, freshly wrapped, along with a flail to help me when the sand flies started attacking the oil lamps.

He placed both items on the bed and was fussing with the cushion when I ordered him out. I must have been more exhausted than I knew from my journey. I thought I watched the Aten sink below the trees, but before the room went dark, I was no longer awake.

Sennemut dominated my dream. I stood facing him in a temple courtyard at 'Epet. I recognized it from the waking world, since it is the only shrine of Khensu left in Qemet. Menkheperre waited beside his obelisk, the largest he had ever created. It rose from the central quadrangle and had an altar set in front of it. I thought it was strange at the time.

As I hacked at him with my sword, Sennemut changed. In a blink, I was staring into the angry face of Khensu, the Night Terror.

My dreams brought the daemon to life. In the dark, two yellow eyes regarded me. It wore the head of a hyena on the thin body of a spotted leopard. Its jaws gaped open revealing uneven fangs that slavered on the tiles as the vile creature crept sidelong toward my bed.

It lunged.

I kicked out at it and rolled to the edge of the bed pad. Pain, like a hot brand, shot through my heel, but my only thought was to avoid the daemon's teeth. I picked up my headrest and threw it into its muzzle as I fell off the tilting bed. I landed on my side and it hurt.

Can a dream be this real?

The upended bed gave me enough cover to block the next attack. It also allowed me time to shake off the sleep that was clouding my defense. I feinted left and dove right to the chair where I had left my sword.

At least I didn't dream *that!*

My sword slid free of its scabbard, and I led with the blade as I swung around to meet my attacker. The daemon stood in the full moonlight across from the balcony, revealing that he was very human indeed.

What in the half light I had seen as the head of a hyena was, in truth, the cat-headed cowl of a leopardskin cloak. My assassin was a priest of Amun!

He lifted a thin ceremonial axe by its curved handle and brought it down hard. I blocked the blow with the flat of my sword and pushed the priest off-balance by twisting into his thrust.

The man was not trained for this sort of extermination work, or he could have countered my move by a simple upward pull to send the corner of the axe deep into the soft spot below my jawbone.

But he didn't.

Instead, he tried a circular swing, aimed at my head. Of course, that is the first part a soldier is trained to protect. I made an inelegant but instinctive defense that hooked the broad axe blade where it met the handle.

The momentum jarred the axe from my would-be murderer's hands, leaving him amazed. Disarmed, he took a step backward and found that he was pinned against a column. I rose from the floor with my sword held less than a span from his body. He closed his eyes and mumbled a prayer to Osiris. In a *deltan* accent.

"Who sent you, priest?" I started to say, but I had barely spoken the first word when he lurched forward onto my sword so that the point sliced through the base of his neck. He gurgled once and crumpled to the floor—dead.

Curse him! And curse the luck! I wanted him alive!

I found the chair and sat until my heartbeats steadied. In my worry over surviving, I had not heard the commotion in the corridor. I called out, frightened that this boy-assassin might not be the only one sent on this errand. I kept my sword high as the door to my chamber opened.

It was Ptah holding a torch. "There was noise, sir."

"I had some unexpected company."

Ptah tended to cleaning up what remained of the young priest while I went downstairs to eat my dinner. I had just finished the fowl and barley bread when Ptah entered the dining hall. He bowed unsteadily and placed his mouth near my ear.

"It is done, master," he whispered. "Now, he floats north with the current."

"I don't want him found."

Ptah grinned, showing all five teeth. "Do not be the least concerned, my lord. The gods have blessed our errand. Especially Set. I believe he will be happy that you've gifted his crocodiles with such a fine meal."

As I nodded in thanks, the old man stepped out of my view and back to his more routine duties. The serving girl poured more thick, heady beer into my cup, refilling it each time I set it down.

Ptah's report had placed the image of crocodiles devouring my assassin's wet and bloated corpse into my mind.

Somehow, I lost my taste for food. That one priest's fate did not account for all the queasiness in my stomach. A portion of the unease was that Death nearly embraced me in the very place I felt the most secure.

Unsettling.

Pushing aside my platter, I got up and strolled into the garden to calm myself. It was cool near the water, and I sat on a bench under the large willow.

My father had put the bench there when I was a child. A beautiful, peaceful spot, he called it "his pondering place."

Now, it was my turn to try it.

"Sennemut remains a prophet of Amun," I said to myself. "And the boy in my room wore the leopardskin and shaved skull of the Karnak priests, and they were the source of Sennemut's power when the Bitch reigned. Could the priests have seen me on the river, or kept a watch on my house—or both?"

"Husband!"

I was jerked out of my thoughts by the happy squeal. I saw the small, slim figure of Raheal running at me from the house. I stood and swept her into my arms.

Her body was hot against mine as she hovered with her toes wiggling above the grass for a long minute. We kissed, and she held me with the grip of a lioness until I let her down onto the bank.

She clawed at my tunic as I ripped the linen of her dress open with my exploring fingers. In the dark, we made ourselves vulnerable and joined together in a welcome release. I heard her cries mingle with my own and felt us fall into the oblivion where the flesh conquers the mind.

Afterward, we walked into our sacred lake, floating there until the cool water restored us. I let Raheal ease onto my shoulder, letting the lake support our weight. She sighed. I thought she had drifted off to sleep, but she opened her eyes.

"You should have sent word," she murmured. "Ptah's wife says you've been here all day."

"Late today. And I was weary. You would never have gotten this greeting while the Aten watched us."

"But Khensu up there is too serious to be excited by our fun?"

"He lights up the dark nearly every night, my love. He must catch us mortals at this sort of frolicking all the time," I answered. "Still, at a time like this, I rarely give the gods much thought."

She kissed my cheek. While her lips were close, she whispered, "Ptah's old woman told of an intruder—"

"It was nothing. A thief. I showed him my sword and he ran off."

"You weren't hurt, were you?" She nuzzled her head into my bare chest. She noticed my arousal and stroked me.

"Do I seem hurt?" I lifted Raheal and rolled her on top of me. With one arm warming her naked shoulders and the other between her thighs, I guided myself into her again.

She twittered, then began moving with a weightless rhythm that sent urgent ripples across the surface of the lake. "Do you want to go upstairs?" she asked finally.

I shook my head and swam the short distance to the bank. She paddled up beside me and we lay, my head on a smooth stone and hers once more on my partially submerged chest.

I pointed beyond the gate to the Nile. The water shone from the orange lights of Karnak. "You were at the palace, I hear."

She pouted and dug a sharp nail into my rib. "Yes. While I thought you were still nursemaiding the barbarians, husband. If I knew you were sneaking back to No-Amun, I'd have been waiting here."

"Yes, I know. You've grown dutiful over the years. Not the wild, untamed pony I married."

"Were *forced* to marry!"

"For that Menkheperre will always have my lifelong gratitude," I said. "I am pleased you spend time with his Great Wife Thelkemina and her sister."

"Don't speak of other women, Amenemhab. In this house, am I not your queen?"

We lay motionless for some time, but exhausted as I had become, I could not dismiss a nagging thought from my mind. "Raheal," I said in a mild voice. "What do you and the royal women do all day when we men are gone?"

"Nothing."

"Nothing?"

She shook her head. "Nothing of consequence. Female things. We talk about the children, play senit or the game of the serpent."

"You hardly ever talked to Ano when you first came. Though, she was solicitous to you, I remember."

"Oh, Amenemhab, that was such a time ago."

I pressed the point. "Ages. But have things changed since?"

"Yes." She sighed. "Menkheperre plans to send her to Yisra-El as wife to the traitor, Jeroboam—"

"Jeroboam is a legal king. Qemet recognizes him."

"Well, in Judah we say he usurped half of our kingdom!"

"The northern tribes defected to him, because that father of yours—"

"His name is Rehoboam! He is a king and deserves some respect, even if you did humiliate him at Megiddo." Raheal propped herself up on one elbow. "Why are we naked and wet and talking politics on your first night home? They'll be enough time for that after pharaoh arrives tomorrow."

"Pharaoh? Who told you he's returning? And how did you learn it was tomorrow?"

"No one." Raheal paused, as if formulating an answer. Her hesitation was so slight—if I had not been married to her and knew her ways, I might have believed her next words. She tried to swallow and couldn't. "You're home, aren't you?"

"That I am. But you've known I'd be here for days. The Lady Ano told you."

"Amenemhab—"

"Don't bother to deny it, woman. You are part of it. Does not the Uatchet Sisterhood train their girls from birth?"

"There is no sisterhood—"

School them in deceit and denial—

"Mere women—"

—And the trickery of the female and the follies of the men who lust after them. Or love them.

"Husband, please!"

"The truth, Raheal! You are a priestess of the Uatchet as your mother was before you," I said as I ran my fingers from her cheek, down the line of her jaw. "And like all of them, you were bred to infiltrate the hidden corners of power as only a woman can—to marry the men who the sisterhood wishes."

Her head shook violently. "No! Think, Amenemhab! It was Menkheperre who gave me to you as wife. Not any secret sisterhood! And you know the god wanted me! Why, then, was I not made his queen? It was because I pleaded with him. I loved you from the first moment I watched you ride into Megiddo. My brave general with the soft heart."

"I *have* thought, Raheal! The god was controlled by his fear of dying and the hope of the Horite Cross. Why would the Uatchets need you in his bed? But I have the army. And I might have become a threat in the future. The threat I am today!"

"Sleep on this, husband. You are fatigued in your mind by travel and strong drink. You'll think clearer in the morning."

"I won't live 'til morning, my love. Not if I sleep with you." I placed one palm behind her head and the other at her throat—and kissed her. "Admit it. You sent that young priest to my room."

"No!"

"Ano and Menkheperre's wife, Thelkemina, are sisters in more than one way. They are Uatchet. In league with Sennemut. You were at the palace when your spies (other women—as invisible as sand) informed you that the cross had returned to Qemet and I was home."

"I had no idea you were here," she whined. "You saw how surprised I was when I saw you at the water's edge." Her chin dropped down, and she opened her eyes wider than I had ever seen them— large as a fawn's. An innocent fawn.

Her voice quivering, she asked, "What does a poor woman know of these things?"

"Enough to return here from the palace after dark."

"I wanted to—"

"No noblewoman can leave the palace unescorted once the Aten has gone west! The guards won't allow it. Pharaoh's orders. And the only reason for you not to sleep at the woman's quarters in the Great House is if you were required here."

"I was! My lord and husband had returned to me!"

"Then, you weren't as surprised as you seemed?"

"I—I . . ." Raheal's lips tightened, and her eyes darted back and forth. Her mouth opened a second time, but she was too confused to speak.

"What happened? Did that smooth-skinned boy you sent fail to report back? You three girls must have been worried that I captured him alive, huh? Did you tell the other two not to worry? Raheal will take care of it. She can simply walk into her own house and put everything right. If the assassin were alive, you could free him—or kill him before he could talk. Then, playing the happy bride, spend the night with me. And late in the hours before the dawn when I am deepest asleep, you'd take your knife and—"

Suddenly, she found her voice. "You're wrong, husband. I and my sisters merely arranged for Sennemut to deliver our sacred object to

Qemet. We will never aid him in his plans for pharaoh. Our only goal is to return the Cross of the Horites to our keeping. This has been our trust and will be for eternity."

I held her to me with all the love I could muster. "Your mission is over, dear wife."

CHAPTER TWENTY-FOUR

Raheal wasn't missed for two days.

Her body floated just below the surface of the sacred lake among a tangle of reeds where a pair of gray cranes nested. Their cries at her intrusion that daybreak might have aroused the stewards, if my Braves had not knocked at the front gates about the same time. Their coming sent all the servants scurrying, and that morning no one took a ritual bath.

As it happened, the commotion put the whereabouts of Raheal out of all the servants' minds. They were too busy feeding the men, releasing the chariots, and caring for the horses to give a mere wife any more than a passing thought.

She must still be at the Great House amusing the royal women, as usual, her maids supposed. And we should thank the household gods she is! We'd never finish all the work the master's given us, if we had to minister to her whims, too!

When a steward eventually discovered her remains, he and the entire staff assumed that my unlucky assassin had killed Raheal when she spied him sneaking onto the grounds. Many believe the story that my innocent bride died in a struggle to save my life.

That is the legend, now, and I have never denied it. To some she is a heroine of Qemet, and I accept that belief is often not reality. Ptah's wife, the only witness, remembered talking to her that night, but since she had been sleeping by the front door, she had no idea if it had been before or after the attack on her master upstairs.

It is a sad fact that the death of my precious wife was shortly forgotten in the turmoil of the next days. I never mentioned her again, even to Rekhmire, who surely suspected mine were the loving hands that held her under the purifying waters until her spirit was cleansed.

I will remember her always. And the legend of her sacrifice for the glory of Qemet and the safety of her home and husband is painted for the gods to see on the walls of my tomb.

But that first morning, it was the rolling rattle of chariots and the spirited whinnies of horses that woke me. It was a sound to vanquish the fatigue of a fighting man. I looked over the balcony and shouted welcome to my six remaining Braves. At the sight of me, they raised up a howl of greeting worthy of a legion.

My captain, Djedeb of Mendes, waved energetically as he ran to greet me. "General!" he shouted so the rest could hear, "where to now?"

"They'll land at 'Epet." I spoke with more assurance than I felt. I ushered him aside to confer.

"The Great Temple?" he asked quietly. "How can you be sure? They've been canny about their destination all the way."

I sat next to him and whispered, "Neither of us are priests, but tell me, Captain, if I happened to mention the moon, what god would it bring to mind?"

"Thoth, of course. The Lord of Right and Truth."

"I would answer the same. But, last night I met with—," I caught myself, "—a young woman, someone who knew Sennemut's purpose. And in quite ordinary conversation, I noticed the moon was nearly full. She, equally offhandedly, invoked the name of Khensu, not Thoth. And Khensu is an old god worshiped at only one temple in all of No-Amun."

"Then, that is where we go," said Djedeb. "But remember, Menkheperre has the Syrian legion with him."

"They'd never be allowed to witness the ritual. I'm convinced the god will keep them on the boat. At most, he'll retain a small escort to bring him to the temple. But no one in the courtyard itself."

The captain grunted. "No matter. We are Braves. Worth a hundred foot fighters."

As soon as the Aten sank below the world, I chose two Braves, young Keret and Djedef, the old campaigner, then set out for the God House of Khensu.

It stood alone at the outskirts of No-Amun, far from the cluster of temples along the Nile. I drove with both my compatriots in one chariot, a light war wagon built for speed.

Earlier in the day, I ordered extra grease on the hubs and axles to keep the chariot as silent as possible, even with the extra load of a third passenger. Keret held on to the spearman's position to my right while Djedef sat cross-legged on the stern platform behind me and snoozed. Our route went along the Avenue of the Rams, where a hundred stone eyes watched us pass from the pedestals lining the road.

Beyond the statues, the way grew dark. Except for a few ritual pyres on the side of the trail and a sailor's lantern glowing from the river's bank, we relied on the moon to see.

I have often thought in the sad years since, Lord Khensu, *Who-Is-the-Moon*, could have kept us from defiling his house if he had only dimmed his light. But the moon was a beacon that night—low and large.

I let the horses run to speed over the rutted trail and, in a shorter time than expected, sighted the torchlights of the temple.

I reined in the team quickly. At the same time, Djedef jumped off to grab the lead stallion and tie him down.

We didn't linger. I kept Keret and Djedef moving in a half-crouch until we faced the eastern wall. It was windowless, and the sides sloped downward so that it resembled the old mastaba tombs of Sakkara.

Keret thought this temple wall was steep enough to climb. If he could, that would bring him above the open courtyard. I thought a bowman might be useful there, so I let him try.

He touched his chest in salute and removed his sandals. Without another word, he scampered up the side, not straight up, but rather at a curved angle starting at one corner and ending beyond the midpoint.

When he gained enough traction, Keret launched himself onto the edge of the roofline, catching a good grip with a hand and a forearm. He hung for a moment, then pulled his body over, and disappeared onto the roof.

"Good lad," I whispered to Djedeb, who grunted with a certain satisfaction since he trained the boy. I told him what was next. "We'll keep the small wadi and the bushes between us and the temple doors. That way we'll see how their men are deployed out front."

Once beyond the wadi, I crawled out to a position beside a date palm.

Djedef followed, hiding himself against the trunk of the nearest tree. From there, the front court of the temple was in full view. It looked deserted except for one guard pacing between the columns.

I was pleased the entire detachment wasn't there to meet us. Pleased, that is, until the torchlight hit him, and I recognized this solitary guard.

Yishaq the Habiru.

I remember I was of two minds. Approaching the temple, I had no plan to speak of, except a vague idea to fight my way inside, even if it meant charging the entire armed force of the Great House.

That all changed when I saw there was only one opponent. Perhaps the simple fact that I was a general and the guard was a simple soldier could gain our admittance without bloodshed.

His or ours.

It might have worked, too, had it not been my hairy barbarian friend standing there. I knew immediately that if the god had given him an order to keep everyone out of the temple, Yishaq would try to bar Osiris himself.

Still, as difficult as the giant would be to pass, his presence confirmed one point I'd simply assumed.

Menkheperre and Sennemut were in there.

I noticed Djedef take a step back. "That's a big one," he muttered. His eyes pinched into slits as he caught my gaze. "Do you think a javelin from here would do it, sir? I'm a fair throw at this distance."

I shook my head. "Takes Habirus a long time to die. Time enough to raise the alarm. No, I think we may have to . . . surrender."

Djedef's jaw went slack. In all of his campaigns under me, he had never heard the word surrender uttered. Ignoring him—I knew he took his cues from me, no matter what—I got up from my crouch and stepped onto the path. Djedef emerged from cover, but I signaled him with an upraised hand to keep back.

"Yishaq!" I called out as I strode alone toward the temple. I kept my hands high, away from my sword. When I was a few cubits away from the Habiru, I saluted him and stopped.

"Lord General," he said in his humble growl, "you left Sidon."

"I follow the god, as you do."

His stance, feet wide apart, fingers clasped to the hilt of his sword,

wavered slightly. His bulk still blocked the door, but I could tell that
he was unprepared to confront me.

"You should go home now, my lord."

"Sorry, friend. I cannot. But I give myself up to your care."

"Sir, they are praying inside, and I have my orders."

"Let me pass, Yishaq. Take my sword if you doubt me. Though,
you of all people know I would never harm him. Menkheperre owns
my heart."

His face shuddered as he fretted about what to do with me. I realized that a quick, fatal thrust of his short sword into my chest was
a definite option for him, but I bet Yishaq might have a problem
explaining my death to his single, nameless god. I decided to up the
wager.

"I must speak with the Tuthmose, *Who-Reigns-as-Horus,*" I said
in my most formal speech. Yishaq straightened to attention as I continued. "This is not a request, soldier."

"B-but, the god was careful to say, you may not pass."

"By name? He said Amenemhab, his oldest friend, may not pass?"

"No . . . no," he answered haltingly. "He and the priest left you
in Sidon."

I shrugged. "See, there? How can you bar Amenemhab from
Khensu's temple if the name of Amenemhab was never mentioned?"

"You try to confuse me. No one may pass, until . . ."

"Until what?"

Yishaq grimly clamped his teeth in anguish. "Until they are finished!"

"Could they be finished now?"

"I-I don't know."

"But if they're done, I can go inside."

His ringlets of hair flew violently as he shook his head. "It is not
my place to decide this."

"I certainly agree, Yishaq. You must open the doors, go inside,
and ask the god if he will grant an audience to his oldest friend."

Yishaq bowed his head. "Forgive me, sir. The-God-of-the-Habiru
will never allow me to enter the house of a Qemetan god."

"Oh, yes." I had him and I knew it. "No god of Qemet welcomes
a barbarian, either. Which means, since you can't ask, I'll have to.
Open the door for me."

"Perhaps a crack. Just to see if they're . . ."

"Yes. I'll step into the entry hall . . ."

Reluctantly, Yishaq flung back the bolt and pulled the copper door ring. The thick wooden doors creaked and strained apart until there was space enough for a man to slip through.

"Good man, Yishaq," I said. The giant's arm dropped to his side to let me pass, but as I did—the dark interior of the temple exploded into day!

Yellow fire rolled from the courtyard like a desert storm, searing my eyes. I tried to turn, then was flung to the ground by a wind that hit me an instant after the intense light.

The door at my back blew outward, striking Yishaq's shoulder hard enough to send him sprawling.

And yet, I swear by all the gods in Duat, I heard not a sound. I couldn't have been on the floor for more than a heartbeat when my senses returned. Now, a fetid yellow haze replaced the sudden flash of light, and the only glow came from past the shadowed columns. I sprang up on aching legs, drawing my sword and pushing ahead into the temple.

Ask for my thoughts at that precise moment, and I cannot remember. In the silvery slickness of far memory, I recall appearing in the temple courtyard without a notion how I got there. Shock can do that, I've learned. No matter. I arrived and what I saw there remains as vivid as the walls in my tomb, painted a day ago.

"Menkheperre!" I shouted. A cloud enveloped me as I stepped into the open court. No one answered, but I saw figures a distance away out of the corner of my eye.

Closer, I realized they were statues of hawk-headed Khensu, shrouded, merely outlines, standing like pharaoh's own soldiers between the lotus columns.

Beyond them towered the obelisk, ghostly as the mist eddied about it in spirals. In the thickening fume, I could not make out the top of it. Or its base.

The granite pulsated with internal fire. Somehow, the stone, glowing orange and black like burning embers, was the source of the light I'd seen. I trod the unseeable ground with care, my sword held out ahead of me.

"Leave here, you young fool!" came a voice within the smoke. Its deep, coarse rasp of a sound unnerved me with its authority. I actually shivered. Instinctively, my blade rose and made a quarter turn so that the sharp edge faced outward, protecting my chest and neck.

Not that I truly expected an attack.

Not from the man who spoke, at least. Not from such an ancient Bitch-lover.

Not from Sennemut!

"Where are you?" I screamed. "Show yourself, priest!"

"In time, son!" The voice came from another place. I swiveled to my right to follow it and would have gone stumbling in that direction if the smoke had not dissipated enough for me to glimpse them near the obelisk.

I ran over and stood above where they knelt. Sennemut cradled the god's head in his thin lap. He stroked Menkheperre over his blank, staring eyes.

Near as I was to them, the cloud obscured their features. Sennemut raised his arm to block me.

"Keep back! You're too late, brave soldier. You cannot stop this without killing him."

I swat his hand away and reached for the god. "Menkheperre! Hear me!" I screamed. The sound was anguished, shrill, and ultimately useless. When my fingers touched Menkheperre's bare shoulder, they charred and splintered into a burst of starlike sparks.

I never experienced such pain. I jerked my arm away, dropping the sword from my other hand and rolling on my side to the floor stones. Then, I dared look at my burnt hand, expecting the worst.

Nothing was there. My hand was perfect. Without as much as a blister!

I looked over my shoulder, and Sennemut was hugging the god to his chest with all of his strength. The mist over them began to snake up the pillar, arcing—imperceptibly at first—into twin shapes. Flattening into—

Wings!

More smoke formed at the center into a birdlike body and lifted from the god's brow. Still lighter than air, it flew to the point of the pyramidion cap atop the obelisk.

The smoke darkened from pale yellow to a mottled gray. Feathers like fingernails grew out of the cloud, minute at first, but widening and elongating with each instant. At the same time, the remaining wisps of smoke were sucked under the feathers in a cyclone of becoming.

Until the Ba stood there, wings aflutter, peering down at us with black human eyes from its imperious perch. It bore the face of Menkheperre—no, that is not strictly true, rather the Ba was the image of the Third Tuthmose.

A regal head, aloof now from Life and fear (which I've realized as the decades pass me, are identical.) The Ba stretched its neck and ruffled its chest feathers, then settled down in a hawkish crouch.

I tore my gaze away and looked at Sennemut, still holding Menkheperre's body. I thought the god dead until his breast heaved, and he rolled onto the grass as if too tired to lift himself.

"Old Prophet, save the pharaoh, I beg you!"

"Hah! Be pleased for him!" Sennemut said, half smiling. "His soul is free! The Second Life holds no terror for him. I've given him all he ever wished."

"Why are you doing this?" I yelled.

Sennemut stood on his withered legs above the god curled up like a hound at his feet. "So, you're doubtful that I'm a simple, old fellow trying to help out in any way I can?"

"Not you! Never you! The curse of Sennemut has fouled Qemet since you first floated down the Great River. You planned this! And not for any selfless motive. Tell me, traitorous priest, are you in the pay of Mitanni, sent to bring us down?"

His mouth cracked into a striated smile, and Sennemut laughed. "Fool! I am not an enemy of Qemet. I am its savior!" He began a tortured walk to the obelisk, ranting to me as he inched along. "But, General, you are correct on one account. I am the architect of all that's led to this. My triumph! I conceived the stratagem, and I carried it out across a thousand leagues and half a hundred years!"

Sennemut reached the base of the obelisk and pointed a crooked finger at the top. Menkheperre's Ba had settled down, still tired, no doubt, from the exertion of his passage into being.

"See that little, preening creature up there? And his shell lying here in the dirt? He's my creation and has been since I allowed him to be born!"

Then, the rumors were true.

(In the chaos of the fourteen years of the Second Tuthmose, it was whispered that Sennemut's new Deltan sorcery empowered the old pharaoh to gift one of his lesser wives with a man-child.

Tuthmose II had produced nine daughters with five of the senior queens, so when he finally sired a son, it was an act considered more remarkable at the time than his revolt against the Ahmose Clan.

But, the birth of an heir mobilized the nomarchs, and the Great Lord was in turn deposed in favor of the infant god.

Even then, my father would tell me, it was confusing when, just

*before the end of Tuthmose's reign, he permitted Menkheperre, a
babe new out of his swaddling, to marry Merytre, Hatshepsut's only
daughter.*

*It was viewed as a simple move to safeguard Tuthmosoid rule. Yet,
now, with all that had gone on since, I detected the hand of Sennemut
behind all of it.)*

"And this is your vengeance on the House of Tuthmose?" I asked.

"No, dear boy. This is how I will rule it!"

"Age has demented you, Sennemut! The army would never allow
it. Even if you were conspiring with Mitanni, every nomarch would
send—"

In a flash, I saw it all. Sennemut was reaching for the rose cross
in the obelisk. He was so very old and, like any Qemetan, had
planned for his Second Life.

But if his scheme worked, Anubis would never weigh his heart,
and he'd never cross the Western Desert to Duat where the dead live
again. No, he would use the magic of the Horites to release his Ba so
that the essence of him could imprint itself on the pharaoh's vacant
soul.

"Yes, General!" cackled the ancient one. "I will be Menkheperre,
the Third Tuthmose. And when he grows old and frail, his heir will
become my vessel, my Ba leaping from body to body and so on, until
time itself is at an end!"

The old man lurched forward as if to embrace the obelisk. I turned
away as he grasped the crosspiece of the ankh, knowing the light of
that godless thing would surely blind me. That instant, I saw motion
on the roof. I'd forgotten the boy!

"Keret!" I bellowed.

My young archer balanced on the edge of the roof with one foot
forward on the timber support.

His arrow sailed.

Its shaft struck Sennemut through the neck as an incomprehensible
brightness leapt off the obelisk. Too late to save the daemon prophet.
Old Sennemut pitched sidelong and rolled off the granite to the grass.

Gurgling.

Sennemut's wizened arm groped for the healing fire of the cross
with every ounce of effort, but he had fallen more than a cubit away.

Too far.

Red and yellow tendrils of lightning sparked up and down the obelisk for a few seconds, then all went still. A rhythmic sound, running, echoing through the temple.

Footfalls came hard and fast toward my back. As Sennemut died, his magic dissolved and freed me to rise. But not quickly enough.

A trunklike arm spun me around, and I faced the flat of Yishaq's sword coming down on my head. Blood rushed in my ears as thundering as the winter flood over the first cataract of the Nile, loud and overpowering.

Dazed, I pulled the hand axe from my girdle and lashed out.

The big Habiru caught it with his swordhilt, but I parried instinctively with a backhand circle that sliced Yishaq's hand off clean at the wrist. My axe continued its arc and struck the red ankh, cleaving it in two. That instant, a spurt of barbarian blood blinded me, so I couldn't see his blade slice into the meat of my shoulder. I felt it. It was the last pain of many that day.

I am told I fell on one half of the ankh, but I have no memory of the entire skirmish.

According to the carvings on the great monuments built in his name, the Third Tuthmose died in the fifty-fourth year of his reign after a long illness brought on by injuries suffered hunting in the forests of Niy. Okheperre, the god's son by his Great Wife, waited the required seventy days of burial and resurrection, then assumed the beard and double crown of Qemet.

We record his god name as Amenhotep, Beloved of Maat, *The-One-Who-Protects-the-Two-Lands, Lord-of-the-Reed-and-the-Bee, Great-in-Victories, the-True-Living-Horus, Who-is-on-the-Horizon.*

A good boy.

Rekhmire and I both think so. And not merely because he asks our advice. Miny, his archery master, told me once that Okheperre is the strongest bowman he ever taught. I myself watched him row a distance of three iteru pulling a thirty cubit oar. And when he moored his falcon-boat, the new god seemed as fresh as when the race began.

Most important, Death frightens him not at all. And the vizier and I have vowed he will never be corrupted by knowing there is a cure.

Young Keret related all I know of what occurred in the Khensu

Temple after Yishaq attacked me. When he climbed down off the roof, the archer was the only one standing.

Sennemut, singed by the eternal fire, was little more than black skin and charred bone.

Menkheperre was curled with his head tucked beneath his armpit, mouth open, tongue lolling in the dirt.

A human hand, a right hand, rested against my forearm as if it were trying to get my attention. Its index finger was gone, lost by the huge Habiru in a campaign of our youth.

The rest of Yishaq had fled.

I was bleeding from my collarbone and my ear. Keret carried me to the chariot, passing Djedef's corpse. My Brave had fought for his life, but probably Yishaq hacked him down during his escape.

But without witnesses, Djedef's courage in the face of a man double his size and with many more times his combat experience could never be proven.

Keret told me that when he lifted me, I had one half of the ankh clutched fast in my hand. I did not relax my grip for two days, and when I finally let go of it, my wounds had healed utterly. Irynufer was amazed that Yishaq's blows had not killed me.

Rekhmire's personal guard cleaned up the blood from the temple and removed any sign that either Sennemut or the Living God had ever visited Khensu's house.

My life-friend Menkheperre was taken to the Great House where he died alone in his bedchamber, save for Rekhmire. I never asked the vizier what happened that night. That is between Rekhmire and the many merciful gods of Qemet.

Menkheperre's tomb is hidden in the foothills of the Western Desert. As is the custom, a hole was chiseled through the ceiling to allow his Ba free access to his body.

I know it is of no use.

The very night I have spoken of, Rekhmire dispatched priests beholden to his clan to the Temple of Khensu. They sang the prayers to summon a Ba home.

Compliantly, they said, it hopped down to them, making it easy to capture. They wrapped the bird-spirit in papyri and sealed it within a cedar box dedicated to Osiris-Sokaris.

During the funeral rites, I beheld with my own eyes the priests place the box within Menkheperre's sarcophagus, where it will stay forever.

In the two days I lay abed healing, the Khensu Temple was torn down stone by stone and its obelisk toppled, but no one found the Horite Cross.

I heard a story coming from Kadesh, the first among Habiru cities, also called Jerusalem, of a giant with one hand who presented a gift of great value to my late wife's father, the villain Rehoboam.

It is told that with Rehoboam at war with the tribes of Lord Jeroboam the Ephraimite, the High Priest placed the object in the Holy of Holies of Solomon's Temple.

Upon hearing of the treasure, Rehoboam left the battlefield for Kadesh where he ran up the steps and into the room of Mysteries at the center. He was discovered there by the priests as they arrived to sacrifice to the carved stones of Amasis which are sacred to the Habiru.

The king had burned to ash.

And yet, nothing else in the room was touched by fire. Perhaps half an ankh was not enough to safely perform the ritual of Eternal Life.

PART THREE

CHAPTER TWENTY-FIVE

He could feel the low droning as a vibration deep inside him long before it reached any audible level. As consciousness grew, he became aware of a disorienting sway that would occasionally shift his body off-center. But it was a calming sensation, making him as secure as if he were being rocked in a cradle.

His memory mixed with strange dreams of Egyptian warriors and their gods. Had he been wounded in a temple courtyard? He knew he watched an old man die. Images of a gaunt priest seemed to merge with recollections of his own father.

Certainly, he thought, he was lying down in a bed, and yet, he knew that he was floating. How else to explain such a thing, except as a dream?

Then, the stunning reality ripped away the haziness. He remembered the knifelike talons and his father and the blood! There was another explanation, a more dreaded possibility than sleep.

He could easily be . . . dead!

With all his courage, Dan Rawlins willed his eyelids to open.

Above him was the silver dome of Heaven. The light was more beautiful and painful than any he had known. He shut his eyes quickly. But he had seen enough to be sure.

He was no longer on Earth.

That settled, Dan drifted back into nothingness. . . .

A muddle of voices brought him back. He felt a jabbing pain in his arm and jerked open his eyes. Again, he saw the silver dome of Heaven, looking even brighter now.

Words swarmed around his ears like gnats. Not exactly words, but guttural nonsense syllables that had the cadence of literate speech.

"*A shlimazal koomt oich a mol tsu nutz.*"

"Wha . . . ?" Dan croaked. His throat was too dry to produce much of a sound.

"Oh," said a male voice, "did you hear us, Rawlins?"

The accent was familiar, and when the man leaned over into Dan's field of view, he recognized Halevi.

"Colonel." Dan managed only a dry whisper. He hacked up a rubbery wad of mucous and tried again. "Were you . . . talking to me?"

"Not unless you speak Yiddish," he said. "I was repeating a favorite proverb of mine. What I said was, 'At times a bit of ill fortune comes in handy.' "

The light was strong behind the colonel's face. Dan tried shielding his eyes, but the strain on his arm was too much. Instead, he felt his head fall back and his weighted lids close.

After another spasm of coughing, he blurted, "Are you dead, also, Colonel?"

Halevi laughed heartily. "Not yet. And neither are you. But you've been through a lot. Perhaps more than you can recall at this moment."

Dan rocked his head to the side and saw Jesus Christ. The white-robed Savior was radiating sunlight and stroking his beard. Dan blinked and squinted at the living icon. He jotted a mental note to rethink his atheism.

"Rawlins?" Halevi's voice probed at him. "You look odd."

"Yeah. I guess I'm a little on the woozy side."

"Understandable."

Dan shut his eyes once more, and when he opened them, Jesus had moved a couple of feet closer. And it was quite a disappointment. Out of the direct sunlight, Christ was only a Hassidic Jew dressed in a white labcoat.

Worse, Dan thought, when he saw the tube end of the man's stethoscope snaking out of his top pocket. Not only was he not a god; he was a doctor!

A doctor. The thought acted like a lightning rod for his memory, discharging its spark in a sudden flash!

"What about my father? I . . . I saw all the blood, and . . ."

Halevi placed a firm hand on his shoulder and kept him down. "Later," he said and the big Israeli left.

The only movement Dan seemed capable of was a lateral twist of his neck that gave his vision less than sixty degrees of arc from center. Except for the filmy privacy curtains around his hospital bed, all he could see was the ceiling. As he was waking, he had seen it as a celestial dome. An honest mistake, since it was metallic silver in color and curved like the roof of a Quonset hut.

After an eternity lasting ten minutes, Halevi returned. He mumbled a perfunctory greeting, then planted himself within Dan's field of view. "Forgive me, I had a situation that required my attention."

Dan appraised him coldly. He tried to move, but could not. "Am I crippled?"

"Hardly," Halevi said, a comforting grin crossing his lips. "We've just taken the precaution . . ." he pulled down the sheet as he spoke, ". . . of strapping you down."

The colonel quickly undid the buckles on the leather restraints. A rush of blood burned into Dan's extremities. "Sorry, I was concerned about turbulence."

Dan glanced up, his expression foggy. "Turbulence?"

Halevi laughed. "You think you're in the hospital? I should've realized you couldn't see with the drapes around you. Presently, we're flying in an air ambulance, rented by my embassy, about twenty thousand feet over the Commonwealth of Virginia."

Dan's eyes widened in disbelief. "Wait—wait! Where are we going?"

"A little place in the Shenandoah Mountains. Really quite lovely."

"Mountains?" Dan sat up. "Why the hell are you taking me to the mountains?" Dan faced the blank steel wall, and when he finally spoke, he was barely audible. "My father?"

"Dead."

"How is . . . ?"

"Your mother is well," Halevi cut in. "She seems to be a woman of rare strength. And her faith is sustaining her."

"Yeah," Dan snorted. "I learned all I need to about God's mercy."

"The Yemenite Jews say, 'The Lord conceals Himself from our minds, but reveals Himself to our hearts.' "

"You look Ashkenazi to me. What do *you* say?"

"I say the saddest thing about religion is that the same beliefs that are such a comfort to people individually can be so destructive when applied to nations."

"Who killed my father?"

"What did you see?" Halevi asked out of the blue.

"See?" Dan had turned to him fast. "I didn't see a thing!"

The answer, Halevi knew, came too quickly. It sprang from guilt, not truth. "My men did. A big bird with a white head, they said. A bald eagle perhaps. Was that what attacked both of you?"

"Your men?"

"I had you watched since that unfortunate incident at the museum. Two agents followed you to your parents' home. Their orders were to protect you and your family, but they didn't expect you'd sneak out for that little walk on the seashore."

The colonel appeared genuinely annoyed. *Is he angry at them or at me,* Dan thought.

"Luckily, they heard screams and were able to get down to the beach in time."

"Not for my father."

"He suffered massive blood loss from a neck wound," Halevi said with shocking casualness. "A quick death. It could have been the same for you. As it was, you were in a coma for sixteen days."

Dan was astonished. "It's been sixteen days?"

"Eighteen, actually. We kept you under sedation for a couple of days to arrange your escape."

"I . . . I don't understand. Escape . . . from what?"

"Have you ever met a Mr. Benjamin Haas?"

Dan shrugged. "Sure. Nassau County District Attorney. I debated him on television once."

"I knew your mind would be sharp. Mr. Haas is—what's that clever term those Christians call themselves?—the Moralizing Majority?"

"Something like that. We did an every-damn-word-written-in-the-Bible-is-one-hundred-percent-true show a few years ago. He's a *putz.*"

"You do know Yiddish."

"I live in New York," he said as if it were obvious. "I met the man exactly once, so why—?"

"Evidently, you made an impression on him. He's charged you with three counts of first degree murder."

Dan sat perfectly still. He recalled Haas now. A pale, thin man with the pink face of an opossum, he had used Biblical truth and what the Bible said about abortion as his issue. The county was liberal, but he won election when the two major candidates split the votes between them.

Their debate, as far as Dan could recollect it, was similar to a hundred others he had participated in. Haas was shrewd, clouding his premise with pseudolegal jargon and righteous pronouncements about the Judeo-Christian ethic.

It seemed to Dan that Haas had a personal stake in being correct, as if his self-worth was tied to it in some way. He'd recognized that trait in zealots before, his father included. "How can this idiot think I murdered anybody?"

"Prosecutors don't need a reason. Haas conjured up a theory that you've been systematically stealing artifacts. Your girlfriend discovered it and was going to turn you in, but the prospect of going to jail so terrified you, you committed murder to cover it up."

"And Carlos?"

"Haas says he and the girl were having a secret affair. Possibly Carlos tried to blackmail you, you went crazy and—"

"C'mon. Marcy didn't know that kid from dirt!"

"I suppose that's why Haas said it was secret! Listen, Dan, he doesn't need proof to make accusations, not when Haas is satisfied with destroying your reputation by innuendo."

"Are you serious?"

"Very. He wants you badly," said Halevi, his words seeming to hang motionless in the air.

"And since I was in a coma, I couldn't fight back."

"He's ambitious, and the polls say he doesn't stand a chance of being reelected. The man would give his right testicle for a sensational case."

"Oh, shit—"

"He has enough for an indictment. You were the obvious link between the museum murders and the death of your father. You knew all the victims, and you were with Dr. Rawlins when he died. The police could only find your footprints in the sand leading to his body."

"Of course," Dan muttered to himself, "it wouldn't leave any *footprints*."

"A fabulous story, when you think about it. Sex, murder, and stolen mystical objects. It made the front page of the *Daily News* three
days straight."

"No!" Dan grabbed the Israeli's sleeve. "They didn't smear this
crap all over the papers, did they?"

"Of course. And television." Puzzled brows creased above his eyes.
"What? Does this surprise you? Could it be you are not aware that
you're a celebrity?"

"I'm well known— for an Egyptologist."

"The great American public doesn't know scientists. They know
people who've been on television."

"Colonel," Dan said, measuring his words, "what's the real reason
I'm on this airplane?"

"I find I need your expertise, sir."

"I'm in no condition to go on a dig, y'know."

"Oh, this will be no physical strain. Only a bit of advice."

"About what?"

Halevi leaned into Dan's space. "You see, an artifact has recently
come into my possession. Half an artifact, actually."

CHAPTER TWENTY-SIX

After dark, the airbus landed a few miles outside Warm Springs at a small strip maintained by Luther Flynn, a cranky old Kentuckian who had flown for the British in Palestine during the Second World War. Flynn married the sister of a Haganah leader and moved back to the States to open a small air-freight business.

It was not by chance, however, that he located less than a half hour flying time from Washington. Since the early sixties, Flynn had received a retainer of five thousand a year from the Mossad to keep a hanger clear, in case.

On board the plane, the doctor had removed his white lab coat and dressed in a top coat, scarf, and hat. He ushered Dan down the five steps onto the weed-strewn tarmac and into a four-door Mercury Grand Marquis.

The doctor whispered to the driver, then shook Dan's hand, and left him alone in the backseat. The car sat on the field for a few minutes as silhouetted figures moved in what seemed to be random patterns outside. Dan thought he glimpsed Halevi talking with a man in uniform, but it was too dark to be sure.

"Nice car," Dan said to the driver, trying to make conversation. "Rented?"

The driver shot a look into his rearview mirror. "Could be."

His southern voice was cigarette-husky and gruff. Although Dan was sure Israel could afford a new model, the big Mercury was at least six years old. The car's main feature was its complete lack of any design flair.

Dan visualized the colonel and his spy minions holding their secret sessions with Ford to see exactly how dull they could make their product so the espionage services could stay out in the open and remain invisible.

The car door to Dan's left opened suddenly. The colonel got in. "Go," he said to the driver, who started off without hesitation. The vehicle reached a main road and turned toward a glow in the distance.

A mile or so down the highway, the colonel opened his briefcase and handed Dan a wallet. Dan opened it and saw his face staring back at him from a Virginia driver's license.

"I'll be depositing you at a safe house," the colonel said, "where one of my best agents will take care of you and allow you to get on with your work with minimum security."

Halevi began placing other identity cards into Dan's new wallet, small pieces of another life to create the illusion of a man. And strangely, those scraps would be all most people would need to believe that Daniel Rawlins was an actuary on holiday from his job in Fort Lee, New Jersey.

Fifteen minutes later, Dan noticed the car was pulling into a middle-class subdivision that a rough stone pylon proclaimed to be Oak Park Estates. They drove directly to a residential street packed with small houses and apartment buildings.

The road curved into a cul-de-sac. They slowed down before cutting into a gravel road that meandered through the woods for a mile and a half until the driver stopped in front of a two-story log house. The house was modest by most standards, but it fit nicely into the rustic setting.

The driver got out first. In the backseat, Halevi held a finger to his lips, and Dan sank down in the seat and stayed quiet. Halevi took the wheel—in case they had to get out in a hurry, Dan surmised.

From the backseat, Dan could see a small automatic weapon in the driver's hand. He kept the gun close to his thigh, ready, but unobtrusive. He climbed the three steps to the porch and knocked on the front door. It opened immediately and he went in, presumably to check the place out.

He returned seconds later, motioning for Dan and the colonel to join him.

"The house is leased to your new identity," the colonel began as they started to the house. "I'm your rich uncle. I provided all this for you. Even the cat. There won't be any trouble. I'll pick up the groceries and such. We passed on the gossip through the neighborhood grapevine that you two are newlyweds, so if you don't go out much they—"

"Hey! Wait a second! What do you mean newlyweds?"

"We couldn't have you living with a man, could we? Not this close to West Virginia. Think of the talk that would generate at the local prayer meeting!"

The colonel held the door for him, and Dan went in. The first person he saw was a dark-tressed woman with her back turned to him. She was brewing a pot of aromatic tea on the gas stove top.

"Oh, here she is now, Daniel."

As the young woman made an elegant turn to greet them, her flowing hair fell across her face like a soft mask.

"Let me introduce you to your new bride," said the colonel, his face grinning impishly. The woman extended her hand to him, and her black eyes locked onto his. Their first touch was tentative, but firm.

"Dan Rawlins," the colonel said formally, "meet your new wife. Her name is Jacinda."

CHAPTER TWENTY-SEVEN

"Ma hadash? . . . en shum hadash . . . bilbel . . ."
"Tov . . . todah rabah. Damned bileam . . . efoh Salameh?"

He awoke suddenly.

Above him, filtering in from a dark space between the ceiling and headboard, Dan heard a muffled conversation. How long the voices had been speaking was anyone's guess, but he assumed the raised pitch, the same sharp sound that woke him, signaled they were getting to the good parts.

He strained to catch the words. The man and woman were arguing in Hebrew, mixing the venerable tongue with American slang as sabras do. Dan pushed his cover sheet aside. The motion startled a thin, short-haired cat sleeping at Dan's feet.

The cat produced an annoyed cry and ran off. Dan shifted his weight carefully, trying to keep the bedsprings quiet, and rose up on his knees.

Finally, he stood on the mattress and braced his back against the wall.

The cross-hatch pattern of the ventilation grate scored his face with shadowy lines. By squinting through the tiny boxes, he saw the couple in the dining area or, rather, evidence of their gesturings, since part of the wall cut off his view of half the table.

Jacinda's head bobbed in and out of sight as she talked to the second person, only a pale, indistinct image cast across the fruitwood paneling by the hanging lamp. She pushed back her chair and stood, clearing the coffee cups. The male arm thrust into Dan's sight and gave a small wave of its hand.

"Lehit ra-ot!"

Dan watched as Halevi came into view. He gave Jacinda a peck on the cheek and left out the back way without another word. She bolted the door after him and went toward the kitchen.

Dan pressed his ear to the grate. He heard the sound of water running and china being placed in the sink.

He sank back on the bed, propping two pillows behind his shoulders. He could barely remember the last week and a half he'd spent in the house.

The pills Jacinda had given him with every meal had kept him in an odd state of exhausted anxiety, until he decided to hide the last three under his tongue and spit them out after Jacinda left.

That was how he happened to be awake to see the colonel. He felt a residual tiredness, but mostly, he just ached. Those little white pills with the beveled corners must have been a strong pain killer, because now, every muscle in his torso seemed to be either bruised or strained. And what didn't hurt, itched.

The door opened quietly. First, the cat sneaked in, then Jacinda peeked inside and was surprised to find him staring back at her.

"Up already?" she asked softly.

"The colonel was here."

"The colonel *has been* here," she said. "He's picking someone up at the airport, so you can get to work. And not a minute too soon."

"Why? Did you run out of knock-out drops?"

"No, I mean I didn't sign on to nursemaid an ungrateful, spoiled little boy. We've been giving you massive doses of vitamins, pain killers—a few other medications—to speed up the healing process. They work better if you're rested."

Jacinda sat on the edge of the bed and touched his side with the deep slash. He winced. "Better?"

"Yeah," he said, brushing her hand away from his stitches. The cat nudged his head between Dan's shoulder and the pillow.

"This is Alexandros. He's a ship's cat, and he misses all the fat Egyptian mice. Say hello, kitty." The cat mewed and brushed his muzzle against Dan to mark him. Dan shoved it off the bed.

"I thought foreign animals were quarantined, or something."

"The colonel arranged diplomatic immunity for him," Jacinda said with a wide grin.

"I heard you and the colonel arguing."

Jacinda smiled. It was as if a light had flicked on. "Oh, sabras talk like that," she said lightly. "It only seems like arguing. It's a very Talmudic trait."

"You mentioned Salameh. Is that the reason the Mossad's taken an interest in me? Well, I've got news. I never met him. My father may have, but he can't help you find your terrorist either."

Her expression darkened. "Calling Salameh a terrorist is like saying Hitler was a bigot. You'd be right, but you'd be missing—What do you Americans say?—the big picture? Salameh is somehow able to bring together all of the Islamic madmen under his banner. Colonel Halevi is afraid Salameh may be trying to be the new Mahdi."

"Yeah, I heard."

"It is written the Mahdi will bring righteousness and peace to the unbelieving world, through the jihad, the holy war that will burn the world in religious fire!"

"Armageddon."

Jacinda nodded, then broke into a grin. "Why don't you put some clothes on while I fix you a sandwich. We can eat and talk, just like a couple of yeshiva students." She patted his hand and left for the kitchen.

Dan threw off the sheet and rooted through the closet for a shirt and pants. He found a spartan wardrobe, heavily weighted toward jeans and work shirts. After dressing quickly, he entered the dining area. Jacinda was placing two plates on the table.

Dan ate his chicken sandwich greedily. He had not had a solid meal in nearly a week, surviving on protein shakes, toast, and pill supplements that made his bowels feel he was connected to a sewage outfall line.

He tasted mayonnaise and lettuce and a bit of chopped onion mingling with the wheat bread and chicken breast. The flavors made his salivary glands ache, but it was wonderful.

"Good?" Jacinda asked between her own bites.

"Jake," answered Dan with his mouth full, "you're one of the great chefs of the Western world!"

"Jake? That is not my name."

"C'mon," Dan chided. "I can't keep calling you Jaw-*cinder*." Jacinda glowered, but Dan continued after one last swallow. "Hey, I'm still weak, and your name has too many syllables. It tires me out to have to keep saying it!"

"I like Jacinda."

"It's a beautiful name, Jake. But if you want to be my bodyguard while Salameh is blowing up the world, you're going to need something tougher."

She busied herself clearing the dishes and placing them in the sink.

She gave Dan a backward glance. She seemed very serious. "Jake? Jake is tougher?"

He nodded.

The corners of her mouth turned up, and she whispered, "Have it your way, Danny, boy."

Dan joined her at the sink and slid his plate into the soapy water. "Then Jake it is," he said, touching her wet hand softly. "But I'll only call you that when I'm in a hurry."

She took his hand and shoved it back into his pants pocket. "Americans are always in a hurry."

They heard a car kicking up the gravel outside, and within a minute, the colonel had ushered a thin, middle-aged Israeli into the dining area.

He introduced the man as Eli Dishon. "He listens," was all the detail the colonel would volunteer about him. He carried his black metal case to the center of the room and dumped out a tangle of wires and a variety of small electronic gear onto the table.

Halevi put the laptop computer he had brought in at Eli's elbow. He peered at Dan through narrowed eyes.

"How is your wound? Still oozing?"

"No," Dan muttered, rubbing the spot. "Never hit a muscle. Mostly I lost flab—thanks to my fondness for pizza and cheeseburgers. Hey, do you scab all the way down or just on top?"

"I think the cells knit together," Jacinda suggested.

Dan smirked. "Feels like they left the knitting needles in."

"Set up the tapes," the colonel said to Eli. He motioned Dan and Jacinda over, and they all took seats around the table. "Eli recorded this tape yesterday in Washington. You'll be listening to Zamir Qader lunching with a Syrian cultural attaché in the sculpture garden of the National Gallery."

Eli slipped a microcassette into a recorder the size of a pack of Virginia Slims. He ran the tape ahead, then depressed the "Play" button.

"... and let me tell you, Hasan, in all friendship," came the distant voice of Zamir Qader. He spoke in Arabic. "Salameh is the Rightly Guided One! And the Messiah of the Jews! And the Second Coming of the Christian Christ! He will raise the dead and rule the Earth for a thousand centuries. You can more easily hold back the searing wind off the Libyan Desert than you can stop Salameh!"

Halevi stopped it abruptly and stared at Dan. "What do you make of this?"

Dan scratched behind his ear. "He believes every word of it."

Jacinda spoke up, an edge of bitterness in her phrasing. "Sounds like typical Arab posturing to me. Fundamentalists like making gods out of their leaders. Nasser, Khomeini, Saddam—each one called a prophet or a god by some faction or other. That's how they can tell all those poor, deluded young boys to blow themselves up in crowded buses so they can have castles and harems in Paradise."

Eli tended to agree with her. "You can't think half of what they say makes sense."

Halevi curled his lip in disdain. "Let's suppose this is part of the half that *does* make sense."

"Excuse me," Dan said impatiently, "The Mahdi, the Christ, the Messiah—no one in his right mind would claim to be all of them. Half the inmates in the mental ward say they're Jesus Christ, don't they?"

"I've met him," said Jacinda. "He's a bright man. Sharp. Sly."

"And yet, he not only makes this wild assertion, but he goes out of his way to offer proof." Halevi hit the "play" button the tape recorder. "Listen to this."

"On the day of the next solar eclipse, there will be a conjunction of three planets and the north star. Look then at the obelisk and see if I am insane. Or if the world is."

"And there's a solar eclipse before the end of the week!"

Halevi turned off the recorder and sat back. "Pretty short deadline, I'd say."

Eli wasn't so certain. "Not really," he said. "A solar eclipse is rare, and there'll be one in five days with that conjunction he mentions, but to see the sign, you have to be standing before the obelisk he mentions. But what obelisk is that?"

Dan started to raise his hand like a schoolboy trying to get his teacher's attention, then thought better of it. Instead, he tapped Eli's forearm. "Uh, where does the umbra fall?"

The colonel and Jacinda looked mystified.

"The shadow," Dan explained. "When the sun is blocked, the umbra is the path of complete darkness."

Immediately, Eli opened the laptop and clicked the phone wire into the wall. "I can grab that off the Internet." And in forty seconds he had. "The shadow umbra won't fall on Egypt or Israel during its circuit. As a matter of fact, it misses the Middle East by hundreds of miles."

"That eliminates Megiddo," the colonel said.

"Does it hit London, Paris, or Rome?" Dan asked.

Eli checked. "Yeah. All of them."

"New York?"

Eli shook his head. "The umbra passes too far south." He looked up with an odd expression. "It will pass over us."

Dan referred to a tiny spiral notepad in his shirt pocket. "Salameh seems to be associated with ancient artifacts. In the picture of the ankh, I saw the cartouche of Tuthmose III. Now, follow this. Egyptian obelisks were taken to Rome, New York, Paris, and London during the nineteenth century. They were called 'Cleopatra's Needles,' then, sort of as a joke. But, I found out one very interesting fact about all of those obelisks."

"What fact, sir?" Halevi said.

"Every one of the obelisks in the major capitals of the world were originally carved and erected during the reign of Tuthmose III."

"Another coincidence—" the colonel began.

"And there are no coincidences," Jacinda interjected.

"Quite true," said the colonel. "Salameh has been sighted over the years in Rome, London, and Paris as well as Egypt. Then, he goes to Megiddo where we find another obelisk."

"If Salameh is crazy enough to think he's a god, he may be planning a godlike act." Jacinda sighed. "Like gassing the subways or nuking the White House."

Her comment brought something else to Dan's mind. "Terror never got Salameh where he wanted to be. What if he gave up on the Old Testament idea of a vengeful God and decided to concentrate on miracles? There is a theory that Jesus set out to fulfill the prophecies of Isaiah," said Dan. "It could be Salameh's doing the same thing. Except, he may be guided by the Egyptian resurrection myths instead of the Bible. Whatever the religious dogma, Eternal Life is granted to man through the grace of god."

"But always different gods," said Jacinda.

"Salameh may be wanting to change that," offered Halevi.

"Yes," said Dan. "That's what I translated from the Megiddo inscriptions. And look at what's happened. Salameh has half of an ankh. I saw the picture. He thinks if he can match it to my father's fragment, he'll have the Horite Cross, which Isis used to raise Osiris from the dead. He sends McMay to steal it *and* a papyrus full of resurrection prayers, which is basically an instruction book that tells you how to get the most out of your ankh once you get your hands on it."

The four remained silent for a moment. Then, the colonel pushed back his chair and got to his feet.

"We have a lot of work to do. You, professor, finish that translation. See if there are any clues to Salameh's intentions. Jacinda, work with Eli to develop any patterns. I'll track Salameh and his friend Qader. Perhaps their movements can help us figure out what obelisk we're looking for."

CHAPTER TWENTY-EIGHT

A dog barked outside the bay window.

Dan bolted up from his work and almost lost his balance on the dining room chair. Quicker than thought, Jacinda's hand was on his shoulder steadying him.

She had been sitting beside him reading from notes the colonel had faxed over that morning. They had been alone together since Eli and the colonel left. Three days of confinement was starting to get to them.

"You are jumpy," she said.

Dan's palm held his side, and he grimaced. "It's what happens when I concentrate too hard. The slightest thing sets me off."

Jacinda focused on the file of hieroglyphs in front of Dan. "Sunday's the eclipse."

"I'm nearly done. I analyzed it all, got the sense of it."

She inched her chair closer and after offering him a cigarette, which he declined, lit one for herself. "Can it help us?" she said taking a long drag.

Dan forced a smile. "The inscriptions talk about ancient powers and secret societies. Just nutty stuff."

"Damn you academics!" Jacinda stubbed out her cigarette, lighting another instantly. "Tell me, please, what does it matter how crazy the ideas are if Salameh believes them?"

"Why don't you just find the bastard, La Femme Nikita," Dan shouted at her. "Then, you can put him in front of a firing squad and blow his belief system all to hell!"

"You go to hell!" she screamed back, then got up and kicked the chair over. Dan made a grab for her arm, but she broke away easily and ran toward her bedroom.

Stupidly, Dan charged after her. With a effortless pivot, Jacinda seized him by his forearm and belt. Before Dan realized it, he was flying through the air ass-first and had bounced onto the queen-sized mattress. He bounced a second time and flipped to his injured flank.

"Why'd you do that?" he screamed when he finally caught enough breath.

She stood at the foot of the bed, her cigarette still in her teeth. "Guess," Jacinda said. She sounded pleased with herself.

Dan tried to move. This time his side really did hurt. He groaned and, out of the corner of eye, he thought he saw a glimmer of concern on Jacinda's face.

So, he moaned again. This time louder. "At any moment during that commando death toss, did you happen to remember that I'm practically an invalid?"

Jacinda sat on the edge of the comforter and checked Dan's bandage. "That's why I aimed you for the bed and not the window."

"Well," said Dan, laughing as he rolled onto his back, "if you wanted to get me into bed so bad, all you had to do was ask."

Jacinda got comfortable, leaning on her elbow, looking soft and languid to Dan's eyes. "I don't like it when people try to stop me."

"From doing what?"

"From doing anything."

"I'm sorry," said Dan. "I apologize."

"This isolation is getting to all of us." She smiled at him. "About the translation. Did anything strike you as odd?"

"Look, Jake, I hesitate to say anything. It sounds too melodramatic. But just between you and me, if the obelisk tells the real story of Amenemhab and Tuthmose III, that would mean that the ancient Egyptians discovered the secret of reviving the dead."

"And this couldn't be?"

Dan was taken aback by her question. "Jake, that's superstition. I assumed they taught you better at spy school."

"Assuming is what we were taught never to do."

He tried to think of a clever comeback, but his mind kept wandering to the second button of her silk blouse, shiny and thin, clinging to her supple skin. Lying on her side, Jacinda's right breast flowed onto her left, making a lovely, inviting crease.

"Are you listening to me?" she queried.

Dan's gaze flew back to her face. "Uh—every word. Now what was that last part? You asked—what?"

"About the cross. Have you seen it?"

Dan shrugged. "I told you. I saw a picture of it."

"What did it look like?"

"Hey," he started, "you've seen ankhs before. It had the same shape as most of them, except about forty percent of it was hacked off at a slight angle. There was a slight distortion at the edges. Maybe it was the picture, but the light seemed to bend around the ankh, like heat waves. The loop on top of the crosspiece was elongated and a little sharper than you see in later representations. That feature tells us it could be predynastic. Are you getting this?"

Jacinda nodded. "Predynastic. Before the kings."

"According to the inscriptions, the thing's supposed to be Horite in origin. They were a tribe, probably from the Sinai. All we know about them comes from the Bible. They were slaughtered by the Edomites."

"And they were—?"

Dan threw up his hands. "I don't know. Some guys from Edom, I guess. Semitic culture's not my area."

"Where it comes from isn't as vital as . . ." her voice trailed off.

"As whether it has the power to restore life." Dan sighed. "Well, it doesn't. It's a myth like a thousand other myths. An allegory, a metaphor, a fable."

"I don't think it's fiction, Daniel." Jacinda's head was down, cloaked in shadow, somehow pensive. Dan was about to ask what might be troubling her when she spoke up. Her voice was even and unnaturally serious. "The colonel thought telling you everything about your injuries would frighten you. He didn't want you to be intimidated by the power of what we may be facing."

Dan heaved a sigh and sat up. He swung his legs over the side of the bed and bent over Jacinda, his head hovering above her ear. "Well, spit it out."

Jacinda took a slow, deep breath. "You were dead."

"What do you mean?" Dan Rawlins asked somewhat urgently. "You mean I went into, uh, cardiac arrest, and they used those paddles you see on the medical shows?"

"The cross saved you." After that, she didn't say a word.

At last, Dan lifted her chin and looked into her eyes. "Hey, Jake," he said firmly, "how's that possible? Salameh's got the ankh."

Inexplicably, Jacinda rose from the bed and walked over to her dresser. She slid open the second drawer from the top.

With her back turned to Dan, she spoke softly. "The colonel saved my life when I was at sea. Salameh's men made a mistake in Egypt, and I was able to take advantage of it. But they almost caught me aboard a ship and, well, that's no matter. I got away. The colonel took me with him to New York. To see you. I was supposed to deliver this—the day after you were hurt, as it turned out."

She removed a black plastic pouch from under a layer of clothing and handed it to Dan. He lifted the flap and found another bag, purple velvet this time, the sort that silver presents come in from the fancy Fifth Avenue shops.

Inside, Dan found Salameh's half of the Horite Cross.

"Let me get this straight," said Dan turning the Horite Cross in his fingers. "You've been hiding what might be the most valuable artifact in the entire history of the planet tucked away in your panty drawer?"

"It had to be kept somewhere," Jacinda said bluntly.

Dan squinted at the ankh. Its clear rose color painted his hands with light. He looked up at her with arched eyebrows. "Ever heard of a safe deposit box?"

Jacinda looked at herself in the mirror above the dresser. She tucked a few stray hairs off her forehead and mussed the rest casually. Deciding nothing could be done without a much-overdue style and cut, she scooped up the cat and returned the to the foot of the bed. Alexandros leapt from her arms, more interested in nuzzling Dan's hand and sniffing at the ankh.

The cat pressed his nose through the loop and must have felt the charge, because the next instant he jumped off the mattress snarling.

Dan looked hard at the cross. "This makes us a target, doesn't it?"

"I'd guess they're peeved," she said, smiling. Then, she leaned over and touched his hand to comfort him. "Although, there's a reason we call this a safe house."

"I'm not worried." Dan placed his hand over hers. He took it as a good sign that she didn't pry his fingers away. "You brought me back from the dead." He sighed. "How much worse can it get?"

Jacinda knew the answer to that question, but her expression remained impassive. "Daniel," she said in a hushed tone, "perhaps I shouldn't have been so quick to tell you about the ankh."

"No, no. I needed to hear it." He glanced down and slowly their entwined hands released. Dan held out the ankh. "I don't know if I believe it. Has it been tested?"

Jacinda shook her head.

"It should be. Just because I started breathing after I . . . arrested . . . well, there are more logical explanations than a five-thousand-year-old chunk of rock."

"Then, we'll test it. Later. Rest now, you're still recuperating."

"I'm fine."

Jacinda was adamant. She began fluffing the pillows behind him. "I'm not a nurse—or a psychiatrist for that matter—still, I know you loved your father and the young girl who died at the museum. You've been hurt both physically and emotionally. Until we deal with Salameh's threat, we both must stay in control and work from our minds and not our passions."

Dan lay back on the bed and murmured as his head touched the pillow.

"Speaking purely from an intellectual point of view, Jake, you being here isn't helping. We're here, together, in the center of a whirlpool, you know. Maybe it's the Stockholm syndrome. Y'know, where hostages fall for their captors—"

"That's not our situation, Daniel."

Dan nodded. "I know, I know that. You're my protector. But events are zooming by so quickly, the feelings are so heightened."

"We've been working very long hours," she said, half-afraid of where the conversation was heading. "When people tire, they get odd ideas."

"As odd as this?" Dan asked while leaning in, violating her personal space and pressing his lips on hers for a long, lingering kiss. Amazingly to Dan, who half expected that another one of her jujitsu moves would send him sailing across the room, she seemed to enjoy it.

When the kiss ended, Jacinda took the Horite Cross in her hand and said matter-of-factly, "Take off your pants."

"What?"

"I want to show you something."

"If I pull them down, *I'm* going to be doing the showing."

Jacinda sneered and unzipped him herself. After exposing his upper legs, she ran her fingers along the three parallel scars across his thigh. "I want you to see this. It might help you understand the stakes of this battle we're in."

Lightly, she touched the ankh to the hot pink of the center mark. It felt warm. She rolled it back and forth in her fingers over the scar, and when she lifted it off, only new white skin remained. Then— carefully to be sure—she placed the cross on the end table.

"You see. Just like new," she said. "If your leg was cut off entirely, I wouldn't be surprised if the cross grew you a new one." She slapped his rump. "You can put your trousers back on now."

The double crescents of Alexandros's yellow eyes were fixed on the glowing ankh. Jacinda and Dan did not notice it, but the cat, who had spent an hour curled up by the casement window, seemingly asleep, was now creeping along the carpet as if he were stalking a bird.

With one silent leap, Alexandros was on the end table, nudging the cross, moving it to the edge with his pebbled-leather nose until the priceless artifact tumbled onto the thick shag of the carpet. If it made a sound when it fell, neither Dan nor Jacinda heard it.

Alexandros scratched at the ankh until he was able to hook the pads of one paw through the loop of the cross and drag it under the window. Then, wraithlike, he temporarily abandoned it to vault onto the sill.

Centering himself on the ledge, the cat lifted up on his haunches, placed his paws high on the glass, and swiped over and over at the latch. It took only a few tries to unlock the window.

Dan rolled over to the right side of the bed and was reaching for his waistband as the cat busied himself opening the window.

Jacinda reached for a pillow and coiled into a fetal position away from Dan to afford him a bit of privacy.

Dan, who was closest to the window, felt a breeze and shivered.

"Caught you with your pants down, eh, boy-o," observed a frighteningly familiar voice.

Jacinda bolted upright.

"McMay!" Dan yelled.

Backlit by the moon, a silhouette of the vulture with the human's head sat perched on the sill of the open window with its wings spread, gloating like a hell's spawned demon.

"So perceptive!" McMay sneered. "Not that I don't realize how unique I am."

The cat mewed, unfazed by the apparition he'd invited inside. Alexandros lay on the carpet in the shadow of McMay's wide wings. The animal had curled his body protectively around the fragment of the Horite Cross, motionless, except for an occasional twitch of his tail.

"Ah! There's what I've been flying aimlessly 'round in circles to find."

Gracefully, considering his size, McMay hopped inside and snatched the ankh in his talons.

"You bastard!" screamed Dan, lunging forward.

McMay swatted him away with a flick of his brawny wingtip. "Now, now, now—let's not get aggressive. I got what I came for, and this little toy ain't worth getting hurt over."

"You killed my father!" Dan shouted.

"I had to do that. Just followin' orders," McMay heckled. "I kinda like ya, kid, and if you hadn't stuck your big face into it on the beach, you'd be a lot healthier now!"

It took an instant for Jacinda to take in the uncanny situation, but then her training took over. She rolled off the far side of the bed, landed on her back, and rose immediately with a shotgun in her arms. She pointed the muzzle at the bird-thing that had invaded the room. She pumped a cartridge into the chamber and took aim at McMay.

"Stay back!" she barked at Dan.

Between the first and second word, Alexandros sprung at her like a ravenous tiger. The animal in midflight imposed his body between the barrel of Jacinda's gun and its target—McMay's head.

She fired, blasting the cat full in the belly. It virtually melted into a splatter of blood, fur, and viscera spreading out until it covered Dan, the bed, the walls—and what pieces of feline were left, hit Jacinda in the face, blinding her long enough to make another quick shot impossible.

"Oh, dear," said McMay in his clipped accent. "Hostile environment, what?"

He turned to Dan, gore-speckled against the pillows. As he took flight, McMay added, "Perhaps you'll introduce me to your bird . . . er . . . *lady friend*—no pun intended—when I'm not so strapped for time. Got to fly—pun intended that time, boy-o!"

McMay's Ba looked up, the moonlight shining in his eyes. They were sharper, more focused than Dan remembered. And then, the creature was out the window and gone.

Dashing after it, recocking the shotgun, and furiously wiping the blood and clots of cat's skin out of her face and hair, Jacinda saw the huge bird-thing fade into nothingness above the trees.

She fired anyway, pelting a few branches, then dropped the weapon in utter frustration.

"Blast it! Goddamn to hell! What was that?"

Dan laughed without joy, rose, and stood at her side—both of them now bathed in moonlight. "We were just talking about him. That was what became of McMay."

"The appraiser?" Perplexed, she turned to him with too many questions to utter.

"The slaughter at the museum, my father—it was him."

"Why didn't you—?"

"Oh, come on!" said Dan, throwing up his hands. "Exactly who would've believed me? The police? The colonel? *You?*"

"I saw mummies walk," she muttered simply.

Dan agreed with a nod, but declared strongly that it wasn't enough, saying, "And even knowing what I knew, I came up with perfectly reasonable alternatives. Every reason but the supernatural."

"If I had known—"

"Nothing would have changed," he assured her, lifting her chin with his finger and cleaning a smear of blood off her cheek with his handkerchief. "Salameh had a four-legged spy in the house dirtying up our kitty litter, remember? You gave the beady-eyed little shit what it deserved."

Minutes after both of them could have been slaughtered, she remained, Dan realized, a fascinating woman. Poised, yet seductive. He was amazed how Jacinda flashed quicker than lightning at McMay.

Where had she kept that gun? Clamped under the bed frame, he guessed. And if it hadn't been for the cat, she might have blown McMay's head off his feathered neck. He held her in his arms, not to comfort her. How could he manage that when she'd saved his life—twice, if he counted her story about using the ankh on him; once, if he trusted McMay's crap about not wanting to kill him this time.

She was braver than he. Trained. Deadly. Magnificent.

He wished he could protect her. At that moment, when he had to release her, or she might suspect how deep his feelings for her had become, he admitted it to himself. For some inexplicable reason—a magic spell suddenly didn't seem so far out of the question—he loved her more than any woman he had ever known.

Jacinda had a more immediate concern on her mind as she slipped out of Dan's arms and turned for the door.

"The colonel has to be told."

Still a sticky mess, Jacinda rushed downstairs to the fax and sent a somewhat blood-smudged document through to Halevi's contact number. The reply spewed out of the machine a couple minutes later. It was unsigned and contained only one sentence.

"Wait for me."

CHAPTER TWENTY-NINE ☥

O n Jacinda's orders, they stuffed the clothes, blood, and cat pieces into two separate plastic bags, twist-tied them shut, and stacked them in the closet until the day when a Mossad forensic lab might wish to examine them.

Walking to the family room, Jacinda was acting distracted. She curled up on the couch, staring into the fireplace.

Dan wrapped an afghan around her shoulders. He sat next to her, feeling her warmth. "I thought I'd be scared, terrified, y'know. But I'm kind of numb. Is it always like that?"

She didn't look at him and was slow to answer. "You do what's necessary when you have to do it. It's the quiet time afterward—"

Dan couldn't keep from staring into Jacinda's eyes and thinking how they danced with life. However it turned out with her, Dan knew he'd never bother with those graduate student groupies again. In front of him was a vital, fully realized woman who excited him more than he could ever have believed.

"What are you gaping at with that moon face?" she demanded. Her eyes flashed. Lord, he loved it when they did that. It reminded him of something—

Oh, no.

That was his mother's look. The same one she shot at him for thirty years whenever she accused him of being a bad boy. But old Evangeline loved him just the same.

That was hopeful. Maybe, just maybe, that glance betrayed a touch of a similar emotion from Jacinda.

"I was musing, that's all," Dan said in his defense. "It's how I am when I'm thinking hard."

Jacinda frowned, but even then, no deep lines spoiled her beautiful face. "Thinking about what?"

"Cats. Egyptian cats."

"I don't understand what Alexandros was doing. Was he trying to protect that horrible bird-thing, or kill it?"

"They're servants of the gods. A cat's eyes, their shape, are different from other animals because it is through them that the gods see into our world. That's why the Egyptians worshiped them. They even mummified cats just like pharaohs."

Alexandros might've been a dead cat all along, Jacinda thought, recalling the creatures on the ship. *Was it just another mummy Salameh brought back to life?*

The colonel pulled into the cul-de-sac and parked the Mercury in the garage. He rushed in with a single order, "Pack!"

Halevi told Dan and Jacinda to get their clothes together while he collected the electronics from the work areas. The colonel gathered up the papers and stacked them into a couple of valises, then accompanied Jacinda who was taking her single duffle to the car.

While they were loading their gear into the trunk, the colonel turned and asked her to fill him in.

Speaking rapidly in Hebrew, Jacinda began a detailed recap of the bizarre events of the past hours. Jacinda told him everything, blow by blow—except she said Dan was tired, and she wanted him to nap undisturbed upstairs, as an excuse for both of them being in her bedroom.

When they returned to the living room, Dan was waiting with a suitcase and a hanging bag. The colonel asked him the same questions as he did Jacinda. He added a clarification or two, making sure to give Jacinda full credit for her attempt to save the cross.

Dan noticed a slight change in the colonel's blink rate when Jacinda first mentioned the bird with the Irishman's head, but otherwise there was nothing in either his expression or body language that betrayed any shock.

"When are we leaving?" Dan asked.

Halevi checked his watch. "We have time for a drink."

"Tea?"

"If that's what you have."

Dan looked at Jacinda, but when she made no move toward the kitchen, Dan trudged off to brew a pot.

The colonel's second order of business was to inspect the second-floor bedroom. He poked briefly around the window, carefully picking up and examining small shards where the glass and wood-frame splinters imploded into the room.

"I'll order a clean-up crew."

When Dan returned to the living room, the colonel was in the lounge chair, sitting upright and attentive. Over his tea, he asked Dan if he had any explanation for the vulture-man. Jacinda found a place on the thick throw rug at Dan's feet to listen.

"I've been thinking," Dan began. "McMay's the key to understanding both Salameh and whatever powers are in the ankh. When I first met him, McMay was a man—a pretty pushy one as I recall but a human being nevertheless. Now he's not. He's air. He doesn't truly exist—not in our reality."

"He seemed very real to me," Jacinda muttered.

"That's our mistake," said Dan solemnly. "We've been beating our heads against walls trying to reconcile these supernatural occurrences with what we believe is solid and corporeal."

"Corporal?" the colonel inquired.

"I mean real. Look, Colonel, I'm a scientist, and you and Jake, here, are—well, you're whatever you two are—but we're all practical types. I don't believe in voodoo or ghosts or astral projection or any of that channeling shit that's popular now, and I bet neither do you. But that's our failing.

"We don't have the brains to know that there are things that can't be explained down to ten places past the decimal point. We shut ourselves off from possibilities when we conceive this as a battle between reality and superstition. Salameh isn't supernatural. He understands what we don't. We're not fighting the supernatural; all of this is preternatural."

The colonel held up a finger. "I'm not American, sir. What is that word?"

"Preternatural? I'm sorry. I'm going into college professor mode. It means some phenomenon that has no natural explanation that we know of now. Say you're a caveman. Every single day you see this ball of fire moving from one mountain in the east across the sky. You watch it, and it seems to go out when it hits a mountain in the west. You don't know why it does this. You make up supernatural explanations for it. But in fact, it's preternatural. There is an actual scientific reason for the sun to appear in the east and set in the west. It just took a few thousand years for the descendants of that caveman to figure it out."

"Oh, I see," said Halevi. "We are the cavemen."

"Yeah. And what we're dealing with is not magic. I'm sure of that. It's an ancient wisdom, or technology, or both. The Horites, a little desert tribe, discovered it. I don't know, maybe it was a mineral from a meteorite that landed near them—"

"Or came down with an 'ancient astronaut'?" proposed the colonel.

Dan smiled. "We'll never know. What we do know is that it works. It can reanimate long-dead bodies. If Amenemhab's story is true, this technology may work on an atomic level. Evidently, it can organize the electrical impulses of one brain and act as a conduit to transfer them into another. That was how Sennemut intended to take over the pharaoh's body."

"Salameh doesn't use it for that," said Jacinda.

Dan nodded. "Could be it takes the whole ankh to reformat a brain?"

The colonel grunted. "Then, he can do it now."

"But, Daniel," said Jacinda, "you said it yourself. We are discussing myths when we talk of living mummies and this bird creature."

"Yes, we are." Dan was troubled. It had been only a few hours since McMay's attack, and his theories were less than fully formed. "Did you read the story of Isis and Osiris in the translation?"

Both nodded.

"That's a myth, too. But the way it's presented, it could be based on fact. I'm not a physiologist, but the brain is electrochemical in nature, and that seems to be how the ankh works, too."

"This bird," the colonel wondered. "A hoax, possibly? A construction, a robot, like they make for Hollywood?"

Making a waving gesture and shaking his head, Dan was emphatic that the Ba was real, at least if one accepts the existence of the soul.

"Then you believe in Egyptian mythology?" the colonel asked.

"What I'm saying is, if the idea of the soul is created in an electrochemical mind, after death it is released as pure energy that's given form by the person's own belief system."

The colonel placed his cup on the coffee table. When he sat up again, his face wore a puzzled expression. "How does this explain living mummies?"

"It explains angels and devils, as well. And how McMay turned into a *ba*! I'll try to make it simple. The *ka* is the essence of the person that's left after his body dies. His eternal double. That's the part that stays in the tomb, but the *ba* is the soul that's free to fly out of the grave and wander among the living. That could be how Salameh controls him.

"He's keeping McMay's body hidden somewhere. And with the mummies, it's just the opposite. The *ka*, the soul, stays with the body after death. Energy cannot be created or destroyed. The electricity lays dormant until the ankh releases it and reanimates a brainless corpse."

"I suppose it's hypothetical now," said Halevi. "My instinct tells me, he's won. Whatever Salameh intended to do with the ankh, we'll never stop him. Time works for him now. I should've protected that damn cross with every man I could spare, locked it in a vault a mile underground."

"It wouldn't have mattered if the ankh blasted off on the space shuttle," said Dan. "This guy has cats working for him. Mummy soldiers. Maybe some jerk with a jackal's head is gonna pop up next. You can't fight against stuff like that."

Jacinda slammed her cup on the table. "We can't give up! I say find Salameh and rip the ankh out of his bloody hands! Where is he? I'll go alone if I have to!" Angrily, Jacinda stacked the cups and stomped into the kitchen. They heard her turn on the small counter television.

The colonel held out his palms and shook his head at Dan. "Salameh keeps a tight circle. We found Qader at the Syrian Embassy in Washington. If the Syrians are protecting Salameh, it could be a very troublesome matter getting to him."

Suddenly, Jacinda was shouting.

"Colonel! Daniel!" Jacinda called emphatically from the kitchen. From her tone, both men knew to hurry to her. She stood in front of the television, blocking the screen. As they came in, she turned her head and stepped aside.

"Take a look at CNN," she said.

They stopped, aghast. The face of Mahmoud Salameh stared back at them. Jacinda explained in a whisper what had been going on as they listened with one ear to the special report.

Moments before, Jacinda had heard the anchorwoman relate the story, her features grave and her tone portentous. That morning, she told her audience, the news channel received a videotape from the world's most sought-after terrorist. But despite their expectations, it didn't contain a threat. Instead, it was what could best be described as a cinema verité recording of a miracle.

Using a hidden camera, probably inside a briefcase or over-the-shoulder bag, Salameh, dressed in a doctor's white coat, was photographed entering the Children's Hospital in Annapolis, Maryland. In the video, he marched directly to the intensive-care oncology ward and stopped at each bed.

The camera framed dying youngsters, attached by tubes and wires to machinery out of *Star Trek*.

Some kids were coherent; most were not, and yet he spoke with a smile on his face to each for a few seconds. Then, he passed his hands over their bodies before touching them on the lips with his index finger.

The scene switched. This time to a smaller building, an AIDS hospice. Again, Salameh moved from room to room, bed to bed, comforting men and women lying in agony or dementia, some human skeletons, others covered in purple lesions. His hands wandered over each of them as he had done before.

Salameh was seen sitting on a tan sofa in the corner of a room. Nothing was on the white walls to distinguish them from any of a million others. He spoke directly into the camera's lens, but it was as if he were talking to a single individual, not in a pedantic way but rather like a knowing father. In this way, in a voice in barely accented English, soothing and elegant, Salameh presented his message of contrition and hope.

"Moses killed an Egyptian overseer. . . . Jesus fought with the money changers in the Temple. . . .

"They were forgiven.

"I, too, have much to be forgiven for. . . . The time of conflict and confrontation has ended. . . .

"Peace, everlasting. . . ."

CHAPTER THIRTY

H e's raising innocent children from the dead," Dan said, his jaw slack.

"And in public, yet . . . This is not good," Halevi lamented as he turned from the screen.

The CNN special report concluded by intercutting interviews with doctors from each institution. They were amazed that all signs of disease had vanished from every single patient Salameh had touched.

None of the doctors admitted a thing, of course, stating that months, perhaps years, of further study would be necessary before any definitive connection could be made between the two events, and—most certainly—research would be funded shortly in an attempt to ascertain a precise scientific explanation for what might, at first blush, seem to be a supernatural phenomenon.

"The Christian fundamentalists are going to have a field day with this," Dan said, shaking his head. "Laying on of hands, like Jesus—*Jesus!*"

"Gentiles will—what?" Jacinda wondered. "Embrace him?"

"Don't get me wrong. The rank and file won't buy it at first. It's only that there seems to be a heavy strain of opportunism in their leaders' ranks. I saw it when I was having all that trouble with my father. I swear, if the worship of Zeus would make them politically powerful, they'd be wearing thunderbolts around their fat, red necks instead of crosses."

A buzzer cut off the discussion. Dan knew it wasn't the doorbell, but he knew it must be important when he saw Halevi and Jacinda stiffen. "What's that?" he asked.

"Where are the cars located?" Halevi demanded of Jacinda in Hebrew, totally ignoring Dan's question. "Mine's in the driveway out front. I didn't see yours."

"Garage. It's ready."

"Hey, hey, hey!" Dan interrupted. "What's all that noise mean?"

Jacinda drew herself closer to him, her manner becoming precise and professional. "It's a signal from the motion detectors. There are intruders on the property. They're coming here."

"I'm sorry," the colonel said. "It's likely I was followed or monitored."

"Who? Who's coming?" said Dan anxiously.

"Could be nothing," said Jacinda.

Halevi sighed. "Right. It could be a deer, an innocent passerby—"

"An Arab hit squad?" Dan interjected.

"That's why we go through the drill." Halevi turned to Jacinda, then examined the ceiling. "Upstairs?"

"Two charges up there."

Dan held up his hand like he was in elementary school. "Charges? What kind of charges?"

Jacinda yanked him aside as Halevi went toward the stairs. "This is not an ordinary house," she said. "It is wired."

"Like dynamite wired?"

"C-4," said Jacinda. "But the idea's the same."

"Our guest is our priority," the colonel said to Jacinda as if Dan weren't standing at his elbow. Dan started to protest, but the colonel shut him up with a glance.

"Doc, keep your head down and follow each order she gives you to the letter. You'll be all right. Or, if not all right, at least alive."

Halevi returned to the television, tapping the hidden side door which should have concealed the vertical-hold, contrast, and treble controls—the ones no ordinary human could figure out and the main reason the Japanese invented automatic fine tuning—but it didn't.

He ran his fingers over a color-coded pad, and a row of recessed circles popped out. He turned two of the phantom knobs, and a grid map flashed on the screen. It was a schematic of the farmhouse and environs.

Inside the linear layout of the house was a cluster of three yellow crosses. Dan realized their positions corresponded to the colonel, Jacinda, and himself. Evidently, someone knew where he was at all times, a thought both comforting and frightening at the same time.

More frightening were the six small red rectangles converging on the farm from a curving electronic path, delineating the access road and the stone perimeter fence.

"How many's that?" asked Dan.

"A carload," was the colonel's quick response. The answer meant more to Jacinda than Dan. The colonel meant six. A pro team, three to cover the rear and both sides of the house, two to enter the front, and a driver who also keeps an eye on the top floor and garage.

More than an adequate number to kill two agents and a know-nothing archaeologist, Dan assumed.

"Lights!" shouted Halevi urgently.

Immediately, Jacinda dashed for the kitchen and slammed her palm into the main switch on the circuit breaker, plunging the house into darkness. All the lights should have gone off, and the lamps and power were, but the green glow continued from the television.

Maybe it had its own generator or a more sophisticated power source. Dan watched Jacinda's yellow "+" one room away, the colonel's by the set, and his own somewhere in between.

His cross was easy for him to recognize. It was the one not knowing what to do. Halevi took care of that promptly.

"Doc! Get down!"

Dan obeyed at once, but as he did, he was attracted to the screen where one of the red triangles was nearly up to the wall across from the living room window. The colonel turned back to the screen and saw the danger, but was an instant slow to react. As he sprang away into the shadows, a burst of gunfire erupted the glass of the casement window, sending a thousand shards like daggers into the room.

Halevi rolled onto the floor, grabbing his leg.

"Colonel! You hit?"

"Not by any damn bullets," he groaned, drawing his firearm and aiming where the map on the screen said the shooter would be. He pumped three shots through the gaping window, and the first of the red rectangles blinked out.

One down, five to go.

Dan reached the colonel in a running crouch. Jacinda, hearing the commotion, was at their side in moments. She looked down at Halevi, then glared at the still-glowing television screen.

"I thought it was supposed to give us some warning?" She whipped out her gun and aimed it at the TV, but Halevi grabbed her wrist.

"No!" His voice was commanding, but a raspy cough followed it as he finished his thought. "At least this way we know where they are."

"How is it?" She stared at his wound. It was hard to see in the dark, but the wetness of it reflected in the light off the TV.

"Piece of glass, damn the luck." He ripped his belt from its loops and wrapped it tight around his leg, twice around hip to groin. "If it was a slug—but, no, it got me in the femoral artery."

"You'll be okay," Dan said instinctively.

Halevi half laughed, half snorted at the idea. "I can walk with the tourniquet on, but if I did, I'd probably bleed out in seven minutes. Let's make the time count!" He stared at Jacinda for the barest of moments. No remorse. In that look, he was passing the mantle to her.

Dan tried to focus. There must be something he could do? Compress it, sew it up, anything . . .

But Jacinda's face said it all. The colonel was a dead man.

He was still up to giving orders, though. "Hall closet, under the shoe rack!" he shouted. "Bring me everything!"

The remaining rectangles had congregated near the far wall, probably to plan their strategy, giving Dan and Jacinda the minute they needed to tear up the closet floor and toss a shotgun and a sack of grenades over to the colonel.

"How's that?" Jacinda shouted.

"It'll do. Detonator?"

Jacinda lobbed a small metal box with a red toggle switch at him. He caught it like a shortstop. The colonel waved them off. "Go! Go!"

On screen, the red rectangles were on the move again. Two were headed for the front door; two more took each of the rear corners to block any chance of escape through the back.

"It's the garage, then," said Jacinda, handing Dan a Glock of his own from the closet stash.

He just stood there weighing the gun in his hand.

Jacinda asked, "Can you handle one of those?"

"I used to carry a revolver in the desert. Never used it for much more than shooting at beer bottles, though."

"Well, there are five Budweisers coming for us right now. Aim for the labels." She turned on her heels, grabbed his free hand, and led him toward the kitchen. She opened the door to the garage and sent Dan through.

But before going in, she stopped for a moment to glance one last time toward the kitchen and Colonel Halevi. He was on his feet, unsteadily, but upright with the shotgun raised toward the front entrance. He noticed her and smiled his farewell.

"Jake, does . . . does the colonel have a plan?" asked Dan as she joined him in the car.

"He's going to invite them in," she said with a glibness she did not feel. "Into the car, now. You drive."

"No, not yet. We've got an entire hit squad out there!"

He sprang out of the driver's side door, pulling Jacinda by the arm without telling her why. Barreling into the laundry area, Dan yanked the plugs and the hoses from the washer and dryer.

Seeing what he was about, Jacinda helped roll them in front of the only door that connected the garage with the rest of the house. That was when they heard the first pair of shotgun blasts.

The colonel had propped himself between the dishwasher and the center island. His position gave him a good view of the television screen and the back windows. Pumping the shotgun, Halevi fired twice at the rear door and blew it off its hinges. Two red triangles converged on the door, perhaps the killers assumed their partners had stormed into the front of the house. They hesitated at the opening, but when they rushed through, they were met with a pair of fatal head shots.

The screen showed the other three rectangles scattered around front.

Halevi's leg throbbed terribly. He was thankful for the few moments respite before the rest of the squad found him. His eyes closed for a second, but a noise from outside alerted him. He raised his hand gun and swept it in a forty degree arc.

Nothing.

And the red rectangles had not moved at all.

That second, the blade of a sword hewed the edge of the island, missing the colonel's ear by a millimeter.

The colonel pitched forward and fired a fan of bullets over his head. Most struck the log ceiling without damage. Only then did he see his attacker. His long, dark overcoat could not disguise the mummy within the clothes. Halevi knew its strength, attested to from his experience in Lebanon.

Halevi fired a clip into the eviscerated chest.

Staring from black, eyeless sockets, the mummy's head tilted at an odd angle in the style of that RCA dog looking into his gramophone. Dust trickled down its cheeks like tears. Its face was the color of pumice.

A bony hand, filthy wrappings exposing blackened nails on decayed fingers, reached out for Halevi and dug into his thigh with a vicelike grip.

Out of habit rather than fear, the colonel snatched his commando blade from its ankle sheath and jabbed sideways. When it made contact, he twisted the point and ripped up. The razor-sharp edge severed the creature's hand at the wrist bone.

Halevi expected a sound of agony. Instead, the mummy hissed like an indignant rat. It rose up, turning its death's head to stare blankly at the empty sleeve. Watching without eyes, it seemed fascinated as a deep rust-colored dust poured from the stump.

Seizing the opportunity, the colonel lunged forward, aiming the knife at the thing's neck. But it was quick, and its remaining hand caught the spy's forearm and bent it back until the colonel finally heard the screams he had anticipated from the mummy.

Unfortunately, this time they were his own.

He felt his elbow separate as the cartilage tore, the sound more appalling than the pain. The knife flew from his hand and clattered into the gutter.

Unarmed and with the rotten, living carcass crawling onto him, Halevi kicked again, furiously, in a bicycle motion. It wasn't enough. He couldn't get enough traction on the kitchen tile to stop the mummy's advance.

The thing, compelled, pressed closer, onto him. Only two hands between them now, but the corpse was unrelenting, pulling at Halevi's belt and shirttails, its gray corrupted flesh reaching for the colonel's throat.

The mummy reared up. It straightened its arm, seized the colonel's neck so that its thumb compressed the carotid artery, while its fingers constricted the windpipe. The colonel knew he had seconds before it was all over.

No blood getting to his brain.

No oxygen to his airway.

Still, he fought. Until he sensed himself fade away.

Jacinda heard two shotgun bursts and then small-caliber fire. Two shots, close together, then fifteen seconds later, rapid fire. She assumed the colonel had invited his guests into his parlor. Then, an awesome silence again.

"We've got a minute, tops," she said.

"Wait! How is he? What's he doing? Is he—?"

"He's drawing them in. He'll have his hands on the detonator by now."

"If he's still alive," said Dan. Immediately, they heard the sound of splintering wood.

"The two outside are breaking through," said Jacinda. "The spider's attracting the flies. Come on, if we're not out of here in thirty seconds—"

"Okay, one second." Dan had only one task left. He bent over to lock the wheels on the dryer, so its weight would block that way in.

It saved his life.

A metal blade crashed through the thin composite of the upper door panel, slicing off that nasty cowlick on the back of his head that he normally smoothed down with mousse, but hadn't since he'd been brought to the farm.

Jacinda was by the car and whirled around when she heard the noise to see Dan falling.

"Dan!"

"I'm okay," he blurted out as he looked up. He watched the blade withdraw, then crash again into the door, showering him with wood chips.

"Oh, shit!"

"What?" She motioned for him to get over to the car as she got in the passenger side.

"It's a bronze short sword," he said as he ran over to the car and piled in behind the wheel. "They aren't just a carload, Jake. I think maybe they threw a couple of mummies in the trunk along with the spare tire."

"How could that be?"

"Dead people don't show up on the infrared. They've been cold a long time. Hell, there could be fifty stiffs waiting for us on the front lawn. Now, how do we get out of here?"

"Rev the motor. The garage door is fitted with explosive bolts," she said as she reached for something in the glove compartment. "The instant, the *very* instant I blow them, floor it. Then, go straight through the picket fence—it's made to collapse—and into the field, not the road. They'd have blocked that."

"What if—?"

"No time for questions."

Which was true, since the door behind them pulverized, and a very angry-looking ancient Egyptian warrior began hacking away at the Kelvinator washing machine in his path.

Inside the car, Dan revved the car's engine as Jacinda found the switch she was feeling for, and the garage-door opener above them rammed ahead like a rocket. Other charges must have been set at the edges, since everything through the windshield dissolved into flame and powdery smoke.

Dan aimed the car into the middle of it until he could see again. He'd burst through the doctored fence without knowing it and was bouncing along the grassy meadow that led to the main road when the farmhouse flared like a roman candle, literally disintegrating into slivers of wood and metal that were instantly consumed by an immense fireball.

Flaming rain hit the roof and hood, but the wind blew them off the car before they did anything more than cosmetic damage.

They were free. With a last death twitch on the detonator, the colonel had seen to that.

Dan hadn't been paying attention to his rearview mirror, so the sight of an eyeless skull with black leathery skin stretched grotesquely across it and coming at him made him jolt upright in his seat.

The mummy fractured the rear window of the car with a blow from the hilt of his sword.

"Jake!" he screamed, trying to alert her, but she was already shifting in her seat, pulling out her gun.

"I see him!" she said as the determined corpse tried to climb into the seat behind her. She gave the thing two blasts to the face, but it kept on coming.

Dan was frantic. He shouted to her, "Want me to stop?"

"Hell, no!" she barked. "Not unless you want him in your lap! Try to shake him off the car!"

Dan jerked the wheel hard to the left, then made an immediate right, causing the car to skid a bit as it bounced over the rugged terrain.

All that tumult didn't seem to be doing much good as far as jostling the creature off, but Jacinda was having some success in avoiding the mummy's ancient weapon as all three pitched from side to side.

The mummy was hanging more inside than outside the car with only its bony, gauze-bound legs flailing about on the trunk lid, denting it deeply with each blow. Remarkably so, considering the mummy's spindly legs.

Dan watched Jacinda grab the thing by the wrist, under its sword hilt. She was able to force the bronze point into the car's roof where it twisted and slashed the headliner before the mummy made a final mad thrust, imbedding the sword into the metal until it broke eighteen inches from the tip.

It hung there, its razor's edge precariously close to the back of Dan's head. "You okay?" said Dan.

"I'm holding him, but, dammit, shake harder!"

"Damn car almost flipped us over the last time!"

"Well, think of something!"

He did, even though he had a less-than-completely formed idea in his head when he threw the gear shift into neutral. A combination of friction, dirt, and grass helped the brakes slow the car without any sudden momentum to help the mummy further inside.

Before the vehicle came to a complete halt, Dan jammed the stick into reverse and tried to find out if the Mossadmobile could handle zero to sixty in reverse. The car almost flew backwards, faster than Dan thought possible.

"What're you—?"

"Break his hands for me, Babe. I know you can do it!"

She wasn't pleased about being called "Babe," but cracked the mummy's wrists without argument, its weapon hand first.

"Hold tight!" yelled Dan at the snap of the brittle bones, then, with both feet and all his power, pounded on the brake pedal until the back of it whacked the floorboard.

The car skidded out of control for ten car lengths before it lurched to an absolute stop, but as hoped, the mummy was propelled out of the rear window like the rocketman in a Commando Cody serial running backwards through the projector. It almost looked comical until the body finally struck the earth and crumbled into a cloud of body parts.

Dust to dust.

In the car, Dan gulped a big lungful of air and nodded at Jacinda. "Where to now, madame?" he inquired lightly.

"Over there." She pointed in the direction of a gravel access road that led from the field to the main drag into town. "We have to beat them to it."

For the first time, Dan saw the attackers' car. It was still some distance away, following the long driveway roughly parallel to them.

"Determined little bastards," Dan said, returning the lever to "drive" and slip-sliding, pulling forward, in the dirt. He aimed the car at the highway and floored it.

"The colonel did well." Jacinda sounded proud as she stared out the passenger-side window. "Only two in the car," she went on. Evidently she had the eyesight of a bird of prey.

"Two?" asked Dan. "People or mummies?"

"Do mummies drive?"

"Damn, I hope not." The Mercury sped off at an oblique angle to the assassins' car. In a few seconds, the tires found asphalt.

"What do I do now, Jake?" he said driving down the center of the road.

"Find a lane and exceed the speed limit!" she ordered. "About a quarter mile from here is a blind curve. Once we make it, we'll have maybe five to eight seconds before they can see us. This is what I want you to do. After the curve there's a boulder, a large one, shaped like the top of a skull. Pull off the road next to it. Stop. Face front with one foot on the brake and the other lightly on the gas pedal. The next thing you will hear is two shots. The first, very loud. The second, not so loud. Now, this is important. The instant you hear that second shot, gun the motor and cross back onto the road. Get us as far from that boulder as you can as fast as you can! Got that?"

"Second shot, I got it!"

"Good, 'cause it's coming right up."

Dan, who had been around the world and in quite a few potentially hostile situations before, had never faced this—the do-or-die moment.

When it arrived, he surprised himself at how calm he felt. As the bend in the road approached, he decided he should pull off the highway without braking first, afraid that if the red taillights flashed, it would alert the killers and give the plan away.

Jacinda must have spotted this curve earlier in the week, Dan surmised, since she told him this was her first trip to America.

Did she plan her escape so thoroughly for every place she went? Or did her mind simply retain everything it saw? No time to wonder; the turn was on them.

"Here! Here!" It was Jacinda's voice breaking through.

"Pull off!"

"Stop!"

The instant his pursuers disappeared from his rearview and side mirrors, Dan took his foot off the gas and coasted.

The curve, when he got there, wasn't especially sharp, but high brush and a thick copse jutting out from the forest effectively hid the road ahead until the driver almost completed his turn. Then, like a miracle, a grassy shoulder next to the promised boulder materialized in front of him.

He swung the car wide and tugged the wheel a bit further than necessary so that when the wheels hit the shoulder, he could still keep the front aligned. He was terrified of going into a skid, but the Mercury was specially made for the Israelis, so it was armored with antilock brakes and had the suspension of a tank.

The tires kicked up some dirt, and then the car fishtailed some as it ran over the high grass. But the tread crunched deep into the undergrowth as the Mercury headed for the granite wall that shot up from the roadside like the prow of a huge Viking long boat.

The car angled back toward the road and came to a stop less than two feet from the black rock. Jacinda used the opportunity to climb up through the moon roof with her gun out.

"Get ready," she said, then held her breath and aimed the strange, two-barreled weapon toward the curve.

"What're you doing?" Dan asked, sounding hoarse.

Jacinda answered through gritted teeth. "This!"

Dan looked over and saw the Syrians' car take the blind corner at full speed. True to the plan, Jacinda fired twice as soon as they showed. As advertised, her first shot was deafening.

It came meteor-quick the instant the terrorist car rounded the curve—an incandescent blast. The single mortarlike shell struck the driver's side vaporizing his head and shoulders and mutating the rest of him into flaming chunks of stew meat.

The second report came immediately after, evidently from the lower barrel. It was more of a popping sound. To Dan it seemed an afterthought, but later Jacinda's reason for it became obvious.

The first bang took out the driver, but the next caused the blowout that sent the assassins' sedan careening out of control and—

"Step on it!" screamed Jacinda, but Dan's foot was grinding the accelerator into the carpet a heartbeat before he heard the demand.

The Mercury had cleared the shoulder and was sideslipping onto the roadway as the chase car struck the granite face just a few feet from them. It was going at lightning speed when it hit, crushing the hood into the passenger cab at the same instant the gas tank ignited. Straightaway, what had been a car with two men inside flashed into a fiery holocaust of melting metal and cooking flesh.

Down the road, Dan saw the smoke and flickering flames in his rearview mirror. "Are we safe now?" he asked pointedly to Jacinda. She was back in her seat with her eyes closed, the gun cradled in her lap.

"I wish I knew." She sighed. "We're alive for a while, but we may never be safe again."

CHAPTER THIRTY-ONE

The two-hour-forty-minute drive to Washington, part on two-lane farmland roads and part on the Shirley Memorial Highway, passed mostly in silence. The colonel was dead, and it affected Jacinda profoundly once the adrenaline of battle wore off.

The road was straight when they turned onto the highway, and the monotony of the drive gave Dan a chance to digest all that happened and maybe decide what to do next. Jacinda offered Dan no choice of destination.

Salameh was last seen in a Maryland hospital. Finding Salameh would be the easy part. He was starting his PR campaign; he wanted to be found.

"Just a thought starting to move around in my head. About Salameh. He's making himself known. That's a dangerous time. It's as if he's started on his ministry after spending years in hiding or exile—you name it. It was sort of like he was preparing himself in the wilderness. Like Jesus."

Jacinda snickered at the idea. "Preparing for what? To be an anti-Christ?"

"That's not what I mean." Dan tried to explain. "I'm thinking this Salameh's got a god complex. He might be trying to fulfill the New Testament. Be the Messiah. Be Jesus returned to Earth. And to do it, it could be he's following the general pattern of Jesus's ministry. Remember Jesus seemed to follow the prophecies of Isaiah and Elijah. He healed the sick; he fed the poor."

"You can't be serious. He's a murderer. No one's going to believe a thing he says. People are put in asylums for saying they're god!"

"None of them had the ankh. None of them knew the secret of Osiris's resurrection. I'd say that puts Salameh into another category altogether."

It dawned on Dan that if the Syrians knew they had escaped from the farmhouse, they might send another hit squad after them. Washington would certainly be on alert for them.

He began checking out men and women in the passing cars, but no one looked like a threat. Of course, an assassin who looked like an assassin wouldn't last very long in the political murder business.

Jacinda didn't seem worried. It was money, she said. She doubted if Syria had enough ready cash to fund all these hit squads.

In time, through the windshield, a huge white spike came into view.

Dan touched Jacinda on the shoulder. "There it is." He couldn't take his eyes off it. That was where the ceremony would be held the next morning. It was the focal point of the most powerful city on the planet.

By law, no building in the city could be built higher than the Washington Monument.

"It's the largest obelisk ever, Jake," he said reverently, then he paused as another thought struck him. "That has to mean it draws more psychic energy into the cross than any other. Dammit! That's it!"

"What? Not another revelation."

"My father kept saying it the night he died. We were talking about the words on the Megiddo obelisk, and he said a strange thing. They were practically his last words—*it's the shape*—he told me."

"Which means?"

He pointed through the glass as the monument grew closer. "Look at what caps the thing. You don't think obelisks have pyramids on top by accident, do you? Hah! I bet I can even figure out why the Old Kingdom pharaohs built the pyramids! You wait. After this is over, I'm gonna write a paper on it!"

"Daniel," Jacinda said indulgently, "I honor the enthusiasm you have for your work, but we've got a lot to prevent and not a lot of time to get it done!"

"Okay, Jake, sure. I was just thinking out loud."

She huffed. "Babbling's more like it. And I'd rather not waste what little time we have."

"We'll have plenty of time."

"I hate to contradict you, darling, but we'll probably be dead in a few hours."

"You called me darling," he said, grinning ear to ear. "Oh, don't be so pessimistic. I expect we'll have a long and happy life after we've taken care of this jerk—."

"Whom I wouldn't underestimate."

"Agreed. Remember all that crap a few years ago about pyramid power? Y'know, how fruit wouldn't spoil under a pyramid. People even started sleeping under these stupid pyramid frames hoping it would keep them young."

"This means something?"

"It's vestigial knowledge. Somewhere down through the ages, people got the idea that pyramids can do this weird stuff. It must go way back, 'cause, in a way, the Old Kingdom pharaohs had to think the same thing. Otherwise, why build pyramids at all? It was only after the priests saw that all of the pyramids were robbed that it dawned on them that this pyramid-power thing didn't work. I mean, the bodies didn't look much better than the corpses they buried in the desert."

Jacinda had been rummaging around the glove compartment searching for a city map and found one in a pouch with money that must have been the colonel's survival kit.

"Obelisks have pyramids on top!"

"Yes, Daniel," said Jacinda, not really paying attention. She unfolded the map until she pinpointed where they were. "We have to find a hotel."

"Maybe I'm not making myself clear. That's where *he's* going. That's where we'll find Salameh. Inside the Washington Monument. At the top. At the center of the pyramid! That's where all the power will be directed, so that's where he's taking the cross!"

CHAPTER THIRTY-TWO

D an circled the block in the Mercury while Jacinda was inside the Israeli Embassy trying to speak with the Mossad duty officer. After the third circuit, he discovered her waiting outside the high iron gate looking like a small, abandoned child who had no more tears left to cry.

"What's the problem, Jake?" Dan asked as she slipped in beside him.

"They don't know a thing, or they won't admit it if they do."

"What about the colonel? Didn't you tell them the Syrians killed him? We're talking 'international incident' here!"

"We have to talk. But not here," Jacinda said, then shook her head without allowing her thought to progress much beyond that.

Dan accepted her state, deciding not to ferret out what had unfolded inside the spies' offices until they found a place to spend the night.

She must have been quashed there—so Dan believed—and it had to be a new experience for her. The motel he chose was just across the border in Maryland. It was situated in a rural area off the interstate where Dan assumed the locals wouldn't recognize his face from his PBS shows or the pages of *Archaeology* magazine. Even so, he let

Jacinda pay for their room at the counter while she told the clerk her husband was getting the luggage out of the trunk.

Dan was surprised, but actually, because of some standard spy procedure, there was a plain black garment bag tucked next to the wheel well.

The Mossad evidently made it policy for their agents to keep at least a change of clothes in their cars in case they needed a quick getaway or had to stay on the run for a while.

When Jacinda returned with the keys, she got in and they drove around to a first-floor unit. Jacinda opened the motel room door, went in, and flopped facedown on the bed closest to the window.

When Dan threw the bag on the other bed and opened it, he found a couple of wrinkle-free dresses, women's underwear, and soft shoes folded into a very small space.

Underneath, he found his own clothes. Somehow they had found their way from his closet at home.

The idea that shadowy people had been inside his apartment made him queasy, at first. Then Jacinda showed him what was in the hidden compartments and his stomach flipped over entirely.

Not only was there another gun—an automatic with three clips next to it—but also a lethal-looking blade and a wrapped bar of Ivory soap which Jacinda said was actually C-4 plastic explosive.

"Did you find the engagement rings?" she asked innocently.

"What engagement rings? Jake, are you trying to tell me something?"

She directed him to a small case packed in a corner. Opening it, he found three gold rings with nice-sized diamonds in them.

They're worth about six hundred each," she said. "It'll get you fast cash from any pawn broker without having to explain yourself, and you can carry the rings in your pocket."

"They must think of everything." Dan hung up the garment bag and lay down on his bed. He faced Jacinda and asked, "You want to tell me what happened at the embassy, now?"

"We're out in the cold, Dan," she murmured, then lazed onto her back and propped up her head with the bolster. "I charged right inside and, as it happened, the Section Chief was in the lobby. I recognized him. I had seen his photo once when I was being briefed in Tel Aviv."

"So, you got to see him at least."

"Oh, yes. He was very cordial."

Dan grunted. "So what did 'Cordial Man' say? Not good. I'm guessing."

"Correct. He listened carefully and took a few notes, but when I explained that the colonel had died trying to capture Salameh, his eyes sort of glazed over."

"You didn't tell him any of the weird stuff, did you?"

Not likely. It wouldn't matter how many code words I know, one mention of that vulture-man, and I'd be talking to you from under a butterfly net."

"But, the Section Chief must've wanted to capture Salameh."

"He said since Salameh's been performing miracles, the politicians are chasing their tails trying to figure out how to handle him. My countrymen in Israel are scared to death to take action against a man who could proclaim himself the Messiah at any moment."

"Yeah. And it's only a few years since the Pope cleared you guys of killing Christ," said Dan ruefully. "The spin doctors on all sides are starting to work overtime to excuse the minor fact that he's a murdering terrorist."

Dan switched on the television and found an MSNBC news-magazine show. Salamah was the only topic of discussion. He turned down the volume and flopped onto one of the beds in utter frustration.

"See! 'Salamah made a few bad choices when he was young, but he's a changed man. A holy man. He's saving children, curing the sick. What kind of terrorist is that?' "

Jacinda finished unpacking and joined Dan at the foot of the bed. "Are we the only two people who believe he'll use the ankh to hold the world hostage?"

They sat for an hour debating options, but except for their over-weening ambition to obliterate Salameh from the face of the Earth, they couldn't come up with a specific plan. Without the help of the Mossad, there seemed no logical way for two ordinary human beings to overpower an immortal.

"He intends to bring back Divine Right enforced by an army of revived corpses," Dan elaborated. "And he'll probably make that army from the bodies of people like us who dare disagree with him."

"That's a lovely thought."

Finally, Jacinda grew tired and curled into her blanket. Dan flicked off the light switch, letting the light from the TV screen fill the room with a blue-white glow.

The flicker from the set calmed him, somehow. It was on a primal level, probably a reminder of a boyhood spent in tents under lantern light.

He used the remote to turn up the volume a bit. The sound was a little cackly like a shortwave. Dan kicked off his shoes, and they rolled to the foot of the second bed where Jacinda dozed.

He eased onto the pillow and turned to the side facing the television. His eyes were half closing when he realized the Washington Monument was on the screen.

"Jake!" Dan blurted, reaching for the remote. "Look here!"

Jacinda stirred, then sat upright. "Make it louder."

"I am, I am!" He hit the button at least four times until the sound became audible. They had blundered onto the end of a weathercast. According to the stout fellow in front of the animated map of the East Coast, it was fast becoming the hottest summer recorded in the District.

The Washington Monument, it seemed, had been closed to tourists for three days due to over-taxed air conditioning and, with the temperature approaching one hundred degrees the next day, the Parks Authority decided to keep the landmark shut at least until the end of the week.

Jacinda's inspection of the screen was over. "He'll be alone at the summit when the eclipse comes," she stated matter-of-factly.

Numbly, Dan agreed. "My father said it was the shape of the obelisk, but the Washington Monument is only the conduit that focuses the power—it's the *timing* that's critical. Maybe daylight scatters whatever energy source the ankh uses. The darker it is, the less interference. Whatever he's up to, it has to be done during the solar eclipse. Which means, if we can only delay him—"

"Until when?"

"You never know, Jake," Dan said. "Somebody might actually believe us next time."

She gave him a look that said, *You honestly think there'll be a next time?*

Dan saw no profit in talking about what could be their impending deaths. Salameh and his minions had tried to eliminate any possible threat to carrying out their ritual to reenergize the ankh.

His father.

The colonel.

And there had to be others, probably in the Middle East, that Jacinda had failed to mention. They were next. Salameh wanted Jacinda and himself destroyed. Utterly. He tried at the safe house, and he would attack again the instant they surfaced.

Dan had not known Salameh's grand design until he compared his evidence with Jacinda's. In time, the governments of the world would correlate what they knew about Salameh's plan, but by then, Salameh would be unstoppable. They had one chance, tomorrow at the monument.

One chance in a billion.

He turned off the television and looked over at Jacinda. She was so luminous in the half-light of the motel room that he felt she might be a fragment of his fantasies.

Maybe two chances, he thought.

CHAPTER THIRTY-THREE

The thin motel sheets lay twisted in coils, oily with part-dried sweat, at Dan's feet. He slept in the center of the bed as the first rays of the sun sliced through the venetian blinds, striping his body with bands of gold and shadow.

The light worked its way across his eyes, signaling him to wake. He shook off the sleep and rolled out of bed in one motion. The sink was three steps away in a little alcove by the toilet and shower. He ran the water and splashed great handfuls onto his face before he realized he was alone.

"Jake?"

Met with only silence, Dan looked around. Jacinda's handbag and clothes were gone.

Dan was worried. Of course, she could've gone out to get the morning papers or maybe breakfast. That was an intriguing thought. Nothing like an Egg McMuffin to get you ready to do battle with the forces of darkness.

He shaved and showered with one ear straining for the sound of a turning lock, but an hour and a half after he was dressed and ready, the door knob still hadn't budged. Dan knew that because he was checking it once or twice a minute all that time.

He lay on the bed in front of the television watching the local morning show for a while. He learned how to make a cream and dill sauce for poached salmon and what exercises he could do in a chair that would make his abs rock-hard before he hit the remote and consigned the image to the oblivion it deserved.

Waiting in general was god awful, but Dan really hated not knowing what he was sticking around for or how long that nebulous result would take to arrive.

Not long after Dan began to sense the unsettling feeling of abandonment, he heard a car horn outside the window. Two blasts at first, then it became more persistent. He went to the door and peeked out of the side curtain.

Out front, parked sideways and taking up nearly five spaces, sat an ivory Cadillac limousine.

He stepped out of the motel room cautiously to get a better look. As soon as he did, the mirrored rear window of the limo glided down, and Jacinda waved at him. "Close the door and climb in," she told him.

Dan slammed the door to the room and made sure it was locked. By then the limo door was open and waiting for him.

He slid into the jump seat across from where Jacinda was sitting and only then noticed another presence in the car.

"Mother?"

Evangeline sat by the passenger-side window, quiet as a sculpture. Her gaze fell on some middle distance beyond the tinted window. *Click, click* went her fingernails against the glass. She paid no attention when her son entered the vehicle and, in a moment, closed her eyes seemingly lost in thought.

Her lids, Dan noticed, were filled in with a hint of foundation makeup and dark liner. His mother in eye shadow amazed him.

Eva Rawlins, who never wore anything on her face except sun block, looked like a Dowager Empress.

"Mother?" he repeated. Only then did she fix her eyes on him. Her head bobbed a bit to the side as she gave him that pursed-lipped smile he knew so well.

"What are you doing here?"

"Isn't it obvious? I'm here to take you to the meeting." She reached over and stroked the back of his hand. "You're looking so much better than the last time I saw you," she teased. "Obviously, being a fugitive from prosecution is good for you."

"Thanks for reminding me. I'd actually put Haas's murder warrant out of my mind. I thought I only had to look out for terrorists. I forgot about the cops!"

Jacinda leaned forward and tapped the partition. The driver tipped his cap and drove the limo out of the parking lot. Dan, facing backward, steadied himself by holding onto the doorstrap.

"Uh, isn't this yacht a little conspicuous?" Dan asked. "People are searching this town for us with lint brushes."

Eva smiled. "We're going to the obelisk, Daniel, where we'll be one of a hundred limousines dropping off dignitaries. Once we drive inside the perimeter, everyone has to be credentialed."

Dan's sneered. "We won't have credentials, either. Did you ever think of that?"

"Your mother has thought of everything," said Jacinda. She whispered a few words to Eva, but Dan couldn't scope out what was said. He kept silent, watching the streets recede from him through the rear window.

Having Evangeline near always disrupted the delicate balance of Dan's social behavior. He discovered early in life that he had trouble making coherent sentences with her standing over him.

They could go at each other like a pair of territorial tomcats when they were in private, but in most public settings Dan deferred to her experience and eloquence—two qualities that, subconsciously at least, he felt he lacked despite fifteen years in the field and hours of hosting television programs. Such is the legacy of a childhood among giants.

Dan heaved a sigh as the limo turned, and he spotted the White House about a mile away. And then, there it was, the shimmering shaft of the Washington Monument.

"How did you find us, Mother?"

"You have a very special young lady here. Jacinda contacted me at my hotel. She arranged for the limo and came along to make sure we weren't followed."

Dan grinned in Jacinda's direction. "She's special all right."

On the last turn, Jacinda sidled over to Eva, and again they spoke in a confidential tone. Eva nodded, then shaded her brow with her thin fingers. Dan felt left out once more and reacted by crossing his arms and pouting.

"Excuse me," he said with obvious irritation, "do we have a plan here, or are we just blundering ahead blindly?"

"You're the plan," Jacinda responded.

"And—is letting me in on it completely out of the question?"

Eva spoke calmly. "You've been in training for this day all of your life."

She turned her stubborn gaze to the scenery outside. The limo was only inching along now, boxed in by the heavy commuter traffic off 17th Avenue leading to the Ellipse.

Dan was gloomy. "C'mon, you wait until I'm right in the shadow of the monument to tell me I have to go up against one of the most dangerous men on the planet?"

Jacinda stopped him. "No. That's my job."

Eva agreed. "Yours is to bring me the ankh."

"Yeah, even if it kills me."

"Yes, you'll lose, if you fight the man," said Eva. "Your only chance is to save his soul."

Dan faced the two women squarely. "Why do I feel like a pawn trapped by two queens? What aren't you telling me?"

"There are some truths, son, you can only believe if you learn them on your own."

"Why would Jake go to you for help, Ma? Who are you two?"

A strangely intimate look passed between Eva and Jacinda before they concentrated on Dan again. "It is all explained on the obelisk, if you know where to find it," said Eva.

"I didn't see your name mentioned."

"Tell him, Mother," said Jacinda.

Eva bowed wearily.

Jacinda focused on him. "You read the part about the group of priestesses in the delta who were keepers of the mysteries of the ankh?"

Dan nodded, a look of puzzlement clouding his features.

"Imagine possessing the key to life and death. No man, not even a king, could be trusted with such primacy. It fell to the women to guard the Horite Cross, but to their great shame, they lost it. Ever since, they have been preparing for this day when the pieces of the sacred ankh are united once more."

"And you . . . ?"

"I am one," said Jacinda.

Dan glanced over to his mother.

"But, your mother, Evangeline," Jacinda went on, "is the *Buto-on-Earth*, the latest high priestess of the Sisters of the Uatchet shrine."

CHAPTER THIRTY-FOUR ☥

Zamir Qader darted like a mouse in traffic in and out of the
crowd of pilgrims arriving at the Mall.

He had parked in the lot of the National Museum of Natural History on 14th and Madison. The walk to the Washington Monument
was about 1500 feet as the crow flies, but he was early and spent half
an hour strolling under the cherry trees that lined the Tidal Basin
before turning north toward the towering obelisk.

Qader halted by the bridge across the north tip of the Basin and
nervously patted his breast to make sure the scroll was still in the
inside jacket pocket. Salameh, the new Messiah, placed it there himself the night before when he bade Qader to his quarters at the Syrian
Embassy.

In the two days he had been in Washington, Qader stayed in an
attic room roughly the size of a monk's cell. His host, dark and mous-
tached with a military bearing even in a purple jogging outfit, was
clearly a member of one of Syria's twelve branches of secret police.
He explained that Qader couldn't leave until summoned, and, he
remarked with finality, he had not received word as to when that
might be.

But Qader knew.

He had been studying the texts. The ritual, according to the Book of the Dead, must occur no later than Sunday morning when the tallest obelisk on Earth would be shrouded in the shadow of a solar eclipse, blocking the light of the Aten and focusing the entire force of the ankh on Salameh.

An instant later, the new Horus would be born to have dominion over the Earth.

And Qader was his first and most beloved disciple.

With that thought bright in his mind, Qader came upon the monument. Its monolithic size was only possible to see up close—so high, Qader couldn't see all of it without snapping off his neck at the third vertebra.

Walking from the bridge, Qader found unhindered admittance to the grassy rise leading to the Washington Monument. Private security was scattered about, he noticed. He wouldn't have given the guards a second thought if he hadn't been so nervous.

They were probably armed, but they only watched out for crazies and Qader consoled himself that he looked more like a jolly old uncle than a problem.

Qader stepped around cliques of people chatting on the grass. He fell in behind a small group generally heading where he wanted to go until it merged with the Muslim conferees in their section near the base.

He sank down into a metal folding chair and tried to seem bored. A handful of women delegates floated in and away from his orbit, their black robes whipping in the wind. This sort of dress was designed to make them scxless, or at least less of a sexual lure to the male faithful. It affected Qader in exactly the opposite fashion.

Whenever he saw these women, his mind filled with the mystery of them. He saw himself running his hands under the thin fabric, hands separated from skin by only the merest hint of silk.

He grinned, running his tongue over the back of his teeth. Damn, they made him horny. He fished in his pocket to check the scroll again.

Soon, he thought, he'd have any of those deliciously shrouded women he could want. But for now, the women were keeping to themselves. He sighed and turned away from them. No one was paying him any mind. That was good. Arab garb would have been a better disguise, though. Of the almost fifty men in his sight, close to three-quarters wore the traditional keffiyeh and abayeh.

There were, however, enough pilgrims in suits and ties for Qader to fit in.

He stayed head-lowered and quiet for twenty minutes. A few persons greeted him as they sat nearby. Offering Allah's salutation to strangers was a Middle Eastern custom, and he returned their wishes with a polite *Alechaim salaam.* Qader, head down, listened to the voices coming from the gathering assembly. He sensed anticipation in the sound. If they only knew.

Soon. Soon now.

He glanced at the dial of his new watch. It was digital, a Timex Indiglo.

Salameh suggested it. He liked the big green numbers. Easy to synchronize. And he said if all went as expected, they'd need a timepiece that could withstand an apocalypse and keep on ticking.

CHAPTER THIRTY-FIVE ☥

"Ma, I thought we were Presbyterian."

Dan's mouth was open, and his stare was wide and blank. His head drooped over, his eyebrows knitting tightly. Out of one eye, he checked on his mother and Jacinda. Both women were watching him with similar amusement.

"Y'know what?" he said. "I've decided I'm never going to get up to speed on this thing. Everybody seems to know more than I do, so I'm just gonna go with the flow. My mother's a pagan priestess— hey, I can accept that. I live in New York. I've seen weirder stuff."

The limo eased into an area reserved for the cars of dignitaries— of course, Evangeline Beecham Rawlins qualified—and parked. When the limo stopped, the privacy screen lowered. "We're here, ma'am," said the chauffeur in a sweet, high voice. "We can proceed whenever you're ready."

"Thank you, Annie," said Eva.

To his surprise, Dan observed that the driver was, indeed, a woman. With her close-cropped hair and powerfully compact build, mistaking her for a man from the back of her head was logical.

Is she another Uatchet sister? Almost certainly.

Annie seemed a masculine woman, perhaps a competitive body-builder when she wasn't guarding his mother, but Dan rejected the stereotype that she was a lesbian.

Somehow sex life was not an issue when it came to the sisterhood. He stared out the window at the crowd and pondered how many of the women they passed were his mother's acolytes.

He wouldn't have time to ask. A policewoman opened the barricade and guided the car into a restricted area. Annie saluted her and parked the limo in the cordoned-off section of Constitution Avenue. Moments later, she led Dan and the women toward the Washington Monument.

The monument fit so well in the landscape that pictures of the obelisk betrayed its enormous scale. It dwarfed the four of them as they hiked silently toward its unexpectedly small entranceway.

Eva was delivering the keynote address, so the group had an ace-in-the-hole that would get them into that inner, roped-off area before the morning service was to begin.

According to the schedule printed in the *Washington Times,* she would be called to the podium after clergy from over fifteen different faiths gave short invocations and blessed the assembled, each in his own language, each without restriction.

Is that when Salameh intends to make his presence known?

Dan envisioned him stepping up slowly, disguised beneath the robes and white beard of a mullah or the black coat of a Lubavitch rabbi, then casting them off dramatically, declaring he was the Living Horus.

Perhaps he'll do what Napoleon did, place the twin crowns on his own head and proclaim himself king of the world.

After a moment's thought, Dan dismissed the idea. Being considered a madman was one thing—proving it in front of an international television audience was another. Dan wagered with himself that Salameh had a more spectacular show in mind.

Dan paced the large woman, looking imposing in her uniform, and when Annie stopped, Dan did as well. They let Eva and Jacinda go ahead as Annie scanned the crowd in steely silence, as still as a statue among the meandering delegates.

Dan observed her for a few seconds, then decided to check the throng in the other direction. If he hadn't, he would certainly have missed the sudden movement.

A vertical movement, not the lateral human traffic he expected. A roundish man at the back of the Syrian sector bumped a veiled woman as he was getting out of his chair. The woman's husband shoved back, but the man bowed and made a gesture of supplication that ended the fracas.

The fat man turned and was swallowed by the assembly, but in that microsecond when his face was visible, Dan recognized him from the picture the colonel had showed him the day they met.

He was Zamir Qader.

"I got one!" Dan shouted at Annie as he ran off after him.

"No!" she snapped. "It's too soon!"

Dan didn't hear her, or pretended not to. He moved quickly through the pilgrims who were gathering closer to the podium, perhaps responding to Evangeline Rawlins's arrival.

Qader, too, was traveling against the flow of the crowd. He passed the circle of flags and went directly to the doors of the monument. Dan was barely twenty yards from him.

Qader seemed to falter in his gait, but continued inside.

Dan sprinted after him. He managed to reach the door before it had fully closed. There he stopped; part in, part out. He exhaled a long and scraping breath—he was definitely out of shape—and allowed his eyes to adjust to the low level of light inside the huge obelisk.

The interior brightened gradually as his pupils widened, as if the dimmer switch were being turned up. It looked to him like the first act of a play was about to start.

"Hello, sir. May I help you?" asked a ruggedly cute young woman in a tan Parks Ranger uniform. For some reason most of the Interior Department personnel at this gathering were female.

More sisters?

Dan never believed in conspiracy theories. He knew that few human actions were ever actually planned. Mostly, people fell into situations and explained away either their successes or failures with the excuse that it was all a plot and not dumb luck.

That used to be his belief, at least, until he dropped head-first into the world Jacinda and the colonel inhabited. Now, all he knew was that he knew nothing. But if answers were going to be found, they would be discovered here in this brick monolith.

Dan's eyes searched the squarish room. There was a desk, an elevator, and the entrance to the stairs with a sign on it warning cardiac patients that climbing up to the summit was forbidden.

Other than that, the inside was oddly utilitarian. Dan didn't know what he had expected, but this made him a bit sad. The Washington Monument was, after all, a product of the Victorians. And yet, it retained little of that notably ornamented style.

"I'm sorry if you wanted to take the tour," the ranger continued, "but we've suspended them today because of the prayer servi—"

Dan heard a sound from above and made for the stairs to see where it was coming from.

The ranger blocked him. "I'm sorry, sir!"

Dan stopped, flustered. "I was just—"

"I'm sure you understand," the woman began officiously, "that we do not allow people to walk up the stairs in any case, so please step away from there. We have guided walking tours from the top down, but we won't be back to our regular schedule until tomorrow."

"But if someone wanted to, they could get by you. There was a man who came in just before I did—."

"I didn't see anyone," she replied. "I could arrange a ticket for you tomorrow, sir."

"You must have seen him—shaved head, big belly, about fifty or so."

She shook her head, but Dan pressed her. "C'mon. Weren't you at the desk over there? You can see everything."

"I couldn't as a matter of fact," she said. "I was at the supply cabinet getting a few forms."

"So he could've gotten past you."

"I guess."

"On the elevator?"

"Oh, no," she said pointedly. "I'd have heard if he got on that thing. It's pretty rumbly."

"He took the stairs, then." The ranger shrugged at the idea. Dan did, too. Where else would Qader be?

"I think I'll need your name, sir," she said.

If she is one of my mother's girls, Dan thought, *she isn't being very helpful. Unless Eva placed her in the monument to delay me.*

How paranoid should he be? He remembered the old saying, "Even paranoiacs have enemies."

"My name's Daniel Gunther Rawlins, Jr. I am a fugitive from a murder charge in New York City. I'd suggest you get all the security within fifty miles in here as soon as you can." With a wave, Dan made a dash for the staircase.

"Hey—hey!" she shouted after him. "You can't go up there!"

"Have 'em follow me to the top, sweetheart. I'll be there." Dan took the steps two at a time. On the third landing, he waited and listened for the *clink-chink* of someone climbing above him.

The brick interior walls of the monument proved a good sounding board and sent the sound echoing down to him. Vibrations on the handrail confirmed it for him. Qader was heading for the top.

Minutes later, Dan had gotten about halfway up. He didn't like the stairs; they were oddly placed—a bit wider than he was used to. They were probably built that way to accommodate those ample 1880s-style skirts and bustles.

He read somewhere that the first elevator inside the monument was considered so dangerous that only men were allowed to ride in it.

The women were left to walk up all 897 steps wearing their fifty-pound dresses and high-buttoned shoes. Dan was sure no men ever died on the elevator, but wondered how many women stroked out using the stairs.

With four hundred or so steps behind him, Dan knew how those Victorian women felt. He was puffing, his calves were knotted into painful lumps, and his throat was as parched as a dry well.

He bent his head down and held his knees in his palms. The air was cool inside the shaft. He let it fill his lungs before he dared stand straight.

A thought crossed his mind. *I should've caught up with Qader!* The man was fifteen years older than Dan was and outweighed him by thirty-five pounds. Why wasn't Qader the one sitting winded part-way up?

He summoned his strength and walked up another twenty steps when the lights flickered. He looked around at the odd little industrial fixtures mounted in unexpected places on the walls.

Then, the lights went out.

"How can we leave him alone up there?"

Eva answered bloodlessly, "He was born for it, Jacinda. We can't help him. Not until he confronts this destiny for himself."

Eva had Jacinda by the elbow and was guiding her through the delegation of Austrian Lutherans—a very fundamentalist group, anti-Catholic, pro-Fascist, although they would never admit that publicly.

A few of the Aryans threw a glance at Jacinda's dusky skin and exotic Jewish beauty as she passed them. Most of the men smiled with an appreciation that transcended their own prejudices.

Jacinda noticed. She noticed everything. The two women gravitated to the front where the Americans, as representatives of the host country, were seated.

Annie moved parallel to them, a few steps along the aisle. As she neared the podium, a big man—he must have been three hundred pounds of beer-belly—stopped her and planted a huge, yellow foam, ten-gallon hat on her head. It read: "Christ's in the Heart of Texas." Annie whipped off the cartoonish Stetson and jammed it back into the man's stomach.

"No, thanks, cowboy," she said and walked on quickly. When Annie arrived at the dais, she spotted Jacinda with Eva Rawlins. Both women were looking up at the towering obelisk above them. She saw they were busy visiting, so Annie held back.

Eva Rawlins turned immediately and demanded her presence with her eyes. Eva's gaze returned to the pinnacle of the monument. "Clouds are low," she said sullenly. "Have you noticed?"

"No." The thought crossed Annie mind that this was not the time to chat about the weather. "It was clearer earlier. Are you afraid of rain?"

"That's not what I meant. Any fog should've burned off by this time of the morning. Perhaps it's only the sky spirits coming down for a closer look."

"I used to think what a benign place this was . . ." Jacinda sounded distressed. She didn't seem to be speaking to anyone in particular until she bowed her head in Eva's direction. "You know," she went on, "they use pictures of the monument on television so often as a symbol of Washington, I thought it was in a lovely, clean park—so perfect, so geometric. Now it reminds me of a stake in the heart."

Eva was staring up in space to a point somewhere higher than the obelisk's peak. The sky had become pearlescent in the last moments as if the sun were diffusing over the pyramidion cap. It all seemed to interest her exceedingly. Jacinda thought she hadn't been listening until Eva faced her and patted her hand.

"You're worried, I know. We all are," Eva said.

"Let me help him. I can go in—."

"Not yet. Not just yet. Not until he senses who he's truly up against."

Jacinda, exasperated, but trying to hide it, said, "How can we leave him inside alone? I've been with him day and night since he was attacked, and I know him. He's not up to this kind of fight."

Eva reacted calmly. "I've trained him all his life for this task. Blame me if he's not ready."

"But so much is at stake, Reverend Mother."

Eva nodded. "Yes. That's why I've given my only son."

CHAPTER THIRTY-SIX ☥

It was as dark as he'd ever experienced, darker than the time his lantern bulb went out in a cave he was exploring a few miles from the Valley of the Kings. Even there, after the few anxious minutes it took for his eyes to get accustomed to it, Dan saw faint light filtering in from the cracks in the rock above him.

The monument isn't hermetically sealed. So where is the daylight?

How can I be in the center of Washington on a bright day and not be able to see a thing?

Dan suddenly felt woozy. He grabbed for the railing but couldn't find it. He started to step forward then thought better of it. Falling down a hundred stairs in pure blackness didn't appeal to him, and Dan decided to wait where he was. He inched back until he touched the wall.

His hand moved, and he felt metal—plaque. His fingers ran over letters and above them then brushed over a sculpture in low relief.

Probably a face, he thought.

If he were one of those blind characters he remembered from the movies, he might be able to figure out whose face he was groping.

He let his fingers crawl past the plaque to the masonry. His foot tried venturing up another stair. If he could get to the next landing, he would have a good solid platform where he could rest and wait for the lights to come back on. He didn't want to be rattled when he met Salameh.

A decent plan, except the stair wasn't there. It wasn't that he was disoriented or misjudged the height of the riser. No, he was standing on the stairs when the lights went out, and the next stair simply had to be right above the last.

Except, it wasn't. He lifted his foot and let it come down where a stair should have been, but it continued down to exactly the same level. Dan slid his sole further and further, but the next stair never stopped his toe.

The only explanation was that he had, without realizing it, reached the next landing. And yet, it couldn't be. The landing had been ten or more steps above his head when the darkness hit.

Another strange thing: The bottom of his shoe felt gritty, as if he had tracked in sand from the beach. Dan did that all the time when he was a boy at the Montauk house, and he recalled the feel of it. Dan bent down and tested the floor with his finger.

The sand yielded down to his second knuckle. Dan paused before standing up again. It was like he was kneeling in a sandbox, not on a metal stairway somewhere high inside the Washington Monument.

What the hell is going on?

He eased a step or two backwards and found the wall. Feeling his way, Dan touched metal. Another plaque, he assumed. Yes, it had letters along the bottom and a sculpture in low relief. A face, it seemed. A nose, eyes. A high forehead. If he were one of those blind characters the movies were so fond of portraying, Dan might be able to figure out whose features he was groping.

Instead, the metallic plaque grew colder in his palm. Again, he ran his fingers over the face. He was certain it was rounder now, as if the low relief stretched away from the wall.

A random thought: Michelangelo once said, inside every block of stone there was a human form straining to get out. That was precisely the way it felt; the head getting rounder, rougher; changing from the slick chill of metal to the coolness of stone until it arched away from the wall and seemed to transform into a free-standing bust under his hands.

The mind plays tricks in the dark, Dan thought. The monument was beginning to seem like a different place to him. Drier. So dry, his throat could have been coated with hard clay.

Then, he caught a glimpse of a light overhead and wondered if his eyes were being affected. The murky shimmer was approaching in a slowly curving trajectory toward him.

He instinctively flattened his back against the wall and waited. Again, Dan fell to his knees. His shins sank into a cushion of sand.

Once more, his hand brushed the sculpture. He touched its face. It was now as if the low relief had pulled completely away from the wall. He knelt by it trying not to breathe.

He looked up. The stone itself seemed to strain higher. The statue was at least five feet in height and provided a protecting shadow from the advancing glow.

Perhaps it is a Parks Serviceman with a flashlight—that occurred to him first, but watching carefully, Dan noticed that the light had an odd quality about it. For one thing, it was hotter and it moved— like a flame.

The mind does play tricks.

Dan stayed low behind the statue, trying to avoid the circle of orange cast by the—torch? No, it was a lamp, Dan recognized it. Made of fired clay, it was a dish-shape with a floating wick inside and a lip for a handle. A simple, elegant design. The museum owned hundreds of them.

Variations on it had been in use since prehistory, and men were using it until kerosene replaced oil. The particular lamp approaching Dan was of an early period, he was sure. If it were closer, he could be more precise about the date, not that it mattered under the cir- cumstances.

What am I doing? Bucking for curator?

If Salameh were holding that lamp, Dan knew he would *be* history, not studying it. From his hiding place, Dan focused on the man with the torch.

At first, his features were obscured in the half-dark and flickering fire, but then, he reached a niche carved in the wall and sat the torch in a holder. The glow spread out, reflected by the whitewash of the panel, and bathed the man's round, jowly face in light.

Dan recognized him immediately.

The person in front of him had been the subject of a monograph he had written for the Harvard Press five years before. There were small differences, his skin was more careworn than he expected, cracked by a life in the sun; his eyes surrounded with puffy, ash-gray folds.

Otherwise, the face was the same as on the famous portrait-statue excavated from his tomb during the early years of the century.

Impossible, but, yes, it was him. Unmistakably, the man with the torch was Rekhmire, the grand vizier under Tuthmose III of the Eighteenth Dynasty.

Rekhmire beckoned to a figure on the stairs twenty feet away from him and, taking the steps confidently two at a time, the man hastened to his side.

He was younger; that was immediately evident from his quickness. His physique, amply displayed under his thin tunic and accented by the light general's armor he wore, reminded Dan of an aging quarterback.

Lithe, but mature.

Dan strained to see the second man's face, but it was difficult since he was watching from such a low angle. Yet, even when Dan caught a glimpse of him straight on, his features seemed to have an unformed quality to them.

It was as if the soldier were standing at the edge of a dream where his presence was felt, but all the details were waiting to be sketched in.

Rekhmire spoke. Dan had never heard the Egyptian language uttered aloud, but he understood most of it. Like Hebrew, the tongue of the pharaohs was written without vowels.

Pronunciation was often just guesswork to archaeologists. However, there was enough of Coptic in it—a language he was fluent in—for him to get the gist of the vocabulary.

The grand vizier addressed the young general by name.

Amenemhab.

Dan had been familiar with his exploits long before Zaннu had sent him the chronicles. Amenemhab, childhood friend of Pharaoh, famed leader of the elite corps known as the Braves and, now he knew, guardian of the ankh. Half of it, at least.

Rekhmire called Amenemhab over to the altar. The vizier sat crosslegged and patted the ground so that Amenemhab would join him. The general shook his head and instead leaned against the wall right under the torch.

When he finally saw Amenemhab in the light, Dan's jaw went slack.

Shocked, he fell against the vizier's statue; staring, disbelieving.

Except for the deeply tanned skin and eyes burdened with their own history, Amenemhab's face was precisely—conspicuously—the image of Dan's own.

CHAPTER THIRTY-SEVEN ☥

Dan drew in a breath as Amenemhab passed not a foot in front of him. The general rested his palm on the pedestal of Rekhmire's statue and gazed down into the niche where Dan knelt. Only then, with Amenemhab staring right through his body, did Dan realize that, to these shades of the past, he must be invisible.

His fear of discovery gone, Dan listened closely to their nearly familiar words. The body language, however, was easier to read. Rekhmire appeared distraught, running his hands over his face and bald skull repeatedly during the conversation.

"Sweet General," he began, "you come to me with only part of the prize. How do you expect me to react?"

"With rejoicing, Vizier," answered Amenemhab. "Now the ankh has lost its power over our lives."

"Don't be a fool! Its power hasn't leaked out like water from a frayed bladder. The halves need only be reunited."

"Then cleave my half to dust, I say! Such power is a curse from the evil mind of Set."

"Power is not so easily surrendered."

Amenemhab glared back with large, alert eyes. "War's my profession, my old friend. Menkheperre himself taught me the value of surrendering ground to obtain a greater advantage."

Rekhmire sighed. "Life eternal is a formidable loss for an old man. You young pups have no idea."

"What I do know is, whole, the ankh will destroy us. The gods present life to us as their gift. Prolonging our time on Earth is an affront to them."

"Facing Anubis, *the Jackal-Who-Weighs-Your-Heart*, I tend to disagree."

"Please, Vizier—you know the truth of it," said Amenemhab with determination. "Maat—*balance*—is why we are supreme among nations. To disturb Maat is to invite the destruction of Qemet!"

Rekhmire brought his fist down hard on the altar. "I want the ankh whole! Not for me—I cringe to think of having it in my hands—but it frightens me more to envision any other kingdom wielding it against us!"

"The lost half is back with the Habiru. Shall we invade? If you suggest another campaign, I will take my Braves and loot and burn every one of their cities. If," he uttered derisively, "if the new pharaoh has the stomach for battle."

"No." Rekhmire snorted. "Let the boy have his time of peace."

Amenemhab approached the older man, who had turned toward the altar and was resting, resigned, alongside it. He reached out and caressed the vizier's shoulder. "Better this way," he said.

Rekhmire grunted. It was impossible to tell if he agreed. "Write about this in here, on the tomb walls, on the ceiling. Tell the gods how you restrained yourself when you could have lived forever. I'm sure they'll make you a god, in gratitude. Like Im-ho-tep."

"Im-ho-tep was a builder," said Rekhmire forlornly, "All I ever built was this hole in the ground."

"And built a jumble of nomes into a unified Qemet, stronger than any nation under the gaze of Amun."

Rekhmire shrugged. "Unions are ephemeral. Stone lasts forever."

"You'll be remembered for eternity. No doubt," said Amenemhab comfortingly.

"I wonder," said Rekhmire.

Dan rose uneasily from his hiding place and crept along the wall, making for the stairs.

This is the ankh's doing, he thought.

The thing was somehow projecting its own history up the height of the obelisk until it reached the present—or perhaps the future?—where time converged inside the pyramidion.

That was where he had to be—at the very top—and soon!

He recalled that the torchlight had seemed to outline an escape route. He remembered that stone stairs led up and out of the tomb, but would those stairs even be there? And if they were, would they lead him to the ankh or just disappear?

Not having too many alternatives, he decided to try it. He pressed one foot on the carved stone slab. It held. He feared it might not, not if it had been created out of dreams. But that stair and each subsequent one took him higher and farther from the darkness of the vizier's tomb.

CHAPTER THIRTY-EIGHT

I'm following him up."

Jacinda could not endure being out of the action any longer. Eva had assumed her place on the dais while waiting to be introduced. Annie was positioned, like the other security drudges, to the sidelines.

"She said—," Annie began.

"That it was written the son of Buto will confront the daemon alone. But," countered Jacinda, "one second later, I'm going to be there." She pushed through the crush around the podium with Annie behind her.

"Hey!" Annie shouted when Jacinda was nearly at the monument's front door. "How do you expect to get up there?"

"Well, damned if I'm going to walk it! Not when it's got a perfectly good elevator!"

Jacinda burst into the monument's main floor, hitting the door with her back and swinging about as she confronted the wide, empty space. She waited merely a second until the same Park Service Ranger who'd spoken to Dan ran up to her.

"I've got to get to the top, miss," Jacinda said.

"Call me Natalia." She used the European pronunciation, but Jacinda being foreign herself, didn't catch it. "The meeting's outside," she went on. "No one is allowed in here! There are no tours today!"

"I'm with Israeli security," Jacinda said with great authority. "Did a man go up a while ago?

Natalia shook her head, looking puzzled. "I don't know—."

"Tall, dark-haired guy," Jacinda cut in.

"Oh, him."

"Take me to the lift," demanded Jacinda.

The ranger nodded and led Jacinda to the elevator. "I think I can handle this by myself," said Jacinda when the ranger joined her in the car.

"No, I can't let anyone go up alone." She closed the door and pressed the button under "OBV" signifying "Observation Level."

The ranger waited for the cables and winches to start lifting them before she turned around. One hand went to her collar and undid the top three buttons of her starched shirt. Inside, next to her skin, she touched a gold pendant hanging from a chain around her neck.

She took it out and showed it to Jacinda.

"I thought you might like to see this," she said, "coming from the Middle East as you do. Maybe you could help me with something."

Jacinda nodded. "If I can."

She held out the amulet. "See. It's Egyptian. Do you know what the inscription says?"

"Sorry. It's written in hieroglyphics. Even most Egyptians wouldn't know. They speak Arabic."

"Oh." The young woman seemed very disappointed.

Jacinda, trying to be helpful, said, "The man we're looking for, *he* reads hieroglyphics."

"Oh, good." She slipped the chain off her head and handed the gold udjat to Jacinda. "It was a present from a guy I know. Here, take a good look at it."

Jacinda gazed at it. "Beautiful," she said. Even by the dim elevator-dome light, the gold shone. It was captivating to the eye. "A gift from your boyfriend?"

"From a man who means the world to me."

"Officer," said Jacinda, passing the amulet back to Natalia, "this is important. When we reach the top, let me out and stand clear of the door. I'm not sure what I'm going to find, but you shouldn't be a part of it."

"Yes. Whatever you wish." Natalia's eyes clouded, and her lids closed halfway. "You can fly right out to meet your professor—and the Mahdi. Just like the funny Irishman." She arched her back and pointed an accusatory finger at Jacinda.

Jacinda stood back warily. "Then, Natalia," she said, "you haven't been with the Park Service too long."

"Don't worry, hon," Natalia said, fondling Jacinda's shoulder with a series of friendly little squeezes. "You won't die too much. And your feathers, they'll be real pretty colors. Here, listen, I'll tell you a secret—."

She cocked her head, as if to whisper a confidence into Jacinda's ear.

Instead, Natalia's deep brown irises rolled back in her head, replaced by yellow cat's eyes. She touched Jacinda's shoulder with the tips of her stiletto nails and ran them around to the front of the neckline on Jacinda's blouse, then quickly down to where her breasts met above the sternum.

The plan was to inject one nail fast into Jacinda's aorta, but at the first sting of the ranger's fingers, Jacinda reacted. She reared back and jammed an elbow into Natalia's stomach. Natalia spilled backward across the small space into the elevator wall.

Jacinda kicked her jaw and leapt onto her side with all her weight on one kidney-crushing knee. Grabbing Natalia's hair in one fist, Jacinda pulled the assassin's head back and rammed her free elbow into the hollow of Natalia's throat.

It was over in under four seconds.

Jacinda checked the woman. She was breathing, but the deep bubbling sound from her chest told Jacinda that she was hemorrhaging into her lungs and would be dead soon. The amulet was on the floor, peeking out from under her trouser leg. Jacinda yanked it out by the chain and stood up with it in her hand.

It had a solid heft to it.

She faced the elevator door and put the necklace into her pocket.

Suddenly, Natalia was standing behind her. She lunged at Jacinda in a fury, her jagged incisors bared and her claws extended.

A mouth full of teeth struck hard plastic as Jacinda jammed her cell phone down the ranger's throat and followed through with a strike to the gullet with her thumb. It crushed Natalia's windpipe and sent her sprawling backward into the control panel.

Not your average civil servant, thought Jacinda as she quickly stopped the elevator, opened the door, and tossed the body out.

CHAPTER THIRTY-NINE ☥

The darkness only got deeper the higher he went until it was almost an entity unto itself. Dan felt carefully for each step, because he soon realized they were coming irregularly, one stair differing slightly from the next until each footfall became an unnerving experience.

Where will this path lead?

Might the entire staircase collapse, and he find himself hurtling off the stairs and into the black oblivion below? But the stairs held. And with each foot, he rose closer and closer to Salameh.

Dan focused his attention ahead. Above him was a tiny rectangle of light, and he headed for it. A good fifteen minutes had passed since he had left the presence of his ancient double, Amenemhab, and the noble Rekhmire. Time enough to doubt the experience ever happened.

He felt like Scrooge confronting Marley. Those Egyptians were probably an undigested piece of cheese—as good an explanation as any. At least, that solution had the merit of not being so much metaphysical crapola.

The idea of seeing his own face in that of a long-dead general had held, most likely it seemed to Dan, psychological implications.

He'd heard about chemical hallucinogens and stress-induced psychoses causing people to see things. Salameh was a terrorist, after all. Presumably, he knew how to poison a city's water supply. What would keep him from pumping a few pounds of oddball gas into the Washington Monument?

The source of the light was clearer now, but he was traveling in the deepest shadow with only hints as to what might be around him.

The stone steps beneath his shoes sounded different, clanking instead of the gritty thud he'd listened to a floor below. He reached out to the wall and found a metal railing under his hand.

The staircase, he assumed, must be resolving itself back to what it had been. He must be back in the monument.

He stopped after another two flights and sat panting on a step. For only the second time since he began his climb, Dan wondered about Zamir Qader. Had Zamir moved through to the past? Stood in that tomb?

Dan doubted it. Somehow, he knew those particular visions were his alone.

Time. It was all about time. The eclipse was coming fast, and Dan wanted to be in that pyramid room that topped the monument when it arrived.

Not that he was sure what he was going to do. Even having the features of some long-dead general, Dan hardly felt like a military man. Brute force wasn't going to work for him. And, frankly, he wasn't sure what would.

Maybe, if he could delay the ceremony somehow. He knew the moment the sun disappeared, Salameh would join the two halves of the ankh and start to intone the resurrection prayers.

How long can that take?

Not very long, he wagered.

Hell, he thought, *it only took a couple of seconds to splatter Kennedy's brains over that pretty convertible—and that changed the world. Imagine what bringing him back from the grave might do!*

Dan saw the outline of a door. It was sitting a couple of flights up with a corona of light around the edges. His forbidding goal was right above his head. Involuntarily, his hand went to his throat. He swallowed hard.

Another few steps.

Closing in on the summit, each fresh step upward filled Dan with dread. Yet, though every inch felt as if his feet were weighted with lead, he refused to slacken his pace.

More stairs.

Higher and higher. Unprotected. Unarmed. Still he continued. The final landing was a smallish rectangular grating made of black iron, all cross girders and rivets—nineteenth-century Eiffel Tower–chic. In front of him was the partially opened door. He walked closer.

The light which had been his beacon glared so intensely he had to shield his eyes with his forearm until his irises could constrict to pinpoints.

Fortunately for him, his eyes were protected, because at that exact instant, the door flew wide flooding him in a torrent of harsh, blinding light. Disoriented, Dan stumbled through the portal.

He expected a square room, pyramid-shaped, with eight undersized windows. Instead, when his sight returned, Dan faced a vast courtyard, open to the sky at its center, and bordered with tall painted columns, capped by papyrus stalks like the ones at Karnak—except, these were laid out in unending rows.

Again, he was someplace else.

In the middle distance, he perceived a tall, straight form—figuring out actually how far was next to impossible, and on closer inspection he saw it was an obelisk carved from pale rose granite.

That was it. That was where it was destined to end.

Dan shuddered. Being so close to the obelisk brought with it more danger than he wanted to think about. Instead, he focused on the reason he started his climb.

Qader.

Where is he?

Dan hadn't passed Qader going up. Even in the dark, it would have been impossible to have overlooked him. So, he had to be here—right? Unless, of course, he missed this trip to Never-Never Land entirely.

For all Dan knew, this whole courtyard could be a delusion. Stepping in the middle of it reminded him of those Doctor Who shows he used to watch when he was a kid in London. The Tardis, the Doctor's time machine, was a phone booth on the outside, but inside it was huge, the size of a shopping mall.

Ever since, Dan was fascinated with the concept that something could be bigger inside than out. That could be another clue that this strange temple where he stood was all a dream.

Dan imagined Qader hanging out in the Washington Monument's observatory taking in the sights like any other tourist. And what about himself?

Dan considered that his body might not be in the temple at all. What if he were lying unconscious on the stairs midway up the monument, knocked out, gassed or—suddenly, the idea hit him.

What if I've been murdered?!

He could be dead, walking around Heaven—or, maybe in this case, Duat—without being aware he'd been killed. Shaking his head, Dan tried to rid his brain of that morbid idea. He felt like slapping his own face. Here he was, a scientist, conjecturing over supernatural possibilities he had no belief in.

"If I'm dead," he whispered nearly in silence, "show me proof."

Dan peered through the smoky atmosphere of the courtyard, searching for any sign of movement. He held back, keeping to the shadows until he made certain that every niche in his vicinity was clear.

Clear of life, that is. Not empty.

Recessed between each pillar stood a different statue of an Egyptian deity; each sculpted out of dark basalt and polished like glass in the exquisite Eighteenth Dynastic style. Thoth, Nephthys, Bast—on and on every few feet until they disappeared into the fog.

Dan made a mental note that Isis, Osiris, Horus, Amun and Re weren't among them. Likely, they were farther on, masked by the smoke.

"Closer to the action," he surmised out loud.

Carefully, Dan rounded the back of the closest column.

The archaeologist in him made him slide his hand over the surface. Like the tomb, it seemed real enough. Only newer. And brighter, washed in blues and pinks and yellows.

He glanced at the glyphs etched in the stone. At once, he recognized the words from the *Book of the Dead*. A resurrection prayer. Looking left and right, the other pillars bore similar inscriptions, each probably entreating its individual god or goddess to grant life eternal.

The damn place had all the makings of a way station to Duat. He didn't like that idea in the least. The more like Heaven it was; the nearer Dan came to getting proof he really was dead.

Worse, he'd always visualized the Temple of Eternity, where the souls waited for Anubis to weigh their hearts, exactly in this 1950s MGM musical sort of way. He half expected Vera-Ellen in a chiffon gown to descend on a cloud singing "Stairway to Heaven."

"Well," Dan sighed in resignation, "that sinks it. I'm dreaming up this lemonade stand."

It was a stretch for him, but he had finally bought the notion that the ankh could raise the dead. Hanging out in the anteroom of Egyptian Heaven was another matter entirely.

"None of this is real," he repeated to himself as he slowly wove his way around column after column. A minute later, he found himself in the niche dominated by a black image of Tefnut who bore the head of a lioness atop the shoulders of a woman.

Outside the cover of the niche, the temple had dissolved into gray. Dan couldn't see two feet beyond the great pillar.

He debated in his mind if he should go on, when he caught sight of a disturbance in the smoke. The upheaval swirled in a figure-eight pattern before its source became apparent.

A huge winged creature floated out of the whiteness and landed on Tefnut's mane.

"McMay!" Dan cried.

Liam McMay hopped onto the statue's shoulder, fluttered a bit, and sniffed the air before turning back to the corner where Dan waited. "Professor, I wanted to see how you were feeling. All healed and ready for more, I see."

"You planning on finishing the job on me?"

McMay scratched his nose with a wing feather. "No, no," he said. "The boss has one of those mind sets, you know, 'if somethin's gonna be done right, he's gotta do it his-own-damn-self.' You're his this time, boy-o!"

"That doesn't get you off the hook, birdman," Dan spat. "I should throw you into a stock pot and make chicken soup out of you!"

In deference, McMay clucked. "I just love ya when ya get all macho, Professor. Thing is, I bollixed up my dealings with you badly. By rights, Son, you should be moldering in a pit along with yer daddy."

Dan leapt up, grabbed McMay's thin bird legs, and yanked hard.

"Yee-oww!" McMay yowled in pain as he thrust out his wings to their full six-foot span to try and regain his balance.

He flapped and flapped.

The wings struck Dan like the blades of a ceiling fan, but he held firm onto McMay's ankles, twisting them until McMay's human head whacked against the stone goddess.

"That hurt!" he bellowed.

"It was meant to!" Dan raised his arms, and McMay's body flipped over until Dan had him dangling over the floor.

"Let me up!" McMay demanded. Upside down, without use of flight or his talons, McMay was helpless. He felt his legs being pulled apart, painfully.

"Make a wish, Irishman!" Dan said.

"Okay! Okay! What do you want?"

Dan eased McMay to the ground. The bird creature's talons were still held firmly high and away from Dan's face.

"Yeah—yeah. That's better," sighed McMay.

"Then stop flapping."

McMay nodded vigorously. "Sure, sure. Merely a reaction to stress. You can understand that. Now, let me up, you asshole. You want to give me an aneurysm?"

Dan bounced McMay's head off the floor—twice. "Then you'll really be a birdbrain."

"Now, now, now! That's a cheap shot. Let me up, we'll talk a bit."

"You can talk fine from where you are."

McMay shrugged his wings. "Okay. You think I ever wanted to hurt you and your da? Naw, but it was the only way I was gonna get out of my fine-feathered predicament. You understand my position?"

"Should I care?"

"Lad, I'm an earthbound spirit. And as such, I've got no prospects of gettin' back to myself without Salameh coming out on top. If the dead rise, I get my body back. If not, I'll be screwin' chickens for the rest of eternity."

"I could bash your head in!"

"Ya want the truth? That might not be such a bad fate, considering some of the alternatives." McMay paused for a second, looking contrite.

"Look, let me go," he said. "I don't know all the particulars, but now that you made it to this dimension, the only way Salameh can deal with you is through ritual. No one can die here."

"But hurting is still possible?" Dan twisted McMay's claw, and he yelped like a wounded puppy.

"Yeah! Real possible. Now, stop that, will ya?"

"Okay, what can you do for me?"

"I'll lead you to the bossman, and you two can work it out. I tell ya, whichever way it breaks, I'll accept it. Man—bird—corpse—however I end up. How about it, mate?"

Dan scowled at the monster, then kicked it in the wing.

Swiftly, his foot came down on the Ba's throat. "I could snap your damn neck!"

"I know," said McMay, panting. "I know. Believe me."

"And if I let you go, you won't start slashing?"

"Pinky swear, Danny boy."

Dan lifted his boot from McMay's neck. "Okay," he said, then released its ankles with a hard shove that sent the bird creature sprawling into the center of the courtyard.

"Hey, easy now!" yelled McMay.

Dan walked over to where McMay was flapping to his feet. The Ba hopped up on one claw and threw a murderous look up at Dan.

McMay raised the other foot and scratched his nose with the sharp talon of his middle toe.

"Tell you what, I'll fly up ahead—if you didn't break one of my damn wings—and tell the new Messiah you're coming."

"Well, Salameh must've known I was coming, so giving him a warning shouldn't matter." Dan squinted into the cloud of fog and waved his hand. "But how am I supposed to find anything in all this?"

"Follow the yellow brick road," McMay answered.

Immediately, he rose into the air, buzzed the center of the courtyard, and blew off some of the low fog to reveal a line of tiles. Dan saw that every yard or so the tiles were emblazoned with the cartouche of a different pharaoh. Dan knew the king lists by heart, or nearly so. The god-king at his feet was Ptolemaic.

That pharaoh's father was next and so on as far as the fog would allow him to see. The bricks pointed toward the distant obelisk, but they were also leading back in time from the New Kingdom to Middle Kingdom, down through the dynasties all the way to the first pharaoh, Nārmer.

Dan lost sight of McMay after a minute, but continued to move warily. Occasionally, a king-name would deviate from what he and other archaeologists presumed was the truth.

Yet even when he thought the lists were horribly shuffled, Dan realized that the additions or deletions had a certain internal logic to them.

Another vote for reality. If this whole thing's a scam, he reasoned, its the best one he'd ever heard of. The fog grew more dense the farther he went.

From all sides, he began to hear low, stifled sounds—guttural noises, then others like the lowing of cattle, except deeper and strangely ominous.

The voice of ox-headed Hathor?

Dan hurried on, passing those particular niches quickly, suspecting the god-statues within them were straining to life.

Suddenly, he had to stop. There was a whiteout, and he just

couldn't see. He went down on his knees and scattered the heavy mist from the brick.

Then, he crawled a few yards until he came to Narmer's cartouche. As first pharaoh of Upper and Lower Egypt, his should have been the last brick, but it wasn't. The king-names trailed onward into Egypt's tribal past.

Dan quelled a desire to get out a notebook and take down names, and he continued on. The fog thinned a bit, and he was able to see the ground again while standing up.

How far would the list of unknowns go? With whom would it end?

Probably, with Osiris, Dan speculated to himself. If the inscriptions on the obelisk were right, Osiris was a real human being, a warrior prince who ruled a thousand years before Narmer united the Two Lands.

Dan raised his eyes from the tiled floor. The colonnades surrounding him appeared as ghostly giants, more imagined than seen. Out of the pure white, without sound or preamble, a figure approached him.

"Professor Rawlins?" The accent was Egyptian. "My name is Zamir Qader. The Ba thought I should escort you."

"My last mile?" Dan kept his distance as a round shape formed out of the cloud.

"You're late," Qader scolded. "We've been holding up the ceremony."

"Ceremony? What kind? Human sacrifice?"

"Not even a fatted calf," he answered. "No call to worry whatsoever."

Dan held out his hand to keep Qader back. He shrugged and stayed about fifteen feet away—far enough so that the mist shrouded him like a restless spirit. "How can I be late? I didn't know I was going to follow you up here until I spotted you in the crowd downstairs."

"The Mahdi says all is preordained."

Qader half turned his body from Dan. His chubby fingers beckoned and, cautiously, Dan followed. They walked closer to the columns. Qader halted under the statue of Thoth.

"He's here," said Qader.

Dan wasn't certain if Qader were speaking to him or alerting someone hidden by the statue. Qader turned to him, bowed like a butler, and backed away into the fog.

As he watched Qader leave, Dan heard a sound. Turning toward it, he beheld a tall man advance into the courtyard from Thoth's shadow.

Veiled by the haze, he greeted Dan with a raised arm and an open hand. "We've never met, Professor Rawlins," he said, "but your reputation precedes you."

"Mahmoud Salameh?"

"That is one of my names."

The revelation hit him like a thunderbolt. He was not speaking with a terrorist. Oh, Salameh was there, but another shared his soul. "One of your names," Dan repeated. "Would Sennemut be another?"

Salameh smiled. "Come ahead. I can't see you very well."

Dan ventured forward a couple of paces. He wanted to feel out his adversary, get him talking, so he glanced around at the columns and statues and asked, "What is this? Mental projection? Virtual reality?"

"As real as I can make it. Can't you smell the heavy air off the delta?"

"It's dank and foggy, if that's what you mean. Where are we supposed to be, anyway?"

"A place with great history, sadly long departed," said Salameh. "This is the Temple of Isis at Mennufer. Or my best recollection of it. It stood a thousand years before Tuthmose's time."

Dan nodded. Yes, the Temple Island. It was as he pictured it, except for the quality of the statuary. The original temple existed in prehistory, but Sennemut would have populated it with the Eighteenth Dynasty sculpture he knew. "You chose the site where Isis rose Osiris from the dead."

"Appropriate, I think."

Salameh edged closer, but Dan's head was bowed, and he didn't notice him approach until he was less than five feet away. But when Dan raised his head, it was Salameh who was shocked.

"You! That face—the young general!"

Dan decided to use the moment. "You've a longer memory than I have. *Chwaja* Salameh, you seem like a reasonable sort of megalomaniac. Why don't we take the elevator—wherever you hid it—and forget about this crap with the ankh. The whole idea never made any sense."

Salameh listened, then folded his arms and looked amused. "Ha! You may look like the noble Amenemhab, Professor, but you don't act like him. He'd be rushing at me with a short sword by now."

"Well, I don't know why I look like him, but maybe it was so you'd listen to a voice of reason you'd recognize. No need for anything sharp. No one has to die. Give back the ankh, and you can go on just like before."

"Being hunted as a terrorist, you mean?"

"I could arrange something. I have friends in the Mossad. They'd swap the ankh for your freedom. I'm certain of it."

Salameh laughed. It was cruel laugh with little joy in it. "So, let me understand what you're offering, Professor. Instead of being the Messiah to millions of people and worshiped as the Messenger of God by the rest of the world, I would be—what?"

"Alive, for one thing. You don't believe people are going to allow you to take over, do you? This isn't the simple world of 3000 B.C. anymore. There are hundreds of governments, thousands of religions, smart bombs, cable TV—"

"Now that I've had a chance to study you, Gener—that is, Professor—I fail to see how you expect to mount an effective opposition. Frankly, you don't seem very formidable."

Salameh turned his back and, with Dan trailing behind him, he strode toward the obelisk. In its glow, near the base, he confronted Dan again.

"You could be part of this. I hoped your father would join me. Of course, that ended badly, but why should you pay the penalty?"

"Penalty?" Dan wondered. "And that would be death?"

"That's why I'll succeed, Professor." Salameh pressed his fingertips together in a prayerful gesture. "Consider this. When living forever's an option, death becomes a terrible prospect, indeed."

Keep him talking, thought Dan *Keep him talking.*

"How about you consider this one I don't care if half the population of the planet thinks you're the Messiah, the Mahdi, and the Tooth Fairy all rolled up in one. People have to die! The damn world's got too many people as is! How do you keep them all from starving?"

Salameh shrugged. "Oh, sterilize the women. Proclaim mandatory birth control. Kill a few, abort a few."

"The Catholics and the religious right won't like that," said Dan.

With three millennia to devise his plan, Sennemut through Salameh, was prepared. "Has the question ever been posed in this way: Either you die or the fetus does?" he said pleasantly. "You see the elegance of that, don't you? If an anti-abortion zealot decides to bite the bullet, so to speak, I'm well rid of her. And in the process, of course, the little bag of cells she thinks of as her baby dies with her.

Absolute control creates its own simple solutions to these pesky problems."

Make him explain—keep him talking!

Dan waved away the thought as if it didn't chill him to the marrow. "Not so absolute. You're nothing to the Chinese. Buddhists and Confucians don't have much interest in the Messiah or the Mahdi—and they make up half the world!"

Salameh actually grinned. "That's why the gods in their wisdom created nuclear weapons. To paraphrase Johnny Cochran, 'If they don't supplicate—incinerate!' "

"They might bomb you first."

"Haven't you learned a thing?" Salameh said sternly. "The ankh eats energy. It could take a split atom and transform it into the very essence of life. You of all people should know, as long as we have it, nothing can harm us."

"You're taking a lot for granted. The Chinese—"

Salameh stopped him. "The Chinese? What do we say about the Chinese, Liam?"

McMay swooped down between them. "Hey, if they can't take a joke," he said, "Let 'em stir *fry!*"

Dan made a tentative move toward Salameh, but McMay hissed, "Keep yer distance."

Zamir Qader returned from his sojourn to the obelisk carrying a smoking brazier. "We're ready for you, sir," he said to Salameh. "We can start the countdown at any time."

Dan was incredulous. "Countdown? You kidding?" he said. "You expect the monument to take off like the space shuttle?"

"No. The eclipse is coming," Qader reminded. "We're keeping track of that."

McMay soared into view again. "Yeah, boy-o. And we've only got ten minutes, twenty-eight seconds by that digital watch old Zamir bought us."

Salameh raised his wrist with a rocking cupped hand that suggested to Dan how the Queen of England waved to the tourists.

Around his wrist he saw a Timex Indiglow Ironman Triathlon watch, the kind that gave off a strong green light in the dark. Its digital numbers were easily readable even from where Dan was standing.

Ten minutes—ten minutes to stop this thing. But how?

"Professor!" A grin was settling over Salameh's face, not a big grin but enough to show that he was pleased with the progress of events.

"When I was a boy, my father worked in the museum in Cairo. Cleaning floors mostly. Sometimes he would bring me and one night, curious as children are, I found myself locked in a storeroom. I found my soul there. When I left that room, I was no longer eight. I had lived for three thousand years. Do you have any memory of the last time we met? In Qemet?"

"I read the story on the obelisk."

"This time will not be like the last. No archer on the roof, no sword in your fist. Why don't you sit down."

"I'll stand."

No sooner were the words out of his mouth than Dan slammed to the ground on his knees. A flash, more of energy than light, flared from Salameh's pupils.

A spasm of agony coursed up Dan's legs to his spine and then spewed into his brain. Evidently, there are persons one does not say "no" to, and Salameh proved to be first among them.

"Stay there, I said!" Salameh clenched his jaw and stared unblinkingly into Dan's eyes. For a transitory instant, Dan felt a devastating intimacy between his mind and Salameh's. Dan touched, then shrank back from, the ancient evil within the terrorist's body.

Salameh let out a deep breath. "Ah, don't worry. You have a box seat. Relax and watch the world change."

Dan strained at his invisible bonds. He couldn't move from the spot. The power of suggestion, black magic—whatever the force, it shackled him to the floor as if he were lashed with chains.

Salameh gave Dan a quick nod, turned, and walked confidently toward the obelisk. Qader on the ground and McMay above fell in behind their messiah.

Dan closed his eyes and bowed his head. It had come down to him—frozen—unable to do a thing against energies he hardly believed in and definitely did not understand. Perhaps there was never any chance he could win.

What insanity made him expect that any strategy could bring down an immortal?

He looked up as the chanting began. Through the veil of mist, Dan made out the towering obelisk, and at its base, he thought he saw twenty or more ghostly figures encircling it. Some had huge heads. Helmets? Masks? Perhaps. He could see few clearly, but those in the circle looked like—as much as Dan wished to dismiss the idea—the pantheon of ancient Egypt.

Cow-headed Hathor, Jackal-headed Anubis, Cat-headed Bast—the true gods of Qemet together again for their last chance to dominate the world of Man.

Salameh drew close to the obelisk. In the half-light, he dropped his robe and stood naked before the assembly. Above, McMay glided in lazy loops, his wings hardly moving at all. On McMay's nearest pass to him, Dan glimpsed one half of the ankh, pulsing red, gripped in the Ba's talons.

Below, he saw Qader place the lighted brazier in front of Salameh, then wait at the side of the obelisk. Qader disappeared for a second, then returned with the other half of the ankh.

He was fidgeting. His face, illuminated in the ankh's Halloweenish light, was tight with strain.

Does he have doubts?

Dan wondered if he could exploit that somehow. Like a vampire, Qader would have to die before he could taste eternal life. Dan was not sure if he had the courage to face death on just a promise.

Twenty feet away, Salameh sank to his knees in front of the brazier and lowered his head. The incantations grew stronger, more insistent. The chorus of gods turned toward the spire, focusing the sound toward the altar.

First Salameh, the vessel that embodied the soul of Sennemut, would assume the Horus. With the power of Duat in his grasp, he would use the strength of the ankh to raise an indestructible army of the dead.

How would he reveal himself, Dan wondered. Would he dress in the golden wings of Horus drifting down the side of the Washington Monument—attended by Liam McMay buzzing around his head—to bring the good news of resurrection to the thousands below?

Or, maybe, he would just go on television.

It wouldn't matter. Who would pass up the chance to live forever? Certainly not that sanctimonious crowd downstairs.

Most of them had been peddling eternal life as a business—whether they were true believers or scam artists—and everyone knew salesmen are the easiest marks.

In response to an insistent drumbeat, Salameh spread wide his arms and, leaning forward, touched his chin to the ground in front of the obelisk.

As he did so, the stone before him changed color. A light, a deep rose light, came not from an outside source shining on the face of the obelisk, but somehow from inside the granite as if it were from an internal fire.

Dan, stuck in midcourtyard, powerless, remembered the ritual from Amenemhab's obelisk. The general, his erstwhile twin, had fought Sennemut once and won. But then, Amenemhab had surprise and loyal troops on his side.

Dan watched alone, embarrassed that he was caught like a fool in the evil magician's web.

Am I so weak? Or is Salameh's power of suggestion so strong? Or is it a physical force that restrains me?

The practical part of him liked the latter assumption. If David Copperfield could fool him, Salameh, a conjurer with three thousand years to figure out how to do it, could trick a mere mortal into believing any damn thing he thought up—even this private world of his.

As hard as Dan tried, he couldn't lift his arms. He was able to stretch his neck a bit to get a glimpse of what was going on.

"Salameh!" Dan shouted, "Let me up! I don't buy any of this crap! I know it's a trick!" He wasn't certain if he could be heard over the din of the ritual. He inched forward, but only with great difficulty.

He sighed and sat back to wait. If he were destined to be at this great event, it seemed it was to be as a spectator.

The chanting ended abruptly.

Qader lay his portion of the ankh on the altar. From high over the obelisk, partially obscured in mist, McMay dove down with his piece firm in his claw. He hovered at the last moment and dropped it beside the other half.

Spaced no more than two inches apart on the altar, the two red crystals stirred. The ankh's broken edges grew small shafts, tens of them, each shaped like miniature obelisks.

The quartzites moved toward each other, crisscrossed, then fused. The ankh, the very symbol of regeneration, was renewing itself.

CHAPTER FORTY

Annie slipped under the cordoned-off entrance to the Washington Monument with the help of two District policewomen who were also Uatchet sisters.

They guarded the doors as Annie checked inside. She found Natalia and called for a clean-up crew on her radio. Then, she drew her gun and ran up to the first landing.

"Jacinda!"

She waited for an answer, and when none came, Annie climbed four more steps and looked around. Above her, the stairway dissolved into an unexpected coal blackness. The sight chilled her.

She glanced across at the elevator shaft and heard a mechanical shudder from somewhere in the high shadows. Within seconds, Annie heard a pounding from the same spot.

"Jacinda!" she shouted up the pillar.

Inside the stalled elevator, Jacinda struck the wall repeatedly with her fist. All that did was vent her frustration and bruise her knuckles. "Damn it to hell!" she fumed.

She slammed her palm against the "Up" button two, three times.

Nothing happened. In a fury, she kicked the door. The base was dented from the last time she tried to get the lift moving. It hadn't helped then and battering the interior wasn't doing a thing to improve the situation.

Jacinda sighed, then slumped with her back against the wall and slid slowly to the floor. She sat there for a moment, feeling trapped. Her eyes bounced from corner to corner, but there seemed to be no easy way out.

"Okay, then I'll get out of here the hard way."

In her imagination, Jacinda mapped out the cube that held her. Thirty-eight rivets secured the ceiling, but only six screws fastened the access panel to it.

She found a metal nail file in her bag and stretched herself on tiptoes to reach one of the screws. The file's curved back fit into the slot, but it slipped out when Jacinda couldn't get high enough for good leverage. On her third try, the screw moved a quarter turn, but on the fifth attempt the file buckled and snapped off at the end.

She cocked her head and glared, first at the door and then at the ceiling. *"Ben kelbah!"* she cursed in her native tongue.

Thrusting her arm into her bag, she gripped her gun by the handle and whisked it out. Continuing the motion, she aimed at the offending screw and blew its head off.

Annie was circling the ground floor when she heard the shot reverberate down the shaft. She ran to the elevator doors and tried to pry them open with her fingers. They wouldn't budge.

"Jacinda! I hear you!" shouted Annie. Detecting no response, she called out on the radio. In seconds, Eva was on the line.

"A shot was fired in the elevator, Mother. Jacinda's caught inside—"

"You can't help her," interrupted Eva. "Once the ritual has begun, the Uatchet cannot interfere."

Annie watched the elevator doors vacantly and bit her lip. "Can I at least bring in a squad to attack the false Messiah if the son of Buto fails?"

"Come outside for a moment, Annie. Just step out the door."

She complied, keeping her ear to the receiver. The two women guarding the door took notice of her, then returned to their vigil.

"Look up," ordered Eva's voice. She did at once and saw that low clouds had blown in from the direction of the Potomac. The sky had changed from blue to slate gray, and most important, the darkest clouds lingered at a height two-thirds the height of the monument. The top was wholly obscured.

"I see it, Mother." She squinted into the chalky haze, frightened but undaunted. "What can we do?"

"The hardest thing," said Eva. "Wait and do nothing at all."

Bracing her palms on the handrail, Jacinda kicked her legs up to the ceiling and booted the center of the access panel. It gave way and fell into the elevator. The panel clattered to the floor an instant after Jacinda swung back to the wall.

"About time, you *momser!*"

She picked up her gun and jammed it into her waistband. Making a grunting noise deep in her throat, she leapt into the dark hole above her and grabbed the edges. Jacinda paused to gather her strength, then pulled herself into the shaft.

The light from inside the elevator allowed her a view of the ancient mechanism. A series of greased cables rose from the rim. She chose one, doffed her jacket, and wrapped it around the line for traction. Then, hand over hand, she started to climb.

Less than twenty feet up, the light faded and she continued scaling the wire in the dark. Jacinda developed a cadence. She felt her way, bracing her legs against the shaft wall like a mountaineer ascending a rock face.

Another ten feet higher, she overreached her jacket, as she had done since the climb started. But as Jacinda tried to get her handhold, she missed.

The slide was short, less than three feet, but she wrenched a wrist and scraped her knees as she twisted to a stop. Panting, she stared up into the unending blackness as her brain slowly accepted the impossible.

The taut cable, which held her and the elevator car below, disappeared a foot or so above her head.

It simply didn't exist.

She hung there for a long minute, like a fakir doing the Indian rope trick, deciding what to do.

Continue.

That was her only option. Whatever abyss of time and space lay before her, Dan was there, too—with Salameh.

Jacinda hauled herself to the horizon between dimensions and probed the elevator shaft with her foot. The wall disappeared at the same height as the cable. She couldn't tell if it left a brick edge that would give her a handhold if she transferred to it, but it was her only bet.

She mumbled a prayer and vaulted into the nothingness—a true leap of faith.

CHAPTER FORTY-ONE

Below, bathed in the red glow from the altar, Salameh remained bowed in supplication. Dan watched the muscles quivering in his back.

That close to the ankh, at least when it formed into a whole once more, Salameh would be at his most powerful; and yet, from Dan's vantage point, seeing him naked and bent over, he looked so vulnerable.

With effort, Dan pushed his knee forward. The movement was easier than the last time he tried it.

Is Salameh relaxing his mind link?

Dan was convinced he could break free, even if the invisible leash only frayed a little. Given five seconds, less if he were lucky, Dan could run at the altar and make a grab for the ankh.

And then what? Dan thought. *Salameh's not going to stand aside and let me get away with the ankh. I should've brought a gun to this party. I won't stop Salameh with a crooked smile and the force of my personality!*

Dan crept forward again. Three minutes. Six more inches.

At that rate, Dan sighed to himself, *Salameh will be sitting in the Pope's See at the Vatican before I can crawl over to that altar.*

Discouraged to his soul and near exhaustion, Dan sank onto his haunches. Oddly, his first thought in defeat was of Jacinda. With death so close, he realized how vital love was in a person's life. How twisted one might become without it—and, suddenly, he had an idea!

"Salameh!" Dan shouted. "Got a second?"

He got no immediate answer and didn't really expect one, although he did hear a snort from overhead and assumed it was McMay reacting. He half expected to feel something wet hit the top of his head, but that indignity never came.

He tried once more. "Prophet!" Did you love her?"

No answer, but he saw the back of Salameh's head twitch a bit to one side. He heard.

"It was all for her, wasn't it! Raising the dead, finding the ankh. You loved Hatshepsut, and you couldn't bear watching her sicken and die, could you?"

McMay swooped in front of him. "Better quit that, boy-o. You're stickin' your nose in forbidden territory."

Dan paid no mind to McMay's squawking.

"Think about her, Prophet!" Dan yelled at Salameh's back. The terrorist turned his head toward him for a second, then went back to the altar.

"That's right, Salameh. I'm not talking to you. Sennemut's still in there, someplace, isn't he?"

Again, no reply.

From the altar, the ankh began to glow with red intensity.

"Hatshepsut's in Duat, Sennemut. These thousands of years she's been waiting for you! But if you let that damned bastard, Salameh, do this, you'll never see her again. She's spirit, Sennemut—and you'll be flesh forever!"

Qader ran over to Dan. "Keep your mouth shut, Daniel," he pleaded.

"Are you so scared of dying, Qader? Living forever—that scares the hell out of me."

"Quiet down!" Qader screamed. "We're in the middle of—"

"I know what you're doing. But you've all been impotent so long that power's clouding your heads! Can't you see? Sennemut and all of us now know that there's an actual Heaven. The ankh proves it. Maybe some call it Duat, and others call it Paradise, but damn it—it exists!"

"So what?" cawed McMay.

"I'll ask you," said Dan. "Why give up a chance at Heaven to rule here on Earth? You'd be stupid enough to renounce an eternity of peace and love for all the crap this world's got to offer? A pretty myopic bargain, it seems to me! You hear that, Sennemut?"

Still bent at the altar, Salameh clenched his fists in anger and cocked his head. He watched Dan try to stand.

Suddenly, a bolt of energy shook Dan and threw him once again to his knees. At the same instant, a fire seared down his throat. His hands clutched at his neck, trying to quell the pain.

"What are you trying to keep me from saying, Salameh?" said Dan, his voice raspy. "Do you want me to say that Hatshepsut wasn't your love? Was she—Queen or not—only a whore to you? Is that the way you feel? That when she died, you were well rid of her?"

"Never!" Salameh rose at the altar and swung around to face Dan. "How dare you! When I rule, no man will speak such . . . such—"

"Truth?"

"Your prattle will not stop this, Professor! When I have the ankh—the instant it's whole—." He let the rest of his thought drop.

Dan crawled forward. As he hoped, the psychic hold lessened as Salameh's anger grew. "Then, why not let me talk? If Duat exists, Sennemut, so does Hatshepsut! Alive in spirit. Waiting for you—waiting."

"NO!"

Dan pulled himself ahead, his fingernails scraping the stone floor. Five yards from the altar, he was bathed in the rose-colored glow from the ankh. "Then she *was* your whore! All right—be the Messiah, Sennemut. Be the Mahdi and the Second Coming! Take revenge on the world! What will you gain if your only love is lost to you forever?"

Grudgingly, Salameh circled back to the altar stone and drew the smoke from the brazier into his nostrils. "You will not speak for her," he whispered.

With his back to Dan, Salameh peered down at the ankh. The tiny shafts at the edges were knitting well. It wouldn't be long before the two halves melded. There wouldn't even be a seam to prove it had been split.

"You know, Professor," said Salameh, "you might've been valuable to me. I could use a fellow who had a television show. I heard you had a good TV-Q, and your kind of sincerity could make the transition to the new world so much easier. I saw you as a spokesman—Aaron to my Moses, that sort of job. But now, I doubt you'd have your heart in it."

Salameh lifted his head regally until he spotted McMay flying a circuit of the obelisk. "Liam!" he barked as he pointed at Dan. "Go kill him."

Talons bared, McMay performed a high pass, then dived directly at Dan's head. Dan, locking eyes with Salameh, never saw the Ba drop from the sky, but he heard it coming. That same fierce howl of wind assaulted his ears the moment before his father was killed.

Dan expected death. Instead, from behind him, three gunshots in quick succession echoed inside the temple.

The first impact struck McMay in his right wing. But since he was diving with his wings tucked close to his body, the bullet hardly affected his fall.

The next ripped into his chest and sent him spinning. The third smashed into his left cheekbone and ricocheted from sinus to brain, killing him instantly.

If it hadn't, crashing into the tile floor at sixty miles an hour would have.

McMay splattered like roadkill five feet away from where Dan was kneeling. Qader screamed, high-pitched like a hysterical woman, and stumbled behind one of the empty temple niches for cover.

He needn't have worried. The ensuing shots were aimed at Salameh. Four tightly spaced bullets burrowed into the altar a fraction of a second after Salameh pitched sidelong to the ground.

Salameh blinked. With his thoughts otherwise occupied, his spell on Dan vanished. Finally free, Dan looked back.

He saw Jacinda.

She stood high up on the entablature between two columns. The smoke from her gun obscured her face, but Dan knew she was smiling.

Dan made a dash for the obelisk. He grabbed for the ankh, blocking Jacinda's line of fire. In that narrow window of opportunity, Salameh pounced from behind the stone.

He slammed one hand down hard on the crosspiece, clutched the handle with his fingers, and tried to pull the ankh to him.

Salameh had the ankh—it was off the surface—when Dan telescoped his wrist and thrust his right hand into the loop of the ankh.

He tugged back. Both men stood across the altar, staring into each other's eyes, each gripping the pulsating red quartz, neither giving ground.

After a second of silence, Salameh grunted. There was irony in the sound. "So, little General, you had another archer on the roof after all."

"No fault of my own," said Dan. He fixed his stare and tightened his grip. "There's time for us to get out of here alive. All of us."

"Yes, all alive," Salameh muttered derisively. "Holding the ankh, who can destroy us?"

Salameh curled his upper lip. Dan wasn't sure if it was a sneer or merely his muscles tightening in their cosmic tug of war.

Around them, the obelisk and the temple enclosing it cracked. Not only the granite and the tile and the obsidian but the very air and smoke that made up the illusion of the place chipped and fell away.

And behind it could be glimpsed the plain square observation tower of the Washington Monument.

"Let it go, infidel!" shouted Salameh with all the venom in him, "Or I'll—"

Then, strangely, he relaxed his shoulders—*not his grip*—and smiled as if greatly amused. "Or I'll what? Killing each other doesn't seem to be an option. Should we flip a coin for it?"

Dan looked down at the ankh. "Hard to do with one hand. And while we're going at it, who do we trust to hold onto this thing?"

Salameh shrugged. He cast a glance toward his chief of staff who was cowering in a shadow, his cover gone. The niche where he took refuge had dissolved into a plain concrete corner.

"Mr. Qader seems unoccupied at the moment," he said.

Dan nodded. "I don't suppose you have a deck of cards. We could cut for it."

"Smacks too much of gambling, I'm afraid. All those religious types downstairs would never approve. I remain open to suggestions, though," Salameh said lightly.

A few seconds later, as if to answer him, Jacinda walked out of what remained of the fog, her gun drawn. "Step away from him, Daniel," she ordered.

Dan stayed in place. "Calm down, Jake," he said. "You could empty that gun into his brain, and he wouldn't even get a headache."

Qader piped up insanely from his corner. "Kill him, Mahdi! He has no right to sabotage your glorious design."

"It's a standoff, then," said Dan.

"In that case, you lose, young General," Salameh hissed. "Haven't I proved I can wait an eternity for what I want? But I won't have to, not when so much of the ankh's power is surging through me."

Suddenly, he jerked his head around to what was left of the obelisk. With one intense look, the rose granite reformed, taller, straighter than before.

"You see?" he said, returning to face Dan. "And once the harmonics of the god's voices begin and the influence of the Aten is blocked, nothing you can do will stop me!"

Dan glanced down at Salameh's digital watch. "The way I see it, you've got about five minutes, or you'll miss the eclipse for another lifetime!"

"If I miss it, Professor, I'll have no reason to keep you breathing!"

"If I stop you, I won't care!"

Salameh shrugged. Then, he heard a sound behind him and smiled. The figures of the Egyptian gods surrounding the obelisk had resumed their unearthly chant.

Dan feared that even with only half the ankh's energy available to him, Salameh might muster just enough to perform the miracle he promised to the faithful assembled in the shadow of the Washington Monument.

The chanting grew louder in Dan's ears. Salameh seemed to have forgotten him and was concentrating on the artificial world he had constructed.

This time it was brighter.

The clouds were blowing away. The temple appeared to be in the center of a huge complex of buildings, pylons, and sacred lakes.

The gods, returning to their somnambulant dance around the base of the obelisk, seemed more real.

That done, Salameh turned his attention back to Dan. He furrowed his brow and glared into Dan's eyes as he had before. A shock struck Dan, but it was a pinprick compared to the psychic blow that had first sent him crashing to the temple floor.

This assault made his scalp twitch but hardly more.

The ankh was protecting him, too.

Frustrated, Salameh gave out a grunt and shook his head. "I have no time for this, little General!" he grumbled testily.

No time . . . no time . . . TIME! Omigod, I've been so stupid!

The idea rocketed into Dan's brain. It was ill-formed, and he wasn't at all certain if he could take and extrapolate it into a coherent plan.

But Dan knew he had to convince Salameh that what he was thinking was true. An impossibility. Except that—it wasn't only Salameh in that body.

Dan started tentatively. "I study Egypt, you know. I have one question."

"Make it quick," Salameh said. "There's less than four minutes."

"I don't want to speak to Salameh," he began. "He's a thug and a man of no honor."

"A thug, am I?" he said lightly.

"Not you!" said Dan, his voice laden with venom. "I know nothing of you, except that you murder the innocent and plan to kill more. No, I want to talk to Sennemut."

The man across the altar grew somber. His eyelids closed heavily for a second or two. When they opened again, they were the eyes of another.

"I am always here," he said.

Dan raised his brows. "Are you? I can't believe it. I know Sennemut. I've studied him since I was a child playing at Luxor. My father wrote the book on him. He always told me there was greatness in that man."

"Should I thank you?"

Dan's mind was rocketing now. "The Sennemut I learned about," he stumbled about trying to get his thoughts out, ". . . seized opportunity. His humble beginnings didn't stop him."

"You had a question to pose?" said the ancient one. "I'll answer it, but hurry; there's not much time."

"Okay, sure. Archaeologists assume you and Hatshepsut were lovers, or else she wouldn't have allowed you absolute authority over her empire. You were lovers, weren't you?"

"That is rather personal, Professor."

"It wasn't my question," Dan noted. "Sex or not, what I want to know is—did you love her?"

"A different life," he said distantly. "She was not a mere woman and was more than a Queen. Love her? She was Isis on Earth. I worshipped her."

The venerable Sennemut paused, then averted his gaze for a moment to think of those shrouded years.

"Her mummy's never been found, Sennemut. You can't ever bring her back."

"Two minutes, Professor. Why don't you slip your hand off the ankh and let me end this. I've brought back the dead with only half of it, so I can still put on a show for them on the ground. There's no time for this. We can't stay in this ludicrous position forever."

"You have a tired look, Sennemut," Dan suggested. "The sadness of an old man remembering when youth and joy ruled his life."

"A minute and twenty seconds."

Dan saw it was too close to dance around his theory; furthermore, he had to make the old priest believe him—fast before Salameh asserted himself again. "I figured it out," he offered.

The Egyptian ignored him.

"The ankh—I know how it works. Here!" He tilted it in Sennemut's direction as a sign of his good intent. "Humor me. Grab the loop with your other hand."

He did so without argument. "Now," Dan continued, "set the ankh up straight, using the handle part as its base."

Moving deliberately, Sennemut helped right the artifact atop the altar stone. "And that done," he said, "what does it prove? Is there a best angle for resurrection?"

"That's the mistake we've been making—the ankh was never meant to raise the dead. Resurrection's only a side effect."

"Raising the dead is not enough, then?" Sennemut, perplexed, but obviously interested, said, "Explain yourself. You have one minute."

Dan charged ahead. "I believe my involvement in this madness was orchestrated. Why else would I have Amenemhab's face? It couldn't be a coincidence. I, a scientist, was meant to be here."

"For what reason?"

"To prove to you what I'm saying is right. This has to be for your benefit, Sennemut. Who else met Amenemhab? Only a man who walked the streets of Luxor three thousand years ago. You know, since I first heard about the ankh, I wondered—like any scientist would—how could it bring back the dead? And what was its purpose to begin with? Then, when you started to go on about how little time we had that was when I know."

Interested, Sennemut whispered softly, "Its function? Which is—?"

Dan sucked in a lungful of air before he answered, "Time travel."

"Ridiculous." Sennemut was stunned. He had never considered that.

"Don't you see? How else can dead tissue regenerate? The answer is, it can't! What happens is the ankh expands brain power somehow—that's how you can make this fantasy world real—and uses that energy to create a temporal shift that moves the dead material back to a time when it was alive. No magic. Technology."

Sennemut noticed McMay's remains.

"Ah, there!" he said smugly. "No technology explains the Ba."

"I don't know."

Jacinda stepped up to the altar. She took the ba-shaped amulet from her jacket pocket and showed it to them. "They used this on Mr. McMay, I think."

Seeing the red quartz at its center, Dan said, "A chip from the ankh. See, too little to bring more than part of him back. But maybe enough to splice his genes with a lower form."

Sennemut frowned. "Where could such a marvel come from, if not from the gods?"

"I don't know. From the far future—or maybe from the distant past. But whatever its origin, I believe that once, on a voyage to ancient Egypt, the ankh was lost and when it was found, its powers became fundamental to the religion it spawned."

"And your face? How was that accomplished?"

"My parents found half of the ankh and had it for fifteen years before I was born. Maybe they tapped into Amenemhab's soul. Maybe the ankh replicated his DNA, somehow. I'll have to ask my mother about that. But I'd be proud to have any part of a great Egyptian warrior in me. Even if he did spoil your plans once."

"And again you try. Thirty seconds."

"Sennemut, you hate this world, admit it!"

"I do."

"You'd return to Qemet in a second, if you could, right?"

"I never dwell on the impossible."

"The Cross of the Horites can send you home, Prophet!"

"I said—'impossible!' "

"And how imaginable is it that you'd be alive after thirty centuries? Has all hope been drained out of you in that ocean of time? Believe again, Sennemut," Dan implored. "Believe that this incredible machine can grab your essence, your energy, your uniqueness . . . your soul—and fling it back into that young priest walking on bare feet along the Nile, back to Hatshepsut's Great House the first time you held her, caressed her, ran your rough hands over her blossom-scented skin."

"You defile her when you speak like that."

"Here—" Dan directed. "Hold the loop with your other hand. I'll let you. Then, stare into the opening."

"Ten seconds."

"Try it. Your mind makes it work. Dream where you want to be."

"You're trying to distract me."

"Do it," Dan begged. "If I'm wrong, what's the harm? Ask it, Sennemut. Ask it to return you to her."

Sennemut hesitated. The ankh was poised inches from his face, but three thousand years of frustration and hate blocked him from speaking.

"Ask it," Dan pleaded. "She's waiting for you."

Sennemut sighed. "I do wish it."

"Concentrate on it."

Sennemut shut his eyes. Almost immediately, Dan noticed the color of the ankh shift from rose to violet. Dan's fingers tingled with an electricity he had never felt.

That was when Sennemut's visage changed.

He began to alter: first, an Egyptian terrorist; then, to the ancient prophet and back again—until the two men in the one body seemed to vibrate within each other's skins.

"Use both hands," urged Dan. "Here, hold onto the ankh. Trust me. I'll let go of it."

Footfalls on the tile. The hammering steps closed in from the side, out of their sight. The sound worried Dan, but he couldn't unlock his stare from the old man. Then, they heard a shout, hysterical and shrill.

"Infidel! You're ruining everything!" It was Qader. He was less than ten feet away and about to make a desperate lunge for the ankh.

Jacinda spun and ran at him, catching Qader with a barehanded blow to the cheekbone that sent him careening sidelong into the stone base of the obelisk.

He leaned there motionless for three seconds or more before sinking into a splayed clump and remained there, a problem solved.

With sudden resolve, Sennemut's fingers tightened over the edge of the upper curve. "I do dream. I've dreamt for centuries." He placed his forehead square against the loop. His eyes grew wide in their sockets as he watched whatever it was the ankh allowed his mind to see.

For the first three seconds, nothing happened. Then, Sennemut jerked back, his spine rigid.

"It's draining me," he whispered hoarsely.

"Let yourself go," said Dan.

"I don't know. I don't know," Sennemut murmured. "If only I could."

Sennemut placed his jaw even with the altar stone and gaped through the empty hole in the ankh. "I see her," he said.

Dan drew back. He had taken a desperate chance, but he no longer held the ankh.

Instantly, particles of crimson light splashed over Sennemut and, like a beacon, led him closer to the opening. There, in a charge of tiny sunbursts and whirling dust, the essence of the old man split from the body he occupied and was sucked into the hollow teardrop formed by the head of the ankh.

Dan dropped below the stone and covered his head while the ankh bucked and shimmered over him.

A massive burst of white exploded from the loop. It lasted a fraction of a second, but in that time the part of the man that had been Sennemut blew away.

Salameh screamed as the ancient one ripped out of him. He looked stunned as he jerked his hands off the ankh.

He turned a bit, looking oddly exhausted, and abruptly collapsed onto the altar.

Dan and Salameh were lying head to head below the stone. An anticlimactic silence pervaded the temple.

Suddenly, pieces of unreality began to crack and crash to the ground. When each chip of the temple or obelisk or sky shattered, it erupted into a pale dust before disappearing entirely.

Dan watched Salameh's open eyes for a sign that he knew the Egyptian world he constructed was rupturing. Jacinda rushed in from the fast-dissolving courtyard and stood over Salameh with her gun aimed at the center of his skull.

"Salameh," Dan called over in a sharp whisper, "he's gone. And you're all alone."

"Back to being a simple terrorist," interrupted Jacinda. "Now, that's my line of work. C'mon, Mahmoud, get on your feet. The good Lord willing, we can get you extradited to Israel before Yom Kippur."

Salameh made no reply, but strained to his feet to face Jacinda's gun. *"La ileha illa 'lloh, Mohammad Rasoul 'lloh,"* he muttered, head bowed, in praise of Allah.

The three of them, Dan, Jacinda, and Salameh, regarded each other as the world around them changed. Salameh repeated his prayer over and over.

"Qif!" shouted Jacinda and, in response, Salameh stopped.

In moments, the facade of the temple complex dislodged, the rose obelisk pitched forward, and the entire fantasy world shattered into points of glitter.

Then, at once, it dropped like a shimmering curtain until no trace of ancient Egypt remained.

They found they were again in the observatory of the Washington Monument, standing in the middle of the square room in front of a display case of monument memorabilia.

Of all the evidence of Qemet, only the ankh remained. It sat on the glass top of the case where the altar stone had been.

"I guess I'll check if the elevator's running," said Dan. "I'd rather not make that walk again."

Jacinda pushed Salameh ahead, shadowing Dan over to the elevator. The eclipse had started, and the observatory was growing dark. Dan summoned the car and held the door for Jacinda and her sullen captive.

Dan said, "You take him down. I think I'd better clean up in here before the cops start nosing around."

"You sure?" Jacinda asked.

"Yeah, I'll be fine."

"You'll take care of the ankh?"

"Sure," said Dan. "I'll hide it in my pants."

Jacinda grinned in her naughty way and said, "That seems like a very good idea."

"Just watch out for Salameh. He's tricky."

Jacinda shook her head. "Not anymore."

It was true. Salameh was not the same man. Without the intelligence and cunning of Sennemut to direct his rage, Salameh, the terrorist, was defeated.

His future would lie in an Israeli prison followed by a show trial and a dispassionate execution. And never once in all the political maneuvering and legal harangues would the name of Sennemut be mentioned.

When the elevator doors closed, Dan realized how dim the light had become. His plan was to gather up Qader and whatever remained of McMay and clear them out of the monument.

Whatever cover story Jacinda and the Mossad would conjure up to explain Salameh's capture, the presence of Qader—and especially, McMay's strange composite remains—certainly would cause more speculation than their alibi could reasonably support.

The last thing Dan relished was scooping up the chunks of McMay left after his collision with reality, so he peered around for a bucket or a Hefty bag, but he couldn't find anything useful in the dark. That was when he first heard the chanting.

"*Neb tekenu qed Amun ni nefer mataiwut pi-eesh ishi Iunu-meht . . .*"

"Who is that? Qader?"

The prayers grew even louder and stronger. In the progressing blackness, Dan could make out the crimson glow of the ankh. He rushed over but halted at the sight of Qader leaning over McMay's carcass with the ankh gripped white-knuckle tight in his hands.

Qader ignored Dan and continued his monotonal chanting. Dan squinted into the dark. Qader, it seemed, had lifted what was left of the Ba on top of the display case between the ankh and the lighted brazier.

McMay's wings twitched as the prayer Dan recognized from the *Book of the Dead* continued.

Suddenly, Dan heard a deep, raling sigh as new breath again entered McMay's lungs. A second later, he was flapping his wings and trying to hop upright.

"Okay, the freak's back. Now give me the ankh," Dan ordered.

McMay howled with laughter and rose to ceiling height for his first flight after returning to the world. Dan was waiting for that before confronting Qader.

"The cops, the Feds—I don't know, maybe the D.C. meter maids— will be swarming up here as soon as Jake turns over Salameh," Dan said. "They'll think he was going to blow up the monument, I suppose."

Qader hesitated, then his eyes dropped below Dan's gaze. When those eyes leveled at him the next moment, they were cold. "Police can't stop me," he said.

He called for McMay, and the Ba swooped down and grabbed the ankh in his talons. The creature floated overhead for a pass or two, taunting Dan by keeping the ankh tantalizingly out of reach. Qader, his face over the brazier drawing the incense into his lungs, continued the final prayer.

"*Fe-em saloh ma-hishta bu eni husu nesmeen jeht tomeetet . . .*"

"Trust me," said Dan. "You're making a huge mistake here."

Qader paused in midincantation and chuckled. "Wait. As soon as the eclipse is over, that very second, I'll be the immortal! I'll walk out of here with the Ba flying over the crowd and announce that *I'm* the Mahdi, *I'm* the Christ—I'm the *Messiah!*"

Now it was Dan's turn to laugh.

"C'mon. Salameh might've gotten away with it. He's got that Charlton Heston, larger-than-life quality. But you—you've got that male-pattern baldness, too-many-donuts quality. 'Master of the World' just doesn't work for guys like you."

Qader peered out one of the windows. "The sun!"

"I guess my mother was right," Dan barked. "We don't know the reason the Horites had for inventing it, but the price is that the ankh turns people into power-hungry assholes!"

Qader wasn't listening. His face was pressed against the glass. "I see the light," he exulted.

"See this!" yelled Dan as he drew back his fist, yanked Qader by the collar, and slugged him in the jaw. Qader yelped in pain as the punch landed just below the bruise Jacinda left on Qader's cheek earlier.

The new god was caught by surprise, and with his mouth open, Qader pitched backward and skidded on the floor before crumpling into one of the display cases. Dan shook off the pain in his hand and, in the graying end of the eclipse, tried to find where McMay had flown off to.

"Okay, bird, where are you hiding?"

"Just flitting around, old son," came the replay from above. "Nice right you got there. I used to do a bit of the boxing myself—in the days when I had arms, that is."

"McMay! Pass the ankh over to me. I promise I'll do what I can to get those arms back. And any other parts that you think you can use."

"Is that sexual innuendo, boy-o?" asked McMay. "It's been so long, I forgot."

Dan stretched out his arm as high as he could. "The ankh, Liam!"

"No thanks. I'd as soon have the magic in my own keeping," McMay replied from on high.

"Suit yourself," Dan said. "But how do you expect to get out of here?"

In the dim light, Dan glimpsed the shadow of the Ba circle the observation room, then aim for one of the windows. The monster hit the glass once. It didn't break, but a small, lightning-shaped crack formed from the center of the pane to the glazing at the upper corner.

McMay flapped his broad wings and zoomed to the peak of the pyramidion. Then, he banked and tucked his wings for a second, more emphatic pass at the window.

This time, Dan was ready.

He ran to the window as McMay hammered against the glass. In an almost poetic motion, Dan grabbed the brazier off the display case and heaved a spray of fire and burning coals over McMay's wing feathers.

"NO!" screamed Qader from behind Dan's left ear. Qader lurched in front of him, pushing him away from the window in the process.

The shove probably saved Dan from some severe cuts, because at that instant the window burst into razor-sharp daggers of glass. The Ba crashed through, aflame, but at that instant, Qader jumped for the ankh and clutched the crosspiece with both hands.

Dan was covering his head from the shower of shards, but he assumed later that Qader never expected the Ba to be so strong. McMay's momentum propelled his body out into the rarified air above the Washington Monument.

And Zamir Qader, with a literal death grip on the ankh, launched through the window along with him.

In the half-light of the waning eclipse, the Ba who had been Liam McMay plummeted like a fiery meteor to the ground, scant feet from the dais.

Below, Evangeline Rawlins saw the streak of fire with the rest of the awed congregation, but she darted from the podium before the bird landed.

In the confusion, she managed to be the first at the small crater where Qader and the ashes of the Ba struck the ground.

Eva was crying as she tried to minister to the crushed body. She finally had to be carried away from the scene. Remarkably, a red crystalline ankh was safely tucked in the inside pocket of her jacket.

EPILOGUE

The leisurely drive to Montauk took Dan and Jacinda less than eighty minutes, because he had picked her up at her hotel after rush hour, a period which could last for eternity in New York. Somehow, as night fell, the house on the beach, that house of memories, seemed to Dan lonelier than he had ever known it.

It was Dan's first trip back to the Point since his father had been killed.

Nine months after the great man's death, an association of fundamentalist churches that he had assisted over the years got permission to set a heavy stone plaque in the sand to protect the almost sacred spot where Gunther Rawlins sacrificed himself for his religion.

The money was raised in less than four hours of tearful pleas over the Christian cable networks. To say that Dan resented the entire idea was the understatement of the millennium.

He'd been tempted to go on some talk show and denounce the whole thing. *60 Minutes* offered the air time, as much as he wanted within reason, but his mother convinced him otherwise.

As usual, Eva was right.

What could Dan say on TV? Who would believe that Salameh had been the vessel of an evil magician from ancient Egypt?

No decent news footage of McMay surfaced despite a story about him in the *Star* that actually had a couple of its facts right. Most people assumed a poor bird had blundered by and was immolated by chance during Qader's suicide.

A thimbleful of ash was all that was left of him. The rest had blown away in the wind, perhaps wafting westward to Duat.

District Attorney Haas was forced to admit that he had been duped by terrorists, but he tried to explain that with the evidence he had at hand—even though Dan was lying in critical condition in a hospital bed—his indictment was justified.

The voters didn't agree and threw him out during the primary election. For Dan, the only thing to do was to accept his father's martyrdom.

That chapter had been edited out of his life.

Jacinda el-Bahri disappeared without a word a day after the events at the Washington Monument. Dan wondered if this was her decision, the Mossad's, or perhaps the Uatchet Sisterhood's.

That summer, Dan moved to Phoenix to write a biography of Gunther Rawlins. Occasionally, Dan was asked out on a dig to the endless Indian mounds bordering the city, but he always refused. "I'd rather not disturb that," was his usual answer. But Dan remained an archaeologist. He still taught a master class in Dynastic Egyptology at Georgetown.

Then, one day, Jacinda left a cryptic message on his answering machine. She said she would be in New York in a week, and Eva had invited both of them to dinner.

He called his mother immediately, and she confirmed the summons. When he asked why, all she would say was, "Unfinished business." Seven days later, he flew into JFK, rented a car, and drove to the Plaza. Jacinda waited outside. It occurred to him that she might not actually be registered there.

Once a spy . . .

She kissed him tenderly and gave him a big hug. She looked the same, except for a new scar that cut through her left eyebrow.

"What's this about, Jake?"

"I wasn't told," she said. "But I'm glad the call came. I missed you."

They had dinner early, with Evangeline fixing elaborate gourmet fare spiced as the bedouins did. Dan loved it, but he knew he'd be living on Rolaids and Gaviscon for a week.

After the meal, Jacinda admitted she was jet-lagged, and Eva suggested she take a nap in the guest room.

"When you're refreshed," said Eva, "come down for tea and cake."

With Jacinda resting upstairs, Dan joined his mother in the kitchen and helped her load the dishwasher. While her son poured the liquid detergent in its trough, Eva made coffee.

Dan set the mugs down in the family room as his mother finished brewing the coffee on the stove. Alone together, Dan and Eva brought their steaming cups, along with a plate of Orange Milanos, out to the porch.

Dan sipped carefully. His mother always managed to serve coffee a hundred degrees above its natural boiling point. For Eva's part, she enjoyed testing every new flavor of International Blends on her guests. This brew bore a distinct hint of cinnamon.

Dan set his mug down on the rattan table beside him as his mother made small talk. When there was a lull in the conversation, Dan said, "I'm glad we're here, Mother, by ourselves. I've been thinking about all that happened. None of it seems real anymore."

Eva placed her hand in his. "But it was. I haven't told you, but I was so proud of you."

Dan's other hand enclosed his mother's. "Why did Dad have to die?"

"I swear, Daniel, I tried to protect him. I placed sisters all around, but he wouldn't listen." Evangeline's features sagged perceptibly, showing her age. "I asked Gun to play along with Salameh only until we'd regained the cross—."

"But he was a lowly man?"

"A prideful man. An honest man. I thought he was safe out here. I sealed off the access, the whole neighborhood. How could I know about the Ba?"

"I used to stare at all the women who lived around here. I thought the beaches were like a lesbian hangout or something—like Fire Island is for guys. Now I know better. They're all sisters."

"Many are. More than you'd suspect." She drank the rest of her coffee.

"And what do they call you, Mother Superior?"

"Buto. Each Mistress of the Uatchet Sisterhood inherits the goddess, as the pharaoh inherits the Horus. The Protectoress lives inside of me."

Dan shook his head. "How is it possible, Mother? How can a secret order go back that far? Did it really start with Isis?"

"Before that. Once all gods were women. We're symbols of fertility, you know. But it wasn't until Isis resurrected Osiris that we received our mission to guard the sacred Ankh of Life."

She paused and looked over to her son. "What's that grin doing on your face? Did I say something amusing?"

"I was thinking about poor Halevi. There he was, deluded into believing it was his own Mossad operation, when it was yours all the time."

"The Sisterhood's waited for Sennemut to reappear for centuries. When he did, it was prophesied he would become the Living Horus. How else could he do that in modern times when the major religions were fighting each other? Sennemut would need a conduit to all the fundamentalists."

"That's why Dad became born again. Did he know you were using him as a spy for the Sisterhood?"

Her expression grew darker. "Gun came from a deeply religious family. I used that."

"And I spent five years hating his guts."

"Your reaction was what made it work. Don't you see?"

"Yeah. But do I have to like it?"

"No, but I pray you'll forgive me, Son. I regret that. You don't realize how much, but I want you to know—every day of those five years my sisters hunted for the ankh. And I will always curse my stupidity. I let my guard down when Jacinda found it."

"So, Jacinda was a sister from the beginning," he said, the words confirming it to himself.

"You have to ask?"

"No. None of it bothers me—except that my mother's a goddess, and I'm destined to be surrounded by her vestal virgins for the rest of my life."

"That's not even close to being a decent analogy, Daniel." Then, in a whisper, she added, "Especially the virgin part. Sex is too powerful a tool to remove from our arsenal."

"Hey, none of my old girlfriends were part of your little club, were they?"

Evangeline smiled enigmatically.

"Okay," Dan conceded, then changed the subject. "You wouldn't care to tell me where the ankh might be, would you?"

"Secured. To be preserved, but rarely, if ever used. That's our obligation."

Jacinda came onto the porch carrying a bowl of fruit. Dan made room for her on the chaise.

"Is anything the matter?" asked the Uatchet sister. "You two look so serious."

"No," Dan replied, looking deep into Jacinda's eyes. "Nothing's the matter. I was just trying to figure out how I'm going to handle all the new women in my life."